THE CITY OF STRANGERS

Michael Russell read English at Oxford, before spending three years working in farming in North De...g to get someone to pay him to write. He ...ed for Yorkshire Television as a Script Editor, on *Emmerdale Farm*, working his way up to Series Producer. He also spent several years in the Drama D...... first as Script Consultant then Producer, be... leaving ITV to write full-time. He was a regular co...ibutor to *Midsomer Murders* and scripted the la.. ever *Touch of Frost* which topped the ratings. He li.es in Ireland with his family, where he is doing what he al...ys wanted to do, writing novels.

F...l out ...e about Michael Russell and his writing:
v.......aelrussellforgottencities.com
f...book.com/michaelrussellforgottencities
@...rgottencities

Also by Michael Russell

City of Shadows

MICHAEL RUSSELL

The City of Strangers

AVON

This novel is entirely a work of fiction.
The names, characters and incidents portrayed in it are
the work of the author's imagination. Any resemblance to
actual persons, living or dead, events or localities is
entirely coincidental.

AVON

A division of HarperCollins*Publishers*
77–85 Fulham Palace Road,
London W6 8JB

www.harpercollins.co.uk

A Paperback Original 2013
1

A catalogue record for this book is
available from the British Library

ISBN-13: 978-1-84756-347-7

Set in Minion by Palimpsest Book Production Limited,
Falkirk, Stirlingshire

Printed and bound in Great Britain by
Clays Ltd, St Ives plc

MIX
Paper from
responsible sources
FSC www.fsc.org FSC C007454

FSC™ is a non-profit international organisation established to promote
the responsible management of the world's forests. Products carrying the
FSC label are independently certified to assure consumers that they come
from forests that are managed to meet the social, economic and
ecological needs of present and future generations,
and other controlled sources.

Find out more about HarperCollins and the environment at
www.harpercollins.co.uk/green

For
Anya, Seren, Finn, Coinneach and Marta
And the Silver Meteor
To the Pennsylvania Station

Send but a song oversea for us,
   Heart of their hearts who are free,
Heart of their singer to be for us
   More than our singing can be.

       'To Walt Whitman in America'
       Algernon Charles Swinburne

RPACN FEBSA HOGYH VTNOY IKSAO RYHOI
VAUAR OAOIR OKWGQ MWAYA IERIL IETTM
NNSTN ATAUA OIETH ARGTR YLHRA NASRI
FOOAA AIALL TINYN LMENV NOOYG EEHOS
OAOET GECTN: List of spies noted. Am
forwarding it to Intelligence Director
for his information. Are you able to
carry out annihilation of all spies?
From *Decoding the IRA*

PART ONE
Uptown

Mrs Leticia Harris, aged 53, who resided at 14 Herbert Place, Dublin, disappeared some time after 6 a.m. on Sunday, 8th March. The following morning her car was discovered at premises in Corbawn Lane, leading from Shankill to the sea. There were numerous bloodstains inside the car, and the police later in the day found a bloodstained hatchet in a shed adjoining her house, and also bloodstains on the flower borders in the garden. The police theory is that Mrs Harris was murdered in her own home and the body taken away in her car. Mrs Harris is the wife of Dr Cecil Wingfield Harris, 81 Pembroke Road, Dublin. The Irish Times

1. Pallas Strand

West Cork, November 1922

The storm did not come suddenly. All day the wind from the Atlantic had blown hard and cold and fast against Pallas Strand. The grey sky sped past overhead, heavy, thick, turbulent. The noise was unceasing, humming and roaring, loud and soft, and loud and soft again, but always there, along with the beat of the sea crashing endlessly against the white curve of sand. The farm lay back from the strand, behind a scattering of tufted dunes and a row of wasted trees, bent and twisted from long years of bowing and creaking before the wind, yet somehow always strong enough to stand. Indoors and out the blast of the wind battering the farmyard and the buildings had been constant, but still the rain hadn't come.

The boy was in the yard, leaning into the wind to stand, scattering leftovers from a bucket to the ruffled and bad-tempered hens. He was seven; it had been his birthday only a week ago. He shouted and laughed as the puppy that had been his birthday present danced around him, darting and leaping, behind, in front, through his legs, trying to snatch the bacon rinds before the hens could get them. His father was in the barn, milking the three black cows. His mother was in the kitchen, peeling potatoes. He didn't hear the two vehicles driving along the track from the main road. The wind was blowing the sound away from him. It was only as the dog turned sharply from the scraps and started to bark that he saw them.

He knew them well enough. The long, sleek Crossley Tourer came first, with its top open even in the wind, and its battered leather seats. He loved the Tourer and its white-walled tyres, despite the men inside it. The other one was different; a Rolls Royce armoured car with its squat turret on the back and its .303 Vickers machine gun sticking out through the letter-box sights. As the dog zigzagged angrily round the wheels of the Crossley, snapping and snarling, it stopped; three uniformed men got out. The boy knew them too. It wasn't the first time they had driven into the farmyard at Pallas Strand.

There was a young lieutenant and two great-coated Free State soldiers. The lieutenant smiled; the boy didn't smile back. No one got out of the armoured car; its turret moved in a slow, grating arc as the machine gun scanned the yard. The puppy kept up a furious yapping, now round the feet of the intruders, but a kick sent him flying across the muddy yard. The boy turned to find his father standing behind him. There was another man too, his uncle. Where his father was calm and steady, he could see the fear in the other man's eyes. And his mother was there now, in the doorway of the house, wiping her hands dry with her apron. The lieutenant stepped towards the boy's father.

'You've heard what happened on the Kenmare road?'

'I heard something.'

'So where were you yesterday?'

'I was here. Where else would I be?'

'You were seen in Kenmare the day before, with Ted Sullivan.'

'Who says?'

'I do.'

The boy's father shrugged.

'There's a Garda sergeant dead at Derrylough. A mine,' said the officer.

The boy's father shrugged again.

'Someone said something about it.'

'There was no mine on Tuesday. The road was clear.'

'I wouldn't know, Lieutenant. That'll be your business.'

'But Ted Sullivan would know, I'd say.'

'That'll be his business then. You'd need to ask him so.'

'Maybe you'd know where he is then?'

'Well, he wouldn't always be easy to find.'

'Unless you were an IRA man.'

'There'd be a lot of IRA men in West Cork. You'd know yourself. And it's not so long ago you fellers would have called yourselves IRA men.'

The boy's father smiled. It was a mixture of amusement and contempt. It was a familiar conversation, empty, circular, quietly insolent; all the lieutenant's questions would go unanswered. But he knew that. He turned to one of the soldiers and nodded. The man walked forward and slammed the butt of his rifle into the farmer's stomach. As he collapsed to the ground the boy stepped between his father and the soldier, saying nothing, but glaring hatred and defiance. The soldier laughed. The boy's mother ran forward across the yard, but her husband was already struggling to his feet. He looked at her sharply and shook his head. She stopped immediately. The boy turned to his father.

5

The noise of the wind rose and blasted. The man smiled, despite his pain, and put his hand on his son's head, ruffling his hair. The lieutenant put a cigarette in his mouth. He hunched over his hands for several seconds, trying to get his lighter to catch it. After a moment he straightened up, drawing on the smoke.

'Let's see what you've got to say at the barracks.'

The soldier who had knocked the boy's father down took his arm and dragged him towards the Crossley Tourer. The other soldier covered him with his rifle. The turret of the armoured car creaked slowly as the machine gun swept round the farmyard once more. The boy watched as his father was pushed into the back seat of the car. Neither his mother nor his uncle moved. They had seen it before; it was always the same; the same questions and no answers. He would come back, beaten and bruised, but he would come back. The soldiers got into the car. Then the Crossley Tourer and the armoured car swept round in a circle in the farmyard, through the mud and the dung, and drove up the track towards the road to Castleberehaven, the dog chasing behind, still barking and snapping.

The woman walked forward. She took her son's hand and smiled reassuringly. It would be all right. These were the things they lived with, that they had always lived with. Even at seven years old he was meant to understand that. The soldiers who had taken his father away were traitors; men who had sold the fight for Irish freedom for a half-arsed treaty with England that was barely freedom at all. Traitors were to be treated with contempt, not fear. Then his mother turned to his uncle, his face white, his fists clenched tight at his side. The fear was gone; now his face was full of anger.

The boy had once asked his mother why his father seemed

to have no fear and his uncle, sometimes, had to hide his shaking hands. 'A man can only give what he has,' she told him. 'If he gives it all, no one can ask more than that.' She was very calm now. None of it was new to them. Three years ago it had been the English Black and Tans; now the men in uniform were Irish, but the same sort of shite. Rage was to be nurtured, as it had been for centuries. There would always be a time to use it.

'You take the bike and go up to Horan's. They'll get a message to Brigadier Sullivan. He'd better know. And we'll finish milking the cows.'

The boy's uncle nodded and walked quickly away. The woman and the boy went into the barn. For a moment, as his mother put her arm round him and squeezed, the boy smiled again. He did know it would be all right.

They waited all that evening, wife and brother and son. The rain had finally come just before dark, beating in from the sea, and the wind began to drop. As night fell a more welcome car pulled into the farmyard. The IRA brigadier said the man was where they expected him to be, in the police barracks in Castleberehaven, on the other side of the peninsula. The Crossley Tourer had been seen driving in through the gates around four o'clock. The IRA had someone inside the barracks; when the man was released they'd have the information immediately. He would be collected and brought home. The Free Staters had pulled in a number of volunteers that afternoon; it was the usual game; most of the men were already home. They only had to wait.

When the boy went up to bed there was no sense of anxiety in the house. The rain was falling outside, but the storm was quiet. Lying in his bedroom under the eaves, listening to the rain rattling comfortably on the roof, he drifted off to sleep thinking of the days when he would hold a rifle in his hand and fight the fight his family fought now. But when he woke abruptly in the early hours of the morning, he knew something was wrong. The rain still fell, but the house wasn't at its ease any more. He could hear voices downstairs; his mother's, his uncle's, and others, a woman, several men. He could make out no words, but the voices no longer echoed the assured tones of the brigadier. There was anxiety; he knew what that was. The voices grew louder and then someone said something to quieten them; but the quiet wasn't really quiet; it was a series of harsh, adult whispers that only intensified the anxiety.

He got out of bed and crept across the room. He knew where each floorboard creaked; he stepped slowly and carefully. At the door he turned the knob and opened it just a crack. The lamps were still burning downstairs. He didn't know the time, but he knew these were the early hours of the morning. The voices were still unclear. The broken words and overlapping phrases that came up the stairs wouldn't fit together. 'Five fucking hours ago – they drove him out, he was in the car – it was ten o'clock – no, the ones at Ardgroom were from Kenmare – Gerry Curran didn't even pick up a gun – they pulled him out of bed – they already knew where the explosives was buried – so where is he?'

The voices stopped. People were moving downstairs. The door into the farmyard opened. The boy tiptoed to the window. He pulled back the curtain and looked down. Two men were walking across the farmyard. They carried rifles. His uncle followed, a few steps behind; he stopped and turned back to the house. His mother was there now, standing in the rain. His uncle stepped back. He put his arm round her and pulled her to him. It was the same gesture of reassurance the boy had received from his mother as they walked to the barn to milk the cows, but everything about the way his mother stood now, unmoving, unaware of the rain falling on her, said that she wasn't reassured.

His uncle picked up the bicycle that lay on the ground by the door. He got on it and rode away. Ahead of him the two other men were on bicycles too, their rifles slung over their backs, their hats pulled down on their heads. The three of them rode out of the farmyard and within seconds the rain and the darkness had swallowed them. The light from the open door shone on his mother as she watched them go. The boy looked down from the bedroom window. It seemed a long time before she turned away from the darkness, back into the house. The door shut. She did not come upstairs.

He let the curtain fall back across the window. He stood in the dark room. He could hear no sound from the kitchen below, but somehow he knew that his mother was standing, just as he was, and that she was crying, just as he was. He could feel the tears now. He understood nothing, except that there were reasons for tears, and reasons to be afraid. He walked to his bed and knelt. He crossed himself and clasped his hands together, closing his eyes tightly. 'Holy Mary, be a mother to me. May the Blessed Virgin Mary, St Joseph, and all the saints in heaven pray for us to the Lord, that we may be preserved this night from sin and evil. Good Angel, that God has appointed my guardian, watch over my Daddy and protect him from harm.'

The rain stopped very suddenly, just before dawn. The sun had been up for over an hour when the boy woke. He wasn't in his bed. He was sprawled across it where he had finally fallen asleep in the middle of the prayers he had repeated over and over again. He got up and walked to the window to pull back the curtains.

The sun was low in the sky but the morning was clear and bright already. Outside he could hear the familiar sounds of the cows in the barn, waiting to be fed and milked. The cockerel called across the farmyard, loud and urgent. But the only other noise was the shrill sound of gulls, flocking overhead. It was a moment before the anxiety of the previous night pushed the morning aside, and he remembered.

He ran to the door and downstairs. There was no one in the kitchen. The door to the farmyard was open. The door to the sitting room was open too, but there was no one there. He ran back upstairs and burst into his mother and father's bedroom. It was empty; the bed had not been slept in. He knocked on the door to his uncle's room across the landing, then opened it; it was empty too and the bed was unused. He raced down the stairs again. He put his raincoat on over his pyjamas and pulled on his boots.

The farmyard was empty. He stood outside and looked around him. It was as if everyone he loved had simply disappeared; for a moment it was bewildering rather than frightening. But he knew the emptiness around him meant that the darkness of the night had not been swept away by the dawn. He looked at the sky. The noise of the gulls was very loud now. A great crowd of them rose and fell on currents of air over the sea beyond the dunes, tightly bunched, angry somehow.

He ran towards the sound, through the farmyard, past the haystacks, on to the track through the dune field, up on to the tussocky dunes. He stopped, looking out at Pallas Strand and the sea, and the crowd of people, away at the far end of the beach, where the gulls were flocking and diving and screeching overhead.

He ran towards the crowd; twenty-five, thirty people in a loose group. Some stood silently, looking towards the sea, away from something. Some stood with their heads bowed in prayer. Some were simply staring down at the sand. No one seemed to see him coming. As he reached the crowd and pushed through the onlookers, still none of them seemed to notice him.

His father's head and shoulders rose out of the sand of Pallas Strand.

He had been buried up to his chest; his hands were by his side, somewhere beneath the sand. His head was facing out towards the sea. And where his eyes had been there were two pits of black and red pus.

The boy stared, not able to understand what he was looking at. It wasn't real; it wasn't a real thing at all. The first thing that came into his head was the face of the vampire he had seen at the cinema in Castleberehaven, when he had crept in at the back with Danny Mullins during *Nosferatu* a month ago; they had watched in open-mouthed awe, for all of five minutes, before they were yanked out by the ears. But he knew what he was looking at, of course he knew. And then it was gone. His uncle's coat dropped over the head and covered it, and suddenly, as if a still photograph had sprung to life, everyone saw him.

His mother turned and came towards him. He didn't see her; he was still staring down at the sand and the coat that covered his father's head. She pulled him to her, standing between him and his father's body, folding him in her

11

arms before she pulled him away. He didn't resist as she led him back towards the farm.

He didn't even try to look back.

No one would let him look at his father's face again. On the day of the removal, when the coffin rested all day in the farm's best room and friends and neighbours walked from all around to drink tea and shake his hand, his mother's hand, his uncle's hand, the coffin would be shut. But in reality he would always see it; the black tears of blood on the wet cheeks. And as he walked silently along the strand with his mother now, the gulls were still screaming and baying for the feast they had been driven away from.

His father had died a hero. But life had to continue; there was a farm. Yet down the years of growing up in the farm behind Pallas Strand, he saw his father's face whenever he heard the sound of hungry gulls. And though he had been told a thousand times that his father was already dead when the Free State soldiers buried him there, as a reprisal for the dead Free State sergeant at Derrylough, and as a brutal warning, he would still wake at night in terror, from dreams in which he couldn't move his body, his legs, his arms, and he felt himself gazing helplessly at the waves moving towards him across Pallas Strand, where no one could hear his screams over the wind roaring in the darkness.

Grief would be softened as the years went by, but not rage. It was a secret strength. Rage had to be nurtured; there was a time to use it.

2. Fulton Market

New York, March 1939

In the Fulton Fish Market, below the Brooklyn Bridge on the Manhattan side of the East River, an Irishman was sitting at a coffee stall. He was a little over forty; tall, fair, with a little bit more weight than was entirely good for him. It was eleven o'clock in the evening and the place was gearing up for the night, as it did every night, its busiest time. It was as cold inside as it was outside. Lights shone fiercely over the stalls stretched out in every direction, but wind from the East River blew in through the open doors, and the crushed ice that was everywhere made it even colder. Fish was still arriving, in boxes and baskets, carried by porters and piled high on the forklift trucks that raced along the market aisles, blasting horns.

The air reeked of blood and the sea; the floor swam with melting ice and fish guts; the occasional live eel squirmed between the stalls, struggling for the doors and the smell of the East River beyond. The price of fish was shouted out with competing, overlapping cries that echoed endlessly round the building. The prices were called in English, but the profanities that accompanied them were in all the

13

languages of New York: English, German, Yiddish, Italian, Greek, Chinese, Spanish, Polish, Russian, Armenian; like the varieties of fish, no one could count them all.

Captain John Cavendish, of the Irish army, Óglaigh na hÉireann, had been in New York for the last two months as an advisor on security during the construction of the Irish Pavilion at the World's Fair, across the river in Long Island's Flushing Meadows. He had also spent some of his time talking to the American army about weapons and training and munitions, and was compiling a report on all this to take back to Ireland. As far as both the ambassador in Washington and the consul general in New York were concerned, his previous role as an officer in Military Intelligence, G2, had nothing whatsoever to do with his presence in America. The fact that he was in New York at all, where the current IRA bombing campaign against Britain, now in full if ineffective swing, had been largely planned and financed, was no more than a coincidence.

It was a coincidence too that he was in New York while the IRA's chief of staff was in America, selling not only the new war against the old enemy, but the idea that the bigger war that had to come, sooner or later, between Britain and Germany, would bring the IRA back to a position of power in Ireland itself. It would be a war that would chase England out of the corner of Ireland it still held on to; it would put an end to the toadying Free State that had found the temerity, under the leadership of the Republican turncoat Éamon de Valera, to almost call itself a 'republic'; and it would reunite the island of Ireland.

Captain Cavendish perched on a stool at the coffee stall counter. He wore a dark grey lounge suit, a blue shirt, a silver tie, a navy blue overcoat and a pale grey fedora. He should have looked out of place among the porters and stallholders in Fulton Market, but nobody took any notice. The man he was chatting amiably to at the counter ought to have looked equally out of place, in a black cashmere overcoat and a black homburg, a half-smoked cigar clamped between his teeth. But men in overcoats and hats were no strangers to the market in the middle of the night; it was run by the Mob, after all, and the men in overcoats took a cut on every box of fish that came in and went out.

The man John Cavendish was talking to carried a .38 under his jacket, and he was important enough that the man in the brown homburg who had come into the market with him, and was now helping himself to boiled shrimps from the next stall, carried a .45 to make sure his boss had no need to use his .38. The man in the black homburg raised his hat to the captain and walked away, followed by his protection. He had a word for every stallholder he passed; the replies all contained the word 'mister'.

John Cavendish looked at his watch; the man he was meeting was late. He had a good idea why and he didn't much like it. But he had no choice but to wait. The army officer held out his empty coffee cup for a refill. And he liked the market. It was an old building that offered relief from the streets of towers and skyscrapers that stretched through Manhattan. It was a manageable place. It reminded him of the South City Markets in Dublin; it had the same red brick, the same arched windows, the same broken gabled lights in the roof, the same vaulting interior and battered, shabby, workaday appearance. Living in the future, as he had been told he was many times since arriving in New York, he liked to touch the past.

The man he was waiting for had docked at Pier 17 on

the Hudson River two hours earlier. There were piers by Fulton Market too, but there were no grand Atlantic liners there, only the fishing boats from Long Island and New England, and the ferries to Brooklyn. Donal Redmond's ship was the French Line's SS *Normandie*; he was a steward. He would have picked up the message he was delivering, as he always did, when the boat stopped at Cobh on its way from Le Havre to New York. And before the delivery was made at the other end he would give it to John Cavendish to copy.

'You're late.'

'I'm here, what else do you want?'

'You'd be better off out of the White Horse every time you dock.'

'If I didn't have a few in there, they'd think something was up.'

'You've had more than a few.'

'I've been on that boat six fucking days. What do you care?'

'I don't,' said Cavendish, getting up off the stool. 'Have you got it?'

Donal Redmond nodded. He followed the army officer through the maze of stalls, out to the back of the market, where the boxes of fish were loading and unloading. Trucks and cars, horses and carts, barrows and forklifts were everywhere. Money was changing hands outside as it was in, and arguments were still going on about prices that had started at the stalls and carried on out to the street; hands were spat on and shaken; illegible dockets and receipts were scrawled out and dropped into the slush of ice and blood and litter.

John Cavendish sat with the steward in the front of his red and white Crossley. In all the noise and the constant movement of vehicles a man scribbling something down in the front of a car looked like any other wholesaler or restaurateur totting up his bill.

The two letters, on thin copy-paper flimsies, had been rolled up tightly into straws and buried in a tin of Jacob's shortbread biscuits. On each of the two pages were several paragraphs of typed capital letters; the letters grouped in neat columns, each five letters wide, with a space between each group. Cavendish copied both pages, laying the letters out exactly as in the typed originals. He rolled up the pages as tightly as they had emerged from the tin, then twisted the top and bottom of each one. The other man pushed them back under the biscuits, pressed the lid down tightly, and turned to stuff the tin into the duffel bag that was now on the back seat of the captain's car.

'Do you want a lift over to Queens?'

'OK. Suits me.'

John Cavendish took five ten dollar bills from his wallet and handed them over. The steward put them in his pocket and grinned. It was done.

'Merci, mon brave. Quelque chose à boire?'

Cavendish reached under the dashboard and pulled out a silver and leather hip flask. As he started the engine he handed it to Donal Redmond. He drove from Front Street on to Fulton Street, past City Hall and up on to the Brooklyn Bridge, over the East River to Long Island. He drove through Brooklyn into Queens. Redmond said nothing now; their business was over. Two blocks from the call house in Woodside, at the corner of 58th Street and 37th Avenue, where the ciphers would be delivered, the army officer stopped the car. The steward got out, hauled his duffel bag from the back seat and walked away.

As he disappeared from sight Cavendish reached for the hip flask and drank the remaining whiskey; as he put his hands back on the steering wheel he realised they were shaking. He pulled out into the road. A horn blasted angrily. The Irishman smiled to himself and tutted, 'Cavendish, Cavendish!' He drove on. He'd said he'd meet her an hour ago. He was heading for La Guardia now, for the Triborough Bridge, and then Harlem.

It was one o'clock in the morning in Small's Paradise on 7th Avenue and 135th. It was hot, however cold it was outside. The downtown whites with the appetite for it had left the restaurants and bars of Lower Manhattan to join the black crowds in Harlem now, where the music was always louder but more importantly always better, much better, and you could dance with a woman in ways that would have got you thrown out of the Rainbow Room for even thinking about. The mix of black and white customers was a natural thing in Small's; it was natural enough that nobody thought very much about it; Ed Small was black after all. There were white-owned, Jim Crow Harlem clubs, like the Cotton Club, where only the waiters and the musicians were black. But there were black clubs and black clubs of course; Small's Paradise was just about as black as Manhattan's more adventurous white downtowners and midtowners could comfortably cope with. John Cavendish was happy enough to be there for the music, which he had grown to love during his months in New York. He'd heard a lot of it now and he never tired of hearing more. It was like nothing he'd known, and whatever he'd heard before, on records or the radio, was only the palest reflection of what it felt like to be in a room with it. He was easy there; he would have been happy just to listen.

The Irish woman he was with, Kate O'Donnell, was maybe thirty, tall, with blue eyes that had the habit of always looking slightly puzzled. Her hair was cut just above her shoulders, blonde enough not to need bleaching, and with enough curl not to need perming; sometimes she even brushed it, but not so often that it looked brushed. She was dressed well, but if you'd asked her what she had on, she would have had to check. She wasn't easy sitting there. There was an edge of anxiety about her. She needed one of the trumpeters in the band with her when she talked to John Cavendish tonight.

If the captain was going to help her, she wanted him to help her now. She had started to feel he was putting it on the long finger. They needed to talk harder again; the captain, her, the trumpeter; they needed to move.

But talking to the trumpeter wasn't the only reason they were there at Small's Paradise. It was safe, safer than anywhere else. Harlem was the right side of Central Park, that's to say the wrong side; it was nobody's territory, at least nobody she knew, nobody who mattered.

The black trumpeter was playing now, standing up for a short, final solo as the band came to the end of 'Caravan'. Cavendish knew it; he'd been at Small's once before when Duke Ellington was playing. He liked swing; it was the sound he heard everywhere in New York. But the man at the piano, with the immaculately slicked hair and the faintest pencil-line moustache, went further than swing. What he played wasn't just music, it was the city itself; it was as delicate and ephemeral as it was hard and sharp and solid. The piano was the night air in Central Park one moment and a subway train the next. As the trumpeter sat down to a scattering of applause, the piano and the brushed cymbals took over. Cavendish took an envelope from his pocket and pushed it across the table to Kate. The music was louder again now as the band played the last, almost harmonious chord, and the whole club focused on Ellington and his musicians, clapping and shouting.

'That's the passport I promised,' said Cavendish. 'Two. If she needs to travel under another name, there's not much point you travelling under yours. It's unlikely she'll want it going into Canada, but with what's going on at the moment you don't need a problem.'

Kate picked up her handbag and put the envelope in it.

'My problem right now is she's still there, locked up in that place.'

The set had finished now, and the fading applause followed Ellington and his band off the stage. Another musician made his way to the piano and started to play, more quietly. Dancers drifted off the floor; the volume of conversation grew; trays of food and drink were coming at greater speed.

Jimmy Palmer, the trumpeter, pushed his way through the milling customers and waiters and cigarette girls, and sat down at the table with Kate O'Donnell and John Cavendish without saying a word. He lit a cigarette.

'So where are we, Kate?' he asked.

'John's at the Canadian border. I haven't got her off Long Island.'

She smiled as she said it, but it wasn't a joke.

'You really think he's going to come after her?' said Cavendish.

'We've been having this conversation for a month, John.' Kate was tired repeating herself. 'You've talked about helping us, and then you've talked about helping us, then you've

20

talked about it a bit more. He won't let her just go. How many times do I have to say it? She wouldn't be there in the first place if he was happy to let her go. If you're not going to do it –'

Jimmy Palmer just drew on his cigarette and watched.

'I need to be sure how careful we need to be, once we get her out of New York,' the army officer continued. 'The answer's still very. So you get her away from Locust Valley and I'll make sure you cross into Canada. I'm not trying to find a way out of it.' He took out a cigarette himself now; he caught the eye of a waiter and gestured for another round of drinks. 'I've said I'll use my car. There's not going to be anybody around to make a connection between you and an Irishman taking a little trip upstate –'

'I can get a car.' It was Jimmy who spoke now. 'I can do the trip.'

Kate smiled, reaching out her hand fondly to take his. He spoke with determination. It mattered to him in the same way it mattered to her. It was different for Cavendish; of course it was. He was there for what he could get. But he was the one they needed. He had the false passports.

'I know, Jimmy. But there's too many connections already. He knows you too. Anybody he sends after Niamh is going to know you. And people are going to notice a black man driving two white women around upstate.'

'Poor old Jim Crow, eh?'

He gave a wry smile. It didn't make the truth any easier. Harlem was his place; he was somebody here. Outside Harlem he wasn't anybody at all.

'I guess I know you're right.'

He shrugged; you couldn't argue much with how things were.

21

Kate turned back to Cavendish.

'I have talked to her. I've told her what she has to do. It's not easy. Once she's out of there it'll be different. Once she can breathe. Half the time she's so doped up she doesn't know what I'm saying. I don't know who's listening either. I am sure she can do it. It's just getting her to walk out –'

'That bit's down to you,' said the Irishman quietly. 'When we're out of New York it should be fine.' He picked up his drink. 'But I still need what I need from her. I need her in a state where she can think clearly.'

She nodded. He held her gaze for a moment. Maybe there was a part of him that was doing this because he had started to care now, about Kate and about her sister. But that wasn't why he was there. And Kate knew it.

'Niamh does know that. She has got the information.'

There was silence. Kate picked up her drink. She was tense again. Jimmy Palmer looked at them both. Whatever they were talking about didn't include him.

'Does know what?' he said, his eyes on Kate. 'What's this about?'

'It doesn't matter, Jimmy.'

She was awkward rather than dismissive, but it came across as dismissive anyway. Cavendish wouldn't want her to talk about any of that.

'It matters to me. And it sounds like it's going to matter to Niamh.'

The trumpeter turned to Captain Cavendish again. He didn't know him. He didn't know why he was involved, why he was giving out passports and booking liner tickets. He didn't like the fact that he was taking things over, in ways that weren't explained, ways that seemed to be about something a lot more than helping Kate O'Donnell and her sister because he was a nice guy. He had only met the captain three times; he didn't always feel like a nice guy. He watched people too much. 'So this'll be some li'l thing the nigger don't need concern hisself with, that right Massa John?'

'Come on, Jimmy. It's nothing of the kind,' said Cavendish.

'Maybe this nigger should know about it, Kate,' snapped Jimmy.

'He's not helping us for love,' said Kate, shaking her head. 'You must have worked that out. He wants something out of it. You know what Niamh was doing on the boats. You know she wasn't just any old courier either. Why should the captain do anything for nothing? Why should anybody? He's a soldier, an Irish soldier. You know what I'm talking about too.'

John Cavendish wasn't comfortable with what Kate was saying, but he didn't stop her saying it. He looked across at Jimmy Palmer and nodded.

Jimmy didn't like it but he could work it out, enough anyway.

'We can't do this on our own,' said Kate. It was all she could offer.

The trumpeter stubbed out his cigarette. The waiter arrived with the fresh drinks and passed them round. Palmer downed his bourbon in one.

'If there's a deal, then you do your part, Mr Cavendish. She can't stay there. And days, not weeks. Kate's seen her. She can't take much more.'

'I'm ready to go.' John Cavendish looked from Jimmy to Kate.

Jimmy was looking at Kate now too.

She nodded.

Ellington's band was straggling back on stage.

'I got the taxi,' said the horn player, getting up. 'Just give me the day.'

Kate nodded again. She picked up her drink.

Cavendish raised his and smiled.

Jimmy reached out his hand. John Cavendish shook it.

Kate smiled at them both. It wasn't much of a smile. She looked tired.

The trumpeter walked back to the stage.

'Do you want a lift, Kate?' She shook her head.

'No, I'll get a cab.'

'Sure?'

'It's better we're not seen together outside work.'

She was right.

Suddenly Duke Ellington's hands hit the piano hard. The drummer crashed the cymbal and top hat. Jimmy Palmer's horn was loud and liquid.

Outside it was cold. Kate O'Donnell slipped away, with no more than a last smile, a stronger smile now, and hailed a cab. John Cavendish watched her go for a moment, conscious that he had been delaying things. He didn't know what the consequences would be, that was all. There was no obvious connection to make between a woman escaping from a sanatorium on Long Island, where she was virtually a prisoner, and the IRA's courier system and its ciphered messages to and from America. But if the IRA was as careful as it ought to be, someone could decide changes were in order anyway, and that might mean his interceptions drying up. He pushed away all that and walked towards 7th Avenue to get his car. It was time to act; a file full of ciphers nobody could read was no use to anybody. He needed Niamh Carroll now.

The night was bright and noisy all around him; car horns,

laughter, singing, angry voices, somewhere a saxophone, the rattle of the trains from the el. It was still Ellington's music, all of it.

At the corner with 7th Avenue there were a few people standing in front of a small black man, not old but with strikingly white hair, who stood on a box speaking. In front of him there was a placard: The Ethiopian Pacific Movement – the Struggle between the New Order and the Old. People drifted by. Some paused, then walked on quickly. The night swept round the white-haired man. John Cavendish did stop, listening to his words. He had seen the man before.

'You think there's going to be change while those sonovabitch Jews run things? Even the white man's starting to listen now. Even the white man's got someone telling him what's righteous. You heard of Adolf Hitler? Now, he's a man got those sonovabitch Jews on the run. When he's kicked their butts, well, the white man can have Europe, that's all Hitler wants. He wants us to have our place and whitey to have his. Black place, white place. That's the world we want. So Herr Hitler is fighting our battle for us. He's fighting against white democracy, because white democracy is the biggest shit lie the Devil ever put on the earth. And you know what Herr Hitler's going to do? He's going to take Africa from the British and give it to the black man. That's coming brothers, believe me! And we got other friends too, not just Mr Hitler. We got the Japanese now. They want to kick the white man's ass out of the Pacific, like Hitler will in Africa. They'll kick it so hard you won't see a white man or a fucking sonovabitch Jew for dust!'

The words puzzled Cavendish now as they had puzzled him before, but the light of truth shone in the black man's eyes. He was looking at Cavendish, with a slight smile, only now registering his only listener. The captain smiled back amiably, pulled his hat on tighter, and walked off.

*

When Donal Redmond left John Cavendish's car in Queens he had walked two blocks to Lennon's Bar, the call house where the messages he brought from Ireland were dropped. He walked in through the bar, nodding to the barman and the two or three customers who were there, and headed straight for the back room. He knew the place; he knew the routine. And there'd be a couple of drinks afterwards. He opened the door into Paddy Lennon's office.

The old man was sitting at his desk, a green shade over his eyes, totting up figures. The room was tiny, lined with ledgers and files, the desk piled with skewered bills and receipts. Paddy raised his eyes and pushed up the shade.

'You're late.'

'Why the fuck's everyone always telling me I'm late?'

'Maybe it's got something to do with the time.'

'Is there a clock on this?'

Paddy Lennon simply smiled, but it was an odd sort of smile.

The steward put down his duffel bag and got out the Jacob's tin.

The bar owner took it and put it in a drawer in the desk.

'You should stay off the booze till a job's done, Donal.'

'I don't take orders from you. I deliver and you collect. That's it. I get my orders in Dublin. The job is done and that's that. The way it always is.'

'The way it always is,' said Paddy, pulling down his eye shade.

26

As Donal Redmond walked back to the bar there were two men standing in his way. One of them was a uniformed NYPD officer. The other man wore a grey raincoat and still had his hat on. He was a policeman too, a detective. He didn't need a uniform for the ship's steward to know it.

'Mr Redmond?' It was the detective who spoke.

'That's right.'

'I'd like a look at your passport and your papers.'

'What for?'

'Some sort of mix up, that's all.'

'What sort of mix up? I'm straight off my ship.'

The detective ought to have sounded apologetic; he didn't.

'We can give you a lift down to the precinct house. The sergeant just wants to look over the details. You can be on your way then. Will we go?'

There was something odd about the way they were looking at him. It wasn't unpleasant. It wasn't anything. But it was the same way Paddy Lennon had been looking at him in the back room. Donal Redmond knew he didn't want to go with them. The detective opened his coat to pull out a packet of cigarettes. As he did Redmond saw the shoulder holster and the gun that sat in it. The detective didn't take a cigarette from the packet. He was making a point. And the point was made.

As the three men left the bar, conversation among the customers resumed, as if they had never been there.

*

It was two days later that John Cavendish, sitting in the coffee bar across from the Irish Pavilion at the World's Fair, reading *The New York Times*, saw an item at the bottom of page seven. A man's body had been pulled out of the Hudson River. He had been identified from papers in his pocket as Donal Redmond, an Irishman who had only just arrived in New York; he had worked on the French Line boat, the *Normandie*, as a steward. It was believed that he had fallen into the Hudson from the ship, docked at Pier 17, when drunk.

It seemed that the captain's source had dried up now anyway. There would be no more IRA ciphers. He had to hope that they had enough to find out what was going on, and he had to hope that Kate O'Donnell's sister Niamh could give him what he needed most of all, the key to break the code, because no one was getting anywhere with deciphering the stuff in Dublin. He had hoped to get a bit more out of Donal Redmond though. He was disappointed; but probably not as disappointed as Donal had been himself.

3. Kilranelagh

West Wicklow

Garda Sergeant Stefan Gillespie was walking slowly down the stairs in the stone farmhouse below Kilranelagh. He was tired. The first ewes were lambing; he had been out in the haggard field behind the hay barn with his father till five in the morning, and now it was only eight. The smell of new life and morning frost was still in his nostrils; the clothes he'd lain down in were spattered with blood and urine, stiff with the grease from the ewes' fleeces. Four twins, two singles, and only one born dead, strangled by its umbilical cord before he could get his hand in to turn it. There was a frail, dark triplet the ewe would have no milk for, to be reared for a time by the kitchen stove.

He had only been half asleep as the telephone started to ring. If his father was in bed and his mother was in the kitchen, it might ring till he answered it. It sat on a shelf by the front door, still looking very new, its black Bakelite shining; it had been there for almost a year now and it was polished more than it was used. It rang rarely enough that when it did Helena Gillespie would emerge from the kitchen and look at it for a few seconds, with an air of mild trepidation that she had not yet quite shaken off, before picking it up and speaking into it, slowly, carefully and loudly. She was coming out of the kitchen now, drying her hands on a tea towel. She smiled as Stefan arrived at the phone at the same time she did, and turned to go back to the breakfast she was cooking.

Tom Gillespie, Stefan's nine-year-old son had got up from the breakfast table and was peering out. 'Who is it, Oma?' His grandmother shrugged. 'It'll be for your father. It always is.' And it was. Superintendent Riordan was calling from the Garda barracks in Baltinglass.

'You're to go up to Dublin, Sergeant. They want you at headquarters as soon as you can get there. There's no point coming in here. You'll need to shift if you're going to catch the train.' Riordan was oddly formal. He would normally have called his station sergeant by his name, but since the message he had just received came from the Commissioner, this was a standing-up sort of phone call. There was also a hint of irritation in his voice; he didn't like passing on a message from the Garda Commissioner to one of his officers when no one had had the courtesy to explain anything at all to him.

'What's all this about?' asked Stefan.

'If you don't know, I'm sure I don't.'

'Well, I haven't got the faintest idea, sir.' Stefan smiled; he heard the irritation now; the 'sir' might help. He looked down at the clothes he was in. No one expected him in at the station today. 'I'd better put a clean shirt on.'

'The Commissioner wants you at eleven, so don't piss about.'

The phone went down at the other end before Sergeant Gillespie could ask any more questions. Stefan walked into the kitchen, puzzled. Tom was eating his bacon and egg slowly, peering across the plate at the book he was reading, *The Adventures of Tom Sawyer*. Once he had grasped that the call was what most calls were at Kilranelagh, for his father, just another message, summons, query, instruction from the Garda station, he had lost interest. Helena was about to put another plate of bacon and egg on the table. Stefan reached out and picked up some bacon with his fingers and popped it in his mouth. That would have to do for breakfast.

Her lips tightened as she looked at his clothes.

'Jesus, could you not have taken those off when you came in?'

He winked at Tom; Tom laughed.

'Do you like making work for me, Stefan?'

'You know I do, Ma!'

She turned back to the stove with a puff of irritation and a smile.

He leant across her and took another piece of bacon.

'Have we got no plates now?'

'Sorry, I haven't got time.'

'Why not?'

'I've to be in Dublin. I'll only just get the train.'

'Why?'

'I don't know. They want to see me at Garda HQ. They didn't tell Gerry Riordan what it was about. I could see the expression on his face coming down the phone line at me!' He laughed again, grabbing an apple from the bowl on the sideboard. He looked down at the lamb, sleeping in a cardboard box by the stove. 'And don't forget her, will you Tom?'

'I won't,' his son nodded, still reading, not looking up.

He ran upstairs a lot faster than he'd come down. He

wasn't tired now. In a place where not much happened, anything happening was an event.

In the farmyard David Gillespie was driving a cow and a calf into the loose box next to the barn. Stefan took the bicycle that was leaning against the wall by the front door and cycled out round his father and the cow and calf; the cow stopped, bellowing darkly, and nudging her wobbling calf away.

'I don't know what time I'll be back, Pa. I've to go to Dublin.'

His father nodded and tapped the cow's backside.

'Your Ma said.'

'Ned Broy wants to see me. And pronto, apparently!'

'What have you done?' said David with a wry smile.

'He'll be worried about the sheep stealing again, I'd say, Pa.' He rode out of the farmyard, down to the road.

His father watched him for a while, remembering the years that had passed since his son was last called to Garda Headquarters. At the end of all that Stefan had left his job as a detective in Dublin, and had come back to Baltinglass to work as a uniformed sergeant in the small West Wicklow town. It had been his own choice, driven as much as anything else by the responsibility he felt to his own son. Tom was only five then, living with his grandparents on the farm, seeing his father once a week, sometimes less. The four years that had passed since then had been happy ones for the most part, but in a family where emotions were sometimes as deeply hidden as they were deeply felt, David Gillespie knew that what his son gave to that happiness came at a price.

It wasn't a price Stefan begrudged, but it was still a price. His life had been on hold. There were things that weren't

easy; there were corners where the comfortable content-
ment the Garda sergeant showed his Wicklow neighbours
was less than comfortable. He lived in a place he loved,
with the people he loved. It was what he had felt he had
to do; it was not all he was.

For Stefan's mother it was simple enough; all that was
missing was a woman, not to take the place of her son's
now six-years-dead wife, Maeve, but to fill the empty places.

David Gillespie knew it went further than that. A long
time ago he had put his own life on hold, for very different
reasons, and he had come back to the farm above Baltinglass
to give himself the space to breathe. He had breathed the air
that came down from the mountains very deeply, and like
his son he loved it, but it was a narrower life than he had
wanted, with all its gifts. David had found a way to calm
what was restless and dissatisfied in himself; perhaps he had
nowhere else to go. But he recognised the same restlessness
in his son; he recognised that it went deeper too.

He looked round the farmyard for a moment, then up
at the hills that surrounded it, Keadeen, Kilranelagh,
Baltinglass Hill. It was a great deal, but it would not be
enough, not the way it had been for him, even if Stefan
had persuaded himself it could be. David Gillespie shrugged,
and turned back to the suspicious cow and her calf, driving
them into the loose box.

Inevitably some of the same thoughts came into Stefan's
head as he cycled through Baltinglass's Main Street and
along Mill Street to the station, but it was easier to think
about the present than the past. As he sat on the train
following the River Slaney north towards Naas and Dublin,
he looked out of the window and thought how little what

he'd been doing in recent weeks could interest the brass in the Phoenix Park. He smiled. Sheep stealing really was about as serious as it got.

There was the new Dance Hall Act, of course, which required all dances to be licensed in light of the moral dangers the Church felt were inherent in dancing. A spate of unpopular raids was taking Stefan into the courthouse in Baltinglass on a weekly basis now. Yesterday he'd been giving evidence against the Secretary of the Dunlavin Bicycling Association and the Rathvilly Association Football Club. Admittedly the Dance Hall Act was causing considerable anger among the unmarried guards in Baltinglass who, when they weren't raiding the dances, were dancing at them.

Then there was the pen of in-lamb ewes he was pursuing, that had disappeared from Paddy Kelly's farm on Spynans Hill in February. Christy Hannity had bought them from Paddy at a farm sale and swore blind the old man had put them back on to the mountain while he was in the pub. It wasn't the first time Paddy Kelly had played this trick and got away with it. All he had to say now was that mountain sheep had their own ways and Christy was too drunk to remember what he'd done with them.

And there were two days wasted on James MacDonald who had assaulted the Water Bailiff, Cathal Patterson, after refusing to give up a salmon found in his possession by the Slaney. He claimed the salmon was a trout, which he had since eaten. As for the Water Bailiff's nose, didn't he break it himself, tripping over a dead cat as he was walking out of Sheridan's Bar?

It was hard to push the past out of the way altogether as Stefan walked from Kingsbridge Station through the

Phoenix Park to the long, low stone building that was part eighteenth-century army barracks and part Irish country house. Nothing very much had happened in the last four years; most of what had, had happened to his son. He had no problem with that; it was why he had left CID, why he had left Dublin, why he went home. But the thought of how easily and how completely he had left behind the job he had always wanted, since the day he joined the Gardaí, had never struck him as starkly before as it did in the few moments he spent waiting outside Ned Broy's office.

It hadn't only been about Tom of course. He had also left because it suited everybody, the Garda Commissioner included. He had been involved in investigating two murders that in the end nobody wanted investigated too publicly. There had been justice of a kind, finally, but it had been a rough justice that the Irish state didn't want to know about.

For a time it had been easiest for Detective Sergeant Gillespie to become plain Sergeant Gillespie in a country police station. No one had really meant him to stay there so long. He hadn't intended that himself. It just happened, because that was what was best for Tom. Now, as Stefan sat in Ned Broy's office again, he could feel an awkwardness in the Garda Commissioner. Sergeant Gillespie's submerging in a backwater had not been what he had intended either.

Whatever was urgent, the Commissioner's opening words weren't.

'So, how's West Wicklow?'

'Quiet enough, sir.'

'You're keeping Gerry Riordan in check, I hope.'

'Well, mostly he does what he's told.'

The Commissioner smiled. There was a moment's silence.

'You've been there a long time.'

'Four years doesn't seem so long. Time goes fast enough.'

'Bollocks, you're not old enough to say that yet.'

Stefan laughed. They were only words, but the Commissioner was looking at him quizzically now, remembering what had happened before.

'Your father's well? And your lad?'

The Commissioner had a good memory at least.

'We're all grand.'

'And you're happy down the country?'

'Happy enough, sir.' Stefan was aware that the polite remarks, whatever was about to follow, meant nothing to Broy, but it was the first time anyone had asked him such a direct question about his job, and by extension his life. The answer he gave was the answer any Irishman would give to such a question; an answer that could mean anything from despair to exultation, and everything in between. He was aware that he was avoiding a direct answer, not for the Garda Commissioner's sake, but for his own.

'A woman is missing.'

Broy suddenly stood up and moved slowly towards the window that looked out on to the Phoenix Park. The trees were still bare. Spring wasn't far away now, but it still felt like winter.

'There is every reason to believe she's dead, and that she was killed.' He turned back from the window. 'The fact that she's missing is the only thing that's been in the newspapers so far. We can keep it like that for a little longer. And it's helpful that we do, for various reasons. She is a Mrs Leticia Harris, with a house in Herbert Place.'

'I think I did read something about it, sir.'

'The evidence from the house, along with Mrs Harris's car,' continued the Commissioner, 'indicates that she was

36

the object of a very brutal attack in her home. Her car, however, was found in the grounds of a house close to Shankill, by the sea in Corbawn Lane. It's clear she had been in the car, or her body had. At the moment we believe she was killed at the house in Herbert Place, or at least that she was dead by the time she reached Corbawn Lane, where the body was probably taken from the car and thrown into the sea. What the tides have done with her is anybody's guess at this point.'

It was odd, but Stefan could feel his heart racing slightly. It was an unfamiliar feeling. It was excitement. It was four years since he had worked as a detective, but the instincts that had made him good at his job were still there. He felt as if a light had just been switched on inside his head.

'Mrs Harris has a son. Owen. He's twenty-one years old. I don't think we know enough about him to understand what kind of man he is, but we know his relationship with his mother was very difficult, in all sorts of ways. Some of those ways had to do with money. Mrs Harris has lived apart from her husband for a considerable time, over ten years in fact. He's a doctor, of some note, with a practice in Pembroke Road. From what Doctor Harris has told detectives, I think you'd describe the relationship between mother and son as highly strung, which is a polite way of saying they were a bloody peculiar pair. Superintendent Gregory at Dublin Castle is in charge, but it's a big operation, involving detectives from several stations, as well as Special Branch. The short version is that we believe Owen Harris murdered his mother and dumped her in the sea.'

'And where is he now?' asked Stefan. The Commissioner's tone of voice told him that wherever he was he certainly wasn't in Garda custody.

'New York.'

'That was quick work.'

'He left from Cobh two days after his mother disappeared.'

'So is he in custody? In New York?'

'No, but we know where he is.'

The Commissioner sat back down again, his lips pursed. It was more to do with irritation than anything else. Stefan could already sense this case was about more than a suspected murderer. Broy opened a file on his desk.

'Mr Harris is at the Markwell Hotel, which is somewhere near Times Square – 220 West 49th Street to be exact. It's felt there's no need for his arrest or extradition.'

Stefan was aware this was a slightly odd way of putting it, as if it wasn't entirely the Commissioner's decision.

'He's agreed to come back to Ireland voluntarily to be interviewed, as soon as possible, as soon as practical. That's why you're here, Sergeant.'

This may have been the most interesting conversation Stefan Gillespie had had in a police station since he went to Baltinglass as station sergeant, but so far its purpose was as clear as mud. He looked at Broy blankly.

'The business of bringing this man Harris back from New York is a delicate one. It's all going to cause a stir when it comes out here, and the powers that be would rather it didn't do the same thing in New York. Since he's agreed to return, as I say, simply so that we can talk to him, the decision has been made not to involve the police in New York. Mr McCauley, the consul, has seen him, and there is a feeling that his mental state is – well, I think unpredictable is the word he used.'

Stefan nodded, as if this clarified things.

'Mr Harris is in New York with the Gate Theatre. He's some sort of stage manager. They're on a tour and they're about to open on Broadway.'

The expression on Broy's face indicated that this explained something else; it didn't but the presence of the past, and of conversations in the Commissioner's office four years ago, was closer.

'This Gate tour coincides with the opening of the World's Fair in New York. You'll have read about that, I'd say, and the Irish Pavilion? It's de Valera's pride and joy.'

'A bit,' replied Stefan.

'You won't have read how much the fecking pavilion's costing.' Broy gave a wry smile. 'There aren't many state secrets more secret than that one.'

'I see,' said Stefan, though he still didn't.

'It's all about punching above our weight, that's the thing. That's how our leader sees it anyway. There's a pavilion from almost every country on the face of the earth, but we're not there to show what great fellers we are on our Emerald Isle. We're there to show the way, to the small countries of the world. Dev wouldn't want you to think we're spending all that money we don't have just to boost the holiday trade. It's a grander scheme altogether. Aren't we God's living proof that the great empires are dead and it's the independent nations that will inherit the earth?'

'Well, I wouldn't put too much money on it at the moment,' said Stefan. 'What do they think about that in what's left of Czechoslovakia?' The presence of what the newspapers had been full of for weeks, Germany's dismemberment of at least one of those small nations, was hard to ignore.

'Well, they might not have got a country, but I think they've got a pavilion at the World's Fair,' shrugged the

Commissioner. 'The future may be a long way off so. But I'm telling you why what happens in New York is important, to Dev anyway. And while we show the world what we've done since we kicked out the British Empire, a bit of theatre on Broadway will add to the kudos. The Gate tour is all part of it, but the whole thing's a performance. Nobody wants headlines about an Irish actor who stopped to murder his mother before he set off for New York. We need your man Harris out of America and back here as fast as we can manage it, before he turns into the spectre at the feast. You're going to New York to fetch him.'

It was an unexpected proposition.

'I assume there's a reason it's me, sir.' Stefan couldn't think of one.

'Mr Harris is in a hotel room. The consulate's keeping an eye on him, but the people looking after him are his friends, other actors. No police, no heavy hands. I think it's all a lot riskier than the politicians do, but that's the decision. Mr Mac Liammóir is the one who has persuaded Harris to come back. It's his company after all. I don't imagine he'd be any more enthusiastic about the wrong sort of headlines than anyone here. Everyone wants the man out of there quietly. And in Mr Mac Liammóir's words he doesn't want some bollocks of a Dublin detective putting the shite up him. In a police force staffed mostly by bollockses – you were the least like a bollocks he could think of.'

Sergeant Gillespie smiled. It was four years since he'd last spoken to Mac Liammóir, the actor and director who was the Gate Theatre's founder, but he didn't need to be told those were his words.

Four years ago the body of a young man had been found

buried in the Dublin Mountains, close to the body of a woman who had recently disappeared. It had been a Gate theatre ticket that had helped identify the man, but the investigation had taken Stefan Gillespie a long way from Dublin, to Danzig and the heart of the European crisis that was now threatening to spill into war. It had brought him face to face with what mattered most in his life. It had led him to the only woman he had come close to loving since the death of his wife, Maeve, six years ago. When it finished the thread of passion that had held Stefan Gillespie and Hannah Rosen briefly together had broken. It had been inevitable.

The investigation itself had concluded in the dark corridors where unwanted investigations were given an indecent burial. Micheál Mac Liammóir was a memory from that time, but Stefan remembered him as a man who had looked for discretion and trust from him, and had found it. Clearly those same qualities still mattered.

'So everyone's pretending he's not a murder suspect, sir?'

'We're dealing with this at a distance.' The Commissioner ignored the question. 'The conversations are in telegrams and even they're at second or third hand. The decision not to involve the New York police is a political one. Extradition could drag on for months if Harris digs his heels in. We'd a feller embezzled six hundred pounds as a tax collector in Kerry. It took nearly a year to get him extradited from Boston. Even that made *The New York Times*. If your man takes it into his head not to cooperate and we have to drag him through the courts, well, axe-murderers make great headlines. Not the ones Dev wants. Mac Liammóir thinks Harris is harmless if he's handled the right way. His mother might have had a few things to say about that, but at the end of it all, a policeman who's not too much like a policeman is what we want.'

'Should I take that as a compliment, sir?' said Stefan, smiling.

'Mr Mac Liammóir obviously thinks it is. I'm going along with this because we are relying on the Gate. I don't need to tell you it isn't going down well everywhere. Superintendent Gregory is in charge of the investigation. You know him?'

Stefan knew who Gregory was. 'I've probably met him. I think he was at the Castle, in Special Branch, when I was a detective at Pearse Street.'

'Special Branch is running it. There's no reason to think it involves anyone other than the mother or the son, except that it's already dragging in the government, the Department of External Affairs and my fucking Uncle Tom Cobley. And while I wouldn't say Dev's a friend of the family, he'd know the father. Doctor Harris carries some weight. So there's that too. Put it all together and you see why kid gloves are the order of the day, Sergeant.'

Though Stefan nodded, he wasn't sure that handing the thing over to Special Branch was the answer to that; kid gloves weren't their speciality.

'You fly to New York the day after tomorrow.'

Stefan was surprised; he had assumed he would be going by boat.

'You'll know the flying boat service has just started operating from Foynes. I won't tell you what it'll cost, but somebody seems to think the wrong headlines will cost more. It will get you to New York in less than twenty-four hours. You'll be there two days and then straight back. A boat's going to take more than a fortnight. Right now the kid gloves are yours, Stefan. I don't need to tell you Terry

Gregory thinks this is shite. He may be right, but I'm doing it the way I've been asked, softly-softly. My office will make all the arrangements. There's a detective here to fill you in. He'll take you to see the superintendent.' Ned Broy laughed. 'Don't expect much of a reception.'

As he left the Garda Commissioner's office Stefan was surprised to see that the detective waiting for him was not the surly, jumped-up bollocks from Special Branch he was expecting, but the large and familiar figure of Dessie MacMahon, once his partner in the detectives' office at Pearse Street Garda station. Dessie and Stefan had kept in touch over the years, but it was still a while since the two men had seen each other.

'How's it going, Sarge?' grinned Dessie.

'You tell me, Sergeant,' Stefan answered. 'It is sergeant now?'

'Well, if you sit on your arse long enough –'

'So what's this got to do with you?'

'They're stuck with me. I was the first detective into Herbert Place. The maid called Pearse Street when she went into the house and saw the state of Mrs Harris's bedroom, the blood that is. So I'm working out of Dublin Castle for the time being. But everybody's getting a look in on this one, I tell you. I don't know why. Superintendent Gregory decided the son killed the old lady the day they found her car at Shankill. But you still can't move for inspectors and superintendents and chief superintendents. We've got Inspector O'Sullivan and Superintendent Dunlevy from Dún Laoghaire, Chief Superintendent Reynolds from Headquarters, Superintendent Clarke from Bray, not to mention Special Branch calling the shots at the Castle.'

'You know I've got to bring Harris back from New York?'

'I've to take you to see Superintendent Gregory,' nodded Dessie. 'You know you'll be getting more of a bollocking than a briefing from him?'

Stefan smiled. 'Let's get on with it so.'

'He's busy at the moment. He'll be out at Corbawn Lane later.'

'Corbawn Lane where –'

'Where Mrs Harris's car was. It's where he dumped her in the sea.'

'So what do we do now?'

'The only instructions I've got are that you're a fucking messenger boy and that's how you're to be treated. You're not a fucking detective. You're not part of the fucking investigation. Nobody's to tell you anything about anything, or give you even a sniff of the job. You'll be bollocked when the super's got the time. Apart from that, Mr Gregory didn't tell me to welcome you aboard, but I'm sure if he wasn't so busy he would have.'

They walked out of Garda Headquarters.

'I tell you what I'd like to do?' Stefan gave Dessie a wry smile. It was a long time since he'd been this close to a murder. 'Have a look at Herbert Place. That's where she was killed? So if you were the first one in there –'

'Didn't you hear what I said?'

'Yes, so it'll be more than your job's worth. Is that right?'

Detective Sergeant MacMahon grinned.

'With a bit of luck.'

*

44

'Blood.'

As Detective Sergeant Dessie MacMahon started to climb the stairs of the big Georgian terrace in Herbert Place he pointed at the fifth tread, without stopping. Sergeant Stefan Gillespie did stop, bending to look down at the dark, densely patterned stair carpet; red, black, yellow, thistle-like flowers endlessly repeated. Only the chalk marks showed him where to look; a small brown stain stood out against yellow and red.

'Blood.'

Dessie pointed at two of the uprights on the grey-painted banister. It was a long time since they had been painted. Again only traces of chalk made the smears of brown that could have been almost anything, or even nothing at all, immediately visible.

'Blood.'

As he carried on Dessie's left hand gestured at a chalk circle beside two crooked picture frames. They had been recently knocked askew; an oval, ebonised frame enclosing a sepia photograph of a heavily bearded man in a frock coat; a chipped, gilt square of plasterwork surrounding a sampler that was a map of Ireland with the counties outlined in green thread. Between them another streak of something brown marked the muddy swirls of the embossed wallpaper. Where the frames had moved they revealed that once the indeterminate colour of the wallpaper had been a startling emerald green. There was little wallpaper to be seen however.

The staircase wall, like the walls of the hall and the landing above it, was lined with pictures, maps, photographs; paintings of dogs and horses; faded prints of flowers; maps of Ireland, Britain, India, the Mediterranean.

45

The mostly Victorian men and women who gazed out of the heaviest frames, with a mixture of confidence and disapproval, looked old whatever age they were. It was all heavy, dark, as if the images and colours lining the walls had faded into a uniform smog.

Dessie stopped as the staircase turned to the right, on to the landing, where the repeated pattern of the carpet stretched left and right along the corridor, between the gloomy, embossed walls and the grey-painted doors. It was lighter here though. A window gave on to Herbert Place below. Dessie was slightly breathless. A larger, elliptical chalk circle spread out on to the landing from the top stair; the bloodstains were clearer here.

'She must have been carried out the bedroom. But the body was put down here a moment. There's more blood on the walls up there, and on the pictures.' Dessie gestured to the left, along the corridor, where several more prints and photographs hung at odd angles. 'Either he put her down or he dropped her.'

Stefan looked. Dessie walked on past two closed doors.

The third door was open. Through it was a big bedroom as cluttered and claustrophobic as the hall and the landing. There were clear signs of a struggle: smashed ornaments, pictures knocked off the walls, a broken chair, a table on its side, sheets and blankets pulled across the big bed on to the floor. But where the smell in the hallway and on the landing was of polish and dust and years of airlessness, the smell here was of smoke and burnt wood; not strong but acrid and sharp.

Dessie took out a packet of Sweet Afton and lit a cigarette. Stefan walked into the centre of the room. There were two small rugs, though it was clear the rest of the floor had

46

been covered until recently too. The floorboards were grimy with age but they had only been varnished at the edges of the room. A carpet must have covered the area in front of the bed, though it wasn't there now. Close to the bottom of the bed the floorboards were blacker than elsewhere, charred. Stefan looked at the black patch and bent down. He rubbed something that was like charcoal on to his fingers.

'Just in time, I'd say.'

Dessie nodded. 'When the maid came in there was an electric fire on. It must have been going full pelt for a couple of days. The boards were starting to burn underneath. If she hadn't come back when she did the place would have gone up so. She threw a bucket of water over it.' He laughed and drew in some more smoke. 'She fused the whole house, but it did the trick.'

'So do you think it was deliberate? Starting a fire?'

'I'd say not,' replied Dessie. 'There'd have to be better ways to do that. No, this was where she was killed and there was a lot of blood. Someone tried to clean it up. There's soap mixed with the blood. The story is he put the fire on to dry the floor, then left. But as he never came back –'

Stefan was still looking down at the floor.

'What happened to the carpet?'

'The State Pathologist took some of the rugs and the bedclothes, but the carpet had gone already. Your man must have had it. It would have been soaked looking at what's round the room. Maybe he brought it with him. Maybe he wrapped the body in it. There's not a lot of blood in the car. She was on the back seat, so she must have been covered in something anyway.'

'So with all this blood – she was stabbed? Is there a weapon?'

'I'll show you where the axe was. We'll go out the back way.'

The garden that led down to the mews at the back of the house in Herbert Place was neatly kept, but it was bare and grey. Squares of grass and small, dark rhododendrons; tightly clipped bushes took up the flower beds. When the spring came there would be few enough flowers to give colour. Dessie pointed out several chalk-marked stains on the stone paved path that led to the two-storey mews; a little more blood to mark where the body had been half-dragged and half-carried from the house.

They walked through a door into the gutted stables that had once housed the family's horses, and now smelt of the leaked engine oil that stained the stone floor. There were a couple of bicycles, some garden tools, a workbench full of spanners and wrenches, rusty and cobwebbed. Against one wall was a pile of cut turf, with sticks for the fires stacked beside it. Dessie stood by the turf and kicked at it.

'There was a small hatchet here, under a pile of turf. There's a gardener comes in now and again. He uses it for splitting wood for a bit of kindling. So it was kept in the garage. It had a good wash but there was still blood on it. They think it was maybe hot water, so instead of the blood running away it coagulated. They reckon it must be what killed her though.'

He walked across the empty garage to the double doors.

'Mrs Harris's car was kept in here. So he must have brought the body in, then shoved her on to the back seat. Bit tight in a Baby Austin. Timings aren't very clear. Only one sighting of the car. It was probably dark when he left.'

Detective Sergeant MacMahon opened one of the doors.

'Evening, night?' asked Stefan as they walked out into the lane that ran behind Herbert Place. It was almost empty, as it must have been then.

'Not late. Seven, maybe eight o'clock.'

Two boys were walking slowly along the lane towards Mount Street. Stefan Gillespie watched them for a moment as Dessie lit another cigarette. They were ten or eleven, one of them dragging a cart behind him, the base of an old pram, stacked with broken boxes and cardboard.

He recognised the boys' slow, patient walk from the years he had spent tramping the streets of Dublin as a guard. There were thousands of children just like them. He recognised the odd combination of resignation and anticipation in the way they moved, their eyes alert for any piece of wood, anything that would burn, anything that would keep a fire going in the tenement where there was never any money for coal or turf, or anything else. He recognised the grey clothes drained of any colour they might once have had, too big on one boy, too small on the other, that had been handed down more times than anyone could remember. He knew the damp, dark, rotten, infested houses that Éamon de Valera's new Ireland had still not touched, and he knew the cold, crowded room in one of those houses that the boys would live in.

Suddenly one of them darted across the lane with a shout to grab the prize of half of an orange box. They were laughing. And after the blood and the well-heeled claustrophobia of the house where Leticia Harris had been hacked to death, their laughter was a reassuring sound. Stefan smiled, turning back to Dessie.

'So where is she?'

Sergeant MacMahon shrugged, drawing on his Sweet Afton.

'We've got a sweepstake going at the Castle. They reckon it was high tide when the old lady was thrown in the sea. My money's on Scotland.'

4. Corbawn Lane

Corbawn Lane was a long, straight road that led from the village of Shankill to the sea. There were dark hedges and closely planted trees on both sides of the lane; the trees reached up and arched across the road almost the whole length, sometimes meeting in the middle. Even with the trees not yet in leaf, the straight line of the lane created the effect of a tunnel out of the skeleton branches.

Eight miles south of Dublin, Shankill was a place of small farms and country houses, just beyond the reach of the city's slowly spreading suburbia. Around the village clusters of new bungalows payed homage to a still very English idea of what it was to live near the sea, but they were also a statement that the city had its eye on Shankill's fields and estates. Yet Corbawn Lane was still a long way from Dublin. Every so often a break in one of the long hedges announced that somewhere among the trees there was a big house: Dorney Court, Lisnalurg, Clarebeg, then across the bridge over the railway, Llanmawr, Eaton Brae, and then, where the lane finally ended, hard against the sea and the small cliff beyond, the turning to the right, past the last lodge, into the last house called Clifton.

Several cars were parked in front of the house, among

them the Austin that Dessie MacMahon had driven down from Herbert Place.

It was a grey house; the grey stucco beneath the grey-black roof was grubbily spotted with algae and lichen in various shades of grey, and at the corners of the house it was starting to crumble away. The house itself was empty; it had been empty for a long time. The big downstairs windows that looked out over the garden to the sea were covered by boards that had themselves become grey and stained over the years; upstairs the curtains were closed.

The gardens that led across the lawn to a row of trees and the sea were controlled rather than cared for; someone came to cut the grass and stop the borders going wild but that was all.

Stefan Gillespie and Dessie MacMahon stood at the far side of the garden where a thick hedge separated it from the low cliffs and the sea beyond. The hedge was smashed and broken; the grass around it was muddy and churned; there were the deep ruts of car tyres that had been spinning and spinning aimlessly there.

'I told you about the Baby Austin Mrs Harris drove. She'd only had it three months. It was her pride and joy apparently. She seems to have spent most of those three months driving it around Dublin. And this is where they found it, jammed into the hedge right here. The night she disappeared a friend of hers saw the car coming out of Herbert Place and turning on to Baggot Street. The woman thinks it was Owen Harris who was driving it.'

'So he brought it here? With the body in the back?' said Stefan.

'It's hard to see it any other way. He had to get rid of it. He must have decided the sea was his best bet. It wasn't such a daft idea either. She hasn't been found. Whether he was trying to get the car into the sea as well –'

They both looked up for a moment. There was the drone of an aircraft overhead. A small plane was following the coast, northwards towards Dublin. Across the garden hedge where the cliff dropped down to the beach below, uniformed guards were walking along at the water's edge, their eyes fixed on the sand and rock; offshore there were two small boats. The beach had been searched and re-searched, but every day it was searched again with the tides in case the sea gave anything up.

'We're up and down the whole east coast,' said Dessie, 'from Wexford right up to the North. They're looking in Wales, Scotland, the Lancashire coast. Not a sign of her.'

'It's going to be hard work keeping all that quiet, isn't it?'

'It's a missing woman, that's all anybody's saying.'

'So why here?' asked Stefan.

'It was the family house. Where Harris lived when he was a lad, before the old man and the old lady went their ways. They'd been living apart for years. The father still owns it. So the assumption is Owen Harris knew it, that's the long and the short of it. And he knew it was empty.'

'And he tried to drive straight through the hedge?'

'That wasn't such a good idea. It's some hedge. And he got it stuck. It went through so far, but it couldn't get any further. Then the wheels started to spin and it wouldn't move at all. He couldn't go forward and he couldn't back out. So the story is he got her out of the car and dragged her through the hedge. He pulled her, carried her, whatever he did, and he got her down on to the rocks. Then he shoved her off. It was high tide. Whether that was luck or he knew – I guess he'll tell us that himself, eventually. It did the job. The problem was the car. Nothing was going to move it. Or get the blood off the back seat. He had no choice. He just left it here and he went home . . .'

'Where's the car now?'

'It's in the garage at Dublin Castle. They've had a good go at it, the State Pathologist and the rest. It's given us more blood and it makes it hard to argue Owen Harris wasn't here. Not that he seems to have gone to great lengths to hide that. He stopped a car at the top of Corbawn Lane by the AA box and asked the feller for a ride into town. He got dropped in Ballsbridge.'

'Jesus, what the hell did he look like by then?' Stefan shook his head.

'Let's say he made an impression. It was a couple, a man and a woman. I think when he walked out in front of the car they were too scared not to give him a lift. He told them he was an Englishman from Tunbridge Wells, on holiday. They had no idea what he'd done of course, but I think they were relieved to reach Ballsbridge in one piece. The conversation was a bit one-sided, but they said he apologised for the Norman invasion, the Famine, the Act of Union, the Black and Tans, and the Economic War, and said he hoped political developments would bring a new dawn in Anglo-Irish relations.' Dessie laughed. 'For some reason "new dawn" did stick.'

Stefan was laughing too.

Sergeant MacMahon took out a cigarette, cupping his hands to light it.

'So does anyone know what it was all about?'

'Apart from the fact that the mother and son were both barking?'

'And were they?' asked Stefan.

'They were always fighting the peace out, according to the maid anyway. Mrs Harris was a great one for throwing the delft across the room.'

'Just an ordinary Irish family then.'

'Well, there was definitely something wrong upstairs,' said Dessie. 'She'd come out of a convalescent home six weeks ago. She'd been in there a month. For the rest, according to Doctor Harris. Superintendent Gregory likes to refer to him as the "estranged" husband. They were all a bit strange if you ask me. Anyway, the doctor says she was very highly strung. Fragile nerves. She needed rests like that quite a lot. This time it was after she'd broken into the old fella's house and stolen a canteen of cutlery. She locked herself in her bedroom with it for three days.'

'When did the marriage break up?'

'They hadn't lived together since Owen Harris was seven. That's when they were all here. The old man's in Pembroke Road now. He owns the house in Herbert Place too. She didn't have any money. He kept the both of them.'

'So Owen Harris had a row with his mammy and killed her?' Stefan frowned. 'And that's it. What did she do, throw one plate too many at him?'

'Maybe we'll find out when we get him back,' replied Sergeant MacMahon. 'The maid says they were rowing about money. He wanted some and she wouldn't give it to him. It was to do with this theatre tour in America, the Gate. The actors had to stump up their own fares. So that's what he needed it for.'

'And she wasn't having it?'

'There wasn't a lot of spare money about. She lived on what her husband gave her. He wouldn't be a man to throw it about, so they say.'

'But there was money, wasn't there?' continued Stefan.

'There was a bit Mrs Harris had from working for the Hospitals' Sweepstake. She did a lot of that, but they only paid her expenses. It's meant to be charity. She had an office in a room at the back of the house, and a secretary came in sometimes to do a bit of typing. That's it. There wouldn't have been any sort of living in it at all. Money was the main topic of conversation at Herbert Place, well, how Mrs Harris never had any was.'

'She had a brand new car!'

'She did so,' said Dessie, 'and in a shoebox on top of the wardrobe in her bedroom, she had a box with six hundred and seventeen pounds in it.'

'That doesn't make much sense.'

Dessie shrugged; it didn't.

'So where did that come from?'

'Same place as the car.'

'Doctor Harris didn't buy her that then?'

'No. She bought it herself.'

'And –'

'And what? Nobody seems bothered about it at the Castle.'

Stefan was surprised. He would have wanted to know.

'So Harris killed his mother because she wouldn't give him the money he wanted, and then left six hundred pounds sitting on top of the wardrobe?'

'The assumption is he didn't know it was there.'

'But he did get the money to pay for the boat to New York?'

Sergeant MacMahon shrugged again. Although he had offered no opinions, Stefan knew that he didn't think much of the investigation.

'Couldn't he have got that from the father?'

'No. The old man thinks he's a waster. As for the acting, it's a joke as far as he's concerned. I've only seen the old feller once. Superintendent Gregory brought him to Herbert Place. I wouldn't say he had much to do with them any more, the lad or his mother. He gave them both an allowance of some sort, as little as he could get away with, that's the word.'

Stefan Gillespie was looking down at the hedge and the tyre tracks.

'Did anyone know she had money?'

'She was always short. Bills were never paid. But she had cash when she wanted it. No one else is very interested in what the maid had to say, but Mrs Harris bought clothes she never wore and paid a lot for them. She was fond of fur as well. And when she bought the Austin Seven she paid cash. When she went out to a restaurant with her friends she didn't just go anywhere. And she always paid her share too.'

'You got on well with the maid, did you?' smiled Stefan.

'They had her sitting around at Dublin Castle long enough.'

'So where does she think the money came from?'

'I wasn't in on any of the interviews.'

'But you asked her, Dessie, come on!'

'She doesn't have much doubt about it. The old lady was fiddling the Sweepstake. She collected up the money that came in from abroad. It went to a post office box, but the post office delivered it to Herbert Place. Some days there'd be sackfuls, from all over, England, America, Australia, Canada, New Zealand, cheques, postal orders, and cash. Hundreds of pounds. She took the cheques into a bank in

Baggot Street, cashed the postal orders, and then delivered it all to the Sweepstake office. She kept accounts, but I don't know how they were checked. It wouldn't have been hard to skim a bit off.'

'And Superintendent Gregory isn't looking at that?' asked Stefan.

'They've decided they know what happened. The eejit son killed her and chucked her in the sea. It's as far as anyone needs to look. Or wants to.'

Stefan was puzzled, even after everything Dessie had said.

'And how many detectives are there on this?'

'They're looking for the body, Sarge.' Dessie laughed again. He was still calling Stefan 'Sarge', though he was now a sergeant himself; old habits. He was enjoying this conversation; old habits, old times. 'Nobody's got any doubt about what happened. I don't know whether Owen Harris really thinks he's coming home for a chat, but I'd say he could be coming back for the long drop. As for the Sweepstake business, it's nothing to do with anything, I've been told. I'm not saying they've got it wrong, but no one wants to know any more. If he was here he must have been here with the body.'

Stefan nodded. Maybe there were other things to find out. Maybe for some reason there were things to find out that nobody really wanted to look into. But there were enough facts to make it hard to see beyond Owen Harris killing his mother and dumping her body out here.

He looked at the sea for a moment. He knew the smell of all this now. There were people who mattered in it. There were lids to be kept on things. There was a show to put on at New York's World's Fair that was far more important than a squalid and brutal murder in Ireland. There were reputations riding on it. There were newspaper headlines that Ireland's hard-earned money had bought. Now there was the country's Hospitals' Sweepstake too; it brought in money the country didn't have, to pay for hospitals it desperately needed, money from all over the world; it was money that would dry up in the face of newspaper headlines about laziness, incompetence, fraud. Stefan could see now why the investigation was in the hands of the Special Branch.

There was a crime to solve that seemed to have an easy, ready solution. But it had to be solved in a way that meant it was contained and controlled. Special Branch was there to make sure there was no spillage. He was a part of the politics now.

The Garda Commissioner was sending him to New York because he could bring Harris back to Ireland with the lid firmly on; without giving him the slightest idea he might be coming home to hang.

'Enjoying yourself, Sergeant Gillespie?'

Stefan turned at the sound of a voice behind him. Introductions were unnecessary. Superintendent Gregory knew who he was, that was clear.

'It'll be a treat for you, coming all the way to Dublin on the train.'

Terry Gregory was in his mid-fifties, his face round and red in the way that marked out detectives who spent more time in the pub than the office. He wore a black overcoat that was too small for him, a brown trilby that was too big. The smile on his face was temporary; it would change to a sneer shortly. But the smile, like the imminent sneer, advertised displeasure.

Behind him stood two detectives in belted raincoats and

hats, like leftovers from an IRA demob sale. They were there because Special Branch superintendents never travelled alone. It would not be their job to speak.

'So, you've been specially asked for by Mr Mac Liammóir?'

'It seems that way, sir.'

'Close to him are you?'

'I've met him.'

'You'd be well advised to guard your backs with this one, lads.'

The two detectives laughed; that was one of their jobs.

'Still, you're down in Wicklow with the mountainy men and the sheep shaggers, so maybe you'll be just the man to take our Mr Harris in hand. So what's it about, Sergeant Gillespie? That's what I'd like to know. What are you doing here, and why the fuck is Ned Broy sending you to New York? You're only a culchie station sergeant who couldn't make it as a detective.'

'I'm here because I've been told to be here, sir.'

'And I've told Ned Broy what I think about it.'

'He did say something about that.'

'I see, you think you're a clever fucker as well, do you?'

Stefan said nothing. Gregory turned to Dessie.

'And what the hell are you doing?'

'Nothing, sir,' replied Detective Sergeant MacMahon.

'No, nothing is what I told you to do, Dessie, but what you've been doing is taking our farmer's boy on a scene-of-crime tour, as if he's got something to do with this investigation.'

He swung round to Stefan again; any trace of a smile was gone now.

'I don't like people interfering with what I do. I don't care if they come from Garda HQ or the Taoiseach's office, it pisses me off. Now they're coming from the poofs' paradise at the fucking Gate Theatre. I'm stuck with you because Ned Broy hasn't got the balls to tell the politicians where to put it. So this is what you do, Stevie boy. You get the plane, you look out the window with your eyes agog, and you go to New York. You get back on the plane with Harris and sit next to him until you get off at Foynes next week. I'll be there, and when you've handed him over to me, you get the next train back to Baltinglass. In between you don't ask him anything, you don't talk about what happened, about Mrs Harris's death, about how he killed her, what he did with the body, where he went, who he saw, who he spoke to. You do nothing that could fuck this up. You're the courier and he's the parcel. Is that clear enough?'

'I'd say so. But what do I do about him talking to me?'

Superintendent Gregory had given Sergeant Gillespie his orders. He wasn't asking to have a conversation about it. 'You tell him to shut up too.'

'What about the Gate?' asked Stefan quietly but insistently.

'Would you like me to write it down, Sergeant?'

'He's got friends there. He's been with them since the day after the murder. He's been shut in a hotel room with some of them since he agreed to come back to Ireland. Wouldn't you want to know what he's been saying?'

'I'm sorry, Stevie, I didn't realise Ned told you to take over.'

'It's a simple question, sir.' Stefan allowed his irritation to show.

Terry Gregory walked forward until he was only inches from him. For the first time he spoke very quietly. The whiskey was strong on his breath.

'You might not have much of a job down there, Sergeant, but if you screw this up, you'll be sitting on an island off the Atlantic till the day you draw your pension. Nobody wants to know what you think. Now fuck off.'

He spun round and strode rapidly across the grass. The Special Branch detectives followed him. There was only the sound of the sea breaking slowly, rhythmically on the rocks below. Dessie MacMahon too started back towards the house.

Stefan was still for a moment. It was a peaceful place. The thought of what had happened barely a week ago seemed to collide in his mind with the image of a small boy playing in the garden, running down to the sea. He looked at the boarded-up French windows and remembered a photograph on the bloodstained wall at Herbert Place. He had barely noticed it, yet it had stayed in his head; a boy, freckled, in shorts and a white shirt and sandals, smiling by the same big windows, wide open then, pulling a wooden cart full of sand.

Stefan heard the buzz of the plane, searching for any signs of Leticia Harris's body. He turned and walked on after Dessie.

*

It was just starting to get dark as Stefan Gillespie walked through the fields on the western side of the farm at Kilranelagh, across the Moat Field towards the woods that abruptly fell down the steep escarpment on the far side of the townland. The sheep were thick-coated and filthy with the winter's rain; the grass was bare and poached, still waiting for the spring flush to show. He noted a ewe hobbling painfully, another down on her knees trying to find some grass worth eating. He had meant to help his father with the foot rot at the weekend; he wouldn't be here.

He could hear the sound of children's voices, and he altered his course down the slope towards the high mound that sat just beyond the corner of the field, a cluster of trees rising out of the woods, higher than everything else around it, looking down at the narrow gash of rock and earth and scrappy hazel woodland that was the steep-sided valley they called Moatamoy, after the mound itself.

It was no more than a smooth, round hillock, with a flat top full of twisted trees and brambles and ivy. Eight hundred years ago the top had been surrounded by a wooden palisade. A Norman village of grass-roofed, wattle-and-daub-and-stone houses had clustered at the corner of the field below it, indistinguishable from the grass-roofed, wattle-and-daub-and-stone houses of the Celts the palisaded motte was there to protect its inhabitants from. The Anglo-Normans who had lived here had sometimes fought the people around them, sometimes traded with them, sometimes killed them, sometimes married them, until eventually they had been absorbed into their surroundings so completely that they became, in the words that would always define them, níos Gaelaí ná na Gaeil iad féin, more Irish than the Irish.

Now the sheep grazed where the village had been, but the motte was still a castle, at least in the minds of the children who played there.

Stefan could pick out the voices as he climbed over the wire fence into the ditch that surrounded the motte. Tom's first of all, shrill and enthusiastic and, it couldn't be denied, with more than a hint of bossiness about it when the game was his game. He could hear the voices of the Lessingham children, Alexander who was seven, Jane who was ten, and the voice of the Lawlors' son, Harry. Stefan started up the slope of the mound and found himself grabbed forcefully from behind; an arm was round his neck, holding him.

'Surrender!' The words hissed into his ear.

'I surrender! Just don't choke me!'

As the arm released him he turned, coughing and spluttering, to see a woman laughing at him.

'Be quiet,' she whispered, 'and we'll see if we can creep up on them.'

He nodded and smiled. He was used to it. For a moment the woman looked at him, and he looked at her. They were standing very close among the trees. He bent forward and kissed her lips. It was fond rather than passionate, but its familiarity told a deeper story.

At thirty-four Valerie Lessingham was a year older than Stefan. She lived with her children in the big house across the valley from the Kilranelagh farm. Her husband, Simon Lessingham, was an officer in the British Army, serving with his regiment in East Africa. He had been away for more than two years; absence had not made Valerie's heart grow fonder. There had been cracks in their marriage for a long time; the fact that he was away so much was an excuse not to face them, as it was an excuse not to face other things. Like the cracks in the crumbling house they lived in, and the bigger cracks in the management of the estate that surrounded it, draining money out year after year and bringing nothing back. Lack of attention wasn't a solution to those problems either.

Neither Valerie nor Stefan had looked for what had

happened quite suddenly between them. They had come together for the simple reason that their children played together; their children were more the entire focus of their lives than they cared to admit. And so it happened.

Valerie walked up the slope ahead of him. She had a head of yellow hair to her shoulders. She was thin and tall, and strong enough to stand beside the men who worked on the estate and do the same job when she needed to. The clothes she was wearing, as they often were, had come out of the back of her husband's wardrobe.

Stefan watched her, climbing gracefully and quietly up the slope. He was aware how much he liked her. She had the carelessness that somehow went with her class, even about their relationship, but she had a well of kindness that often didn't. Whenever he thought about her, she was laughing. She laughed with everyone, but he sometimes felt that her laughter only really came from her heart with the children, and the children had come to include Tom Gillespie, more often than not.

The track across the fields from Kilranelagh to Whitehall Grove had become well-trodden by the children over the last two years, and the woods that filled the valley between the farm and the estate seemed to have become their world. At the moment, after the arrival of the film *The Adventures of Tom Sawyer* at the small cinema in Baltinglass three weeks ago, it served as the countryside around St Petersburg, Missouri; the tiny stream at the bottom of the valley, on the other side of the motte, was the Mississippi River. The voices Stefan and Valerie could hear, floating down from the top of the mound, were now those of Tom Sawyer, Huckleberry Finn, Becky Sharp, Joe Harper and, intermittently, of Injun Joe, Muff Potter and Aunt Polly too.

65

'I was at Garda Headquarters today,' said Stefan.

'Be quiet, Stefan,' she hissed again.

'It sounds mad, but I've got to go to America.'

She turned round, glaring, holding a finger to her lips.

'You can tell me later, darling!' The last word meant nothing very much; it was simply the word Valerie called everyone she cared about.

She continued up the slope. He followed, amused. It was a very different reaction from the ones he had got both at the Garda barracks in Baltinglass and at home. The idea of flying to America was, immediately at least, a prospect of such extraordinary wonder that reasons paled into insignificance, especially where Helena Gillespie was concerned. Stefan's father smiled and joined in, but he still thought it all sounded very odd.

David Gillespie, like his son, had a policeman's nose; he could smell the politics too, perhaps as acutely as his son. He had worked in Dublin Castle under the British once, when he was an inspector in the Dublin Metropolitan Police. He picked up the excitement in his son's voice too. It was something he hadn't heard in a very long time. He felt that the wind was changing; he could see it in Stefan's eyes; perhaps it was changing for all of them. He wasn't sure whether that was a good thing or a bad thing, but then the wind and the weather were nobody's to control.

By now Valerie Lessingham had reached the top of the hill. She crouched down behind a fallen tree, and as Stefan arrived behind her she grabbed his hand and pulled him down. There were no voices now, just the sounds of the rooks overhead, a great crowd of them heading home to roost. Then Tom Sawyer appeared among the bushes across the flat top of the motte, in the form of Tom Gillespie; he was holding Becky Sharp, in the shape of Jane Lessingham, by the hand; things were getting very serious.

'Becky, I was such a fool!' lamented Tom. 'I never thought we might want to come back! I can't find the way. It's all mixed up. Don't cry.'

Becky didn't look much like crying. Jane was older than Tom Gillespie and she was quite a bit taller – she felt Becky needed to buck her ideas up; crying wouldn't get them out of the cave they were lost in.

'Tom, if you can't find your way out of here, I will!'

'That's not right, Jane. It's Tom who gets them out!'

'I don't see why it always has to be that way.'

'It's in the film. It's in the book too.'

Suddenly there was a loud whooping noise, then crashing through the undergrowth came Harry Lawlor, as Injun Joe, his belt tied round his head and a pigeon's feather sticking out of his headband, and screaming loudly.

'I'm a-going to get you, Tom Sawyer! I'm a-going to get you!'

'Becky, run, it's Injun Joe!'

Tom put his fist up to defend Becky, who scowled and looked like she was perfectly capable of protecting herself, but before Harry reached his prey a small figure wearing a wide-brimmed, very torn straw hat, flung himself at Injun Joe. Alex Lessingham, more accurately Huckleberry Finn, was coming to the rescue. Tom Gillespie clenched his fists and shouted.

'That's not what happens!'

'Who cares?' said Jane.

She ran. Injun Joe followed.

'Come on, Tom, let's go!' said Huck, racing off. And Tom

ran after them, laughing, finally abandoning accuracy for fun.

Valerie got up, laughing too, pulling Stefan up on to the mound by the hand. The voices of the children echoed through the darkening trees for a moment longer, and then there was silence again.

'Come on, you lot!' shouted Valerie.

'Tom, we've to get back! Tea'll be ready! Harry needs to go too!'

'Jane, Alex, it's almost dark!'

'Tom! I mean it!'

Valerie sniggered.

'What's that for?'

'I mean it, indeed! Sure, don't you put the fear of God into them?'

'They'll have us standing here all night, Valerie.'

'Really?' She took his hand.

He pulled it back.

'Don't be so daft.'

She giggled. They walked on a few steps.

'Did you say you had to go to America?'

'New York.'

'What on earth for?'

Out of the twilight four forms launched themselves at Stefan and Valerie, leaping up and pulling them down to the ground, laughing and whooping, in whatever characters they still carried in their heads. Tom and Harry Lawlor pinned Stefan to the ground; Jane and Alex held their mother down, demanding immediate surrender and a considerable ransom. But after a few moments the hostages were released. As they all got up, Valerie grabbed at the severely battered and torn straw hat that had fallen off her son's head. She frowned a frown of considerable severity.

'And who did this?'

The children looked at one another and said nothing.

'This came out of my bedroom. It was new last year. Look at it!'

'It's like Huckleberry Finn's hat,' muttered Alex.

'It certainly is now,' replied his mother. 'Who did it, please?'

Tom stepped forward, his head hanging down.

'We were going to put it back, Mrs Lessingham.'

'Oh, well, that's all right then.' Her voice was still very stern.

'I only cut it a bit, so it looked right. But it's got quare ripped now.'

'Quare ripped indeed, Tomás Gillespie!'

She put her arm round Tom; then she put the hat on her head.

'So what do you think?'

As Valerie and her children walked down the track through the woods, Stefan turned towards the farm with Tom and Harry. The boys climbed over the fence into the field and walked on. He realised he hadn't explained anything at all to her yet. He called out in the near darkness.

'I'm leaving for New York tomorrow!'

'How long will you be?'

'Five days, six. I'm flying.'

'What? You still haven't told me why.'

'I'll catch you in the morning, Valerie!'

'I don't know what I'm doing tomorrow. I'll see what –'

She was gone from sight; her voice had gone too, fading into the trees. He wasn't sure how much she had heard but when he clambered over the fence it was clear Tom had heard enough. He stood with a look of bewilderment and awe on his face, waiting for his father; it was a look shared by Harry Lawlor too. The Mississippi had disappeared from view.

5. Inns Quay

That evening, after tea, Tom Gillespie brought down the newspaper cuttings he had collected earlier in the year about the flying boats that had just taken to the air, flying out of Ireland, across the Atlantic, to America. It was a wonder that no one could have dreamt of, even a few years ago. There were photographs of the planes, gigantic yet graceful; a great, wide, heavy wing of engines and propellers, with the sleek lines of a ship hanging underneath, cutting down into the waters of the River Shannon as they landed at Foynes. There were men in the navy-like uniforms of Pan American Airways and Imperial Airways, names that on their own conjured up for Tom all the vastness of the earth. There was a map that showed the route the flying boats would take, from Southampton Water on the English Channel across England and Wales, across the Irish sea and all of Ireland to Foynes on the Shannon Estuary; from Foynes over the whole of the North Atlantic, the longest, barely imaginable leg of the journey, to Botwood in Newfoundland; then across the Gulf of St Lawrence and down through Canada and New England to New York, the city of skyscrapers that Tom had only seen in newsreels; a city that felt like it was on another planet.

The atlas was pulled out to join the cuttings, and for more than an hour the farmhouse on the western edge of the Wicklow Mountains was open to the skies and the oceans and a light that seemed to shine on all the distance in the tiny maps and make it almost tangible. David and Helena too were swept up in the adventure that filled their grandson's head, and when Tom finally went up to bed he had exhausted them all with his excitement. He felt as if he was going too.

For a moment even Tom's father had forgotten that the man he was going to bring back from New York, on the return leg of that great adventure, might be coming home to meet the English hangman.

And the hangman was still English. Despite the fact that two years earlier, in Éamon de Valera's new constitution, the Irish Free State had officially been renamed Éire, Ireland, and that it considered itself now, for all practical purposes, a republic, there was still one job no Irishman would ever be asked to do in Ireland. So when that job did need doing it was the English hangman, Thomas Pierrepoint, who took the boat train from Euston, the mail boat from Holyhead, and a taxi from Dún Laoghaire to Mountjoy Prison.

Stefan was thinking about what his journey meant now, as his mother and father washed up. He folded up his son's newspaper cuttings and put them away in the Cadbury's chocolate box that had a picture of a flying boat pasted on it; he closed the box and put it aside to go back to Tom's room.

As he returned to the kitchen the telephone rang. It was Valerie Lessingham, her voice bright as always, pushing away what was in his mind.

'Stefan, I only got a bit of what you said. How long are you away?'

'It's not even a week.'

'I have to be in Dublin tomorrow. So I'm going up there anyway. I thought I might drive you. You said you'd be staying the night. I could too.'

In a relationship that largely revolved around their children, the time Stefan and Valerie had actually spent alone together didn't amount to much. When the chance did arise, Valerie dealt with it simply enough. Where Stefan approached it all with caution, she just got on with it.

He laughed. 'Well, I suppose if you're going anyway.'

It was unlikely she had been going anyway but, like the practical woman she was, there would, naturally, be things she had to do in Dublin.

As he walked back into the kitchen the last dishes were being dried and put away. His father and mother looked round. In a household where the telephone was still a novelty, an explanation was always expected. Stefan would rather it hadn't been expected right now. It was an area of his life where the less said, especially as far as his mother was concerned, the better.

'Valerie Lessingham's got to be in Dublin tomorrow. She's going to give me a lift up.'

David Gillespie nodded and turned to put a cup in the press. Helena's pursed lips told another story. Open skies were forgotten.

'Well, as usual, there's nothing much happens here that Mrs Lessingham doesn't want a part in. I suppose we should be used to it.'

David shot a warning glance at his wife, but she took no notice.

'Normally it's Tom of course.'

'What the hell is that supposed to mean?' said Stefan.

His irritation was defensive; he wanted to tell her to mind her own business. His father shot him the same warning glance he had shot Helena, and it had the same effect. 'Leave it alone, Ma. You know no one could be kinder to Tom.'

'And what does he think about that?'

'What?'

Helena turned to the range, taking off her apron and folding it very purposefully, several times, before she hung it over the rail to dry.

'Think about what? You know what he thinks. He loves being at Whitehall Grove, and he loves it when Jane and Alex come here. They have a grand time, don't they? Leave it at that!' He knew perfectly well why she wouldn't leave it at that, at least he thought he did. 'Valerie gives him more time than anyone outside this house. He thinks the world of her! Why not?'

His mother still had her back to him.

'Why not indeed? I'm sure she's an angel come among us!'

Even David Gillespie thought this was unnecessary.

'Helena, will you come on? That's enough.'

She turned, smiling now, but it wasn't a smile of agreement. It was a smile that said she had more to say, and obviously no one wanted to hear it.

'Probably it is. Trust me to blow out the candle when it's burning so bright.' She walked across to Stefan and kissed his cheek. 'You'll need an early night, son. You've a lot to do. I'm sure there's more to all that travelling than they say. It's still a long way, however quickly you get there.'

She walked out and went upstairs.

Stefan sat down at the table. He looked down at the picture of the flying boat. There had been times, more times recently, even before the call to Dublin, when he had felt he needed to get away. It had nothing to do with Valerie Lessingham, or with his mother's tight-lipped disapproval, or even the slow repetitiveness of his life; it had nothing to do with his family really. It was the feeling that sometimes the mountains around him closed in, watching him grow older, watching his son grow up as he did no more than mark time.

David Gillespie went to the press and brought out two bottles of beer. He stood pouring them, saying nothing for a while. He pushed a glass across to his son and then pulled out a chair on the other side of the table.

'She's thinking of Tom,' he said finally, as he sat down.

'I know what she's thinking of, Pa.'

'Well, that's another thing altogether,' David frowned. 'There is that too. She's another man's wife. We've never talked about it before, whatever we think, but do you expect your mother to be easy with it? Or me, Stefan?'

'Does it matter so much?'

'It matters,' said his father. 'You know it does. I'm sure Mrs Lessingham knows it. It's the children that matter most. You know that too.'

'What do you think we are? I could count the number –'

'You can give each other the explanations. Don't waste them on me.'

Stefan felt the sting in his father's quiet words.

'That's not what really worries your mother anyway. I'm not saying she hasn't got an opinion about it that doesn't reflect very well on you or Mrs Lessingham, but all that can't go on. Sure, you know that yourself.'

For a moment Stefan drank; he did know, of course he knew.

'It'll stop,' he said, gazing down at the glass. 'These things do.'

'These things?' laughed David. 'Is that all it amounts to? Maybe it's when it stops that your mother's worried about. Can't you understand that?'

'For God's sake, I think I'm old enough to deal with it, Pa!'

'I'm glad for you so. I'm glad for Valerie Lessingham too, if that's how it is with her. It's a good job your mother's in bed. If she was here she'd tell you she couldn't give a feck whether you two can deal with it or not.'

Stefan laughed, but he could see this wasn't one of those familiar moments when David Gillespie had been despatched by his wife to say what she wouldn't say herself.

'And what sort of sense is that supposed to make? If she doesn't care, then what the hell is she so angry about?' He drained his glass and stood up.

'Jesus, you're thick sometimes, Stefan Gillespie. He thinks the world of her, that's what you said. Not that it needs saying. You might be able to deal with it when it's all over, do you think Tom's going to find it so easy? She's pulled him into her family, and I've no complaint about that, nor has your mother.'

Stefan gave a wry smile; he wasn't so sure about that.

'Maybe she's a way with strays,' continued David, with a kinder expression. 'But you and Mrs Lessingham have taken a road you can't stay on together. There'll be a parting, and when there is things won't be the same again. Perhaps there'll be more for Tom to lose than you then.'

Stefan stood where he was, looking at his father, as two compartments in his mind opened up to one another, and he realised that not only were they sitting side by side, they looked into each other. He had become very good at keeping things in separate boxes in the years since Maeve had died; he was aware of that. But it was a trick his son had had no reason to learn.

*

In Bewley's Café in Grafton Street the next evening, Stefan Gillespie and Valerie Lessingham talked about the things they usually talked about: first, their children. It was not only what was closest to their hearts, and what held them together, it was where they found the happiest parts of who they were. Tom was at the National School at Kilranelagh, a mile along the road from the farm. Jane and Alexander were at Stratford Lodge, the Church of Ireland school in Baltinglass. But their closest friendships were with each other, and with Harry Lawlor who was at school with Tom and also inhabited the woods between Kilranelagh and Whitehall Grove. Other topics could be almost as amusing for Stefan and Valerie, some of the time, but there was too often something less than funny below the surface that could rise up to still the easy laughter.

The chaos that was the Whitehall Grove estate was never really as entertaining as Valerie Lessingham made it out to be, though she was good at finding the humour in it. The estate was in serious decline, propped up by Major Lessingham's army salary and the selling of assets that had once been considered the family jewels. Valerie still talked to Stefan about her husband with the fond exasperation that she had before they became lovers. She needed someone to talk to; Stefan was a friend first and what else they were to each other now didn't change that. He wasn't sure why she wanted to speak about her husband tonight. It wasn't an unfamiliar conversation, but there was concern behind it, preoccupation, even worry. It was as if she was refocusing her mind, all of it, with a quiet intensity that was unlike her.

'Simon always prattles on about how passionately he's attached to the land and the house. The family's been there for over three hundred years and all that, but he's got no idea how the estate survives. Farming's still a complete mystery to him. As far as he's concerned grass grows, corn ripens, sheep lamb, cows calve, and we all live on it merrily! The fact is it's a business and it's eating up far more money than it's making. And every conversation we have, every letter I get from him, is just another version of: Sure, it'll all be all right. It'll all be grand. It will all sort itself out!'

'He's not an Irishman for nothing,' smiled Stefan.

'Isn't he? I'm not sure what he's an Irishman for at all!'

Stefan didn't reply. He could see the tension behind her words.

'Sometimes I don't know where he fits. In England he's Irish and he champions Irish independence so aggressively he offends all his English friends. When he's at home he defends England and doesn't understand why all his Irish friends just want him to shut up. I don't know where he belongs. I'm English. I never wanted to live here at all really, but I know more about Ireland now than he does. The only place he feels at home is with his regiment, whether it's in England or East Africa or India. He's spent more time away from us since I came to Whitehall Grove than he has with us.'

'You know there's not a farmer who isn't struggling.' Stefan said it reassuringly, but he knew the problems at Whitehall

Grove were bigger than most farmers faced. He had tried to help with advice, but the place had its own creaking system of management that advice couldn't change.

'I wish the IRA hadn't stopped burning down big houses. That would be the ideal answer. I was thinking of approaching Cumann na mBan directly to see if there was a waiting list I could get Whitehall Grove put on.'

She laughed the kind of careless laugh that she was so good at. Stefan still felt it was less careless than usual. But he didn't ask her if anything else was wrong. If she wanted to tell him, she would tell him. They ate for several minutes in silence. Stefan was less easy with his life than he had been two days ago. And somehow it seemed the same for her. He felt it as they spoke. Something was changing.

They walked across O'Connell Bridge and turned along the Quays towards the hotel. They were staying at the Four Courts Hotel on Inns Quay, just along from Kingsbridge Station, where Stefan would be getting the train to Foynes the next morning. It was a cold night. Valerie's arm was through his as it could never have been in Baltinglass. It was such a simple thing; but he missed it; a woman with her arm through his. It wasn't very often that he allowed himself to look at the empty corners of his life. When he did he dismissed them with a wry grin or a few swear words, and usually it worked; but it was always something small that put the thought in his head, something like Valerie Lessingham's arm now. They hadn't spoken for a while. He was easier with silence than she was. But this silence was hers.

'There will be a war. I really think so, don't you?'

She spoke quite suddenly. It wasn't such an odd topic to introduce, but Stefan wasn't really sure where it had come from. Talk of war was everywhere. Most people had an opinion, even if in Ireland they were quick to shrug the idea off and change the subject; it wasn't Ireland's business anyway. What opinions there were, voiced or unvoiced, changed from day to day, with the news from Germany and Britain and Europe.

The belief that once Adolf Hitler's demands were met, surely not entirely unreasonable demands after all, the dark clouds of conflict would blow away was strong in Ireland. The desire not to take sides, in what was increasingly seen as a confrontation between Britain and Germany, never mind the other countries in Europe threatened by Nazi expansion, had become a statement of nationhood. Independence and neutrality seemed to mean the same thing; too much criticism of Germany was seen as forelock-tugging subservience to Britain.

Stefan Gillespie's views on Nazi Germany had little to do with forelock tugging. His mother's family was German; he had been there himself. For him what was wrong in Germany wasn't about Britain. But his opinions were not very popular; he had got used to not expressing them very loudly.

'You know I've always thought that,' he said quietly.

'Simon doesn't think it's going to be very long. His last letter –'

'He's probably right.'

'The regiment's coming back from Kenya. They sail next week.'

'Is that unexpected?'

'They were meant to stay in East Africa till November.'

He nodded, but it didn't feel like this conversation was about the war.

'He won't be coming home. I mean I'm sure he'll come

over at some point when he's back in England, but it feels, well, he says it feels like something's going to happen soon. We all know, we all damned well know!'

There was a stress in her voice that was unlike her.

They walked on in silence again. She held him tighter.

'I can't stay, Stefan. I wanted to tell you —'

He wasn't sure what she was talking about; it felt like it could have been that night, but even before she spoke again, he knew it wasn't at all.

'I think I have to be where he is. I mean, I don't know where he'll be, but in England, I think I have to be in England. I'm not sure it's what I want, for the children, even for me. Whatever's happened between Simon and me, however far apart we've become – we have, I know we have. But I think I have to do what's right now. He doesn't agree. He doesn't want us to leave Ireland at all. Obviously we'd all be safer here, but it matters more that we're where – I mean I – I'm not putting it very well, am I?'

'I think you're putting it very well.'

It was strange, but he felt very close to her now.

'I'm going to shut up the house and let the land. That way the estate will just about pay for itself. It means letting people go, and I'm not very happy about that. I know the children are going to hate it. My mother has a house in Sussex. It's not huge, but we'll all fit, just about. I wanted to tell you. I wanted you to understand. I think he needs us. He'd never say it. Perhaps it's the first time he really needs us. He says he doesn't want me to do any of this. But I am going to do it, Stefan. I hope it makes some sense?'

'You don't need to explain it all to me, Valerie.'

He knew she did of course; they were friends first.

They stopped. She turned towards him. She wasn't a

woman who cried; he wasn't sure he had ever seen her cry. She was always bright, always laughing. Yet there were tears in her eyes now. He held her close. It was what she needed him to do. She turned her face up. They kissed, unaware of people around them, of traffic; unaware, it seemed, of the words just spoken. They said nothing as they walked into the Four Courts Hotel.

*

It was one o'clock in the morning when Stefan Gillespie woke up. Someone was hammering on the door of the hotel room. Valerie, in a deeper sleep, stirred next to him, then turned over. The hammering continued, a fist thumping rhythmically. He got out of bed, fumbling for clothes. He didn't turn the lamp on. The banging stopped and a voice called through the door.

'Wake the fuck up, Sergeant!'

He didn't recognise the voice.

The fist started thumping again, slowly and impatiently. He walked to the door, doing up his trousers. The light by the bed suddenly went on.

'What is it?'

Valerie was sitting up now.

'God knows.'

He walked to the door and opened it slightly. The round, red face of Superintendent Gregory smiled in at him through the crack, so close that Stefan could taste the breath of whiskey and cigarettes coming off him.

'I hope I'm not disturbing you, Sergeant.'

Gregory pushed hard against the door, and although Stefan stopped it opening fully, it opened wide enough for the

Special Branch superintendent to see past him to the bed. Valerie was surprised, but unflustered. She simply pulled the bedclothes up and smiled pleasantly at the unknown man.

'I didn't know you had friends dropping in, darling?'

'What the hell do you want?' demanded Stefan.

'There's a bit of news, Stevie.'

Stefan stared at him, only now really fully awake.

'Still, I did knock, that's something. I'll be in the bar.'

The smile had gone; the last words were an order.

Superintendent Gregory was sitting in the empty bar of the Four Courts Hotel when Stefan came down. He had a glass of whiskey in front of him. The sour, just woken night porter stood behind the bar next to a bottle.

'Will you have a drink?' said Gregory.

'I won't,' was all Stefan replied as he sat down.

The superintendent turned to the night porter.

'You can piss off now. Leave the bottle.'

The night porter put the bottle of Bushmills down on the table in front of the Special Branch man and walked back to the hotel lobby. The superintendent topped up his glass and then lit a cigarette. He took a few moments to do this. Stefan knew the game well enough; he thought Gregory wasn't especially good at it.

'I didn't think there was a Mrs Gillespie?'

'I'm flattered I'm worth finding out about, sir.'

'I wouldn't be too flattered. I like to know who I'm dealing with, that's all. Still, it's a relief to see a Mrs Gillespie of some sort on the hotel register. We've all been a bit concerned how friendly you are with your pals at the Gate, Messrs Mac Liammóir and Edwards. And she's quite a looker.'

The game had to go on, and Stefan Gillespie decided it

was better to let it run its course than to tell the Special Branch superintendent to fuck himself. Gregory was enjoying the fact that he had something on him; it was how the detective branch worked; with Special Branch it was almost the only way they did anything. The more you had on people, your colleagues included, the stronger you were. Stefan knew he used the same methods himself, though perhaps he didn't use them in the same way. Favours and threats, knowing what other people didn't know, the little nuggets of information you carried in your head until you had reasons to use them – it was part of the armoury, and the higher up you went, the more it mattered. If Terry Gregory didn't quite know what to make of this country sergeant who didn't seem to behave like a country sergeant should, it didn't matter. He had something on him.

'My father was always suspicious of Wicklow people. He said they're all in bed with the English too much down there. That was a long time ago, but maybe he was right so. Course, you're a Protestant yourself, aren't you? Well, I suppose that makes it all right, you being in bed with the English.'

Gregory laughed, stubbing his cigarette and taking out another. He knew exactly who Valerie Lessingham was. He wanted Stefan to know he knew.

'Isn't her husband in the British army?'

'I'm glad you've got time to investigate me, sir, when there's so much on, but if there's anything else you want to know, you can ask. It might save you some time. I know you're busy. What's happening with the investigation? Is there any news about Mrs Harris's body yet?'

Superintendent Gregory shook his head.

'Don't try to fuck a fucker, son.'

But the game was over.

84

'Ned Broy had a telegram from Mr McCauley, New York. It seems our Mr Harris wasn't as enthusiastic about an invitation to come home for a chat as everyone thought. Not as I'd want to tell Ned I told him so, but I did.'

'What do you mean?'

'He's gone. Not the biggest surprise, and I'm glad to say one that I don't have any fecking responsibility for at all. I can kick that one upstairs.'

'What happened?'

'He walked out of the hotel, that's all. And why wouldn't he if he's worked out what might be waiting for him in Dublin? So now he's gone, the consul's had to tell the New York police that we parked an axe-murderer in a hotel room with a bunch of queers to keep an eye on him, and never even mentioned it. And they were all worried about what we'd look like if something got into the American papers! I suppose we should be running the rosary through our fingers and praying Owen doesn't get hold of an axe.'

He grinned. He was clearly taking some satisfaction in all this.

'So does that mean I don't go?'

'Oh no, Stevie, the plane's all booked.'

'But I thought you –'

'It's not my mess. The Commissioner seems to think the NYPD will pick him up quick enough, so the job's still the same. You might want to take a pair of handcuffs with you for the journey back though. Of course the NYPD will be pissed off. We've been playing the bollocks on their patch, however much we tell them it was all about Owen Harris doing us all a favour and helping us with our enquiries. They will know better by now.'

'So what am I supposed to do?' said Stefan.

'Turn up and wait till they find him.'

'And if they don't?'

'I'd say they will. No one seems to think he's much in his head. But the lad might want to go easy over there. They're as likely to shoot him as look at him, knowing what he's done.' Gregory laughed. 'The place is full of Irish cops who love their mammies after all. They won't take to him, I'd say. Not that anyone here would be too bothered if he came back in a coffin –'

'I thought nobody really wanted me to go to New York –'

'Now everybody wants you to go, me included.'

'In case it's a fuck up?'

'Got it in one. You're a bright lad, Stevie. But it's already a fuck up. McCauley's fuck up in New York, Ned Broy's here. I don't intend to make it mine. So the grand thing about you is you're nobody. You don't matter.'

'What about the NYPD?'

'What do they care? They'll deliver you a prisoner, or if we're lucky a box. And you've got the trip to look forward to, a hotel in New York. Jesus, you'll be the toast of the sheep shaggers for miles around when you get back to Baltinglass. And it's not all bad news, Sergeant. If you could maybe make it a box, you might even be up for promotion. It'd save on the trial and for my money, well, if I had to choose between being shot and being hanged –'

Terry Gregory drained the whiskey in his glass and stood up.

'It's an ill wind, eh Sergeant?'

He walked out to the lobby and into the street.

In the room Valerie was sitting up, reading. She laughed as Stefan came in.

'What was all that about?'

'The man I've got to bring back from New York has disappeared.'

'So aren't you going?'

'They'll find him. Well, that's what the superintendent said.'

He shrugged. She said no more. As he sat down on the bed she stretched out her hand to touch his back. He sat there for a moment, not moving, feeling her fingers. He was aware how much he liked her. That was the thought in his head that made him smile. It wasn't love between them, it never had been, but it wasn't nothing, for either of them. He turned round and reached across the bed, stroking her hair. As he kissed her she pulled him slowly down on to her. Neither of them needed to speak now to know that this would be the last time they would make love.

6. West Thirty-Sixth Street

New York

Longie Zwillman stood at the counter in the window of Lindy's diner on Broadway, between 49th and 50th. He kept his hat on and his overcoat done up, though it was warm enough in Lindy's. He was thirty-five; he didn't look older but somehow people felt he was older. There was age behind his eyes, and behind the half smile that was almost always on his lips there was nothing that suggested he found very much to laugh at. He was drinking the cup of coffee and eating the cheesecake Clara Lindermann had brought him personally.

It was busy in Lindy's, but there was space at the window where Zwillman stood looking out, seemingly at nothing in particular. The two big men in homburgs who stood behind him would have made sure there was space, because Longie didn't like people too close to him; even in a New York diner he expected the courtesy of space. But they didn't have to make room for him. There was something about the way Longie held himself, and the way he looked at people when they came near him, that ensured he rarely had to ask for anything. He was a courteous man though; he seemed to inspire courtesy in others. Broadway wasn't his territory; neither was Manhattan. He had come over from New Jersey. But he was respected here as he was respected everywhere. The work he had today crossed no lines. It wasn't business. It was pest control, and he had an interest in that.

Outside the window, across the sidewalk, a truck stopped. It was a fish truck, one of the hundreds that pulled in and out of Fulton Market every night. The driver looked through the window at the man in the overcoat, eating the last forkful of Lindy's cheesecake. Zwillman nodded. The truck drove on.

Longie finished his coffee and walked out on to Broadway, followed by the two big men. He sauntered down towards Times Square. He went almost unnoticed in the afternoon crowds bustling up and down around him, but not entirely. Several people recognised him and nodded respectfully. He nodded in return. Several times men walked up to him and spoke, in low tones of respect, asking after his health and the health of his family. They waited for him to stretch out his hand before they attempted to shake his. Two NYPD officers were among those who stopped and received an invitation to shake that hand.

In all the unseeing and indifferent noise of Broadway, Longie Zwillman walked like a secret island of calm and courtesy, or so it seemed. He knew who every one of the people who greeted him was, even out of his own fiefdom; and they were grateful for it. To know him and to be known by him was something. To lose those small favours was something else; after all respect and fear weren't very different.

There was the beginning of darkness in the grey March sky over Times Square, and the lights all along Broadway were beginning to push the trash and the seedy corners out of sight. Crowds jammed around the 42nd Street subway as the people heading home from work met the people coming out to the theatres and movies, restaurants and clubs, or to do what most people did on Broadway, to be there and to walk about.

Pushing up from the subway, through the hundreds of New Yorkers streaming down, was a group of men, a dozen or so, all beered up for the evening in advance. They were rowdy already, laughing loudly and looking around with a kind of purpose and anticipation they seemed to find funny and exciting all at the same time; they were their own entertainment. But there was an aggression in their laughter that was more than just a bunch of guys with too much beer inside them. Several of them carried bundles of newspapers; one carried a furled flag; another carried billboards. Two of the men wore distinctive silver-grey shirts with a large L on the left side, in scarlet, close to the heart; the uniform of the Silver Legion of America. When they stopped on the corner of Broadway and 43rd they were quieter, gathering around the flags.

The newspapers were handed out, the billboards propped against a store front, the flags unfurled. The flag was the red L on silver; L for the Legion, L for Loyalty, L for Liberation. The placards bore scrawled headlines from the newspapers the men were selling: *Social Justice, Liberation, National American*. 'Buy Christian Say No to Jew York!' 'Keep Us out of England's War!' 'The Protocols of Zion and the End of America!' 'Roosevelt Public Enemy Number One!' They moved along Broadway in twos and threes, hawking their papers, and shouting the headlines.

They were all New Yorkers, with names like other New

Yorkers; mostly they were German and Irish names. But they weren't only there to sell; they were looking for the enemies of America in the streets of their city; anyone they thought might be a Jew.

Dan Walker was already bored calling the headlines of the papers he never read anyway. He wanted another beer. Van Nosdall was a lot keener, thrusting out blue mimeographed slips as he moved through the crowds. 'There's only room for one "ism" in America, Americanism!' 'Democracy, Jewocracy!' 'Hey, Yid, no one wants you here! We're coming for you!' As he screamed 'Coming for you!' at an elderly couple, heading to the theatre, he formed his fingers into a pistol and laughed. 'Pow!' Dan Walker yawned.

'Let's get a beer for Christ's sake!'

Then he stopped and smiled.

'See the piece of shit there —'

He was looking at a boy of sixteen or seventeen, with a thin face and large, dark eyes. Anyone would have said he was Jewish. You could always tell a Jew of course, but this one was Jewish Jewish. He was staring at the two men with real anger in his face, and he wasn't moving; he wasn't trying to run the way he was supposed to. Dan Walker walked forward, with new enthusiasm for the slogans he had been leaving to Van Nosdall till now. He walked up to the youth, who was standing his ground, quietly unyielding.

'Read *Social Justice* and learn how to solve the Jewish question.'

The Jewish youth nodded, unexpectedly.

'OK, I'll take one.'

It was an odd response; he should have already been running.

Dan Walker looked round at Van Nosdall.

Nosdall shrugged. He handed over a copy of *Social Justice*, and the youth handed him some change. As he opened the paper the youth glanced at the contents, with a look of deep seriousness. He turned a page.

'I've been reading Father Coughlin's articles about the Protocols of the Elders of Zion. It's certainly some piece of work, some piece of work.'

He folded the newspaper up and put it in his pocket.

'I've never seen shit like it. So this is what I'm going to do – I'm going to take it home and wipe my arse with every last, lying, fucking page.'

With that he ran, out into Broadway, through the traffic.

Dan Walker and Van Nosdall were already running after him. The bundle of papers was dropped. Dan put his fingers in his mouth and whistled shrilly. This was what they were all waiting for, this was real politics. And while a couple of men remained behind to pick up the newspapers the whole gang that had emerged from the subway only ten minutes earlier was racing through the blasting horns in pursuit of the young Jew. They had one now. And as long as they kept him in sight, they would run till they caught him.

He was in west 44th Street now, heading towards the Shubert Theatre. The street was quiet after Broadway and 7th Avenue; the theatres weren't open yet. He looked round. They weren't far behind. The other men had almost caught up with the two he had spoken to already. There were at least a dozen of them. He turned right abruptly, into the alley that ran between the Shubert Theatre and the Broadhurst. The gates were open. He stopped for a moment, catching his breath, and walked between the two theatres for a moment.

It was dark here now, and it was a dead end. At the top of the alleyway Dan Walker and Van Nosdall were standing, watching him. The youth turned round, and stood looking up at them. The other men were there now. They grouped together, extracting a variety of batons and coshes and knuckle dusters from their coats, grinning and joshing one another. They produced a wailing wolf-like howl, all together, and started to walk down the alley towards the Jew.

He seemed remarkably, unaccountably unafraid.

Quite suddenly a door out from the back of the Broadhurst Theatre opened. The youth gave a wave to the advancing party and walked into the theatre. The door closed. The men ran forward. It was a fire exit; it was heavy, blank; it had no lock or handle on the outside. Two of the newspaper sellers hammered on the door.

At first only one man turned round and looked back up the alley. A truck had just stopped there and in the light from 44th Street he could see a gang of men getting out of the back. Some of the others were looking round now; then they all were.

The whole street end of the alleyway was blocked by a small crowd; there were a lot of men there, twenty-five, thirty. They carried baseball bats and pickaxe handles. There was complete silence for some seconds. No one was hammering on the Broadhurst fire door now; no one was laughing. The men from the fish truck filled the alleyway. They moved in a line towards the men from the Silver Legion and the Christian Front, looking for healthy political debate.

On West 44th Street Longie Zwillman's Pontiac passed the fish truck. The driver, closing the back doors, touched his cap as the car approached.

The Pontiac carried on into Broadway.

*

There wasn't much that was old in New York. Keens Chophouse on West 36th Street was as old as most places that were still standing. It had been there long enough that clay pipes still hung from the ceiling where long-dead customers had kept them. It smelled of old wood in a city where that smell was barely known. John Cavendish sat upstairs on the raised platform in front of the small-paned windows that gave on to 36th Street.

It was still early and there were few customers, but those there were, were kept well away from the table the Irish army officer was sitting at. It was Longie Zwillman's table. Cavendish waited. He had been there for half an hour. It wasn't a problem. Half an hour to sit and do nothing was welcome; half an hour to sit and think of something other than what he was doing. He thought of his wife and his children in Rathmines. It would be another two months before he went home. It was hard. He didn't often let himself think about how hard it was. Whatever New York was, there were moments when it really wasn't much at all, if you only stopped long enough to take a breath.

They talked for half an hour about nothing in particular: how old their children were; what was the most impressive thing at the World's Fair; the news from Europe. They were almost strangers but for reasons neither of them was entirely sure about they trusted one another. Each had information the other wanted, or at least had some chance of getting it. As the main course arrived Longie Zwillman took out an envelope. Inside were several small photographs. He fanned them out on the table like playing cards. There was a brownstone building, cars, half a dozen men going into the building or coming out. Some faces were very clear, some indistinct.

'This is the German bookstore on 116th Street. There's a lot of stuff distributed there, not just American Nazi Party pamphlets and Bund papers, but pretty much any pro-German, Roosevelt's-a-commie, anti-Semitic, democracy-will-eat-your-kids crap you can think of. Silver Legion, Christian Front, Social Justice, National American. You've seen all that already.'

'Some of it.'

'You've seen some, you've seen the lot. They got a meeting hall upstairs. Same people, same crap. Some of my boys keep an eye on it, to see who's making all the noise. I got some friends who like me to do that. So it's a favour. Also it's where they get together to maybe go out and beat some Jews up, or just some people they don't like, who mainly happen to be Jews. But that's not compulsory, Jewish I mean. There's a lot of people they don't like. As an American I don't regard that as entirely reasonable behaviour.'

Longie Zwillman shrugged. Captain Cavendish looked at the photos.

'Anyone you know?'

The intelligence officer picked up four of the photographs.

'James Stewart,' he said, laying one of them down again. 'I know him. He's a Clan na Gael man in the Bronx. I wouldn't have said he was that important, but he is close to Dominic Carroll. He raises a lot of money that goes to the IRA. He has a cousin who's an anti-Roosevelt congressman –'

'He's a Christian Front man now as well,' said Zwillman. 'He's not out in the street, but he's been at some meetings where they put together a bunch of street fighters, mostly German and Irish. He says a lot of them are ex-IRA.'

95

'I wouldn't take too much notice of that. Give me a dollar for every Irishman in New York who was in the IRA and I could buy up Manhattan.'

John Cavendish put down another card.

'Joseph McWilliams. I've seen him at a few Irish-American bashes. He's big on anti-British campaigns of one sort or another, that's all I know. But I wouldn't have said he's anybody big in Irish-American politics now.'

'He's big on the German side.' Zwillman spoke again. 'He speaks at a lot of Bund meetings, about Germany and Ireland – together against the British and the Jews. I guess you know how that goes. Maybe he's a useful go-between. He speaks good German too. This meeting was no rally for the masses, though. This was small; a dozen people, Irish and German. He's a somebody somewhere.'

Cavendish nodded; it was good information. He put down the next photo.

'This one's a man called Aaron Phelan. Clan na Gael organiser from Queens, and an NYPD captain. He's also as pally as you can get with Dominic Carroll. And you know who he is now – Clan na Gael president.'

'And the IRA's man in New York.'

'That's him. If Phelan's there, Carroll is involved in it too.'

'So who's left?'

The G2 man put down the last of the four photographs.

'An old friend,' he smiled. 'I knew he was in New York. It's interesting to see he's not just giving speeches at Hibernian Club dinners.'

'Who is he?'

'He's the IRA chief of staff, Seán Russell.'

'So what are they all talking about, the German Bund and the IRA?'

John Cavendish shook his head.

Zwillman picked up the photographs.

'I've got some friends who'll want a look at these too.'

Cavendish knew enough not to ask who Zwillman's friends were.

'What about these women?' said the American.

It sounded like a change of subject, but it wasn't.

'It's going ahead. It'll be the night after Patrick's Day.'

'And will you get the information?'

'She says the sister's got it. She knows the key to the ciphers. She knows how they work. If I can get both of them across to Canada –'

'So when does she deliver?'

'When they're on their way.'

'I want to know what this is about,' said Longie Zwillman. 'So do you. I got someone inside the Bund. A good man. They trust him. But he doesn't know nothing about this meeting with the IRA. Nobody does. That's not how it is. They're smart as hell when it comes to dressing up in brown shirts and Sieg-Heiling it all over New York, but their organisation stinks. It's like a sieve. And you don't seem to think the IRA's far behind them –'

'Some of the time,' replied Captain Cavendish. 'It depends –'

'This has got a smell. That's where it started. You smelt it and I smelt it. But that's all we have, a shitty smell. They got it well hid. That means it's got to be worth hiding. You need to open up those ciphers, Captain. This woman has to deliver the goods. If you can't get it out of her somebody else is going to have to. No maybe. So how about you keep me posted, John?'

The half smile that was always on Zwillman's lips was

still there. His expression hadn't changed at all. But John Cavendish was conscious that he was dealing with a man who was used to getting what he wanted and didn't care what happened along the way. The American wasn't a man to play games with. He had made a mistake telling him about Kate and Niamh at all. It had been necessary to give information to get information back.

It had never crossed his mind that he risked losing control. But the waters were getting deeper. Now he heard the quiet threat in Longie Zwillman's voice.

7. The Yankee Clipper

Foynes, Co Limerick

> *It's the sheer size of it I couldn't believe. It's higher than a house. It's like a liner, sitting in the water, but it's the wings and the engines that are so big when you climb up under them to get in. One minute you're on the water, bumping a bit – bumping quite a lot in fact, and then you're in the air. We were only over Ireland a few minutes, hardly at all, and then we were over the Atlantic. You look down and the sea just goes on and on forever.*

The postcard Stefan Gillespie was writing to Tom was growing in length, and his writing was getting smaller and smaller to fit. He had bought the picture of the Boeing 314 Yankee Clipper at the terminal, but Tom wanted it to be written on the plane and sent from America with an American stamp. The card wouldn't reach Baltinglass till he was back there himself, but it was crucial that it came in the post as far as his son was concerned; that had an authenticity that the picture alone couldn't have.

Finishing the card Stefan gazed down at the Atlantic

again, as he had been gazing on and off for an hour. At 20,000 feet the sky was clear; there was nothing below except the sea, grey and choppy and unchanging, mile after mile after mile, and the long journey was only beginning. But as Stefan gazed down, that unchanging swell had its own fascination. The flying boat felt smaller now, far smaller than it had tied up beside the pontoon on the Shannon.

The cabin of the Yankee Clipper was divided up into small seating areas, with bulkheads closing them off from one another. The seats were leather, still with the smell of newness about them. The floors were thickly carpeted. Halfway along the length of the main cabin there was a small dining room; two stewards, naval-officer navy now exchanged for gleaming white jackets, were setting the tables for the first sitting of dinner, with crisp linen and silverware. Another steward, passing Stefan's seat with a bottle of champagne, stopped and topped up the glass at his elbow.

The journey that was all about bringing a man home to hang perhaps had become no less strange in all the self-conscious elegance of the Yankee Clipper. But it was still hard not to smile grimly at the prospect of the return, a pair of handcuffs linking him and his prisoner across the plush leather, and both of them with a glass of champagne in each free hand. Whatever crap Superintendent Gregory had given him the night before at the Four Courts Hotel, he had taken one piece of advice; on the way to Kingsbridge Station he had walked round to the Bridewell Garda station, behind the Four Courts, to get a pair of handcuffs.

The flying boat was by no means full. Most of the passengers were already on the plane when it touched down from Southampton, English and American; only three others had got on with him at Foynes. The service had been in operation for barely a month and many of the passengers were wealthy people flying for the experience rather than because they needed to get to America fast.

The smell of money filled the cabin of the flying boat as distinctively as the smell of new leather and the steaks sizzling in the galley at the back of the fuselage. Several passengers had eyed him curiously as they smiled and said hello, not because they knew who he was, but because they didn't. There was an atmosphere on board the plane, amidst all the tasteful elegance; if you were on the flight you ought to be important enough to be recognisable; you did have some obligation to be somebody.

Across the aisle from Stefan, in the compartment just in front of the galley, a man in his late fifties or early sixties had been immersed in a pile of newspapers, English and Irish, between scribbling notes in a notebook. He had said hello to Stefan, and remarked on the weather, which was pretty good for the crossing to Newfoundland it seemed, and then he'd got on with what he was doing.

He was a thin man, with a thick sweep of grey, almost silver hair; he had the kind of intense, thoughtful face that always has a frown between the eyebrows, even when it's smiling. From time to time he whistled tunelessly to himself, not loudly, but loudly enough for it to slightly grate on Stefan. The Yankee Clipper was surprisingly quiet, despite the insistent buzz of the four great engines hanging from the wings above them, endlessly turning the propellers. Then all of a sudden the man folded his pile of newspapers together and reached over to put them on the empty seat opposite him. He closed his notebook, put away his pen, and picked up his champagne. He turned towards Stefan Gillespie with a smile.

'Sláinte!'

'Sláinte mhaith,' replied Stefan.

'First time?' asked the man.

'The very first.'

'Quite something,' the man continued, glancing out at the sky.

Stefan nodded.

The man got up and walked across the aisle, stretching out his hand.

'Dominic Carroll.'

They shook hands.

'Stefan Gillespie.'

The stranger sat down in the seat opposite him. There was nothing particularly unusual about the way he delivered his name, but Stefan got the impression that he expected it to mean something. As he continued to smile at Stefan it was as if he was waiting for recognition of some kind to dawn. It didn't, and Dominic Carroll's smile became a grin for a moment, as if he was aware of his own ego, and could find the room to laugh at it sometimes.

'Where are you from, Mr Gillespie?'

'West Wicklow, Baltinglass.'

'I don't know it. I could place it probably. I'm just about from County Tyrone, Carrickfergus. We emigrated when I was four, so you see it is just about. I'm a New Yorker, heading home. And where you headed yourself?'

'New York too.'

'Business?'

'Of a sort.'

'And what sort of business are you in?'

Stefan hesitated. He had had no instructions to keep what he was doing a secret, at least as far as it simply concerned who he was. The details were a different matter. But the fact that he was a policeman didn't tell anybody anything significant; in fact it provided good reasons, without his appearing rude, for him to keep his business to himself.

'I'm a guard, a policeman.'

The effect of this on Dominic Carroll was unexpected. He looked puzzled, and if not quite angry, irritated. He didn't like it at all. Then his expression changed and he smiled, pushing away whatever had been there.

'I know what a guard is, Mr Gillespie. I'm not a stranger to Ireland.'

He spoke easily, wiping out any traces of the feelings that he hadn't been able to hide seconds earlier. But he was no longer as relaxed as he had been, and as the conversation continued Stefan couldn't help feeling he was being watched and weighed up. It was hard to work out what was going on. It wasn't much now, and if he hadn't registered those first, unfathomable reactions from the American, he probably wouldn't have noticed at all. Carroll was suspicious; for some reason he was uneasy that Stefan was a guard.

However, time passed and bit by bit the suspicion seemed to fade. Dominic Carroll was a good talker, and like a lot of good talkers he was used to being listened to. Once it was clear that Stefan Gillespie had nothing to say about his business, other than he was doing a job for the Gardaí and would be meeting some NYPD officers, he left the subject alone, except to announce that he knew almost every senior police officer in New York. As Stefan hadn't got the faintest idea who he'd be talking to, or what would be happening once he arrived in Manhattan, the string of names, all of them Irish, had little effect. The NYPD was soon forgotten but New York was not.

The man who had been born in Carrickfergus was proud of the city he now lived in. He had no doubt whatsoever that it was the greatest city on the face of the earth and that if there was anywhere that represented the future, the future of everything, it was New York, his city. It was no accident that the greatest World's Fair the world had ever seen had just opened its gates in New York's Flushing Meadows. Dominic Carroll had played some part in putting that together. The World's Fair was the world of tomorrow in a box, tied up with red-white-and-blue, star-spangled ribbon and more magical than the stars in the heavens at night.

'When you fly west, Mr Gillespie, you're flying into the future. But it's not just America's future. One day we'll bring that future back to Ireland!'

It was hard not to share his enthusiasm. He seemed to have a lot of business interests, so many that it was a struggle to follow them as he fired out details of his early career, his failures and successes, his various bankruptcies and disasters, in building and finance and property speculation. At one point it seemed he had been responsible for building most of the skyscrapers of New York over the past thirty years personally. He caught the amusement in Stefan Gillespie's eyes, and laughed himself, enjoying his own pomposity and yet happy enough to puncture it.

'It's my city. It belongs to me. Every New Yorker feels like that.'

Over dinner the talk turned to families. Here Dominic Carroll seemed more reticent. He had sons, grown-up sons, but no grandchildren yet. He didn't say much about his sons, for a man of such far-ranging enthusiasms, but it was enough to tell Stefan that the American wasn't as close to them as he wished. Somewhere in there was a failure he didn't want to talk about.

He let Stefan talk more now, and clearly he could listen too when he wanted to, or when the topic of conversation wasn't so easy. Details of Stefan's life on the farm at Kilranelagh absorbed him and amused him, but it was when he told him about Maeve that something changed. Stefan retold the story of his wife's death, six years ago, in the matter-of-fact way he always did. It was simply part of who he was. The American listened intently, then reached out his hands and clasped Stefan's across the table. By now Stefan had had a bit to drink himself; his acquaintance was ahead of him. Carroll shook his head sadly, knowingly. He had found a bond between them. He was a sentimental man; sometimes sentiments shared were a kind of friendship for him.

'My wife died when my eldest was thirteen. It wasn't so unexpected. She'd been ill a long time, and however much money you've got, when they can't do anything, it's no use to you. You keep thinking you'll find a doctor who knows the cure, if only you look enough and pay enough. But you can't pay your way out of God's decisions. You can't pray your way out either.'

As he said the last words he crossed himself.

They walked back to their seats from the dining room with glasses of brandy, quieter than they'd come. Stefan had no desire to continue talking about the past; it was enough to say it. But the American wouldn't let it go.

'You've never remarried?' he asked as they sat down.

'No.'

'You're still a young man.'

'I'm not avoiding it. It's just something that hasn't happened.'

'You should count your blessings,' said the American. It was an abrupt change of tone. Where his words had shown sympathy, consideration, shared understanding, there was a surprising edge now, something almost bitter. He looked away, staring at the window. It was dark outside now; all he was staring at was the black hole that was the night sky. 'You should be careful. It was the biggest mistake of my life. If you want sex, you can buy it. You can buy as much as you want. But if you think you can replace the one love you ever had, if you think you can even come close, forget it.'

Stefan didn't reply. The new tone of voice had unsettled him. It contained an appeal to an intimacy he didn't want and didn't feel he liked very much. Whatever the man was talking about it was his and his alone.

For a moment the American said nothing either. He seemed to realise that he had taken a direction he shouldn't have done and had revealed more of himself than he was comfortable with. He looked up and smiled again. 'That's the trouble with a journey like this. Nothing to do but drink and they chuck it at you like there's no tomorrow.'

Stefan nodded. 'I've had enough. I wouldn't mind some more coffee.'

Carroll called to the galley for two coffees. He turned back to Stefan.

'You don't make much sense to me. You mind me saying it?'

'It depends what you mean,' laughed Stefan.

'I've got your boy, and why you're where you are, looking after him, and I've got what happened to your wife. I've got the farm and your mam and your dad. But I haven't got you. I haven't got you at all, you know that? What are you doing sitting on your arse in a country police station, running in drunks and, what was it, raiding the village hall to see if there's any illegal dancing going on! Jesus!' He grinned, entertained by the idea. 'That's not you, Sergeant Gillespie, not you! I didn't have to talk long to see that.'

'Someone's got to do it,' shrugged Stefan, and attempted a smile.

The look of suspicion was back in Dominic Carroll's eyes. It struck Stefan forcibly that although the stranger was smiling at him, he somehow didn't believe he was who he said he was. They'd talked about all sorts of things. Yet there was a sense now, as he watched the older man watching him, that the American had been probing, trying to find out something when there was nothing to find out. Stefan needed a break from the conversation. He leant across to the newspapers Carroll had been reading and picked one up.

'Do you mind if I have a look at one of these?'

'Help yourself. I'm going to turn in. We'll be landing at Botwood in the early hours. It's best to get some sleep in. You can't sleep through it.'

On each side of the compartment the seats had been made up into beds while they were at dinner, with curtains across them to create small bedrooms. Dominic Carroll got up and took an attaché case from a rack above. He pulled out a washbag and walked through the plane to the bathroom. Other people were starting to appear in pyjamas, dressing gowns.

Stefan felt relieved to be alone for a moment; if nothing else it was a rest from talking. He opened the newspaper. The first thing he saw was a report about an IRA bomb that had gone off in London the day before.

There had been dozens of bombs across Britain since

the beginning of the year. On 12 January the IRA Army Council had sent a letter to the British government, declaring war and claiming it was now the sole representative of the people of Ireland, since the treacherous and toadying government the people of Ireland had voted for several times since 1922 did not have the legitimacy the IRA had inherited, by a process similar to Apostolic succession, from the seven signatories of the Declaration of Independence in 1916.

The quantity of bombs that had followed this declaration of war had been impressive, even if the results had been indifferent. The damage had been minimal; reaction in Britain, despite indignant speeches in Parliament, seemed more like puzzlement than either anger or fear. The targets were sometimes railway or underground stations, mainly in London, and bridges over canals elsewhere; sometimes electricity pylons and gas mains were attacked; sometimes incendiaries were planted, more randomly, in stores like Marks and Spencer, Burton's, Woolworths; one bomb had gone off at the offices of the *News Chronicle* in Fleet Street.

Remarkably, no one had yet been killed, in line with the declared intention of the IRA's chief of staff, Seán Russell. In this most recent attack two bombs had exploded by the Thames, on Hammersmith Bridge. Stefan had heard about it in Dublin.

Two explosions which occurred at Hammersmith Bridge, just after 1 a.m. yesterday morning, are being investigated by Scotland Yard officers. The force of the explosion dislodged two girders in the suspension work of the bridge, and one was thrown across the roadway. Lamp standards were demolished and the middle of the

108

bridge was left in darkness. While investigations at the
bridge were in progress, Divisional Detective Inspector
Clarke left to interview two men at Putney police
station. It was later decided to arrest the two men. They
were Edward John Connell, 22, a salesman, of Elibank
Gardens, Barnes, and William Brown, 22, of Grafton
Place, Euston.

He looked up to see Dominic Carroll opening the curtains
into his sleeping compartment, and looking down at him
with a wry smile as he did so.

'Another bomb.'

'Another bomb,' replied Stefan; it was familiar news
after all.

'They don't seem to be able to do much to stop it.'

'Well, they will if they keep arresting people at the rate
they have been. I don't know what it is now, fifteen, sixteen,
and two more yesterday.'

'You're assuming the IRA's short of volunteers then?'

'There are only so many people who'd know how to plant
a bomb.'

'Well,' shrugged Carroll, 'the British must be shaken up
by it now.'

'I would be,' Stefan nodded. 'I'd be pretty pissed off if I
lived in Barnes and I had to go all the way down to Putney
to find a bridge. I wouldn't put it much stronger than that.
Unless London County Council's very short on lamp standards, I wouldn't say it'll keep anybody awake.'

As this conversation had started there had been a look
of amused satisfaction on the American's face. Stefan
believed he could read it easily enough. He had sat in pubs
with enough American-Irish singers of Republican songs

to know that though 'Up the IRA' was a cry that was hardly on many lips in Ireland, the enthusiasm in New York and Boston and Chicago was unaffected by the fact that the IRA wasn't only at war with Britain, it was still ideologically at war with the government of Ireland itself. It wasn't an argument he intended to start. Carroll could have his opinions.

'You're one of Ned Broy's men all right, Mr Gillespie. Goodnight.'

The words were said with something like a grin, almost with a wink, but there was something colder in the words than anything that had gone before. They were words that no guard could fail to understand, and they came from somewhere that was about more than singing rebel songs.

To be one of Ned Broy's men was to be more than just a lackey of the illegitimate entity that Republicans still referred to contemptuously as the Free State; it was to be an informer, a traitor, a killer. Wasn't the Commissioner a turncoat, like de Valera and all his crew, an IRA man himself who had brought ex-IRA men into the Gardaí to hunt down their old comrades, to imprison them, to torture them, sometimes to kill them? And it was true enough. The men Ned Broy had brought into the Garda Special Branch had done all that. Their reasons didn't make the bare facts any more palatable.

That none of this had anything to do with Stefan Gillespie didn't mean he couldn't feel the contempt behind Dominic Carroll's parting wink, or that he didn't sense now that the man was no idle wearing-of-the-green, up-the-rebels American-Irish tourist. He was a political Republican, and as a wealthy and influential man in New York he probably mattered in Republican politics, whether it was in America or Ireland, and it was likely both.

Stefan remembered that Carroll had expected him to know who he was. If he really was someone, it was unlikely he hadn't had a Special Branch tail on him while he was in Ireland, or that he wouldn't have been aware of it. The suspicion he had shown, on finding a Garda officer sitting opposite him on a plane to New York, with apparently no very good reason to be there, finally made sense.

It was 5.30 in the morning when the Yankee Clipper bumped down into the waters of Botwood, Newfoundland, and was tied up at the end of the long pier at the western end of the small harbour. Stefan Gillespie had not been able to sleep. For a while there had been the rattle of conversation and laughter and the clink of glasses from further down the cabin, where a group of passengers was playing canasta, but it had been silent for several hours now. The soft buzz of the engines, and the occasional grunt and snore from behind the curtains across the aisle, were the only sounds.

It was an odd feeling, cocooned up here, sailing through the night sky. He felt apart, not just from the world below in general, but from his own life in particular. He wasn't in the habit of stepping back from himself, and he wasn't entirely sure he liked doing it, but here, hanging in the darkness, it was hard not to do it. There was a lot in his head. Ned Broy and Owen Harris and Dessie MacMahon and Terry Gregory; Valerie Lessingham and Tom and his parents; the wide-ranging conversation with Dominic Carroll, about Ireland and New York and the prospect of war and Hammersmith Bridge and loss and grief and the sheep on the mountainside at Kilranelagh. And he kept coming back to the question a stranger had asked that he hadn't asked himself in a very long time: what are you doing, sitting on your arse in a country police station, running in drunks?

When the flying boat was down he joined most of the other passengers, pulled on his overcoat, and left the cabin. Dominic Carroll didn't stir, and he left him snoring quietly. He needed air and he wanted to walk. The air was cold enough. It was still dark. The Yankee Clipper was at one end of Botwood's small harbour. Across the water he could see the lights of fishing boats coming into dock; there was only the chug of their engines and the sound of the wind, not strong but beating the rigging slowly, like a pulse.

Botwood was a village in the north of Newfoundland, almost as far east in North America as you could go. The whole of Canada lay to the west, but to the north the nearest piece of earth was Greenland, and to the east it was the Dingle Peninsula in Ireland. The town sat in a sheltered bay, shaped by bare, treeless mountains, pretty much on the edge of nowhere; not very different from a thousand villages scattered along the western coast of Ireland on the other side of the Atlantic. Its buildings were of wood and corrugated iron sheets; most of its roads were dirt; an empty place in the great empty island of Newfoundland, which hadn't even got round to calling itself part of Canada yet.

But Botwood had suddenly become important. By the time the flying boats of Pan American and Imperial Airways got there they were at the end of their range; they had to refuel. And the great and the good of Europe and America, the bankers and film stars, the heirs and heiresses and politicians, the makers and shakers, at least in their own eyes, now trailed regularly along the pier in the early hours of the morning, to drink coffee, eat a breakfast they didn't need and talk about themselves.

Stefan drank the coffee too and spent some time talking idly with his fellow passengers. The conversation of the group, now all sitting together, had taken the turn every conversation did sooner or later, even at the edge of the world: war and the rumour of war. It wasn't a conversation he wanted. He walked back to the sea along the dirt road from the pier and watched the fishermen unloading their catch. The lights of their boats marked one end of the harbour; the lights of the Yankee Clipper marked the other; the Atlantic water was very still in the darkness, full of the lights playing on its surface.

When he got back to his seat he opened his case to take out a pen. He had a postcard of the harbour at Botwood, with a flying boat tied up at the pontoon. Tom wanted an account of everything; writing it now would bring him out of the nowhere the night sky was, closer to home. He looked down at the contents of the case for a moment. Passport and tickets, his warrant card, a typed itinerary from the Commissioner's office, a book, a notebook, three pencils held with a rubber band, a manila file with his own notes, and several envelopes, and the handcuffs; a change of under-wear, a clean shirt. He wasn't a particularly fastidious man, but things weren't the way he had packed them, not quite anyway. He pulled out the file and looked at an envelope that contained a letter from the Garda Commissioner to the consul general in New York. It had been opened.

It had been done very carefully and the flap had been

resealed, but it had not sealed perfectly. He smiled, looking across the aisle to the curtain of Dominic Carroll's compartment. The snoring was a little too regular now. He settled down to write the card. It was odd, but it didn't matter. If Carroll knew his business, he knew it didn't concern him.

As dawn came the Yankee Clipper approached the Canadian mainland and turned to fly south through Canada and New England to New York. Stefan Gillespie and Dominic Carroll said little over breakfast. When the American talked he spoke about what a visitor should see and do in New York. Stefan listened politely to the list of sights, buildings, parks, galleries, museums, department stores, bars, clubs, theatres, restaurants that Carroll threw out at him every time another one came into his head. His enthusiasm for his city was infectious. Dominic Carroll was all charm this morning; there was no hint of the doubt and suspicion of the previous evening. It was clear that he had now put Sergeant Gillespie in a box labelled 'harmless'.

In the early afternoon the plane started to drop and turn. The stewards were clearing the cabin. The Yankee Clipper was approaching New York. As Stefan looked out of the window he caught his first glimpse of the city. There was some thin, low cloud, and for a moment he couldn't make out very much. Then he saw something above the cloud, the top of a building, caught in sunlight, then another, and then another, and then as the plane descended through the cloud he saw the city spreading out below, looking down into Manhattan from the bend of the East River. It was exactly as he had imagined it to be, and yet it was breathtakingly like nothing he could have imagined. He had not noticed that Dominic Carroll had moved across into the seat next to him, looking over his shoulder at the same view.

'The lessons of the concrete, wealth, order, travel, shelter, products, plenty, as of the building of some varied, vast, perpetual edifice, whence to arise inevitable in time, the towering roofs, the lamps, the solid planting spires tall shooting to the skies.' When Stefan looked round the old man's eyes were shining with undisguised pride. 'I wish I'd written it, but Walt Whitman got there before me. You won't know the skyscrapers of course, but maybe you'll get to know some of them before you leave. I know them all, like you know your mountains in Wicklow. They're my mountains. If you do nothing else in New York, just walk the streets and look at them.'

The terminal at La Guardia had been open only months. It was new and everything in it was new; it was the biggest airport in the world. It spread along the East River on Long Island, looking across towards the Bronx and Harlem. The flying boat was moored at the marine terminal, away from the main runway, beside the river. The airport sat right next to the World's Fair at Flushing Meadows, a part of the future the Fair proclaimed to the world; La Guardia was the future now. Stefan waited at the Pan Am desk to be met by someone from the consulate, with that future all around him. Dominic Carroll walked past; a uniformed driver behind him, carrying his cases.

'I'll make sure the NYPD doesn't give you a hard time, Stefan.'

'I'd say I'll manage well enough.'

'Well, you're Irish, which should get you into the parlour at least, but as a Free State policeman you might not just get the seat by the fire.' He chuckled, happily back on his own turf now. 'Still, if you can stand your round, keep your mouth shut and remember to put in a quarter when the Clan na Gael cup comes round, you'll be grand so. It was a pleasure, sir.'

He stretched out his hand; Stefan shook it.

'At least you know who I am now, Mr Carroll.'

The American gave a wry smile. He knew that Stefan knew.

'A shabby business but sometimes I do need to know who people are.'

Stefan nodded as if this was the reasonable explanation it wasn't.

Dominic Carroll grinned.

'Did your man really do his mammy in so?'

'I haven't met anyone who thinks he didn't yet.'

'That's not an answer.'

'No, it's not.'

'Ah, you'd be a man for the road less travelled, somewhere in there.' The American tapped his head and laughed, then he turned away, followed by his driver.

A man in his late twenties, who had been hovering awkwardly in the background, waiting for the conversation to finish, approached Stefan immediately. He wore grey flannels and a tweed jacket; he was pale-faced and intense, and carried the air of a man who should be doing something a lot more important than meeting people at airports. Although he was only a third secretary he was, after all, an acting second.

'Sergeant Gillespie?'

'It is.'

The man reached out his hand to shake Stefan's.

'Roland Geoghegan. I'm from the consulate. I've a cab outside.'

They walked out through the terminal.

'Mr McCauley will see you at four o'clock. There's time to take you to your hotel. We're not far from there. Have a good trip? I'm sure you did.'

'Good enough,' replied Stefan. He sensed that the man would like to have asked him more, but that too much interest in the flying boat didn't accord with his position; such things were nothing to a diplomat after all.

The yellow Chevrolet taxi pulled out of the airport.

'A friend of yours, Mr Gillespie?' said the diplomat, quizzically.

'What?'

'The man you were talking to at the airport.' It was clear from Roland Geoghegan's pursed lips that he had been waiting to ask the question.

'Well, I met him on the plane. Why?'

'You know who he is?'

'I know his name's Dominic Carroll.'

'He's the president of Clan na Gael here.'

Stefan nodded; it all made more sense now. Whatever Clan na Gael claimed for itself in representing America's Irish community, its hallmark was its antagonism towards the Irish government in the face of a revolution not only unfulfilled but betrayed, its bitterness towards Éamon de Valera, once its hero now turncoat Taoiseach, and the fact that it didn't only fund the IRA from New York, Boston and Chicago; it made IRA policy there too.

'I'm afraid politics wouldn't be my strong point, Mr Geoghegan, especially not Republican politics. But he did give me a very long list of places to see in New York.'

117

The acting second secretary was unamused; he was a serious man.

'Presumably you know who Seán Russell is,' he continued.

The context told Stefan who Roland Geoghegan meant.

'The IRA chief of staff Seán Russell?'

'He's in New York now. And he's staying in Carroll's apartment.'

8. Fifty-Second Street

The Hotel Pennsylvania, sitting directly opposite New York's Pennsylvania Station, was something Stefan Gillespie hadn't expected. If it wasn't exactly one of New York's grand hotels it had clearly been booked by someone who hadn't been told that the Garda officer who was coming over was only a sergeant. The room on the corner of the tenth floor looked out over the city to the west and north along 7th Avenue. He had only minutes to take in the skyline. Roland Geoghegan was waiting downstairs to bring him to the consul general.

Another cab took them from 7th Avenue across town to the Irish consulate on Lexington Avenue, through more traffic than Stefan had seen; it was an entertainment in its own right. The city was there as a whole thing before he could appreciate its parts. Traffic, buildings, noise, colour, people; all happening at once; all drive and purpose; yet all just happening because it was happening, according to its own broken rhythms and discordant harmonies, just because the city was alive. Before he had time to take in what it really was, the vitality of New York had overtaken him.

The Irish consulate was four rooms and a corridor in a midtown office block on Lexington Avenue. Stefan was in

119

the consul general's secretary's office. Leo McCauley was busy. Roland Geoghegan disappeared into McCauley's office and came out, shutting the door behind him, leaving Stefan to wait.

'He'll be finished soon enough.'

The acting second secretary left with the air of a man who had a lot to do and was still irritated at having had his work interrupted. Stefan sat on the black leather sofa opposite the desk that took up half of the small room. Several posters on the wall advertised the glories of Killarney's lakes, the beaches of West Cork and the monastic ruins at Glendalough that were over the mountains from where he lived; other posters showed the new Irish Pavilion at the World's Fair, all glass and clean, cut stone and lean twentieth-century lines.

The door from the corridor opened and a woman came in. She smiled pleasantly and let that be greeting enough. He did the same. She walked to the secretary's desk and sat down on the chair, which was the only other chair in the room besides the sofa. She turned it slightly sideways, and crossed her legs. She picked up a magazine from the desk and flicked through it, not exactly reading but with an idle, slightly impatient manner.

Stefan looked at the posters again. He was aware that he had been looking, for a moment, at the woman's face, and at her legs as she had crossed them. She was worth looking at though he wasn't sure why he seemed to be struggling to look at the walls. He wasn't a man who spent his time gazing at women. She was attractive enough but not in any remarkable way. Her fair hair was slightly tangled. Her face was pale; she had almost no make-up on. He felt unaccountably awkward, sitting there, trying to avoid looking at her.

'I'm waiting to see Mr McCauley,' he said, for something to say.

'He's busy then?'

She looked up and smiled, but she didn't want to continue the conversation. She turned away and glanced at her watch.

'I'm just over from Ireland.'

'That's good.' She smiled again and looked down at the magazine.

'Do you think he'll be long?'

He didn't mind how long he waited. It was something to say again. The woman was hard work. The telephone on the desk started to ring. The woman continued to sit sideways on, flicking through the magazine for the second time, faster than the first time, paying even less attention to it.

'I'm sorry,' she said, 'is there something –'

The smile on her face was tighter, less generous than it had been.

'No, I'm sorry,' he laughed. 'I didn't mean to stare.'

'In that case you should make more effort not to.'

It was a rebuke, but it was soft enough; it made him feel less awkward.

The phone was still ringing.

'You've got a very relaxed way with telephones.'

She looked at him curiously.

'Most secretaries answer them.'

'I'm sure if I was a secretary I would,' she replied.

'Oh, I'm sorry, I assumed –'

'That'll be because of the legs and the cute smile, will it?'

'I didn't mean –'

'Don't worry, what else would a woman be doing in an office?'

121

He couldn't decide if that was real irritation or she was just milking it.

'You are sitting at the desk.'

'Next time I'll make sure I cuddle up to you on the sofa.'

The smile was back; he preferred her smiling.

'I'll give you the legs,' he said, 'but I'm not sure the smile's so cute.'

Finally she laughed.

The door from the consul general's office opened. A tall, fair-haired man in his early forties came out. The woman looked round and stood up. She didn't smile. It felt as if she had been waiting for the man because she needed to. Her face was, if anything, slightly anxious now. There was more behind her impatience than boredom. Stefan Gillespie stood up too as he looked from the woman to the man. He recognised him immediately, though he hadn't seen him for four years. The man smiled at the woman; he didn't notice Stefan straightaway. The woman looked at her watch once more.

'I've got to be back at the Fair. I've got some painters coming in.'

'It's all right, I'm going back. I'll drive you.'

'Is everything ready?' She lowered her voice instinctively.

'Of course,' said the man lightly. He touched her arm, moving towards the door. 'We can chat in the car.' He smiled at Stefan now, but without recognising him.

Stefan walked forward, stretching out his hand. 'John Cavendish. I won't say this isn't a surprise. How are you?'

The man laughed, recognising him now.

'Stefan Gillespie! How are you, Sergeant? It is still sergeant?'

'It still is. Is it still lieutenant?'

122

'Captain for what it's worth. If you hang around long enough –'

'So, how's it going? How's the army?' said Stefan.

'Not so bad. I'm over here working at the World's Fair, at the Irish Pavilion, in charge of security. I lock up every night and put the bins out.'

The woman was watching them both. Whatever her business with Captain Cavendish was, she didn't much like it being interrupted like this.

'So what are you doing here?'

'I've got a man to take back to Dublin.'

Cavendish nodded. Stefan could see that he knew something about it.

'You flew then.'

'Someone thought it was important enough.'

'How long are you here?'

'Two days that's all.'

'Where are you?'

'The Pennsylvania.'

'We'll have a drink.'

For a moment he looked at Stefan quite hard, as if he was thinking about something that had nothing at all to do with a drink with an old friend. He held out his hand and shook Stefan's again, quite unnecessarily, and with a purpose that reflected, somehow, whatever it was he had been thinking.

'Good,' he said quietly.

The door from the consul general's office opened again. The consul general looked out and saw the man he assumed must be Stefan Gillespie.

'Sorry to keep you, Sergeant, come in!'

'Thank you, sir.'

As he stepped back inside Stefan followed.

'I'll look you up!' called John Cavendish.

Leo McCauley was still young, like many of the young Irish state's diplomats, though a balding head made him look older than his forty-five years. He had a shrewd face that rarely showed irritation. He showed it now.

'I've had several telephone conversations with the Commissioner of Police here that have been extremely polite, but not over-friendly. Obviously he can't give me the bollocking he'd like to, but I imagine he'll depute someone at Police Headquarters to give you one. The line you take, apart from the fact that you're only here, as a junior officer, to remove the problem of Mr Harris from their city, is that he is simply a witness. Whatever rumours they've got hold of, you ignore. The NYPD won't believe he's only a witness, and they know we don't believe it either, but it's the best we can come up with as an explanation for our silence regarding the said Mr Harris and why we chose not to have him arrested or go through the usual deportation channels. It has the virtue of containing about enough truth to make it possible to keep saying it. So just keep saying it, Sergeant.'

'Have they got any idea where he's gone?'

'There was a sighting of a man who could be Harris. If it was him I'd have some faith they'll find him fairly quickly. Of course we're all at the rosaries hoping that murdering his mother hasn't given him a taste for it.' He smiled. 'Quickly and quietly doesn't seem such a very good idea, does it?'

'And what do I do now?' asked Stefan.

'You'd better go down to Police Headquarters and

introduce yourself. The Headquarters Detective Division is dealing with it, and the Missing Persons Bureau is there too, so, as I say, I think we can hope for rapid results. The man to speak to is Inspector Twomey. As you can tell from the name he'll be Irish enough for the bollocking to be loud but not too painful.'

The bollocking was much as the consul general had expected. Another cab took Stefan Gillespie through the streets of New York, now on his own; this time south towards Lower Manhattan and the unlikely baroque building on Centre Street, part palace and part French town hall, that was the NYPD's headquarters. Inspector Joseph Twomey, despite having been born in the Bronx, had an accent that was unmistakably Irish, and the bollocking he gave Sergeant Gillespie reflected his origins.

What the fuck did they think they were doing keeping the presence of an Irish fucking axe-murderer to themselves and trying to fucking spirit him back to Dublin with a bunch of fucking queers and actors to make sure he stayed where he fucking was? It gave a whole new meaning to a fucking unarmed police force. And before anyone else started telling him the fucking man was only a fucking witness, he already knew better than that, and so did every fucking detective in Dublin. And after making the fucking hames of it they had, the fucking Gardaí couldn't even send over an officer senior enough to give a decent fucking bollocking to!

The inspector stopped, almost in mid-bollocking, and asked Stefan where he came from. He then reeled off a list of a dozen officers whose families Stefan might know in Ireland. He didn't know any of them, though the names of Dunlavin and Blessington and Carlow were being thrown at him, and it seemed like a good idea to say he thought some of the names rang a bell. When Stefan asked the inspector what he wanted him to do Twomey shrugged. There wasn't much he could do, but with a bit of luck there'd be time for a drink with some of the lads before he put the fucking axe-murderer on the plane. And that was it. He handed Stefan over to one of the detectives who was looking for Owen Harris and disappeared back into his office.

Sergeant Michael Phelan was a few years younger than Stefan. He was about the same height, with the same dark hair, but cut very short unlike the untidy mess that was Stefan's. He was another New York Irishman, but with none of Inspector Twomey's obvious Irishness. His accent was entirely American and to anyone who knew, identified him unquestionably as a New Yorker. He seemed more amused by Owen Harris than irritated. It was just another job as far as he was concerned. But Stefan could see that the amusement was part of his style; he took it all much more seriously than the grin and the shrug suggested. He didn't think the Garda sergeant would be sitting around in New York for very long however. He expected Owen Harris to be found fast.

It was Stefan Gillespie's turn to smile, though he said nothing. It was clear the young policeman wanted to show him what a real police force was about. They hadn't been talking for many minutes before Sergeant Phelan mentioned that the NYPD was the best police force in the world. It was said with a wry, self-deprecating smile; but he meant every word of it. And he said it again, twice, before they'd finished talking.

'You've spoken to the people at the Markwell Hotel?'

asked Stefan as the conversation faltered and Sergeant Phelan had temporarily run out of ways to impress him. 'I mean Mr Mac Liammóir and the other actors.'

'I was there myself. Not that they knew anything. The guy climbed down the fire escape. I don't think anybody knew he'd gone for an hour.'

'I'd like to go over there anyway.'

'That's up to you. You think we missed something?' Phelan smiled.

'I'd say that's unlikely.'

'Too right it's unlikely.'

'Is there anything I can do though?' asked Stefan.

'Not unless you know New York backwards. I take it you don't?'

'What do you think? You'll let me know when you get something?'

'You'll know soon enough, Steve. Like I say, it won't take us long.'

'Let's hope so.'

The NYPD sergeant looked at him for a moment, then grinned.

'You want in on it then?'

Stefan looked; he hoped Phelan meant what he thought he meant.

'I mean he could just be picked up on the street some-where, but if there's anything more interesting going on. I mean it's your call, OK?'

'I've got nothing else to do. And I wouldn't mind him in one piece.'

He looked at the gun in the American detective's shoulder holster.

Sergeant Phelan laughed.

'We'll try so. And if there's anything worthwhile, you're in on it.'

Stefan walked out of his hotel and turned north on to 7th Avenue. If he kept going he would come to Times Square and 47th Street. It wasn't a long walk, and it was a good way to get to know where he was. The gridiron wasn't meant to be difficult to follow; that was what it was there for, but the profusion of numbers and the way they combined felt, for the moment anyway, more complicated than just looking for a name. Still, the place itself wasn't entirely new to him, not so new anyway. There were names already in his head, the names everyone knew from the movies and from songs and the fact that New York somehow existed in the air people breathed, even in Wicklow and the streets of Dublin. It was, after all, as much an Irish city as an American city, at least in Ireland.

In front of the hotel, right across 7th Avenue, was the Pennsylvania Station; a great row of simple Doric columns like something from the Forum in Rome that Rome could not ever have built on that scale. Beyond the columns was one of the largest indoor spaces in the world. It was no accident that it looked like a temple; its grubby granite was no longer the palest pink it had been once, but its scale, and even more the scale of the glass and iron inside, was meant to impress. It reminded Stefan of the Brandenburg gate in Berlin, rebuilt on the scale of St Peter's Basilica; he had walked through the Brandenburg Gate into Unter den Linden as a child, visiting his cousins in Germany, and since it had never been out of the newsreels and newspapers since 1933, the connection was easy to make; it was a connection the architect had intended.

As he walked away from the station, he looked up, as Dominic Carroll had told him he should. The shapes that ascended, sheer and straight out of the noise and hustle of the city streets, were calm and still, carving out the skyline all around him; it was that skyline, unlike anything else anywhere, that made this place New York.

He could pick out one skyscraper, ahead of him, to his right, the Empire State building, towering over everything else, and a shape he already knew. He had promised Tom he would go to the top if he could; if he did nothing else, that's what he would do. There were other buildings he thought he might know, that his mind had some pictures of at least: the Chrysler Building, brighter and more delicate; the heavy, solid sprawl of the Rockefeller Center. There were dozens of others, but that was about it as far as recognition went. They were all round him, in numbers he hadn't quite been prepared for; if he got to the top of the Empire State he would be able to say he had seen them anyway.

He glanced down at the map he was holding, then put it in his pocket, and walked on. It didn't really matter what the buildings were called. It was enough to look up and see them.

It wasn't until he came into Times Square, where 7th Avenue met Broadway, that his eyes really looked back down at the streets around him. There was nothing calm or graceful here. There was all the noise and colour he had taken in from the taxi rides, only more. There were restaurants, diners, lunch counters, bars, theatres, cinemas, ticket booths, nightclubs, burlesque shows, parking lots, newspaper stands, juice stands, souvenir stores, carts selling soda and hot dogs, pretzels and ice cream.

The lights that brought the place to life at night,

advertising Planter's Peanuts and Coca Cola, Chevrolet and Four Roses Bourbon, could only twinkle now, unable to turn the chaos into magic. Now there was just the already familiar traffic and the endless stream of people going somewhere in a hurry or nowhere in particular, and the stinking trucks still picking up filth from the night before. Yet Stefan Gillespie thought it was magical enough as he stopped to buy a pretzel and found himself looking down 42nd Street, where the theatres and restaurants spilled out of Times Square; almost immediately the hotels looked shabbier.

It was the last film he'd seen with Maeve, on a rare night out, seven years ago now. Ruby Keeler and Dick Powell. 'Come on and meet those dancing feet. On the Avenue I'm taking you to. Forty-Second Street.'

Five streets on he turned into 47th Street, past the Mansfield Theatre, which advertised Dublin's Gate Theatre, opening with George Bernard Shaw's *John Bull's Other Island*. The Hotel Markwell was two streets up 8th Avenue on 49th.

'Mr Gillespie, we'll have some coffee. The Markwell cockroaches are some of the largest I've seen, but the coffee is better than the Rainbow Room's.'

Stefan sat opposite the director of the Gate Theatre, Micheál Mac Liammóir. They were in two armchairs in the hotel foyer, next to a window that looked out on to 49th Street. Most of the stuffing had long disappeared from the chairs, and there were pieces of peeling tape all over the cracked and stained leather that had been stuck on over the years in vain to hold back the tide.

The Markwell was not one of New York's grand hotels either, but it was a very long way down the list from the

Pennsylvania. However, the actor sat back in his chair, smoking a cigarette, as if he was in the lobby of the Plaza or the Waldorf Astoria. As he spoke he never seemed to lose his focus on Stefan's face, even though his eyes constantly flitted to the street beyond the grubby plate glass and the ever-absorbing flow of people and vehicles outside.

Stefan remembered very clearly now the wry, almost idle half smile that suggested Mac Liammóir found everything and anything he encountered amusing and entertaining. He also remembered the sharp eyes that said the actor and director saw far more than the vague smile indicated. The receptionist, wearing carpet slippers and with a chipped enamel badge that bore the word 'concierge', brought the coffee, which was very good; although as Stefan would discover, there wasn't anywhere in New York where the coffee wasn't good, as there was nowhere in Dublin it was.

'Handy for the theatre of course, and extremely flexible, so flexible that they rent rooms by the hour. I've no idea why, but it did seem a good idea that the ladies should find another hotel. For myself, I wouldn't stay anywhere else.'

Micheál Mac Liammóir laughed.

'It's been a long time, Sergeant.'

'*The Taming of the Shrew*,' replied Stefan, remembering.

'And other things,' said the actor quietly. The dead were the other things; for a moment silence gave them their due. 'You're still in Dublin?'

'I'm in Baltinglass. I have been for four years.'

'And the woman, there was a woman? I'm sure I remember.'

'It's a good memory then.'

'A boon as an actor,' smiled Mac Liammóir, 'a curse as a

human being. But the two occupations have very little in common of course. However, I do recall her with you that evening. She sticks in my mind.'

'She stuck in mine too, Mr Mac Liammóir.'

'I see, but not in your life.'

'She does send me a Hanukkah card every Christmas.'

The director of the Gate smiled.

'Humour always sticks, I think, more than good looks. But it's a long time to carry a torch at your age, well, at any age where men are concerned.'

'Not really a torch, maybe a penny candle.'

'The mess of life must wait, Mr Gillespie. We have the mess in hand.'

'We do, sir.'

'Partly of my making, I'm afraid. Unfortunately Mr Harris was less enamoured of the prospect of the journey home than I thought. It seemed to suit everyone, except him. Quickly and quietly, those were my words.'

'I imagine they were the words everybody wanted to hear.'

'You're kind, Sergeant. And it's true enough. The politics! I never go near politics without burning my fingers. I should have had the courage to ignore it and trust to the old adage that no publicity is bad publicity. I should have called a press conference to announce that the Gate was the only theatre company in New York with a murderer in its midst. Before long every theatre on Broadway would have wanted one!' He chuckled quietly. 'If only we'd been doing *Crime and Punishment*! There's a rather good poster, with me as Raskolnikov, wielding an axe. An opportunity missed.'

Mac Liammóir looked down and shook his head.

'It seemed the right thing to do.'

He looked back at Stefan.

'I don't really know Owen. I certainly don't know whether he's capable of killing someone or whether he isn't. But I think he has a quite fragile grasp on reality, that's the only way I can put it, talking to those who do know him. I'm not suggesting there's a question about his sanity, only that he lives, well, in a precarious place. And as he was with us in New York, for better or worse, I felt the least I could do was to help him hold on to whatever grasp of reality he has. I felt that shackles and police sirens would not be helpful, and that kindness would. And you sprang to mind. Since Mr McCauley at the consulate wanted to do the thing quickly and quietly too, we all took up that cry. And the boy himself seemed amenable. He seemed quite content to go. It was a simple solution to all our problems.'

'So what happened?' asked Stefan. 'Why did he change his mind?'

'There was no indication that he had.' Micheál Mac Liammóir shook his head. 'I think the young man from the New York police was under the impression that we'd been keeping him in a room under lock and key. Of course it wasn't like that at all. I simply left his friends to keep an eye on him, chat to him, play cards with him, whatever was best. Naturally enough the bedroom window wasn't nailed down, so when he decided to go he simply climbed out of the window and down the fire escape. Even that was more dramatic than it need have been. There was someone with him most of the time, but it was hardly like the changing of the guards up there.

And the truth be told he could have just walked out of the hotel, very easily indeed, without any clambering down ladders at all.'

'Did he know anyone in New York?'

'Not as far as I'm aware. Charlie Mawson's closest to him and he doesn't think so.' The actor smiled. 'Harris is always rather keen to tell us who he knows. I think if he had friends here we would have heard about it.'

'Did he have any money?'

'I'm not sure. Some I imagine.'

'Enough to leave the city?'

'I can't imagine it would have been a great deal. He took nothing with him when he left. No one's been paid this week, and we were all on rather short commons on the boat over. I'd say it was unlikely he had much at all.'

'That might fit,' said Stefan.

'With what?'

'The police have a description of a man who was in a diner in Times Square last night, who could easily have been Mr Harris. He ate a meal and then didn't have enough money to pay the whole bill. There was an argument. He ran off without paying at all. The owner said he was English.'

'Yes, he can sound very English, especially when he wants to.'

'If it is him, he hasn't travelled far then.'

Micheál Mac Liammóir nodded; he hoped that was the case.

'You know he really wasn't someone I wanted on this tour. The poor boy can't act to save his life, and as a stage manager he leaves a lot to be desired. He inhabits his own world most of the time. The trouble is we were struggling to cover our costs. We could pay the wages and the hotel, but everyone in the company had to stump up for the passage. A lot weren't able to and in some areas we couldn't be too choosy. Hilton Edwards and I rather hoped Harris wouldn't find the money, but in the end he came up with it. And we did need an acting stage manager. So we took him, without enthusiasm.'

'If he hasn't gone far,' said Stefan, 'it won't take long to find him. And if he's wandering the streets without any money, it'll be even quicker.'

The actor looked at Stefan for a moment, his lips pursed.

'Charlie Mawson doesn't think he killed her you know.'

'Is that what Harris told him?'

'I'm not sure he did, not in so many words. I don't know what they talked about while he was here. And I have the impression that most of the time he'd been talking about everything but what happened to his mother.'

'That's not so surprising.'

'I'm just repeating what Charlie Mawson said.'

'And does Mr Mawson know him well.'

'Better than the rest of us. They had been lovers until recently.' Mac Liammóir said it without apology and without expecting it to be taken for anything other than the straight-forward statement it was. Stefan knew it would not have been something the actor would have said to Superintendent Gregory. 'I don't know what that counts for as far as know-ledge goes. Does it make us more perceptive about the people we love, or less perceptive?'

Stefan didn't reply.

The actor shrugged.

'No, I haven't got an answer either, and if I pursued it I'd probably only find one that depressed me. Let's just say

Charlie's opinion should count for something. I only repeat it because I gather from Mr McCauley that it isn't an opinion, even a question, as far as the Gardaí are concerned. Even the New York detective had no doubt he was looking for a murderer.'

'No one's in a position to make that call, not before Mr Harris has been questioned. No one can know what happened to his mother, not yet.'

Mac Liammóir sat back in his chair.

'You wouldn't make much of an actor either, Sergeant.'

Suddenly his expression changed. He was looking past Stefan and Stefan turned his head to see Sergeant Phelan of the Headquarters Detective Division walking towards him. The easy smile he had worn before was there, but it was broader, and he carried an air of satisfied expectation.

'Didn't I tell you it wouldn't take us long?'

Stefan and Micheál Mac Liammóir stood up.

'We've found him.'

The actor nodded, looking genuinely relieved.

'Where is he?' asked Stefan.

'He's in a club on 52nd Street. He's been in a couple of bars, cadging drinks and drawing a bit of attention to himself. But we've got a tip off now. It's not far, so you might as well bring him in with me. I've called a patrol car. From what I'm told I'd say his first stop is going to be the drunk tank.'

52nd Street had the same kind of busy, sleazy vitality that was everywhere around Times Square, but in the late afternoon, before the night brought it to life, it was the sleaziness rather than the vitality that had the headlines, and even after dark most of that vitality was underneath the dingy brownstones, in the cellars. As Michael Phelan walked from 8th Avenue into West 52nd Street, he was on his territory; he wanted Stefan to feel that. This was the centre of the world as far as he was concerned; whatever you could find anywhere else, that was about what had happened, history; New York was now.

'This is called Jazz Alley,' he drawled. 'It does what it says. There are clubs the whole length of 52nd Street, down in the basements. It's the only place this far from Harlem you'll find black musicians playing with white musicians, or where you'll find anybody black downtown doing anything other than serve food and clean floors. It's quiet enough now, but later on it's full of people you wouldn't want your sister to know, along with the whites who haven't got the money or the guts to go to Harlem. That's along with the more select clientele, you know what I mean, pimps and whores and drug dealers and the usual mob of hangers on. It's a busy place after dark.'

He said it with his laid-back smile and plenty of shrugs to show how everything extraordinary was ordinary in his city. But he said it with pride.

'It sounds like Baltinglass on a Saturday night,' said Stefan.

'I doubt it,' laughed Phelan. 'Is that your nearest city?'

'It is. And second only to Dublin.'

'I've never heard of it,' replied the American.

'Well, you'd want to go on market day to get the best out of it. We're short on jazz musicians as a rule, not to mention pimps and whores and drug dealers, but you can't move for cattle and sheep, and there's always the chance of a bit of set dancing in the evening, with Seamus Maloney on the accordion. Not that we let that sort of thing get out of hand, Jesus no!'

'OK!' laughed Sergeant Phelan. 'I get the point.'

He stopped by a set of railings and steps down to a basement. A sign that wasn't lit up yet, but would shine brightly in blue and white after dark, read 'The Dizzy Club'.

'So what's our friend Mr Harris doing in here?'

'Like I said, getting drunk as far as I know.'

'Hasn't he run out of money? It must have been him at the diner.'

'I guess he's made some friends. You can add queers to the mix up here. I'm sure he'd sniff that out. I got the impression he was. Am I right?'

Stefan shrugged.

They walked down the steps to the club. Michael Phelan pushed open the door. The narrow entrance was dark. There was a small archway into a cloakroom. A door opened along the passage and a heavily built figure walked towards them, in a tuxedo and a shirt that hadn't been white for some time. For a few seconds Stefan Gillespie didn't realise that the owner of the muscular body and the surprisingly soft, feminine face was a woman.

'We're closed. You want to come back in a couple of hours.'

The sound of laughter and clapping drifted up from the club.

'Come on Lois, my pal's come all the way from Ireland for this.'

'Do I know you?'

The detective took his badge from his pocket and flashed it lazily.

'You called us, about a guy we're looking for.'

'Why would I call the cops about anything?'

'My mistake, Lois. It must have been someone else.'

'He's down there.'

She pointed into the darkness, then walked back into the office.

'Who's she?' asked Stefan.

'Lois DeFee. She's the bouncer.'

They walked into the dingy, cramped cellar. Tables and chairs were jammed into every space in what looked like a giant, brown shoebox. There was a small stage at one end, with more tables hard up against it. On one side of the room there was a bar. The only lights that were on were over the bar; the rest of the club was in shadow. There was a group of men, mostly young, some quite big and burly. There was a smell of bourbon, brilliantine and too much aftershave. They stood in a tight group, all facing the bar, laughing, watching. A voice, slightly high pitched and shrill, pierced the laughter.

In front of them stood a young man, his fair hair was slicked back, thick with hair cream, his face was red with the rouge of alcohol, his eyes had a slightly wild, startled look. His brown suit looked as if he had been sleeping in it. Around his neck was a green feather boa that he had picked up somewhere between 49th Street and 52nd Street. He held a tall glass in his hand. And he was declaiming poetry of some kind, in the sharp, crisp voice of the English upper classes, a voice that his audience seemed to find amusing in its own right, irrespective of what he was saying, accompanied as it was by winks and pouting lips, the occasional thrust of his torso, and the sexual innuendo that the poem had never been meant to carry.

'It's no go the Herring Board, it's no go the Bible. All we

want is a packet of fags when our hands are idle.' The juxtaposition of 'fags' and 'idle hands' made the audience laugh louder. 'It's no go the picture palace, it's no go the stadium. It's no go the country cot with a pot of pink geraniums. It's no go my honey love, it's no go my poppet.' More exaggerated winks and pouting lips. 'Work your hands from day to day, the winds will blow the profit.' He pulled the man next to him close and then pushed him away. And then his face suddenly changed. The last words were quieter, and they seemed to be addressed to the darkness in the empty club, rather than to the people still laughing and sniggering around him, as much at Owen Harris as with him. 'The glass is falling hour by hour, the glass will fall for ever. But if you break the bloody glass you won't hold up the weather.'

He stopped abruptly, then laughed himself, and gave a low, sweeping bow. The audience applauded and cheered; it was weird, but it was funny. Behind them Stefan Gillespie had recognised Louis MacNeice's 'Bagpipe Music' immediately; Michael Phelan hadn't; there was a lot more to do in the evenings in New York than there was in West Wicklow.

Owen Harris straightened up and drained his glass. It had been a tumbler almost full of straight bourbon. He held the glass out expectantly, grinning the way a performing seal might have grinned, if performing seals grinned. One of the men reached for a bottle on the bar and filled the tumbler.

'My good man!' exclaimed Harris.

Stefan was still standing in the shadows with the New York detective. Phelan grinned. 'Wow, he's some specimen. I guess that will be him.' Stefan nodded. He had never seen Owen Harris, or even a photograph of him, but he didn't need to. The man might not be much of an actor, but he was definitely a performer. Out of habit rather than necessity Michael Phelan reached his hand inside his coat and undid the clip of his shoulder holster.

9. Centre Street

'Mr Harris?'

It was the NYPD detective who spoke, stepping out finally into the circle of light around the bar. Until then neither the performer nor his audience had been aware of the two men watching them in the darkness. Sergeant Stefan Gillespie stood just behind Sergeant Michael Phelan.

'And what have you come as, dear?' pouted Harris.

Phelan held up his badge.

'Oh, G Men!' the Irishman proclaimed, raising his eyebrows.

The onlookers laughed, though less enthusiastically.

'I'm Sergeant Phelan, NYPD. I'd like to talk you, sir.'

'My goodness, what good-looking policemen you do have here!'

There was another ripple of laughter. Owen Harris was good value.

'If you'd come down to Headquarters with us, Mr Harris.'

'Down to Headquarters! Just like a movie. But a lot more polite. I like that. It's definitely an improvement. Who does write your dialogue?'

Whatever about the dialogue, this wasn't the script Michael Phelan had in mind, at least not in front of Garda

Sergeant Gillespie, who was there to see what real policing was. But for the moment Stefan was enjoying it.

'If you just come along. You'll know what it's about, sure enough.'

Owen Harris grinned broadly; his accent was suddenly stage Irish.

'Sure enough! Sure enough, says he! Bejasus and begorrah, Sergeant Phelan, was your mother ever Irish? God save all here, go away with you!'

The laughter from the onlookers was louder now. It seemed that the entertaining Irishman had the measure of the young detective. They resumed their drinking and topped up glasses. Stefan was aware that like Owen Harris himself they had all been drinking a lot. Who they were, how Harris had met them, whether they were, some of them, all of them, as Michael Phelan assumed, of the faggot fraternity, he didn't know. It didn't matter. What mattered was that the atmosphere had changed.

As the men grinned and sniggered, the geniality that had been there when he had walked into the club with Phelan wasn't there any more. Owen Harris wasn't aware of it; he wasn't really aware of anything except that he was the focus of attention, his glass was being filled, and he was making people laugh. But there was a tension behind that laughter now. Stefan had been on the end of enough pub brawls to know how suddenly things could happen.

Michael Phelan's voice was no longer lazy; he felt it too. The American detective had had no reason to expect trouble in the Dizzy Club at this time of day, but in his eagerness to show the visiting Garda sergeant how things were done, he had been less cautious than he should have been. Now he thought Stefan's presence might defuse the

143

situation. He only needed Owen Harris to agree to go with them.

'This is Sergeant Gillespie. He's here from Ireland.'

Harris looked at Stefan, a slightly puzzled expression on his face for a moment. It was New York, and for a moment it didn't quite make sense.

'A guard?'

'I think you were expecting me, Mr Harris,' said Stefan calmly.

'You're here to take me back!'

There was no suggestion left now of the repertoire of archness, the grins, leers, pouts, sneers, simpers and eyebrow-raising, that had so amused Harris's audience. Now the man in the green feather boa looked frightened.

'No! If you think I'm going with a fucking peeler and the fucking Irish Mafia here, you can fuck yourself. I know what you'll do with me when you get me back there. You don't want to talk to me. You want to fucking hang me! I've done nothing, nothing at all!' He stepped back slightly, into his audience, looking at them with fearful, desperate eyes.

'You just have to tell us what you know,' said Stefan. 'I'm sure you'd want to do anything to help. Didn't you say so to Mr Mac Liammóir?'

'Don't let them take me. Please, don't let them take me!'

He grasped the arm of a thickset, burly man. There was silence now. The group of men, seven of them, were looking at the two policemen hard.

'What's he supposed to have done?' one of the men asked.

'It's not your business,' snapped Phelan. 'Just keep out of it.'

Another man put his arm round Owen Harris's shoulder.

'He looks harmless enough to me.'

'You want to come downtown too?' Phelan held the man's gaze.

They were the wrong words. Another man stepped in front of the NYPD detective. He held up the glass he had just drained the drink from.

'You know what you need to do, Sergeant? You need to walk back up those stairs to 52nd Street and come back with some cops who are big enough and old enough to make those kinds of threats. You got that?'

The man was very close to Michael Phelan, breathing into his face; his stale breath smelt of too much bourbon and of too many cigarettes.

'Back off,' said the detective.

'Why don't you make me?'

Stefan saw two of the onlookers pick up empty bottles. Sergeant Phelan shrugged. It was an attempt at a kind of weary indifference, but he was well aware the situation was dangerous now. He shook his head, and then reached into his coat and pulled out his gun. His movements didn't look fast, but the gun appeared with considerable speed. But with even more speed, one of the men who had picked up a bottle moved out of the shadows and smashed it down across Michael Phelan's outstretched arm. The gun clattered to the floor and spun off under a table.

Stefan Gillespie moved closer to Phelan, but even as he did there was a man in front of him, blocking his path. The man grinned and then swung his fist into Stefan's face. He collapsed to the ground, knocking over a table.

Two men grabbed Michael Phelan by the arms; the man who had spoken to him stood in front of him, shaking his head. He tightened his fist and threw a heavy punch into the NYPD man's stomach. Owen Harris was laughing now, a high-pitched laugh that was almost a scream, an uncomfortable mix of fear and hysterical amusement.

As Stefan tried to get up his assailant was standing over him; he kicked him back down again. 'Stay down there, you bastard!'

The big man punched Phelan in the stomach again. 'Next time bring some real cops, asshole!'

The other men were clapping and laughing now, as if all the geniality that had been there before the policemen had arrived had returned. And there was a new floorshow. The man who had hit Stefan was chuckling too, reaching for his drink. Everybody had forgotten about the gun. But Stefan could see it, close to the table he had knocked over as he fell. He rolled forward suddenly and grabbed it. As the man who had knocked him down caught the movement, he turned round and came for him again. Stefan sat up, pointing the gun straight at him. The man stopped. Then Stefan Gillespie fired the pistol into the air, deafening them, and stood up.

'Do you want to let Sergeant Phelan go now, fellers?'

The men who were holding the NYPD detective let him drop to the ground. He struggled painfully to his feet, but as he did so the smile he wore so confidently was returning to his face, just a little more wry than usual. From outside, drifting along the passageway to the steps, the sound of a siren could be heard over the rumble of traffic. The woman they had spoken to when they entered Dizzy's was standing behind Stefan, smoking a cheroot.

'Someone must have phoned the cops again. They're here.'

Lois DeFee turned back to the office and slammed the door shut.

There was complete silence in the club. Owen Harris's shrill voice had stopped and no one else could find much to laugh about now. No one moved, but then Harris let go of the arm he was clutching so desperately and walked to the bar, as if he was unaware that anything at all had happened. He picked up a bottle of bourbon that was on the counter and filled his tall glass brimful to overflowing. He picked it up with great care and drained it. Still no one else moved, but everyone was watching him. He filled the glass again and drained that, and then turned round with a sigh, to face the room.

'It's been a pleasure, gentlemen,' he said. He took a step forward and grimaced. He cleared his throat and started to sing. 'If you ever go across the sea to Ireland.' He took two more steps forward; they were shakier than the first. 'Then maybe at the closing of the day.' He frowned, as if searching for the words; he swayed a little. 'You will sit and watch the moon –'

Then he passed out.

As he did there was the noise of running feet in the passageway from 52nd Street now, and four billy-club-wielding NYPD officers appeared. They were definitely big enough and old enough. And when Owen Harris was carried up the steps from the club, on his way to the drunk tank, Stefan Gillespie could hear them proving it.

Later that evening the sounds drifting out on to 52nd Street would be jazz, and very good jazz it would be. But there was nothing cool about the noises from the cellar now. No one was going to bother to take the customers from the Dizzy Club downtown and book them. That was too much like hard work. But beating the shite out of a bunch of faggots was altogether different; that really wasn't any work at all.

*

147

Garda Sergeant Gillespie sat in a bare office on the ground floor of Police Headquarters. It was dark. The lights of New York were outside the window, but the blind had been pulled down. The room was lit by a lamp. There was the rumble of traffic. Through the door came the rattle of a typewriter, the occasional shout or curse, the sound of laughter.

Owen Harris sat opposite him, drawing deeply on a cigarette. It was ten o'clock in the evening now. The would-be actor and suspected matricide was a great deal quieter than he had been in the club on 52nd Street. He had spent the last three hours in the drunk tank and was now on his way to a cell. But if he was quieter, he was also surprisingly resilient. Under his eyes the skin was almost black and the effects of a fierce, throbbing hangover still had him in their grip. As Stefan explained that he would be kept locked up for the next two days, until the Yankee Clipper left for Ireland, he accepted the situation with a calmness that seemed to have no relation to the terror he had shown earlier. The idea of the hangman had disappeared, as if it had never been there. Perhaps it had only been there for the audience.

Stefan put the change down to the fact that Harris had been blind drunk and probably couldn't remember anything that had happened anyway, yet it didn't feel like that. It felt as if he was speaking to someone else now, a man who was rational, helpful, perceptive, and alert.

'I understand perfectly, Sergeant.' Harris blew out a ring of smoke. 'Obviously I can't expect you to leave me wandering round New York, not after I've put everyone to such a lot of trouble to stop me doing exactly that.'

'You'll be in a cell on your own,' said Stefan.

'Well, that's more than I was at the Markwell. And the

food's better here too. You'd really think that with a theatre company that has the kind of reputation the Gate has, the dear chums, Micheál and Hilton, could put us up somewhere a little more upmarket. I can cope with the occasional cockroach with the best of them, but it's a question of style. We really do look like the poor relations. And the theatre's not much better, according to Charlie Mawson anyway. The thing is, if you're going to be on Broadway, you need to be on Broadway. Appearance does matter. In the theatre it's everything.'

He spoke clearly, brightly, as if he expected the Garda sergeant across the desk to have an opinion. His accent could have been mistaken for an English one, of the public school variety, but he had abandoned the over-precise, over-shrill voice of his upper-class English impersonation at the Dizzy Club. Stefan assumed this was his own voice; the Irish tones that softened the brittle consonants and sharp nasal vowels were unmistakable.

'You understand that you'll be taken to the plane with a police escort.' Stefan didn't feel it was necessary for him to comment on the Gate Theatre's choice of hotels. 'Once we're on it you won't be getting off again until we get to Foynes. It does stop to refuel, in Botwood in Newfoundland, and most people do get off. However, I won't be able to let you do that, I'm afraid.'

'Botwood, well, there's a place I'd never thought of going.'

'I don't imagine many people have.'

'Not much there in the way of nightclubs anyway?'

'Not much at all.'

'That's no great loss then. Will I be in shackles, Sergeant?'

'Not if I can avoid it. That's really up to you.'

'Ah, so you do have shackles.'

'Handcuffs,' replied Stefan.

'I did intend to come back to the Markwell, Mr Gillespie. It wasn't so much an escape from returning to Ireland, more an escape from the tedium.'

'I'm not sure that's something I can take for granted, Mr Harris.'

'I was so bored in that grim hotel, you see. There wasn't even a view. Just a fire escape and somebody's washing. And I wanted to see something of New York. I'd been shut up in the sodding place since I arrived. I mean to come all this way and not walk down Broadway. It was a frightful waste.'

'Well, you've certainly seen some of New York now.'

'Ah, yes, there won't be many tourists who can say they've woken up in the drunk tank, Sergeant. I mean any fool can take the elevator to the top of the Empire State Building and have his picture taken. But all this!' He gestured round the drab room, laughing. 'If my mother could see me now!'

He stopped abruptly. Stefan could see that he had simply forgotten that she was dead. He knew you could do that. He knew how even when the death of someone you loved filled your head and left room for nothing else, no other thought, no other feeling, you could still, for a moment, just forget.

'Poor old Medea,' said the would-be actor quietly.

Stefan looked at him. He knew enough about Greek mythology to know that Medea was the wife of Jason, a priestess, an enchantress, maybe a witch, but he didn't know that she inhabited Owen Harris's own mythology.

'Medea and Moloch, Mater and Pater, Ma and Pa, Daidí agus Mamaí. The beloved Ps. You know the sort of thing.' Harris stopped and shrugged, shaking his head. 'Familial terms of endearment, old chap. Well, after a fashion. "Sophey pephukas kai kakoan polloan idris." Thou art a clever woman, skilled in great evil, grieving for the loss of thy husband's bed. And Moloch, a different kettle of fish altogether! Thou shalt not let any of thy seed pass through the fire to Moloch! Oh, just an ordinary family, after all.'

There was no extravagant performance in the words Harris quoted. They were familiar words, to him at least, old words, worked and reworked, and usually thrown out to make someone smile, or to make the ordinariness of his parents' ordinarily unhappy marriage and the mess of their ordinarily uninteresting lives, sound somehow extraordinary. But odd as the words were, they sounded tender. Harris looked at Stefan, a half smile on his lips.

'I didn't kill her. It's a simple fact. I hope you'll believe me.'

'I think you should keep what you have to say until you're in Ireland.'

'Why?' It was a simple question.

'For a start we need to know what happened. It can take a long time to do all that. It's a step by step thing, and it's very important to make sure it's right. And there are questions to be asked. I don't know what they all are.'

'Surely one of them has to be, "Did you slit your mother's throat, Mr Harris?" I'm just telling you that I didn't, Sergeant. It seems to be pertinent. In fact I'd say it's crucial under the circumstances, isn't it? For goodness' sake, man, I should have thought the sooner you know all that the better.'

It was a flash of petulance and irritation in the current calm.

It was also exactly the situation Stefan Gillespie had anticipated. The first police officer to talk to Owen Harris was bound to hear things that might not be said again, that might be said differently, that reflection might change and re-order and re-interpret, that a solicitor might want to sit on, or reconstruct, or suggest his client forget about altogether. He already had the sense that the man in front of him was used to giving a performance and that you might not always be sure which Owen Harris you were talking to. He had seen one extreme at the Dizzy Club, frantic, desperate, hysterical; this one was brooding at times, but it was a more reasonable and more circumspect one; he couldn't really know whether it was any less of a performance though.

Micheál Mac Liammóir's observation stuck in his head: a fragile grip on reality.

There were a lot of words coming out of Harris but it was hard to know what was behind them, and he couldn't believe it would get any easier when Superintendent Gregory sat down with him at Dublin Castle. Besides, he had learned a long time ago that if you wanted to get the truth out of a suspect, the time to do it was when the suspect wanted to talk to you, not when you told him to talk to you.

If there was a real Owen Harris to find in there, finding him would come out of some kind of trust, or it would come when he was off-guard, or at least when he wasn't on a stage. A Dublin Castle interview room and a row of Garda detectives would probably be another stage and another audience. But Stefan Gillespie had been told what to do. He had been told to keep his mouth shut.

10. Pennsylvania Six-Five-Thousand

Tom, this is the Empire State Building. I've seen it now. Wow! It's as big as you think and then bigger! But I haven't been to the top. I hope I'll get there tomorrow. I want to go at night. I think it should be something to see, the lights of all the other skyscrapers. Tomorrow is St Patrick's Day. I'll be standing on Fifth Avenue and watching – that should be something to see too – maybe just a bit bigger than Baltinglass. The biggest Paddy's day parade there is! I've got some police friends who'll be marching it. Enjoy your parade as well!

Stefan Gillespie sat at the desk in his room at the Hotel Pennsylvania, writing a postcard to his son. The desk was in front of the window, on the corner of 7th and 33rd, looking out over the Pennsylvania Station and across the lights of a thousand Manhattan buildings, high and low, towards the Hudson River. He poured the last of a bottle of Eichler beer, happy to do nothing except sit in the chair and gaze out over the city.

The radio was playing quietly in the background, the last blue notes of Glenn Miller's 'Moonlight Serenade'. He didn't particularly notice the sombre organ music that followed a bouncy advertisement for Pepsi Cola. 'Pepsi Cola hits the spot. Twelve full ounces, that's a lot. Twice as much for a nickel too.' He didn't register the sombre voice that spoke over it. 'Ladies and gentlemen, we present at this time the regular weekly broadcast of Father Charles Coughlin, pastor of the Shrine of the Little Flower, in Detroit, Michigan.' But the voice that came next pulled his attention away from the window. It was slow, even laboured, but the words were enunciated with a weight and precision that seemed to insist that every consonant, every vowel mattered.

'Good evening, ladies and gentlemen, I ask your indulgence as I return once more to the gruesome subject of war, but it is my duty to disclose to you information which does not level itself down to ordinary people. We Americans have been victimised by invisible forces which are determined to embroil us in war. Is this democracy? When ninety-five per cent of our population abhors the very word "war", is this democracy?' Stefan was looking away from the window, at the radio. It was a curious voice, and curious words; they weren't the words he expected to hear in New York.

'When ninety-five per cent of our fellow citizens have their minds tortured, their passions agitated, by the five per cent of internationalistic warmongers, whose sole, insidious aim is the destruction of the so-called totalitarian states, is this democracy? Are we not used like putty in the hands of those responsible for the half-truths, the warmongering which appears daily in our press? When the catchphrase "unjust aggressors" was used to stir up your wrath against Germany and Italy, were you conscious of the real truth of unjust aggression, of Britain's seizure of the African continent in the last years of the last century, conducted more ruthlessly than any seizures accredited to Italy and Germany in the past two years? Who were responsible for the silence but the scheming internationalists, descendants of the Father of Lies? Did they tell of the crimes of France, that other great democracy? No! See the hidden hand of the internationalists who dominate governments and nations and control the world. Who wants to drive America to play a part in the impending European clash? Ask the leaders of the League for Peace and Democracy! Ask the internationalists who shuttle gold back and forth across the Atlantic! Ask the munitions makers! Ask the Jews who refuse to oppose Godless communism as they oppose Nazism!'

There was a knock on the door. Stefan got up and walked across the room. The voice had mesmerised him for several minutes. He knew little about what was happening in America, its politics and its preoccupations; but hardly noticing it he had left Europe and its dark quarrels behind him. Now that over-precise, rhythmic voice, a voice that had enough of Ireland in it to make him even more uncomfortable, had taken him back to the politics and preoccupations on the other side of the Atlantic. They were all here, of course they were all here; but to listen to such a shrill expression of them was a shock to him. It was as much the tone, cold and dark, as the words themselves. He felt it ought not to belong in this city of towers and lights. But there it all was, in the very air, crackling down out of the night sky.

As he opened the door he was pleased to see that John Cavendish had indeed found him. Cavendish walked in, pulling off his overcoat and dropping it down on the bed. He looked at Stefan for a moment, smiling.

'You haven't changed, Stefan.'

'It's four years, not so long I suppose.'

'No, I mean you haven't changed. The first time I met you, you'd been beaten black and blue. Your face looked like it does now. A bad habit.'

Stefan glanced at the mirror behind him and laughed; he had forgotten the altercation in the club on 52nd Street. The first time he had met the army officer it had been the night after a run in with two Special Branch detectives who had a point to make. His face had probably looked much worse then.

'Your prisoner wasn't in the mood to go home then?'

'It wasn't him. But he'd made some friends in New York. They were reluctant to break up the party. They thought they'd break up some cops.'

Cavendish bent over his coat and took out a half bottle of Bushmills.

'Have you got any glasses?'

He slumped down into an armchair.

Stefan went into the bathroom and came back with two tumblers. Cavendish was looking at the radio. The slow words were still coming out.

'Now that democracy seemingly has failed in America, because it was irreverently wedded to international capitalism, the schemers plan to destroy our form of government and replace it with an absolute dictatorship, by pleading with you ill-informed people to save democracy! Democracy?'

'The Radio Priest! I wouldn't have thought he was up your street.'

Stefan took the bottle of whiskey. He walked across to the desk and turned off the radio; he was glad that the piercing voice had stopped now.

'It just came on after Glenn Miller. Who the hell is he?'
He opened the whiskey bottle and poured out two glasses.

'Father Charles Coughlin,' said the army officer, settling back into the chair and yawning. 'The Shrine of the Little Flower. The best-known priest in the country. Anti-war, anti-communist, anti-Roosevelt, anti-capitalist, anti-British, anti-Semitic, and now anti-democracy apparently. He's got an audience of millions. There are a lot of people who'd like to shut him up, including most of the Catholic hierarchy. He frightens the life out of them. That was him on a quiet day. There's even a song about him. "Yonder comes Father Coughlin, wearing the silver chain – Gas on his stomach and Hitler on his brain." And isn't he a credit to us all?' Cavendish took the glass Stefan held out and grinned broadly. 'You wouldn't be long working out the old bastard's mammy and daddy came from the oul sod itself, would you?'

'You wouldn't so. It's in his voice.'

Stefan sat back down at the desk.

'I was talking to Leo McCauley at the consulate this morning,' said Cavendish. 'He told me there was a guard coming to take your man Harris back. I didn't dream it was you. A bit of a cock up, eh? The NYPD wouldn't have been too happy.'

'Not very, but it's un-cocked up now. It's nothing to do with me anyway. I'm only here because Mr Mac Liammóir thought I'd frighten Mr Harris a bit less than someone from Special Branch. Nobody wanted a mammy-killer raining on the World's Fair parade. I just sit on the plane and make sure he gets back. So what's all this World's Fair about with you?'

'Security and all that. It doesn't amount to much really.

157

The army found me a few other jobs to do here. I was in Washington for a while.'

'No more intelligence then?'

'Well, old habits,' laughed Cavendish. 'I might send G2 a postcard now and again. I keep an eye open so. You meet all sorts in New York.'

He looked down for a moment. Stefan could see he was preoccupied. He took a slow sip of whiskey, and then carried on making easy conversation.

'You're really still down in Baltinglass?'

'When I'm not in New York.'

'You should come out to the World's Fair. It is worth seeing.'

'Isn't it all?' Stefan looked back towards the window.

'You should still do it. It's like nothing else.'

'I've only got two days before the plane leaves.'

'I'll drive you out there. Just spend an hour, you won't forget it.'

John Cavendish stood up and walked towards the desk. Stefan was still sipping his whiskey, but the army officer had already finished his. He poured another one and drank half of it immediately, looking out through the window. There was only the sound of traffic, a muffled music through the glass. Stefan wouldn't have put him down as a drinker when they had met before, but he had already reached out for the bottle again. You couldn't judge those things. And there was something about the conversation that was, well, odd; it seemed easy enough but there was tension in it. It didn't feel like the acquaintances-in-a-strange-town visit that was advertised.

'I want you to do me a favour, Stefan.'

He looked up at Cavendish. The captain was more serious

now. He went back to the armchair. As he sat down Stefan could see he was tired. It wasn't just tired; it was a kind of weariness; the tension was a part of that too, wherever it was coming from. There was more than the Irish Pavilion's security in his head, and more than a drink and a chat about old times.

'I need to get something to Dublin, as quickly, as safely as I can.'

Stefan said nothing; clearly old habits did die hard after all.

'Nothing's going to be any faster than the way you're going, on the flying boat, and I doubt it could be any safer. Even sending something in the diplomatic bag from Washington – it takes forever and even using the damn thing draws attention to whatever you put in it. I've got some material, papers, that need to go to Commandant de Paor. You'll remember him.'

'He was your boss in G2. And maybe still is?'

The captain shrugged.

'I take it this is all material no one knows I've got.'

'You've got no connection to anybody at the embassy in Washington, or the consulate here. You don't know a soul, and the reason you're here is simple. You've got your witness or prisoner, or whatever you're telling him he is.' Cavendish smiled; he was well informed. 'You've got no particular connection to me. Better not to tell the consul general we're old friends.'

Stefan looked surprised.

'I'm not doubting Leo McCauley, not for a minute, but we're all still living in an Irish village sometimes, even in the middle of New York. Everyone knows everyone's business. I try to keep away from all that. As far as my business is concerned, well, some of it – it's better if no one knows.'

Stefan nodded, simply accepting it.

'The trouble is I don't know who does know my business now.'

He stopped, absorbed by his own thoughts. His glass was empty.

Stefan topped up his own tumbler and walked over to fill Cavendish's.

'I'll tell you what I think you need to know, Stefan.' The intelligence officer had decided more was required. 'So if anything happens to me –'

Stefan looked at him harder.

Cavendish laughed.

'I don't mean that the way it came out.'

It sounded like he meant it exactly the way it came out.

'I can't talk directly to Gerry de Paor, and I don't want to write it down at the moment. All I'm asking you to do is get on the plane with an envelope in your bag. But I guess you have to know enough to keep your wits about you, that's all.'

He hesitated, reassuring himself that what he was doing was right once more. He hadn't made this decision lightly.

'I've been intercepting IRA ciphers here for three months now. Messages they're couriering back and forward from Ireland. Some of the material's already back there, with G2, but it still hasn't been deciphered. They're getting nowhere with it, but the more there is to work with the better the chances of cracking it. Though I hope I'll be able to do something about that myself. If I do then I'll risk a phone call to get that information through. But it'll be very important then that they've got everything.' He smiled. 'Still, that's all something I've yet to make happen. Anyway, you just take an envelope –'

'More of the same?' said Stefan.

'More of the same and probably the last of it. My source has dried up. That's the polite way we put it in this game. He dried up in the Hudson.'

'So the IRA knew he was giving you information?'

'They may not know who he was giving it to, but I have to assume, yes, they may know it was me. And if they hadn't clocked me as G2, they probably have now. But the couriers have no idea about contents. They're messengers, that's it. I'd say the IRA would be confident about the ciphers. They've every right to be. We've had people working on them for months.'

'Doesn't that put you at risk?'

'I don't think it would, not normally.'

'What does that mean?'

'Well, the IRA is a lot more popular here than it is at home, but knocking off Irish government employees isn't going to endear them to anybody. There's a kind of unwritten rule as far as the government and the IRA are concerned. Don't embarrass us and you can get on with it. You can send money and explosives across the Atlantic, but don't blow anyone up in America. It's the old Irish village thing again too, just like home. You know yourself. The IRA could put the finger on every Special Branch man and Army Intelligence officer in Dublin, and the world and his wife knows who's on the IRA Army Council. We don't go around shooting each other though,' Captain Cavendish smiled, 'well, not most of the time anyway.'

'But this is different?'

Stefan was still thinking about the word 'normally'.

'I don't know. There are other people involved.'

'Like who?'

161

'Like German Intelligence.'

There was a tight smile on Cavendish's face. Not everyone would have understood how that changed the game. Stefan Gillespie did. He might have forgotten that he did, but four years really wasn't such a long time ago.

'Why?'

'I don't know specifically. I mean there's all the usual stuff they have in common. Number one is keeping America out of the war, that's what brings German Americans and Irish Americans together politically. President Roosevelt is trying to amend the Neutrality Act in ways that would help Britain buy arms here. Congress is probably going to stop him and it's Irish-American senators and congressmen who are making more noise about it than anybody else. And they're winning. Why wouldn't the IRA and the Abwehr be sniffing around all that? But that's merely the stuff of everyday politics. You just heard some of it on the radio. Dear old Father Coughlin on every week to tell his flock the president's dragging the country into a war and democracy's the way to perdition. But there's a lot more going on too. There's the IRA bombing campaign in Britain. Among other things that is meant to show the Germans they can deliver the goods in the sabotage department if there's a war. That's not going well from what I've read.'

'It's a farce so far,' said Stefan. 'The last thing they blew up was a bit of Hammersmith Bridge and a public convenience in Birmingham. I've only been to Birmingham once, and from what I remember of the toilets that one's maybe no bad thing. But sooner or later they'll hit something bigger.'

'The truth is they need to do better, a lot better,' replied Cavendish, 'if the Germans are going to take them seriously.

That's one of the reasons Seán Russell is here at the moment. It's about money mostly, and it's about persuading people the bombing campaign he cooked up with Dominic Carroll isn't the mess it is. But it's also about planning what's going to happen next, in the event of a war. And there's something else on. I don't know what it is, but something here, that's the word. Against all the unwritten rules, they're planning something here.'

'How do you know that?'

'It's from the German end. I don't know if it's the IRA and German Intelligence, or the IRA and some bunch of German Americans, or pro-Nazis. There are all sorts of German-American organisations out there. The Irish have got Clan na Gael and the Irish clubs – the Germans have got the German-American Bunds, complete with brown shirts, brass bands, flags and fuehrers. Sometimes they just drink a lot of beer and eat bratwurst, sometimes they go out and beat up a few Jews. But there's more to it now.'

'Presumably that didn't come from an IRA cipher you can't read?'

'It comes from a lot of things,' said the captain. 'It's in the air too.'

Stefan Gillespie was being drawn into it. He could feel it. It was that sensation again; his heart beating faster. He wanted to know more. But he could see that John Cavendish had gone as far as he intended to go.

'Where does Dominic Carroll come into this?' asked Stefan.

'I told you, the bombs in Britain, the IRA declaration of war and all that bollocks, that's what he and Seán Russell put together. He's got a lot riding on that, and since it looks like all it's going to achieve is to get a lot of IRA men locked

163

up in Britain and Ireland, piss everybody off at home, and demonstrate very convincingly how fucking incompetent the IRA is –'

'I've met Carroll.'

It was Cavendish's turn to show surprise.

'Where?'

'On the flying boat. He was coming back from Ireland.'

'Back from Berlin actually, Stefan. He was there last week.'

'He didn't mention that.'

Stefan turned and poured some more whiskey. As he stood up to take the bottle across to John Cavendish the army officer's head had dropped. He was on the edge of falling asleep. His head snapped up and he grinned.

'I'm banjaxed. I need to get home and get some sleep.'

He stood up, pulling on his coat. He picked up his glass and drained it.

'I'll catch up with you, Stefan. I'll take you out to World's Fair.'

'I'll leave it to you,' Stefan replied.

John Cavendish nodded. He turned away and walked out.

Stefan stood still as the door closed. It was a strange meeting, and it took him to other places than New York. Dublin four years ago, when he was still a detective; the Austrian abortionist from Merrion Square, who had collected information for German Intelligence, beaten to death in an empty house in Danzig; the bodies of a man and a woman buried in the Dublin Mountains because they had loved the wrong people, and because they were in the way of bigger things; the priest who believed Adolf Hitler was the Church's salvation and the sister who thought her

164

brother was; the only woman he had felt he could love since Maeve's death. He had not seen Hannah since.

It had all seemed further away than it really was, all that, despite the constant talk of war. It was close again now, some of it anyway. He wasn't entirely sure what John Cavendish was trusting him with yet. There was something to deliver; but it wasn't only that. The intelligence officer had told him much more than he needed to. Stefan understood that too; he thought he did. It was partly the man's isolation, the fact that there was no one he could talk to about what he was doing. He had decided to trust Stefan with something, then he had decided to trust him with more. It was also the fact that he didn't know where he stood; he didn't know whether he was in real danger or not. Stefan wasn't convinced John Cavendish really believed in that Irish village, where everyone knew everyone anyway and, sure, no one ever had to get shot.

Stefan walked back to the desk and sat down. He poured the rest of the Bushmills into his glass and sipped the whiskey. He looked out at the lights of New York, like a thousand stars, rising up, filling the sky and stretching into the distance to merge with the real stars above. The sight was as exciting, as vibrant, as full of life as it was when he had first sat at the window, but something had changed. The city was darker. It was no longer as magical as it had been. And it was a darkness that felt tired and familiar. There were not enough lights, even in New York, to push the darkness away.

11. Fifth Avenue

*It's a great day for the Irish, with New York's finest
leading the St Patrick's Parade! Forty thousand men,
women and children, are marching to pipes and bands,
heavenly music right from the oul sod. The parade is
reviewed by many notables: there's Mayor La Guardia,
and Jimmy Walker, just like the old days, and Dominic
Carroll, how many of these has he marched in as
Grand Marshal? At St Patrick's Cathedral New York's
new archbishop, Cardinal Spellman, gives his blessing
to New York's Irish. And while half a million
Gothamites, all green flags and flowers today, watch the
tremendous spectacle from packed curbstones and
vantage points in high buildings, the Old 69th, the
Fighting Irish of World War fame, are in the vanguard,
as the marchers swing along 5th Avenue. Sure, what a
celebration tonight!*

When Stefan Gillespie woke up the next day the words
of the previous night felt out of place in the New York
morning, but as he sat reading *The New York Times* over
breakfast in the Hotel Pennsylvania, there wasn't really very
much to keep the conversation of the night before at bay.

At the World's Fair, across the East River on Long Island, the exhibits that had already become its symbols, the soaring, needle-like spire of the Trylon, and the great white globe next to it, the Perisphere, had been attracting more than six thousand visitors a day since President Roosevelt had opened the Fair a week earlier. Inside the Perisphere was a diorama of the City of Tomorrow; elegant, peaceful, full of light and space, with jobs and homes for everyone, said *The New York Times*. It was called 'Democracity', and visitors were carried around the inside of the globe on the world's longest escalators, watching twenty-four hours of the city's well-mannered, utopian day. But that was about all there was of 'Democracity' on the paper's front page.

Elsewhere Adolf Hitler had declared Slovakia a German Protectorate; it was all that was left of a Czechoslovakia he had just dismembered and filled with German soldiers, with not much more than a sour shrug from the world's democracies. The temporary withdrawal of various ambassadors was still threatened of course. Hungary had annexed what had been Ruthenia to finish off the remnants of the Czechoslovak army and mop up the last pieces of the country. Prague was under German martial law, but although the persecution of its Jews was proceeding as expected, the *Times* did say it was in a methodical and orderly fashion, which was something.

Congress was split between condemning Hitler's annexations and minding America's own business. In Brooklyn, meanwhile, kindergarten and high school children of the Jugendschaft des Amerikanischdeutchischen Volksbundes, in storm troop and Hitler youth uniforms, had marched through Brooklyn Heights with mechanical precision, under heavy police guard, to the delight of their parents and friends.

However, stocks were rallying in London and Paris as the immediate threat of war had, familiarly, been postponed once more, and in baseball the New York Yankees had got their revenge on the Tampa Reds, in St Petersburg, Florida, for a recent defeat. But whatever was happening anywhere else, in New York this day was going to be green.

As Stefan finished his breakfast, Detective Michael Phelan arrived. He was in uniform, and it was full NYPD dress uniform, with buttons and cap badge gleaming for the day that was in it. He sat down at the table, his face still showing the bruises from their visit to the Dizzy Club. The waiter brought a cup and poured him a coffee without any need for communication.

'I take it you'll be marching.'

'I will,' said Michael Phelan, full of himself once more.

'I'll maybe see you then. I'll walk up to 5th Avenue and have a look.'

The sergeant pulled a crumpled NYPD cap from his pocket and pushed it across the table. Stefan folded up his newspaper and picked it up.

'I thought your boy might like it.'

'He will too. That's quite something, Michael. Thank you.'

'In the meantime you'll be wearing it yourself,' grinned the detective.

'I'll keep it for Tom.' Stefan shrugged, reading nothing into it.

'You will not! You're going to be marching so.'

'Should I look out for the Wicklow Association?' laughed Stefan.

'You can forget the County Wicklow, you'll be marching with us.'

Two hours later Sergeant Stefan Gillespie found himself in West 44th Street, off 5th Avenue, standing with Sergeant Phelan and maybe a hundred other police officers, beside the NYPD Mounted Unit. Further up were the soldiers and veterans of the Fighting 69th, then the Police Department Marching Band and the NYPD Holy Name Society. Behind, stretching back down 44th Street, as far as he could see, were the uniforms of firemen, marines, sailors, boy scouts and a dozen high school marching bands. Hovering to one side, at the corner of 5th and 44th, were the dark suits and the dark hats of the Irish-American Legislators Association, the city and state and federal politicians who were important enough to march at the front of the parade. They were moving through the ranks of soldiers and police officers, pumping the hands of people they didn't know, with smiles that, if a steady eye had anything to do with it, were every bit as sincere as their firm handshakes.

Above the rumble of conversation and laughter, and the shouted orders of the marshals, there was the strangled wail of bagpipes tuning up; there was the snort of horses and the clatter of their shoes on tarmac. Unusually there was no noise of traffic. Cars, trucks, cabs, buses were a long way from 5th Avenue today.

On the other side of 5th Avenue, on East 44th Street, and along the route at the intersections at 45th, 46th, 47th, East and West, all the rest of Irish New York was assembling, in a city that ranked, after Dublin and Belfast, as the biggest Irish city in the world. There were the sashes of 32 county associations, from Antrim down through the alphabet to

Wicklow; there were Ancient Order of Hibernians boards from Manhattan, the Bronx, Brooklyn, Queens, Staten Island, Long Island, New Jersey and the Hudson Valley, and from Pennsylvania, Connecticut and beyond; school children and church congregations and Gaelic Athletic clubs were ready to step out, along with Clan na Gael chapters and Brian Boru clubs and the Friends of Irish Freedom; there were more uniforms, too, from fire departments, from the Port Authority, from sheriffs' departments, from correction facilities, from the Coast Guard; there were ever more drums and ever more pipes.

Stefan really would much rather have watched than participated, but he had no choice in the matter. When he had reached 44th Street he was introduced to thirty or forty police officers whose names he wouldn't ever remember, and to a few he would, including Michael Phelan's elder brother, Aaron, and his father, Ernest. The Phelans were an important family in a police force where family, especially Irish family, mattered. Ernie Phelan, wearing the eagle insignia of an inspector on his cap badge, would lead out the Police Department guard of honour on to 5th Avenue; Aaron, a captain at Police Headquarters, would be close behind.

And then suddenly it was time; after two hours of standing around, all the waiting was over. The last cigarettes and the last cigars were stubbed out along 44th Street. The horses rode out on to the Avenue. Pipes and drums played. The parade had begun.

Moving uptown from 44th Street, the 5th Avenue of Lower Manhattan, stretching down into the garment district below the Empire State Building at 34th, had already been left behind. The parade was a midtown-uptown affair, and a few streets on from 44th Street St Patrick's Cathedral was firmly located where New York's bluebloods still held sway; they weren't much in evidence today though. Cardinal Spellman stood on the steps of the cathedral, blessing the marchers, and almost to a man, woman and child they crossed themselves as they passed him. There were few enough beside Stefan Gillespie who didn't. He was conscious of it.

There had been times in his life, when he was younger, surrounded by people doing what most Irish people did without thinking, that he had simply done it too, not to stand out. It wasn't that anyone particularly noticed whether you did or didn't; it was simply the consciousness that not being a Catholic brought, and had seemed to bring more and more in Ireland since his childhood; not quite fitting.

As the parade moved past St Patrick's, on towards the Grand Army Plaza and the start of Central Park, this wasn't the territory of most of the people who were marching, nor of most of those who lined the Avenue in their hundreds of thousands to watch, from 44th Street to halfway along the length of Central Park and 86th Street.

If New York's social register had retreated steadily north and east into Park Avenue over the years, and was now heading beyond the city itself to Long Island, there were still old mansions in the streets off 5th Avenue; there were air-conditioned apartments and penthouses in the skyscrapers; there were grand hotels like the Waldorf-Astoria, the Savoy-Plaza, the St Regis; exclusive clubs where you wouldn't want to be too Jewish or even too Irish to qualify for membership, and where, if you weren't white, you might just get in to collect the garbage; there were museums and art galleries that still preferred their patrons to be on the social register and expected them to leave bequests in their wills; there were the shops and stores and restaurants and cafés and night-clubs that required money, real money, if you wanted to indulge: Tiffany's, Cartier, Saks, Bergdorf Goodman, the Rainbow Room, the Stork Club.

But none of that mattered much on St Patrick's Day. And the feeling that New York belonged to everyone who filled 5th Avenue, marchers and spectators alike, was hard to resist. Stefan Gillespie was enjoying his Irishness more self-consciously than he ever did in Ireland, sharing it with everyone else. And wasn't New York one hell of a place to feel you had as much stake in as anyone else, even for a day? Looking at the people around him, in the march and on the street, more than at the buildings, he remembered the words he had read in *The New York Times* that morning, about the opening of the World's Fair, words the city's mayor, Fiorello La Guardia had spoken a week earlier: 'The greatest display of all, at this great World's Fair, will be New York City itself, with its 7,454,995 inhabitants.'

For a few hours the Atlantic seemed much wider again to Stefan; the shrill rumour of war out of Europe slipped away. Maybe there was more to 'Democracity' in New York than just a cardboard cut-out after all. Just now it was hard not to believe it.

The parade ended for Stefan Gillespie where 86th Street met 5th Avenue and crossed into Central Park. Behind him thousands of marchers were still funnelling through the cheering midtown crowds; they would do so for two more hours. The NYPD vanguard broke up quickly, as officers met up with their families, headed for the subways and the els to the Bronx and Brooklyn, Staten Island and Queens, or drifted off to various Irish bars. Stefan walked east along 86th Street with Michael Phelan and a dozen other Headquarters' detectives to the Lexington Avenue Line Subway.

They jammed their way into the subway car, down to the Lower East Side, and then jammed into McSorley's on East 7th Street, where people were spilling out on to the street. Michael Phelan had promised Stefan he'd feel at home in McSorley's, and he did. The dark wood, the dim light, the smell of stale beer, the cloud of tobacco smoke, not to mention the complete absence of women, was familiar enough, even for a man who spent more time raiding pubs to break up out-of-hours sessions than he did drinking in them.

Home wasn't really where he wanted to be when he had barely two days in New York; he quite fancied being in New York as it happened. But the warm, foaming beer was good, and there seemed little point doing anything other than drink it, talk about where he came from, which seemed to interest McSorley's customers far more than their own city, and to admit that, yes, you could be in a pub slap bang in the middle of Dublin.

The sneers about Free Staters, and the Free State Polis, were delivered with good-humour, as it was St Patrick's Day, and it was answer enough for him to shrug and smile. But when Michael Phelan suggested they went back uptown, to crash a party on Central Park that wouldn't feel at all like the middle of Dublin, Stefan was more than happy to squeeze out of McSorley's again and take the subway back to 59th Street and the park.

The parade had been over for hours. The sun was setting; it would soon be dark. New York was coming alight.

Hampshire House was a 37-storey building on West 59th Street, overlooking Central Park, almost exactly halfway between 6th and 7th Avenues. It was a new building by New York standards, and builders were still working on the upper floors, but apartments lower down, with their views the length of the park, south to north, were already filling up. The most distinctive features of the building were the stepped terraces of the top storeys and the steep pitch of the great pyramid-like copper roof that crowned it. The roof bore some resemblance to the roof of a French chateau, hanging in the sky, and it had little to do with the tower below, where a bit of Spanish baroque blended with austere Art Deco and some English Regency here and there. It shouldn't have worked, but it did. Like the rest of New York it threw together all sorts of things from other places and other times to produce something that could only belong, uniquely and spectacularly, to one place and one time: New York, now.

It was in Dominic Carroll's sprawling apartment on the twenty-ninth floor of the Hampshire House that a St Patrick's Day party was in full swing, as Michael Phelan and Stefan Gillespie arrived. There had probably been someone checking invitations at some point, but by now anybody with any claim to be Irish could walk in, let alone anyone in an NYPD uniform, which was, in any case, its own claim to being Irish. It wasn't until he was in the elevator going up to Carroll's apartment that Stefan realised whose party it was. He wasn't sure how welcome he would be, but he had had enough to drink not to be concerned. It did have its funny side too. No one could deny he had a connection; it wouldn't be everyone whose luggage had been personally searched by Dominic Carroll.

'It doesn't get much better.'

Stefan Gillespie was standing at a window looking out

over Central Park. There wasn't much to see of the park now, except for the strings of lights that were roads, and the occasional clustering of a building's lights in the great darkness that was the green space at the heart of Manhattan. But on each side, cut sharply out of the night on the park's west side and east side were the buildings that gave it its rectangular, ordered shape, blazing with light. It was everything he had been looking at since he had arrived, but there were things you didn't tire of looking at. The voice behind him, rising quietly above the voices filling the room, was Dominic Carroll's.

'I'd say not,' replied Stefan, turning round.

'I spent every cent I had on this building. I may never see it all back.'

He heard the pride in those words, yet there was nothing boastful in it.

'It's your building then?'

'Just about. Mine and a couple of banks'. I'm a builder.'

Stefan looked back through the apartment and through the party-goers. There were easily a hundred, probably more, chattering, laughing, arguing, eating, drinking. A series of wide rooms interconnected through folded doors. Everything was black and white, clean and new, but the furniture that filled the rooms was elaborate and fussy; the pictures on the wall were landscapes and still lifes. Like the building itself it ought not to have worked, but it did. In one room there was a bar and a buffet full of food. A black pianist played quiet, soothing jazz. Waiters walked around with silver trays full of drinks and canapés.

There were green, glittering shamrocks and green balloons and green bunting. But the flag that hung in each room was not the tricolour of Ireland; it was the green flag

175

with the golden harp that had been the flag of Ireland before the tricolour. There was a point to be made for those who knew, though for most people there the flags were just a bit of old Ireland. But as far as Dominic Carroll was concerned the tricolour wouldn't fly until there was a republic in Ireland that was a real republic, and Éamon de Valera's statelet was not that republic.

'It was derelict for years,' Carroll continued. 'They started on it in 1931, but by the time the shell was up and the floors were in, the Depression caught up with it. It was boarded up for five years. It just sat. I bought it for where it was. To be honest I didn't care what it looked like.'

'Well, it's not a bad-looker either,' Stefan answered.

'Love's never about looks,' said the American. 'When I finally got it, I didn't have the money to finish it. I let it sit here for another two years until I did. We're still fitting out the top storeys, but it's almost there. I didn't just want to live here. I wanted to make something of it. This is what I made.'

'So what happens now?

'Now, I need to sell it, Stefan!' Dominic Carroll chuckled. 'If I don't, it'll break me. It wouldn't be the first time I've been broken, but I'm getting long in the tooth for clawing my way back. Still, I should get there. Anyway, I'm glad you got here. From what I've just heard, you seem to be fitting in.'

'I guess it's hard not to on St Patrick's day, Mr Carroll.'

'I meant with the NYPD.'

'Still keeping an eye on me?'

The older man smiled. 'Ernie Phelan was telling me.'

He looked across the room in the direction of Inspector Phelan who was talking vociferously to some junior officers, all listening with dutiful attention, waiting anxiously for him to hit the punchline of a very long joke.

'You chose the right man to save from a beating. Mikey Phelan's father's got a long way to go in the NYPD. I'd put my money on him getting to Chief of Department, and not too many years from now. Aaron's already a captain. You've met them all haven't you? Mikey's father, his brother?'

'Yes, at the parade.'

'Mikey's Mikey, of course. He'll settle down though.'

'I don't think he'll be doing that today,' smiled Stefan. 'He's here somewhere, investigating something, but I don't think she was interested.'

Carroll laughed. As a waiter passed by with a tray of drinks he lifted one off. He took a sip and looked at Stefan for a moment, more serious.

'You should think about it yourself.'

'About what?'

'The NYPD.'

It was Stefan Gillespie's turn to laugh.

'Why not? You wouldn't find it so hard to get in either.'

'I'm not looking to emigrate, Mr Carroll.'

'If you've got what it takes, you've got what it takes, and something tells me you have. I don't have a lot of time for the Guards, but I'd have thought even Ned Broy could find something better to do with you than stick you out with the mountainy men.' The American grinned. 'And you know people who matter here already. That's some going in a couple of days.'

'Well, it's a bigger thought than I had in mind.'

'You should think big thoughts, Stefan. They're the only ones worth thinking. That's why I'm standing here, with this, instead of carrying a hod.'

'Maybe someone has to stay in Ireland.'

'Does it feel that much like you've even left?'

'It didn't in McSorley's this afternoon.'

Dominic Carroll slapped him on the back in a way that was almost fatherly; he reached out his hand and grabbed the arm of a man passing by.

'Seán, come and meet Stefan Gillespie!'

The man stopped. He turned a serious, slightly preoccupied face towards Stefan Gillespie, as if interrupted in the middle of something important, though he had been doing nothing and talking to nobody. He was in his late forties, his hair starting to recede; his eyes moved from Stefan to Dominic Carroll, and kept moving, around the room, as if he still had something else on his mind. He wore a dark suit that had seen better days, and had seen them some time ago. Unlike most people he wasn't drinking.

'Seán Russell, Stefan Gillespie. You may know who Seán is.'

Stefan simply nodded. He didn't know what Dominic Carroll expected him to say, but he sensed that the American enjoyed putting people at a disadvantage; the best way to deal with it had to be to do nothing. He shook the IRA chief of staff's hand. Russell's handshake was very quick and slightly tentative. He was waiting to be told who he was talking to.

'Stefan's a Garda sergeant,' the Clan na Gael president announced.

'Well,' said Russell with a curt smile, 'that's unexpected.'

'He says he's not Special Branch, but then perhaps he would do.'

'You're having a good time anyway?' The IRA man smiled

again, more warmly for a moment. He knew Carroll's fondness for mischief.

'I'm only here a few days, Mr Russell.'

'He's on his way home with an axe-murderer, isn't that it?'

He clapped Stefan on the back again, more forcefully, laughing.

'It's a state secret. At least Dev would like it to be, right Sergeant?'

Russell looked puzzled, understanding none of it, as his host led him away, amused, offering no explanation about de Valera and axe-murderers.

As they walked across the room Stefan was surprised to see Captain John Cavendish coming towards him, his path crossing Dominic Carroll's and Seán Russell's. The army officer was in the dark blue dress uniform of the Irish infantry; there were red stripes on the trousers; on the jacket white, starred epaulettes, white braid, a red and white belt. He stopped and spoke to the host and the IRA chief of staff. They all shook hands with studied politeness.

The conversation was short, but there was time for Seán Russell and John Cavendish to exchange a joke. It was clear the intelligence officer and the IRA leader knew one another. The captain walked on, saying hello to several people, working his way to Stefan Gillespie in a way that made his eventual arrival more like chance than intent. He had seen Stefan before Stefan saw him. He reached him by the windows over the park.

'I see you had a chat with the chief of staff.'

'I think it was Mr Carroll's idea of a joke.'

'It's a long time since I've seen Seán myself. We don't move in the same circles normally, but I've bumped into him from time to time. He was my commanding officer once, in 1920, before the Treaty.' Cavendish was more thoughtful, but then he laughed. 'He was a pain in the arse even then.'

'He wouldn't have reckoned much to the uniform.'

'Wasn't it fancy dress then? I always get these things wrong –'

The captain looked out over Central Park and sipped his drink.

'I'll pick you up tomorrow morning and drive to the World's Fair.'

Stefan was immediately aware that this was about the package he would be taking back to Dublin when he left New York with Owen Harris.

'I'd appreciate that. I'd like to get a look at it, however brief.'

The G2 man nodded, turning back to the party, scanning the crowd.

'I wouldn't have expected to see you here,' said Stefan.

'At least I was invited!'

'Well, I came with the NYPD.'

'You're right, that's invitation enough around here. Carroll always has a big Lá le Padraig bash,' continued the captain. 'It's good to see who's at these things. Who's chatting to who, and who isn't! It beats reading about it in the social column. But I'm actually among the guests of honour this year.'

'You and Seán Russell?'

'Quite possibly. There's a thought. No, he asked everyone from the Irish Pavilion at the Fair. Now the thing's open, some people are going home, so we're all here to have our success toasted. And we're not the only ones. There's the

Cork hurling team. I think you can spot them as the lads most obviously destined for a very good night and a very bad morning. At least they're ahead of the game at the minute from what I've seen. The consulate staff always politely decline Mr Carroll's invitation, but then there are even more important bashes for them to go to at City Hall and the like. And other consuls make up for it.'

He gestured idly across the room with his glass.

'The man in the horn-rimmed glasses is the German consul general, Becker, cornered by a gaggle of congressmen and a couple of state senators. A heavy conversation about keeping America out of the war, I think. As a fellow neutral I'm tempted to go and join in. The man behind the consul, in the brown suit, the one who's nodding and not saying much, works in the German Tourist Office, Herr Katzmann. But he's an intelligence officer really, Abwehr. He might not have much to say to Seán and Dominic today, except "Top o' the Morgen", but they'll be down to it soon enough, sorting out the parade past the GPO after Germany's flattened Britain. Or did you think your new pal Carroll was in Berlin for tea with his long-lost Uncle Fritz?'

The pianist had stopped playing. There was a round of applause as a boy and girl in their early teens moved across to the small platform where the piano stood and people began to gather round it. The boy had a bodhrán, the girl an accordion; he started to beat out the rhythm of 'The Lark in the Morning'; toes began to tap and a few hands to clap.

As Stefan and John Cavendish walked forward, away from the window, Stefan noticed two men, in their mid-twenties, staring at them. They both looked red-faced and slightly dishevelled; they had been drinking at a rate that was now

181

catching up with them. Cavendish seemed unaware of them, looking towards the young musicians.

One of the men, small and dark, stepped in front of them. The other, taller, heavier, grabbed his arm to pull him back.

'Will you leave it, Colm!'

But Colm shook off his friend's hand.

John Cavendish smiled at the fierce, glowering face in front of him. He had no idea why the man looked so angry, except that he was very obviously drunk. In fact the young man had been watching Captain Cavendish for a long time before approaching.

'How's it going, lads?' said Cavendish benignly. 'I heard a bit of the match on the radio in the car.' He turned to Stefan. 'The lads were hurling at the Polo Grounds this morning. They thrashed New York.'

He looked back at the two hurlers, laughing.

'And so you should have, coming from Cork!'

The dark-haired man steadied himself, his gaze still fixed. In the background the music continued, and most eyes were on the stage. Stefan assumed, like Cavendish, that they were dealing with a lad who had had too much to drink and just taken an arbitrary dislike to someone. The captain glanced back at Stefan and shrugged; a few more words – then let's walk on.

'The lads are with the Cork team. Did you ever play yourself, Stefan?'

'We're not great ones for hurling in Wicklow,' smiled Stefan.

'What's your name, Mister?' asked Colm, still staring, glaring. It didn't look like the confused anger of drunkenness to Stefan; it was as if the man was trying to put together something that he saw in Cavendish's face.

'I'm John Cavendish.' The army officer held out his hand.

The dark-haired man didn't shake it. If anything he stared harder.

'Were you ever in Cork yourself, Mister?'

'I have been over the years.'

'And when was that?'

'Too long ago!'

Cavendish laughed, but now he looked slightly puzzled as well.

'Come on, Colm.'

The other hurler grabbed his friend's arm again, but as he tried to pull him away, Colm turned angrily.

'Will you fuck off, Ryan!'

He pushed away the hand once more, and stepped even closer to the man in the uniform, into the space where a stranger's proximity starts to threaten.

'West Cork, was it? Was one of them times in Béarra maybe?'

'Do we know each other, Mr –'

'Perhaps you should be telling me, Mr Cavendish?'

'I think this has gone far enough, don't you? You're not in a pub.'

The captain had had enough.

An older man was suddenly there, tall, grey-haired, bearded. There were three younger men with him, clearly Cork hurlers too, the worse for wear but in nothing like the state of Colm. The older man was very sober.

'What's this about, Colm? What do you think you're doing?'

The dark-haired hurler took a step back, and finally took his eyes from John Cavendish. Applause and cheering marked the end of 'The Lark in the Morning' and the boy and girl launched into 'Out on the Ocean'.

183

'I was just talking to Mr Cavendish here! Would you know him?'

'Get out of here and sober up. I'd say it's high time we were going.'

Colm didn't move. He turned back to John Cavendish with a look that was no longer just petulant, angry, aggressive; it was a look of real hatred. Stefan could feel it, even though it wasn't directed at him. He had no doubt that Cavendish felt it too. Despite the noise of the music and the clapping of hands in time, people were beginning to look round at what was going on.

'Get him away and give him some coffee,' snapped the older man.

The other hurlers shuffled uncertainly round their friend. Two of them grabbed his arms. They moved him through the crowd into another room. He went without protest now. The older man was clearly embarrassed, and felt his own responsibility for the scene. He looked from Cavendish to Stefan.

'I'm sorry. I don't know what got into him. Well, I do know what got into him, and too much of it.' He attempted a smile, and both Cavendish and Stefan responded in kind, but they were all uneasy with what had happened; all the more so because it had come out of nowhere.

'It's my fault,' continued the grey-haired man. 'I'm responsible for them. They're just lads that's all. They're not used to all this. I should have put the lid on it earlier.'

'I should forget it. These things happen.'

The captain's voice wasn't as forgiving as he tried to make it sound. He was more unsettled than he appeared. The two men looked at one another. The expression on the bearded man's face changed. He was no longer thinking about what had just happened, but about the man in front of him. It was recognition. Stefan saw it clearly enough. He was sure the man knew John Cavendish.

For the army officer himself there was something familiar stirring too, but it wasn't quite recognition; for a moment it was merely a memory. And it had no place here. It was a memory he wasn't easy with; he hadn't thought about it in years.

Stefan could almost see that memory in his friend's face, whatever it was, wherever it came from. In the seconds following he saw that the two men both recognised one another now. They knew each other. But neither of them was going to say a word about it.

12. The Hampshire House

The grey-haired man walked off through the crowd, pursuing the young hurlers to another room. John Cavendish watched him for a few seconds and then, whatever memory it was that had disturbed him, he shut it away.

'Well, you would have thought congratulating the bloody team on a win would go down better than that. Jesus, I could do with another drink.'

He stepped across to a waiter, standing with a tray of drinks. He took one. As he turned back he almost bumped into a woman in her mid-twenties.

Stefan recognised her immediately; the almost shoulder-length hair, and the pale, almost serious almost amused face. She smiled at Cavendish; she was pleased to see him; Stefan thought she was even relieved to see him. But behind the smile she looked like someone who didn't want to be there. She turned to Stefan; he could feel himself reddening, remembering the last conversation and aware that he was staring at her. But she smiled easily.

'So how's New York treating you, Mr Gillespie?'

'Well enough, thank you.'

'Maybe too well. You look like you've been in a fight.

Not that I'd be the sort of woman who'd judge a man by appearances. An accident was it?'

'In the line of duty, I promise.'

He grinned; she was getting her own back on him. She already knew. It struck him that if she already knew, then she must have asked Cavendish. That wasn't such a bad thought. There was a hint of mischief in her eyes. But almost immediately it was gone, as if a switch had been thrown. The sparkle had gone; she looked at the captain with questioning expectation.

'I've just got a couple of things –'

John Cavendish gave Stefan an apologetic shrug and didn't finish a sentence that he didn't really have an end to anyway. He touched Kate O'Donnell's arm and steered her away. For a moment the two of them were talking in what was a whisper, despite the noise all around them. There was something intense about it that made Stefan think it was a conversation she wanted and he didn't; at least he didn't want it here, in public. The army officer looked at his watch. The woman's whispers seemed more urgent. Cavendish nodded several times. Then Kate walked off. Unquestionably an arrangement to meet had been made.

Stefan turned away from them, looking towards the children still playing music. He didn't know why he had been watching them at all. He had no business doing it. But he did know of course. He didn't like what it seemed to say about the relationship between John Cavendish and Kate O'Donnell. He had only seen her twice, but absurd as it was, he rather wished there wasn't a relationship between her and another man that required whispers and assignations. As Cavendish came back something was different; he was tense now; his mind was elsewhere.

'I've got a few people to talk to, a few goodbyes to say, but I'm going to think about heading home. I'll pick you up around ten tomorrow, if that's all right.'

'That's fine. I think I've had enough myself,' nodded Stefan.

Cavendish said nothing for a moment then walked away. It could have been the conversation with Kate O'Donnell, but Stefan wasn't sure that the incident with the young hurler wasn't still on his friend's mind. It had been unpleasant, and there had definitely been more to it than mere drunken misbehaviour. John Cavendish drifted through the crowd of party-goers, stopping briefly to shake hands, joking and exchanging farewells. Stefan watched him. Whatever it was about, the army officer was distinctly uneasy.

Stefan felt suddenly quite isolated. He knew hardly anybody and it felt like everybody else knew everybody. He walked to the window again and looked out at the night. Part of his own reflection looked back at him. He smiled as he thought of the woman again, Kate O'Donnell. It wasn't that hard to know why he'd been watching her with John Cavendish. He liked her. She made him realise that he needed to be with someone he wanted to be with too.

As he looked out over the park and uptown Manhattan, the room and the party was reflected back at him. He saw the face of Kate O'Donnell again in the glass. He turned to see her a few feet away, looking out of the window too. He was sure she had been looking at him too, via his reflection in the glass. She opened her bag and took out some cigarettes; she put one in her mouth; then she rifled the bag for a lighter or matches she couldn't find. She looked up, irritated, and met his eyes. He saw that mischief again.

'Since you're staring at me, perhaps you can light this cigarette?'

'I'm sorry. It was –'

'I'm old enough to work out what it was.'

He laughed, but laughing seemed all right.

'It's OK, Mr Gillespie. I guess if you've got nothing better to do.'

He took out a box of matches and stepped closer.

'Do you live in New York?' he asked; it sounded harmless enough.

'I didn't say I didn't have something better to do.'

He lit a match and held it out. She bent forward to light the cigarette. It could be a moment of odd intimacy, lighting a woman's cigarette, when the people involved let it be. He felt she was letting it be exactly that now. But as she lifted her head, drawing in the smoke, she was distant again.

A voice behind them was singing now, accompanied by the piano. Kate was looking past him towards the stage. She shook her head with a look of distaste; it seemed even stronger to Stefan; more like contempt.

'Jesus, here we go.' She turned and walked away abruptly.

Stefan looked round to see it was Dominic Carroll who was singing now. 'The minstrel boy to the war has gone, in the ranks of death ye will find him. His father's sword he has girded on, and his wild harp slung behind him.' It wasn't a bad voice, almost in tune, and Carroll was almost sober. People were applauding even as he started singing.

Applause was expected.

'Worth a try, Steve.'

The voice beside him was Michael Phelan's.

'What?'

'Kate O'Donnell.'

'Is that her name? I didn't get that far –'

'You didn't get far at all, did you?'

'It'll teach me not to stare.'

'She's worth staring at some,' grinned the detective.

'You know her then?'

'I wish I did. I've met her though. Pretty stuck up. But I guess she's got a bit to be stuck up about. She works at the Irish Pavilion. I don't know what she does there. But be careful, Steve. She has friends in high places.'

Stefan looked at Michael Phelan, not sure what he meant. He thought for a moment the grin was about John Cavendish, and what he had witnessed himself. Maybe that was common knowledge, but it seemed unlikely, and he'd hardly have called Cavendish a friend in high places.

'She's Dominic Carroll's sister-in-law,' said Phelan, lowering his voice. 'He's married to her sister, Niamh. Not that you're going to see her here. But that's another story altogether. Jesus! Come on, let's get some food inside us. It doesn't look like we'll be getting much else tonight, does it?'

'No luck either?' smiled Stefan.

'Half way there, if she could have got rid of her boyfriend!'

They walked through the crowd. Stefan glanced back at Kate O'Donnell, further along the row of windows, still looking out, still somehow determinedly not a part of what was happening. Dominic Carroll was finishing his song. 'Thy songs were made for the pure and free. They never shall sound in slavery!' The applause and cheers were echoing round the room. The boy with the bodhrán and the girl with the accordion struck up a jig.

There was a buffet table in the next room. Michael Phelan, slightly unsteady on his feet, picked up a plate and joined the line. Stefan stood behind him.

As they waited he saw the grey-haired man with the beard, who had put an end to that unpleasant, seemingly unmotivated confrontation between the young Cork hurler and John Cavendish. The man was sitting at a small table on his own. There was a drink in front of him and a plate of sandwiches. Both were untouched. People moved all round him, talking, laughing, pushing, humming snatches of the jig from the other room. Yet it was as if the man with the beard was sitting in an empty room. He saw nothing around him. Stefan was sure he was crying, though his face was as unmoving as his body. He was in another place. It wasn't a very happy one.

Outside the Hampshire House there was green bunting underfoot and there were green paper flags and green paper flowers in the gutter. It wasn't so late. People were still out celebrating the day, sober and less sober; families from the suburbs were still occupying midtown Manhattan, though they were only the stragglers now. Stefan had found it hard to get away from Michael Phelan and his friends, as more NYPD men found their way to Dominic Carroll's party; he had stopped drinking an hour ago, but they hadn't; they had no intention of stopping. The party had got noisier and more crowded; the big rooms had got hotter. It was a relief to get out into the air.

After everything New York had to offer Stefan found himself thinking about half a dozen tractors parading through Baltinglass and a crowd of children waving the green crêpe-paper flags they had made at school. It was five hours earlier at home; the parade would be long over; Tom, Helena and David would be asleep.

He saw Kate O'Donnell standing at the kerb, trying to hail a cab; the cabs were thin on the ground tonight. She looked frustrated and irritated as several swept by. He watched her for a moment. It was more than irritation. She was upset or worried. It still wasn't his business. He wanted to walk back to the hotel anyway.

'For fuck's sake!'

The voice was Kate's as yet another yellow cab ignored her.

He smiled and turned back towards her.

'Are you all right?'

She looked round.

'Don't worry, Sergeant Gillespie, I've found some matches.'

She took a packet of cigarettes from her pocket. He said nothing as she got one out and lit it. It was another expression of irritation, or whatever feeling it was that she wasn't hiding very well. But she was good to watch. She did irritation well.

'Can I help you get a cab?'

'Do you think I'm beyond calling a cab?'

'I wouldn't say beyond –'

'You try then,' she stepped back. 'Show me how it's done.'

Stefan wished he'd chosen different words, but having chosen them he had to act on them. He stepped off the kerb. Three cabs were heading towards them. He held up his arm and took a few steps further out on to 59th Street. The first cab blasted its horn and swerved out round him. He jumped back, more quickly than he had stepped out.

Kate O'Donnell was laughing.

'How long have you been in New York?'

'Nearly two days! It's not like I don't know my way around.'

'I can see you do, Sergeant.'

'Stefan. It's Stefan.'

'I'm Kate, Kate O'Donnell.'

He didn't tell her he already knew.

She held her hand out. He shook her hand.

'You were talking to John Cavendish earlier,' she said.

She looked more serious, as if she was trying to weigh him up.

'Do you know him well?'

He wasn't sure what he was supposed to say. A conversation at a party was one thing; he wasn't certain it was a good idea to advertise how well he knew John Cavendish.

Despite the fact that he had exchanged only a few dozen words with this woman, there was already something complicated about her relationships that suggested he should be careful. She was involved with Cavendish in some way, probably the way he'd rather she wasn't. She was Dominic Carroll's sister-in-law. That didn't make her a very sensible choice for a clandestine relationship on the G2 man's part. But it wasn't his business, he reminded himself for the tenth time. Or maybe it was. The intelligence officer had turned up in his hotel room to make at least some of his business Stefan Gillespie's business. Where did that stop?

She was still looking at him, but in the end she didn't wait for an answer.

'Do you know where John is?' she asked.

'He said he was going home. That was a while ago —'

'He wouldn't have just gone without —'

There it was again; frustration and irritation, and it wasn't about a cab. It was even more obvious that it went deeper. And alongside all that there was anger, concern, even distress, maybe something like fear too. The smile had gone and the intensity was there again. But she wasn't going to say any more. She had stopped, aware she was revealing more than she wanted to.

'It doesn't matter. I'm sorry.'

She turned back to 59th Street. She held out one arm and put the fingers of her other hand to her mouth. She gave a loud, shrill whistle, and this time a yellow cab pulled into the kerb and stopped. Stefan laughed.

'You'll have to teach me to do that.'

She opened the cab door and got in. She looked up at him.

'I'm going to Queens. If you want dropping in Manhattan —'

'I think I'll walk, but thank you. I need to clear my head. Besides, I'm only here another day, and I want a walk through New York at night for some reason. No reason in particular except I'll probably never do it again. And I think I might remember that more than 5th Avenue this afternoon.'

She looked at him. It was the same kind of look he had seen moments before, when he thought she was trying to weigh him up. This time it looked as if she had seen something she could make sense of. She smiled. She understood perfectly, and she liked the fact that he'd said it.

As the cab pulled away he watched it go. He thought she had turned her head and looked back through the window of the cab. Or maybe she hadn't. He laughed to himself, turning the other way, heading along the south side of Central Park towards 7th Avenue; wishful thinking and a drink too many perhaps. But Michael Phelan was certainly right; Kate O'Donnell was worth staring at. And he was right himself, about that walk back to his hotel through the streets of New York, now quieter and emptier as he went. The New York night had already given him something special to remember.

*

The phone woke Stefan Gillespie up abruptly, though it had been ringing for several minutes. He had been in a deep sleep. Not an easy sleep, and not a sleep that would offer much refreshment; he had had too much to drink for sleep to do anything other than fill up the rest of the night.

His first thought, as he reached out for the telephone, was that he must have said something stupid to the woman, the woman outside the Hampshire House, Kate O'Donnell. It didn't matter much. He wouldn't see her again. He was still pulling himself out of sleep as he answered the phone. He didn't recognise the voice, but there was an urgency in it that pulled his mind back into focus.

'Slow down will you, Roland. And will you tell me Roland who?'

'Roland Geoghegan, at the consulate! Mr McCauley told me to call.'

Stefan looked down at the watch on the bedside table.

'It's two o'clock in the morning.'

'Mr McCauley is already there. You need to get a cab –'

'Get a cab where?'

'He's waiting for you now!'

'What?'

'The NYPD called him straightaway. Just get a cab, Mr Gillespie!'

195

'You want me to go somewhere, I've got it. So how about where?'

'I've already told you where!'

'Then tell me again, Roland!'

'The Hampshire House.'

'The Hampshire House?'

'It's on 59th Street, right in front of Central –'

'All right, I've got it. I was there this – never mind. Why does Mr –'

'I'm not phoning for a fucking chat, Sergeant. Just get off your arse!'

The cab couldn't stop at the front of the Hampshire House. There were vehicles all along the kerb. They included three police cars and an ambulance. There were policemen everywhere. Stefan got out of the taxi and walked to the kerb.

A uniformed police officer stepped in front of him.

'Move along, buddy, this is a crime scene.'

'I'm looking for the Irish consul general, Mr McCauley.'

'You must be Gillespie?'

'That's right.'

'Over there, down the side of the building.'

He gestured over to the left. Stefan walked along the front of the Hampshire House. Where the building stopped there was a black gap and some shining, aluminium gates, now open. There were more policemen. He saw the consul general in conversation with a senior officer. He recognised him as Inspector Ernie Phelan. He had last seen the inspector singing 'Wherever Green Is Worn' round the piano with Dominic Carroll, just before he left the party.

Leo McCauley looked relieved to see Stefan. Ernie Phelan nodded a curt, business-like greeting, then turned away to shout at a group of uniformed officers. 'Someone get me a fucking coffee here!'

The consul walked across to Stefan. 'You know what's happened?'

'No. I was just told to get here fast.'

'You were here with John Cavendish last night?'

'I was talking to him, at the party –'

McCauley said no more. He walked to the dark alleyway between the Hampshire House and the next building. A group of NYPD officers stepped aside to let them through the silver gates. A little way down the black valley between the high-walled buildings was a blaze of light. Dark figures and their shadows moved in it.

Stefan walked beside the consul; McCauley spoke quietly and calmly; he gave no explanations, no instructions.

'The party broke up around midnight, but apparently he'd left some time before that, quite some time. But you were there yourself, isn't that right?'

'I left around eleven. He'd already gone, maybe an hour before.'

'I need to know what's going on, Sergeant. I need to know what's happened. The best thing is for you to liaise directly with the police. You seem to have got on the right side of them, which is helpful. I've spoken to the ambassador in Washington and he's agreed you delay your flight. I don't know how long this will take, but Mr Harris can stay where he is. There may be staff from the consulate who need interviewing, as well as the World's Fair pavilion. We have to be as helpful as possible.' He was silent for some seconds. 'Captain Cavendish spoke to me about you. A short conversation but he trusted you. If he trusted you you're the right man to keep an eye on all this. It may be no more than a terrible accident. Let's hope it's just that.'

They had reached the floodlight that illuminated the end of the alleyway, where it turned a corner to the back of the Hampshire House. A police photographer was taking pictures of a body that lay where it had fallen from a terrace some thirty storeys up. Detectives and uniformed officers looked on. Flash bulbs lit the scene more brightly than the floodlight for a fraction of a second, then again, then again.

Stefan already knew whose body he would find as he passed through the group of detectives. Captain John Cavendish lay on his back on a mound of builder's rubble, brick and broken concrete, in the dark blue dress uniform with its red stripes, its white braid, its white belt. He was staring up at the night, his dead eyes wide open.

PART TWO

Upstate

Seán Russell, stated to be an Irish Republican Army leader, has been detained in Detroit. Federal agents arrested Russell as he was about to enter a taxi-cab in front of Michigan Central Station. According to a Detroit newspaper, Russell's companion, who was not arrested, is Mr Dominic Carroll, of New York, said to be known as IRA leader in the United States. Detroit, where Russell was arrested, is just across the river from Windsor, Ontario, where the King and Queen are today. Dominic, adds the newspaper, described himself as an 'old friend' of Russell. He said that Mr Russell was in America to visit relatives in the Bronx, New York, and they had gone to Detroit to see friends. He denied that their visit had any significance. The Irish Times

13. Locust Valley

Every Saturday since arriving in New York, Kate O'Donnell had taken the Long Island Rail Road from Woodside in Queens to Locust Valley in Nassau County on the island's North Shore, changing trains at Jamaica for the Oyster Bay Branch. She knew the journey now; it should have been enjoyable, but in the months she had been working at the World's Fair she had grown to loathe it.

As the train moved east and north from Jamaica, the city of New York was left quite suddenly and abruptly behind. There were bright clapboard houses, and close-cut lawns; there were neat farms with tidy bar-fenced fields; there were thin, scattered woods and narrow two-lane roads edged with trees; then eventually, beyond the trees, there were the long, empty beaches on Long Island Sound that they called the Gold Coast. The Oyster Bay Branch Line stopped at the small towns that nestled comfortably between the low hills and the coast and described themselves as villages and hamlets; Albertson, Roslyn, Greenvale, Glen Head, Sea Cliff, and Locust Valley, the last stop before the end of the line at Oyster Bay.

There was quiet order in the timber-fronted stores that lined the Wonderful-Life Main Streets; and in the countryside beyond, ever closer to the sound of the sea, there were the homes of the wealthiest New Yorkers. There was old money here, which was always preferable to new money on the North Shore. There was so much money in fact, and it had been here so long, that the wealthiest people of all spoke a language of their own, just to show that their money, like their families, really had been around since time immemorial. It was called Locust Valley Lockjaw, a slow, tight-lipped, consonant-dropping drawl, consciously or unconsciously the exact opposite of the accents of New York City itself, that were only ever fast, furious, urgent, shrill, loud. Those other accents were beginning to find their way up the Long Island Rail Road, but money could always absorb more money, even money that spoke with Irish, Jewish, Italian accents, as long as there was enough of it. The privacy all that money gave was a precious commodity only miles from one of the biggest cities on earth; there was more than one reason to want it.

For the last month Kate O'Donnell had changed her routine. Instead of coming in the afternoon she came in the evening and stayed late. With the imminent opening of the World's Fair, she said she was working every Saturday, along with everyone else at the Irish Pavilion. Sometimes, when the Woodside train got to the Jamaica interchange, she walked down the steps to Beaver Road and got a taxi all the way to Locust Valley, and had it wait to bring her back. It was expensive, but it meant people got used to her arriving in an out-of-town taxi and to the sight of a black driver in a Queens cab. And they did get used to it, though the nurses still thought Kate had some serious moxie to sit in a car with a Negro all that way, and at night too.

It was a big house that lay at the end of Kate O'Donnell's journey, surrounded by lawns and trees like all the other big houses. It was past eight o'clock when she arrived now, and it was already dark. This time the Jamaica taxi had been waiting for her in Beaver Street. The driver was the trumpeter, Jimmy Palmer; the cab belonged to the friend of a friend who didn't ask why Jimmy wanted it. They said very little as the car drove out of Queens into the countryside. It had all been said. Now it had to be done.

In Locust Valley, coming out of the town that called itself a hamlet, past the drugstore and the bank and the filling station, on to Birch Hill and Horse Hollow Road, they passed the driveways to half a dozen big houses and signs to the country clubs that serviced them, the Nassau and the Piping Rock, before the cab turned into a driveway that seemed like all the others; high hedges, dark shrubs, pine trees. It didn't particularly stand out. All the estates were shut away from prying eyes. But behind the hedges here, among the trees and the rhododendrons, the high wire fencing that was invisible from the road made a more serious statement about being shut away.

A hundred yards along the gravel road there were heavy iron gates, with none of the frills and flourishes of the other wrought-iron showpieces off Horse Hollow Road. They were opened by an elderly man in a dark green, guard-like uniform. He tipped his cap to Kate who was sitting in the back of the cab. He knew her well enough. As the taxi drove on he closed and locked the gates. There was a small sign at the lodge: Bayville Convalescent Home.

The house was as big as a Locust Valley house should be. It was wide and high, with white-rendered walls and grey stone-mullioned windows, lit now by two spotlights where the driveway turned towards the stone columns of the porch. The grey shingles of the high-pitched roof matched the stone. Once the house had hosted Astors and Vanderbilts, Guggenheims and Rockefellers, Roosevelts and Du Ponts, but its owners hadn't had quite enough old money to fend off the Depression, and it had quietly and discreetly become a convalescent home for the wealthy. Yet it still hosted members of the New York aristocracy occasionally. There were several of them in the secure wing at the back of the house, where the windows had bars and there was a locked security door to the country-hotel-like reception area. It had been hosting some of them for a considerable time.

The Bayville Convalescent Home dealt with the kind of convalescence that nobody talked about. The term most heard in the consulting rooms was 'nerves', and the Bayville's patients suffered from nerves of various kinds. Alcohol-induced nerves were probably at the top of the list, although the nerves created by Benzedrine and cocaine and heroin featured prominently too. People dried out and cleaned themselves up here, sometimes because they wanted to, sometimes because they were locked in until they did. Either way a lot of the patients were very regular visitors; they came and went, willingly and unwillingly.

There were other problems the Bayville Convalescent Home handled just as discreetly, although no one needed to put you in a barred room because you had gonorrhoea or syphilis. Sometimes, of course, like sexually transmitted diseases, nerves weren't so easy to get rid of, even when the drugs and alcohol had been flushed out. Insanity wasn't a word much used at the Bayville, but no one wanted a wife, a sister, a brother, a child, to join the thousands of cuckoos in the fortress hell that was the 'Psych Center' at Long Island's Kings Park. You didn't want to commit them to being plunged in and out of baths of near-freezing and near-boiling water for the rest of their lives, or put them on the wrong end of the other varieties of curative care; electro-convulsion, insulin-induced seizures, ice-pick lobotomies. No one would choose that for a loved one, let alone in public. But at Bayville nerves of that kind could be kept in check, and kept out of sight. And the nervous could vegetate happily enough in a room that didn't remotely resemble a cell, while the patient was pumped full of drugs very like the ones that their fellow patients were having pumped out of them.

'So, we're going to do it. Today, Niamh. It has to be now.'

In the pink-washed room at the back of the Bayville venetian blinds hid the iron bars on the windows. There was a bed, a wardrobe, a chest of drawers painted pale blue, a desk with a radio and a vase of fresh flowers on it; there were two armchairs on either side of a coffee table piled high with magazines; a door opened into a bathroom. The door to the corridor had a small pane of wire-meshed glass in it. There was a painting of trees in the fall, somewhere in New England. The radio was on, playing music quietly, a Beethoven piano sonata; it was always on, even through the night, though Niamh Carroll was never really conscious of listening to it.

She was thirty-six, almost eight years older than Kate. The sisters had been close for a very short time, when Kate was young, but age had pushed them apart; Niamh had left home when Kate was only nine, and she had only rarely come back. She had lived her life away from Ireland, and the life she had lived had been her own, separate life. It had taken her away from her family in ways that had nothing to do with distance, for no special or extraordinary reasons; just because it's a lot easier to get lost than it is to find your way back home.

'I don't know if I can do it. You didn't say it would be today.'

'It has to be one day.' Kate took her sister's hand. 'And it's today.'

Niamh shook her head uncertainly. She was confused, already tearful.

'Jimmy's outside, Niamh.'

The words were met with a frown of disbelief.

'I told you he would be.'

'He's here? He can't be here.'

'Niamh, we've talked it through a dozen times. It will work, I know it will. You have to be strong, that's all. All you have to do is walk. No one's going to want to talk to you, no one ever does. There's one locked door to go through, then there's the reception desk and the front door. You walk through it, straight to the taxi. Jimmy's there. You can do it.'

The idea of strength was not something Niamh Carroll found it easy to think about. Thinking at all was something she had got out of the habit of doing. She had been in this room for nearly eighteen months, though she had little real sense of how long herself. The days were always the same, the music was always the same, the magazines were always the same, the nurses were always the same; it was a dull haze, much of which she spent asleep. But she didn't sleep so much now. She had stopped crying for reasons she didn't understand; she had stopped screaming in the night when she woke up; she had stopped eating her food with her fingers and then pushing the same fingers into her throat to make herself sick.

They had cleaned the heroin out of her a long time ago now, and though she thought about it occasionally, she didn't want it the same way any more; it was a desire for comfort now not a craving that ate at her stomach and her mind. And they had stopped the drugs. They still gave her sleeping tablets, but as she was behaving, as she was calm, they didn't always watch to see she took them. She had been flushing them down the toilet as Kate had told her. Sometimes she still took them; sometimes it was worse to be awake than to be asleep.

There was a knock on the door. A middle-aged woman in a crisp, pale green nurse's uniform pushed it open and looked in at the two women.

'I'm going in a minute, Mrs Carroll, is there anything you need?'

'I'm grand thank you.'

'Goodnight then,' smiled the nurse. 'Goodnight, Miss O'Donnell.'

As she left, Kate turned back to Niamh.

'They'll be changing shifts in half an hour. You have to go before they do. It won't be hard, it really won't. Come on, you need to get ready.'

Niamh closed her eyes and shook her head.

Kate ignored her. She got up and walked to the bed and opened a small travelling bag she had brought with her. She took out the clothes that were in it. A grey polo neck sweater, a straight brown skirt, a long tweed jacket, a pair of black, low-heeled court shoes, a dark-green hat with a narrow brim; there was also a wig that was the colour of the hair she had deliberately left longer and unstyled for over a month now, and a pair of heavy-rimmed glasses, identical to the ones she was wearing today, though she only needed them for reading. Everything she had taken out of the bag was identical to what she was wearing herself. The two sisters were about the same height and build. Although there was a family resemblance it wasn't particularly strong, but Kate was wearing make-up in quantities she would never normally have used; she had to believe it would be enough.

'Come on. It's a long time since you played dressing up with me!'

Niamh laughed; it was a rare laugh that really did let Kate see the big sister she remembered in that anxious, always tired face. She took the bundle of clothes and pulled Niamh up out of the chair and into the bathroom. It had to happen very quickly; it had to happen faster than Niamh could think.

Ten minutes later a woman walked out of Niamh Carroll's room. Almost anyone who had seen Kate O'Donnell enter the room forty-five minutes earlier would have seen Kate O'Donnell leaving it. But it was her sister who took a deep breath and walked tentatively along the corridor to the locked door that closed off the secure wing from the rest of the Bayville Convalescent Home. The door to her own room wasn't locked, though it had been until a month ago. Good behaviour had earned her certain privileges. She could use the sitting room now and talk to other patients who had also demonstrated their good behaviour, though she never went in there; she could use the kitchen to make herself coffee or tea; she had the freedom to walk up and down the main corridor and to look out of a different barred window to the one she looked out from in her room.

As she turned the corner into the corridor that led to the security door a black woman, mopping the floor, smiled at her. She knew the woman, Sally; sometimes she cleaned her room. She smiled back, keeping her head slightly down, but feeling a kind of exhilaration; she was feeling stronger, just a little stronger.

When she reached the security door she hesitated, but she took a breath again. Jimmy was outside. It was still almost impossible to believe it, but he was there, waiting for her. She pressed the buzzer. A woman's face appeared at the meshed-glass panel. Niamh didn't know her. She was very young, twenty-two or twenty-three. She wore a nurse's uniform, but she was a receptionist; the only business she had with the security door was who went in and who came out. She had opened the door for Kate O'Donnell an hour earlier and now she was opening it again. It happened every Saturday. In so far as the receptionist had any opinion about Kate, she didn't much like her. For a woman who had a nut job for a sister she seemed to think a lot of herself; not that she had ever exchanged more than a few words with her.

'OK?' were the only words the receptionist had to say tonight.

Niamh nodded, too afraid to answer the clear, confident 'Thank you, goodnight!' that Kate had told her to. 'She doesn't know you, and all she'll hear is an Irish accent. So lay it on thick!' It didn't matter anyway. As Niamh walked through the door the receptionist was already on her way back to her desk. She sat down and picked up the telephone; she had been interrupted in mid-conversation.

Niamh was walking across the hallway to the front door now, and suddenly she was standing in front of it, right in front of it. She was trembling, trying hard to do what Kate had told her so many times. 'Open the door and walk out. That's all. That's all you have to do.' She could feel her hand shaking as she reached out to the handle. She was afraid to touch it. She couldn't move. She stood there completely still.

'It's open, all right!' The receptionist's tone was irritable.

Niamh grasped the handle and opened the door.

'Thank you, goodnight!'

As she walked out into the night and the door slammed shut behind her, the receptionist returned to her telephone call, shaking her head.

'Some of them, I tell you! They got so many people chasing after them, they stand at the door waiting, like they don't know how to open it!'

The cab was waiting in the shadows, under a tree, out of the floodlights that lit up the front of the building. Niamh walked to the car, forcing one foot in front of the other, waiting for the sound of a voice telling her to stop, and the hands that would drag her back inside; they had to come. No one would let her leave. Wasn't she still too sick? That's what Dominic had told her; she might never be well enough to leave. But suddenly, moving out of the light, she was looking at the face of Jimmy Palmer, grinning at her through the open window of the car, a barely glowing cigarette end between his lips.

She stood looking at him, waiting for the moment she would wake up in the pink-washed room. A lot of the time dreams were most of what happened in her days in that room; she slept and dreamt because it was all there was to do. And Jimmy was often there, painfully there, in those dreams.

They hadn't seen each other in almost two years. There was nothing to say. For a long moment they stared. He was still smiling; she was frightened he would suddenly be snatched away. He got out of the cab, dropping the cigarette butt and stubbing it out. She moved towards him, needing him to hold her; that was all she wanted now, not words; his arms holding her.

'Don't touch me, baby. Just get in.' He looked around. There was no one there, no one to see. 'You get in the back and you crouch right down between the seats.'

He pulled the rear door open. She did what he'd told her to do.

'Right down. OK? As small as you can, Niamh.'

She crawled into the gap between the front and back seats.

Jimmy leant in and pulled a blanket across the seat and draped it over her. As he tucked it round her he let his hand stay still for a moment against her shoulder. Then he slammed the door shut and got back in himself. He started the car. He pulled round in front of the colonnaded porch and down the driveway to the gates. The guard saw him coming and stepped out of the lodge. He unlocked the gates and pulled one of them back; one was enough.

Jimmy slowed down as he pulled past; his window was still open.

'She's still in there. I'm going into town to get some gas before they close. Maybe get a cup of coffee too. I'll be right back for her though.'

The Queens cab drove out towards the road. The lights of another car were coming round the bend from Horse Hollow Road. It was a taxi from Locust Valley. Jimmy Palmer pulled over to let the other cab pass.

211

As the Queens cab moved on towards the house the gate-keeper waited; it would be coming back out in a couple of minutes. He stood by the open gate, watching Jimmy Palmer's tail lights disappearing, filling his pipe and chuckling to himself. Miss O'Donnell's driver might be just about all right for some gas now, if he put his foot down, but if Susie Maitland was still serving coffee at this time of night, she surely enough wouldn't be serving it to no Negro cab driver.

Thirty minutes later Kate O'Donnell walked out of her sister's room. She left the radio and the nightlight on and she had stuffed pillows and clothes into the bed so that anyone looking in through the window would see some-thing; a shape in the bed would do; there was hardly any light. As she walked along the corridor towards the security door the two nurses who had taken over the night shift were sitting in the kitchen smoking and drinking coffee, which was mostly all they needed to do; any patients who weren't behaving had been dosed up with their drugs. They called goodnight as she passed and she called back, trying to sound as nonchalant as she could, despite a racing heart.

She pressed the buzzer on the security door and the night porter came to open it; the receptionist had left. He was barely twenty, working his way through college, doing this at weekends to make some money. He had got used to Kate leaving later Saturdays. He liked her in the way that made him redden when she smiled and left him wishing he could have thought of something funnier to say when she'd walked out through the door. He had been on the end of some of Kate's best smiles in recent weeks.

'How's she doing today?' He always asked the same question.

'She's had a good day, I think.'

'That's good. That's something, isn't it?'

He always said that too, and she always nodded as if it mattered.

'I didn't see your taxi there, Miss O'Donnell. There was a Queens cab going out. So if you want me to get one up from town, there's one just –'

'I'm sure he's gone to get some gas, don't worry.'

He walked to the front door and opened it for her, as he always did.

'See you next week. You take care.'

'You too. Goodnight.'

Kate walked out on to the drive, heading down towards the gate lodge. She knew he was watching her. She heard the heavy door shut behind her.

At the gate the old man saw her coming and stepped out.

'He's down at the gas station, that's what he said.'

'I thought so. I'll walk on to the road. He'll be on his way back.'

'You can wait in the lodge, Miss.'

'I'm grand,' she said breezily. 'Sure I could do with some air.'

She followed him to the small wicket gate next to the lodge; he opened it and held it back for her. She walked through, trying not to hurry, walking the way she thought she always walked. She could hear an engine; the lights of the cab lit up the bend in the driveway. Jimmy Palmer pulled across the drive and stopped. Kate waved back at the gatekeeper and got into the back of the cab. Jimmy turned the car and headed back towards town.

'You can get up now,' said Kate, laughing. She pulled the

blanket and the coat off her sister, squeezed down on the floor in the footwell next to her.

Niamh pushed herself up between the seats. She was shaking. She sat next to Kate now, dazed, still frightened, looking in something like wonder at the two people she loved. Kate put her arm round her and pulled her close.

'We did it, Niamh! I told you we could!'

Jimmy Palmer looked in the rear view mirror.

'Christ, if you two aren't one of the scariest things I've ever seen!'

The two women looked at one another, dressed as they were in the same clothes, with the same hair, the same make-up, the same glasses. They both started to laugh at once. Kate pulled off Niamh's wig. Laughing more, Niamh leant forward and put her arms round Jimmy. Kate's arm was still round Niamh; she buried her head on her sister's shoulder. Jimmy let out a great whoop of exhilaration; he was still laughing. And Niamh and Kate were both crying, as Jimmy drove past the Long Island Road signal tower that marked the end of the town, across the rail tracks, and out of Locust Valley, heading for Route 25A and Queens.

14. Central Park

Two days had passed since Captain John Cavendish's body had been discovered at the side of the Hampshire House after falling from a terrace thirty-two floors up, close to the top of the building. It was the first time Stefan Gillespie had stood on the terrace, looking down into the narrow chasm between the Hampshire House and the next building on West 59th Street. Most of the terrace looked out on to Central Park, but where it faced the adjacent tower there was a low brick wall, no more than two feet high, between the patio and the drop of more than five hundred feet to the ground. A section of wrought-iron railing, newly painted and intended for that wall, was leaning by the doors out to the terrace; the railings overlooking Central Park were already in place. It wasn't easy to stand by the low side wall where the railing had not yet been fitted, staring down. Stefan got as close as he could, watched by Sergeant Michael Phelan, a few steps behind, smoking a cigarette and clutching it tightly in the buffeting wind; New Yorker as he was, he showed no desire to get very much closer to the edge.

'It wouldn't be difficult, would it?' said Stefan quietly.

'If it was dark and you'd had a few,' agreed the NYPD detective.

Stefan turned back towards the open doors into the apartment and walked in. The high room smelt of fresh paint. Their voices echoed loudly.

'So what did your forensic people find?'

'Nothing at all, other than a few cigarette butts. One of them was probably Cavendish's. The rest were just, well, the builders are still up here finishing the place off. It's the usual sort of rubbish you'd expect to see.'

Stefan thought there was very little of the usual sort of rubbish. Everything looked remarkably neat. The concrete floor was clean and free of dust. He knelt and ran his finger across it. Maybe they were very tidy builders.

'Footprints?'

'Not really, no.' Phelan shrugged and got out another cigarette.

'Would there have been lights on?'

'The electricity was off.' The detective lit the cigarette.

It had taken Stefan Gillespie more than a day of sitting around at Police Headquarters to get up here. Everybody said there was nothing to look at anyway, except the view and the drop. There wasn't. On the terrace there was the low wall. Inside there was no furniture, just a series of bare rooms. There were wires hanging down where the electricians had been working; there were cans of paint in a corner with the decorators' ladders and trestles. They were three floors up from Dominic Carroll's apartment, where Stefan had last seen John Cavendish alive, in a part of the Hampshire House where fitting out and decorating was still going on.

The Headquarters Detective Division had been happy to let Garda Sergeant Gillespie tag along in their investigation into the death of the Irish army officer; he would also

216

provide any liaison that was needed with the Irish consulate. But Stefan had quickly found himself kept at an amenable and good-natured distance from whatever it was that was happening.

Inspector Twomey had tried to dress it up to look better than that. Captain Aaron Phelan had made a point of issuing him with the same gun they all carried, a Colt .38 Police Special. That got a round of applause, but it had taken more time than Stefan felt was convincing to establish exactly which floor the Irish army officer had fallen from. It had taken even longer for the forensic team to clear the thirty-second-floor apartment so that he could see it himself; they had been a very long day finding nothing. Talking to people who had seen John Cavendish at the party and trying to put a time on when he had left and who saw him last, was proceeding at a leisurely pace that felt very out of step with the wham-bam ethos of the Headquarters Detective Division. And Michael Phelan, the detective who had been assigned to keep Stefan in touch with everything, had spent most of his time taking him for coffee, or for lunch, or for yet another drink in McSorley's after work.

It was clear the general consensus was that Captain Cavendish had wandered up to the thirty-second floor, maybe drunk enough to have lost his way, and had walked out on to the terrace where the railing hadn't been put up. Then he had taken a step too far in the dark. If it hadn't been for the fact that only a few days earlier an Irish seaman, who happened to be passing IRA ciphers to Cavendish, had fallen off a transatlantic liner into the Hudson River, after just taking a step too far in the dark presumably, after having a bit too much to drink presumably too, Stefan might not have questioned that consensus.

217

'So why was he up here, Michael?'

'Your guess is as good as mine. We don't know.'

'Are you any nearer a time?'

'We still can't figure exactly when he left the party.'

'How easy was it to get to this floor?'

'The elevator would bring you. So would the stairs.'

'So he just went to the wrong floor?'

'There are no-access notices all over the elevator and the stairs,' said Michael Phelan with a shrug, 'but the electricians were in here the day before. It wasn't locked up the way it should have been. They were coming back to work the weekend. I guess it shouldn't have been so easy to get here, but then you wouldn't assume anybody was going to be wandering around.'

It didn't sound like the NYPD sergeant was being evasive. But Stefan knew him better than that, even after four days. These were lazy words; they bore little relation to the man who believed he worked for the hardest, sharpest police force on God's earth. It wasn't his case; he was there to mind Stefan; but he knew more than this. Stefan Gillespie knew he wasn't trying.

'He didn't seem like he was pissed to me.'

'The Medical Examiner said he'd had a bit.'

'So much that he didn't know where the fuck he was?'

'I'm just telling you what the report said, Stefan.'

'Well, you're right. There's nothing here. What about the body?'

'Sure, I can take you to the morgue now.'

It was something else that seemed to have taken longer than it should.

'Let's see him then.'

Stefan headed for the lifts. He was irritated by what was

going on, or what wasn't. There seemed to be no reason at all why he wasn't getting the information and cooperation that Inspector Twomey had been so enthusiastic about telling him he would get in spades, at every stage in the investigation. Something else was going on here. Whatever about the best police force in the world, Stefan knew bullshit; as bullshitters the NYPD only rated average.

The morgue at Bellevue Hospital was like any other morgue; cracked and crazed white tiles and a row of white porcelain body-sized slabs on metal legs; the smell of putrescence almost but not quite hidden behind a wall of disinfectant. It wasn't one of Manhattan's finest sights; it certainly had no view of the future as far as John Cavendish was concerned. His body lay on a slab at the far end of the long, cold room. Two other bodies kept him company on adjacent slabs. The Medical Examiner was in court when they arrived; Stefan had the distinct impression he'd probably stay there until they left.

The smell of rotting flesh was already strong as the mortuary assistant, smoking a black cheroot, pulled back the sheet that covered the G2 man. The body was bruised and the skin was broken; the legs and arms had been straightened, but in places twisted bones pushed the flesh out at odd angles, and in the right leg the shattered femur had burst through the skin.

Stefan walked slowly round the body. He remembered the first time he had met John Cavendish, the intelligence officer who had been so bad at following him through Dublin four years earlier, and had handed him a card that said 'Lieutenant Cavendish Military Intelligence'. He didn't imagine the soldier had handed out many of those in New York; that didn't mean there weren't people who knew he was doing more than check on the door and window locks at Ireland's World's Fair pavilion. It didn't mean he hadn't had too much to drink and fallen off a skyscraper either.

He looked at Cavendish's face and realised he didn't have the faintest idea whether the man had a wife or a family. He knew nothing about him. They had met only half a dozen times, but there was something, a bond, that meant no one else in New York knew who this man really was; except perhaps for the woman, Kate O'Donnell. He wondered if she knew he was dead; she must have heard. Everyone at the pavilion in Flushing Meadows had to know by now.

'Did you know him well?' asked Michael Phelan.

'No, I hardly knew him at all. I was just talking to him at the party.'

Stefan didn't quite understand why he was lying. He had done it without thinking, instinctively. He remembered the conversation he had had with John Cavendish at the Hotel Pennsylvania, the day before he died. Lying probably had no purpose at all, but whatever the intelligence officer had intended to trust him with, it felt as if saying nothing about any association, past or present, was how he would have wanted it. As for where that was, the envelope that had to go to G2 in Dublin, it could be that only the dead man knew; or it could be in other hands now, and maybe the same hands had pushed the intelligence officer over the wall at the Hampshire House.

His eyes moved down Cavendish's body from his face; a lot of bruises. He wasn't sure what falling thirty-two storeys did, apart from killing you; you'd expect bruises. It occurred to him that no one seemed to have asked whether John Cavendish was alive or dead when he fell. He looked harder at the dead man's face. He bent closer. Bruises told all sorts of tales.

'What do you think about the bruises?' Stefan asked.

'What do you mean, what do I think?'

'How many dead bodies have you seen?'

'More than you probably,' laughed the detective. 'Human, that is. You've maybe got the upper hand when it comes to dead sheep, right?'

Stefan smiled, still looking down at the corpse.

'You know when a man's been beaten up then.'

'I guess I would.'

'Wouldn't you say he was in a fight? Look at the facial bruises.'

'For fuck's sake, the man fell thirty-two storeys! How the hell is anybody going to know whether he had a couple of bruises first? Maybe he did, maybe he didn't. If he did, maybe he fell over when he was pissed. You've seen the autopsy report. The injuries are consistent with what happened to the guy. He's a mess. Jesus, what else would you expect?'

'It's still a question. Is anybody asking it?'

'Every question that needs to be asked will be asked.'

Sergeant Phelan was tight-lipped now. Somewhere the young NYPD detective had a feeling this case wasn't being pushed the way Headquarters detectives pushed, but if it wasn't that was because there was nothing to push. He had been told to keep the Irish policeman out of the way, because he was getting on people's nerves, people with better things to do. Sergeant Gillespie had seen the reports. The man was drunk and he fell. But he kept pushing, as if there was something missing, as if there was something he didn't think the NYPD was doing properly. The man wasn't even a detective, just a hick who was in New York because he was the other end of a pair of handcuffs. Michael Phelan had kept his jokes about sheep and cattle and crime in the Wicklow Mountains to good-humoured banter; maybe Stefan Gillespie needed more serious pointers to the difference between rural Ireland and what happened in New York.

Stefan looked at him with a smile; he could feel a wall going up.

'I've just got a job to do, Michael. I didn't ask for it. I've the consul general on my back here and I'll have to put in a report to the Garda Commissioner when I get back. Whatever fucking questions I get, I'll have to have an answer. I don't know anything about Captain Cavendish's family, but you know how these things go. If he's got a wife, she's going to want to talk to someone who was there, someone who's got answers, even if they're not great ones. That means me, doesn't it? Have you never had to do that?'

Michael Phelan nodded; he had. He knew how it felt.

'I get you, but when there's no answers there's no answers.'

'I know,' said Stefan. 'Let's get out of here.'

He looked at John Cavendish one more time, with a faint nod. It was all he had to offer. Before long an undertaker would be doing what could be done to slow the body's decay and would seal him in a coffin. A closed car would carry him through New York to one of the piers on the Hudson or the East River. He would be loaded into the hold of a liner. All the way across the Atlantic, somewhere above him, hundreds of people would eat and drink, dance and sing, laugh and quarrel, sleep and make love. At Cobh he would be loaded into the guard's van of a train, en route to an undertaker's by the Grand Canal, and eventually, before his removal to the Church of Our Lady Immaculate, Refuge of Sinners, to his home in Leinster Road, Rathmines.

In the main office of the Headquarters Detective Division, Stefan Gillespie sat at Michael Phelan's desk and typed the bare bones of the report he would take back to Ireland. He had spoken to the consul on the phone in Inspector Twomey's office, and in a conversation that remained elliptical, partly because of where he was and partly because that's how Leo McCauley wanted it anyway, he confirmed what he already knew.

There were questions to be asked about people who had spoken to John Cavendish at Dominic Carroll's St Patrick's Day celebration, but none of those questions could be about the reasons a G2 man was in New York that had nothing at all to do with the World's Fair. Whatever he wasn't getting from the NYPD, there were things he wasn't giving them. The police questioning of party guests had been slow and unmethodical. It had, so far, involved only a few people, including police officers who had been at the Hampshire House that night. Most of them didn't know who John Cavendish was, and none of them knew anything about the time he left the party. Stefan had been there when the staff working at the Irish Pavilion at the World's Fair were questioned. They all knew Cavendish; some of them had spoken to him in the course of the evening; none of them had seen him leave.

Kate O'Donnell was someone Stefan had particularly wanted to talk to; she was the only person who obviously knew the army officer well, and she had clearly made some arrangement to meet him. But he didn't say that. He had been cautious about saying anything except that he had the impression the two of them knew each other as colleagues at the World's Fair. But Miss O'Donnell hadn't yet been interviewed; she had been uncontactable the previous day and since there was no urgency about any of this, no one was in any particular hurry to find her.

Stefan had raised the odd encounter between Cavendish and the Cork hurlers. In what had seemed like no more than some random, drunken misunderstanding he had still not forgotten the look of hatred in the face of the young man who had spoken to John Cavendish so aggressively. The idea that someone needed to follow up a kid the captain didn't even know, with too much whiskey in him, didn't impress anyone in the Headquarters Detective Division. A detective had spoken to the team's coach, but all the bainisteoir could tell them was that the player in question had spent most of the night back at the hotel throwing his guts up. Now the hurlers had embarked on the *Normandie* and were on their way back to Ireland. But the questions that couldn't be asked, because Stefan Gillespie couldn't talk about them, were the ones that really made John Cavendish's death suspicious.

Nothing could be asked about Seán Russell and what the IRA chief of staff knew about the captain's activities in New York; certainly nothing could be asked about what Dominic Carroll knew. Nothing could be asked about the German intelligence officer who was in the apartment that night. John Cavendish had joked about the Abwehr man, Herr Katzmann, but if the relationship between the Nazis and the IRA in America was as real as the G2 man thought, there might not be much to laugh about. Cavendish not only possessed IRA ciphers that a man had already died for, he had told Stefan he was about to find the key to cracking the code that would let them be read. If these messages mattered, wasn't that something worth killing for?

As his two fingers typed up his empty report, Michael Phelan appeared with two cups of coffee and a look of some surprise on his face.

'You know we couldn't get hold of the broad yesterday?'

Stefan looked up.

'Kate O'Donnell.'

'Is she coming in?' asked Stefan. This was more interesting.

'Oh, yes. Eventually!' grinned the detective.

'What does that mean?'

'You thought she was up to something with Cavendish, right?'

'I didn't say that.'

'Don't kid me! Anyway, fuck that. She was up to something all right!'

He looked across the room and chuckled. Several detectives were grouping around Inspector Twomey and the uniformed captain, Aaron Phelan, Michael's brother, who had just come out of the inspector's office with him.

'She's got to be some piece of work,' continued Michael.

'What are you talking about?'

'If Mr Carroll ever gets hold of her –'

Inspector Twomey walked forward, into the middle of the room.

'Listen to me, men! We've got a missing persons –'

There was an irreverent groan from the detectives still at their desks.

'It's not just any missing person. It's a serious matter. It concerns Mr Carroll. You all know he's a friend of this department, and always has been. Some of us are privileged to call him a personal friend. So there will be officers who know that his wife has been sick for a while, for quite a while. There's no good playing around under the circumstances. She's been in a hospital in Long Island, and basically she's under lock and key. She's had the kind of problems we wouldn't wish on anyone in our families, and it's a hard thing for Mr Carroll. But the truth is Mrs Carroll is a danger to herself and to other people. Yesterday night, two other people got her out of the hospital where she was being cared for, I guess in the mistaken belief that they were helping her. One of those people was her sister, Miss Kate O'Donnell. She's an Irishwoman, working at the World's Fair. The other person involved was a Harlem Negro called Jimmy Palmer, a trumpeter.'

There was a buzz of conversation round the room; there were several sniggers and not a few raised eyebrows. It was already an odd story, and the presence of a black man made it odder. And if some officers knew a bit more about Niamh Carroll's story, they also knew a bit about Palmer.

'We don't know where they are,' said Twomey, 'but we need to find them. As I've said, Mrs Carroll is unpredictable, and she could be dangerous. According to Mr Carroll she's hysterical and she could do anything. I don't know what the fuck her sister thinks she's doing, but Palmer is dangerous too. We know he was probably supplying Mrs Carroll with drugs in the past. He's got connections with all sorts in Harlem, pushers, pimps, racketeers. I don't know what they're trying to do, or where they're trying to get. I'll maybe know a bit more when I've talked to the Nassau County Police Chief –'

There were more groans, and this time a ripple of laughter.

'We won't be leaving it to the Nassau County hicks, that's for sure,' smiled Twomey, 'but I'm being polite to Abram Skidmore. I doubt they're still on Long Island anyway. They dumped the taxi they used in Queens. I'm not leaving it to Harlem either. Some of you need to get uptown and find out what you can about Jimmy Palmer. Someone's got to know what he's doing and where the fuck he's doing it. Get off everything else and get on to this. Captain Phelan's going to coordinate with Missing Persons and uniforms.'

Inspector Twomey walked back into his office. Aaron Phelan was spreading a map of New York City out on a desk. Half a dozen detectives were standing round him. Others were grabbing their coats and heading out.

'Probably a good job she wasn't biting, Stefan. You could be in some shit now if she had,' laughed Michael Phelan. 'She springs someone from the crazy house, with a fucking nigger in tow. What the hell's that about?'

The officer at the next desk was pulling on his jacket. He grinned.

'That's what they always said about Mrs Carroll.'

'What?' asked Sergeant Phelan.

'Well, it's a risky business marrying a woman half your age, but I don't imagine Mr Carroll knew what he'd bought himself when he got her.'

'Crazy you mean?'

'She might well be crazy, but that's not what she's locked up for.'

The officer took his gun from his desk drawer and put it in its holster.

'She liked fucking niggers too much,' he smirked, shaking his head. 'That's what I heard in Harlem. And if Inspector

Twomey wants to know what it's got to do with Jimmy Palmer, he's the nigger she was fucking.'

As the detective turned round, still finding it all funny, Aaron Phelan was standing in front of him. He hadn't noticed that his words had stopped the conversation at the desk across the room, or that Captain Phelan had left his map. The captain grabbed the officer by his jacket and propelled him several yards, slamming him hard up against a window that looked down on Centre Street. Aaron Phelan's face was inches from the detective's now.

'You see the window behind you, Eddie? You see it, don't you?'

As the detective could hardly breathe, he could only nod.

'If I hear any more filth like that coming out of your mouth, I'll push you straight through it. You got that, Eddie? Straight – fucking – through it!'

Captain Phelan let go. He turned back to the other detectives in the now silent room. He walked back to the desk where he had spread out the map.

'Respect, gentlemen,' he smiled. 'Mental health is a sensitive issue.'

The silence was broken.

They all returned to their work, grinning.

'I'll have to get on this too, Stefan,' said Michael Phelan.

'OK. There's not a lot more we're going to do anyway, is there?'

Stefan fixed his gaze on the NYPD sergeant as he took the sheet of paper out of the typewriter. He put it into an envelope, and then got up and put on his jacket. He slipped the envelope into his pocket and shrugged.

'I'm just going down to the cells to tell my prisoner we'll be here a few more days. Not that I'll be adding much to this report at the end of it though. Anyway, it looks like you've all got something to do now that's more important than finding out what happened to Captain Cavendish. Why don't I leave the greatest police force in the world to get on with that?'

*

Stefan met Consul General Leo McCauley in Central Park, at the gate to Center Drive. Now they were walking by the pond. Behind them, across 59th Street, was the Hampshire House. The consul general was uneasy about a lot of things. The fact that Captain John Cavendish had been keeping an eye on IRA activity in New York wasn't something he didn't know about, but he knew about it in a way that he kept at some distance from his diplomatic role. The ambassador in Washington may have known more about it, but not much more. The Irish diplomatic corps didn't carry the baggage of military attachés, let alone intelligence officers dressed up with other titles and fictitious roles. Ireland took the business of diplomacy seriously, and as a country that proclaimed its neutrality in the face of what was happening in Europe at every opportunity, it had no intention of playing the games the great powers played. It was the embassy's job to know what was going on diplomatically and to represent Ireland's interests, nothing more.

The fact that New York, along with other American cities, was a refuge and support for people who didn't recognise the legitimacy of the Irish state and wanted to replace it with their own vision of Ireland, by force of arms if necessary, was a fact of life that was mostly to be ignored rather than challenged. It was the business of Irish diplomats to ignore it, at least publicly. It had been John Cavendish's job to collect information, but at a distance from the work of the diplomats. Leo McCauley wasn't easy that that hard-won distance might have been bridged by what had happened. Cavendish's death was distressing in itself, but it was unpleasant, even unfortunate, if it drew attention to things that nobody cared to have attention drawn to.

The consul general was more inclined to accept the version of events coming out of NYPD Headquarters than Stefan Gillespie had expected. But it wasn't hard to understand that whatever Leo McCauley knew about John Cavendish, however upset he was personally, like others in New York he rather hoped the captain's death was simply the tragic accident that it appeared to be.

'I think you're overstating the case, Sergeant,' said the consul.

'I just feel they don't want to look.'

'You're assuming there's something to look for.'

'Isn't that what we're supposed to assume until we know there isn't?'

'There are questions, I realise that. Seán Russell's presence –'

'I doubt the IRA chief of staff goes around pushing people off buildings personally these days, but you know an IRA courier was killed.'

'I don't know that. All I know is that an Irish seaman died.'

'I'm just telling you what John Cavendish said, sir.'

'I can't go anywhere with this,' said McCauley. 'I am by no means convinced the NYPD aren't entirely right in their conclusions, and if there is more to it, I don't see how we begin to suggest that without announcing that at some level Ireland is involved in activities that are not going to endear us to anybody. Captain Cavendish was collecting information that I'm sure he believed was important to the state, but if any sense of that gets out I know exactly what Dominic Carroll and Clan na Gael, and every other Irish organisation in America will do with it. I'll have Irish-American senators and congressmen breaking down my door to demand why we're spying on patriotic Irishmen, including American citizens, in America. You've only been here a few days but as you've spent that time with the NYPD you know this city supports the IRA more cheerfully than it supports the Irish state!'

'So I might as well be on the plane with Mr Harris,' said Stefan.

The consul general walked on in silence for a moment. He didn't relish his involvement in this, but he couldn't ignore the thing completely.

'You've no idea where this material is – these IRA messages?'

Stefan Gillespie shook his head.

McCauley walked on for a moment.

'I think we ought to at least try to find them, Sergeant. As far as John knew you were going home yesterday. He wanted to give you an envelope?'

'He said he'd drive me out to the World's Fair. I read that as him saying he'd give it to me the following morning, after St Patrick's Day.'

'Well, if we assume he didn't have the stuff with him at the Hampshire House,' continued the consul general, 'then it was either at his apartment, or in his office at Flushing Meadows. You'd best try and find it.'

Stefan's surprise showed. It was an abrupt turnaround.

'You're a policeman, aren't you? Presumably you know

a lot more about searching than I do. And you have a perfectly good reason to be in his apartment and his office. I'm asking you to look through his possessions, before they're packed up, to see if there is anything of a personal nature that you feel should be taken back to his wife and his children. It's a job that somebody has to do anyway, of course, because I'm very sure there will be.'

Stefan said nothing. He looked up at the Hampshire House. There would have been telegrams now; back and forth across the Atlantic. Mrs Cavendish would know of course. He wondered how old the children were.

'Inspector Twomey sent the contents of his pockets to the consulate,' said Leo McCauley, taking a small envelope from his coat. 'These are the keys to his apartment in Brooklyn. The address is on it. I can arrange for someone to be at the Irish Pavilion to let you into his office. After the Fair closes I think. There's no point drawing more attention to this than we need.'

Stefan walked through the park, parallel with 59th Street, heading for the 7th Avenue gate. As he stepped on to the West Drive he caught a glimpse of a man behind him, quite close. He recognised the brown suit and the round features. It was the man John Cavendish had pointed out to him in Dominic Carroll's apartment, hovering attentively behind the German consul. He didn't have the name for a moment, but it came; Katzmann, the man from the German Tourist Office who was really an Abwehr agent. Herr Katzmann smiled, speeding up, and Stefan stopped. It was obvious the man was going to speak to him; it was equally obvious that this meeting, with someone he didn't know, and who could have no reason to know him, was hardly a coincidence. As for the consul general's desire to meet where nobody would observe them, Stefan had no doubt at all that Katzmann had been watching.

'Mr Gillespie, Sergeant Gillespie,' smiled the German, raising his hat.

Stefan said nothing, but he nodded in return.

'You don't know me of course, but I saw you in the park and I recognised you from Mr Carroll's party. I wanted to express my condolences, over the death of Captain Cavendish. It was most unfortunate.'

'It was,' said Stefan quietly. And indeed it was, as people kept telling him; variations on the word 'unfortunate' seemed to be the first words on almost everybody's lips when it came to describing John Cavendish's death.

'I happened to see you talking to the captain that evening.'

'Did you?' Stefan replied.

'Of course.'

It didn't explain how Katzmann knew who he was, why he remembered him so clearly, why he had been watching him in Central Park.

'You're an Irish policeman I understand.'

'That's right.'

Stefan offered no more. It was for the German to offer an explanation. But it was already certain that the Abwehr man must know something of his watching-brief on John Cavendish's death; it wasn't difficult information to get, but he had spoken to somebody. It was also obvious that the German agent had been following him. He didn't know how long, but whether it was from the Hampshire House, Police Headquarters, or his hotel, he had been followed to Central Park. Now Katzmann had decided to reveal himself.

'Did you work with Captain Cavendish?'

233

'No. I didn't know him.'

There was a broad, unbelieving smile on Herr Katzmann's face.

'I'm being very rude, Sergeant. I should introduce myself.'

He took a wallet from his jacket pocket and handed over a card: Mr Rudolf Katzmann, German Tourist Office; with an address on Broadway.

'I had intended to talk to him that evening. Just a chat, you know, to catch up. So many people there! And I didn't! And suddenly, he's not here.'

'You knew him at the World's Fair then, Herr Katzmann?' Stefan decided it was his turn to ask questions. The conversation was oddly stilted; yet it had to have a purpose.

'No, we were barely acquainted, strangers in a strange city, you know how it is. Germany has no exhibition at the World's Fair. Our Fuehrer feels that if anyone wants to see the future of mankind they don't need fiction. There is the whole Reich to look at. Germany is the real World's Fair.'

Katzmann said it with an unctuous smile that could have been wry, knowing, condescending, even contemptuous; but whether his contempt was for what he had just said or for Stefan Gillespie because he wasn't a part of mankind's real future, it was impossible to tell.

'I'm sorry we didn't have that conversation now,' Katzmann continued. He looked harder at Stefan, as if he was waiting for something. 'I assume someone will have to take over from him. I thought perhaps you –'

'I have no connection with the Fair, none at all.'

The Abwehr man nodded, as if he expected a lie and had got one.

'Well, we are fellow strangers in New York, my condolences again. If you feel there is something to say, when you have thought about it more, you know how to find me. At the moment you must be shocked by what has happened. Understandable, of course. But the world goes on, Mr Gillespie.'

He raised his hat and walked towards the gate and 59th Street. Stefan waited a moment, until he had gone. It had been a conversation about nothing, except some of the things two strangers might have said about a man neither of them was much acquainted with, who had died in a city neither of them was much acquainted with either. But the German had wanted more. Stefan had felt the gentle push in his words. When he had asked if Stefan was working with John Cavendish, it wasn't about the burglar alarm system at the World's Fair. It was an invitation to reveal something more; a question hardly there and yet insistent.

Rudolf Katzmann not only knew who Captain John Cavendish was, he knew they were both in the same business. And since the G2 man's business had been to find out what was going on between German Intelligence and the IRA in America, it was difficult to see what the two men had to chat about at the Hampshire House on St Patrick's night. Now the Abwehr man had not only been asking about the enquiries into Cavendish's death, he had been asking about Stefan too. He had followed him but he had been unperturbed that Stefan would be able to work that out. He had assumed Stefan was working with John Cavendish and had somehow wanted to talk about it. Of course the German's assumptions weren't all wrong. There was a sense in which he was taking over from John Cavendish; he had instructions to find the documents for G2 in Dublin, documents that he was sure must contain information about Germany and the IRA.

But how many people knew that?

Stefan Gillespie turned away from the West Drive and walked back the way he had come, across the park to the 5th Avenue subway. It seemed like a good idea to go to Cavendish's apartment now; he would phone Leo McCauley later to make arrangements to get into the office at the World's Fair. But he wouldn't go straight to Brooklyn. He would not be so easily followed through New York again.

*

Two hours later a cab carrying Stefan Gillespie crossed over the Brooklyn Bridge from Manhattan. It was dusk. His circuitous journey had involved cabs, subways and els, a walk through Bergdorf Goodman and half an hour in the Metropolitan Museum of Art, looking less at the exhibits in the Egyptian collection than to see if any faces kept recurring from his journey. He had picked up a street map along the way and in Brooklyn the cab dropped him outside the Brooklyn Public Library in Grand Army Plaza. He went into the library through one door and left through another, then walked along Underhill Avenue to Prospect Place. It was a street of flat-fronted brownstone houses and stunted sidewalk trees. He walked up the stoop of number 292.

One of the keys on John Cavendish's key ring opened the front door. It was dark inside the hallway; there was a steep flight of stairs in front of him; to the left was a heavy door with the number 1 on it.

On the street floor, below where Stefan Gillespie was standing, an elderly man was listening to his footsteps. He had been at the window, pulling on his coat, when he saw

236

Stefan outside, looking up at the house, checking the address on a piece of paper. He didn't know the man but he heard him enter with a key. He knew the door the stranger was standing in front of in the parlour floor hallway; it was the Irishman's apartment again. He heard that door open too. Then he walked to his own door to the street and took the stick he used. He came out on to Prospect Place and turned left towards Vanderbilt Avenue and the drugstore telephone. He had more to say now. Maybe he'd get more. But ten dollars was still good money for a phone call.

Stefan had pushed open the door and slipped inside, closing it behind him almost noiselessly; at least that's what he thought. He was standing in a sitting room; heavy armchairs, a table, a dresser. The curtains were open, but there was little light now; it was almost dark outside.

He could hear something. There was movement. He saw a door on his right, half open. Someone was in there. There was a noise that could have been a drawer opening. Then something heavy fell. Silence. Then a light went on. It wasn't bright, probably a lamp. Stefan walked quietly to the door. He could see quite clearly now. He stood looking through the open door into the bedroom.

He knew the slight figure crouching down, pulling out the bottom drawer of a chest. She wasn't easily forgotten. He pushed open the door and walked in.

'You know every policeman in New York's looking for you.'

Kate O'Donnell spun round and got up. The shock lasted only seconds. She shrugged, as if she did this kind of thing every day of her life.

'You didn't bring them with you then?'

'I didn't think. I wasn't expecting to find you here.'

She looked at him as quizzically as he was looking at her.

'Ditto, Mr Gillespie. Obviously New York's smaller than we thought.'

15. Flushing Meadows

'I don't know how we're going to do this, Miss O'Donnell, but maybe if you tell me what you're looking for, I could help you find it. That's if it's something you should be looking for in the first place. What do you say?'

'Are you going to tell me what you're looking for, Sergeant?'

'Who says I'm looking for anything?'

'You mean you're just here to make sure nobody else is?'

'It's not my business why you've got a key to his apartment.'

'There could only be one reason for that, couldn't there, Sergeant? I was running short of underwear and I always keep a great drawer full here.'

'Like I said, it's not my business.'

'The caretaker let me in as a matter of fact. He already knew what had happened. I'm afraid I told him I was John's sister. It sounded more convincing than lover. That's such a dopey word I've always thought, even when it's not true. I think sister got more sympathy, which was the point.'

Stefan could see that the words weren't a reflection of what she felt. Behind the smile and all the couldn't-care-less answers, she was afraid.

'I don't mind what the point is,' he said gently.

'I don't know how this happened. I needed him. We needed him. He wasn't here. The night we – he was meant to be here. He was to drive us –'

Stefan walked across to her. There were tears in her eyes.

'He said he trusted you,' she said suddenly, looking at him.

'What do you mean?'

'He just said it, at the party, when I asked him who you were.'

'I don't know what you're doing, but I was at Police Headquarters earlier. They're looking for you, and your sister, and a feller, a black feller who helped you get her out of some hospital. Is that it? Is that right?'

She nodded. The tears that had started had stopped.

'And I mean looking for you,' he continued. 'Everything else is on hold. What did your sister do, kill someone? That's what it sounded like. They're going to find you, you know that? It can't take long. And here you are, wandering around Brooklyn, going through John Cavendish's flat!'

'We shouldn't be here. We should be on our way to Albany.'

She looked helpless now; she had no words to throw back.

'He said he trusted you.' She said it again, looking at him, as if it would make something happen. He knew she was asking him for help.

'What is it you're looking for?'

'The tickets for the boat. John had to do that, to match the passports he got us. We were meant to come here, to drive to Albany for the train. It's all we need, the tickets. Jimmy's found a way to get us out of the city now.'

240

'Jesus, it better be a good one. I tell you the way the police —'

She smiled. He hadn't said a word about helping; she knew he would.

'I have to find the tickets, Mr Gillespie.'

He hesitated another moment, but he knew he would help her too.

'I'll search the room. Why don't you tell me what this is about?'

Whatever it was, it wasn't just Kate O'Donnell and her sister and a black trumpet player. It was John Cavendish too. Stefan wasn't at all sure he wanted to know any of it, but it seemed less and less likely he didn't need to.

He started to work his way through the apartment, starting in the bedroom, working quickly, tidily, thoroughly. He needed to find every envelope and every piece of paper anyway. As he worked Kate talked.

It didn't all come out at once. She spoke a few words, then stopped, watching him. Some of the words were for him; some of them were just her own. She stopped and started again, walking round the flat, following him.

'You have to understand that there's nothing wrong with my sister. Niamh's been locked up in a glorified asylum for over a year, for nothing, not because she's crazy, but because she married a man she should never have married, because she got herself in a mess, in her head. I don't know why she married Dominic. He was so much older. I think it was a way out of something, or she thought it was. She'd got involved in things when she was working on the boats. She was a waitress first, then she started working as a singer with some of the bands. I don't know everything she did, but she was smuggling, drugs

241

sometimes. She started taking them too. And then she met Dominic, and he was a way out for her. Only he wasn't. I know she did have a breakdown. Then she started drinking and taking drugs again. He didn't help. He put her in that place, locked her away. She did nothing, nothing!'

Stefan had searched the bedroom first. He was moving out into the sitting room. He closed the curtains, switched on the lights, started again. He looked behind cupboards and reached down the backs of chairs. He pulled drawers out and looked inside them. He opened every book in the bookcase.

'I had a plan that when I finished working in New York I'd get Niamh out and take her back to Ireland.' Kate began again. 'I tried to talk to Dominic, to get him to let her come home. He didn't want to know. He didn't really believe she was in there to get help. He said it all the time, but it was where he wanted her. So the plan got crazier. It got Jimmy involved and then it got John Cavendish involved. I don't know how. But he could do things. He could get false passports and use them for tickets. He had a way to get us into Canada and away while they were looking in New York –'

'Can I ask a question?'

'Of course you can.'

'Why did John Cavendish decide to do all that?'

'What do you mean?'

'About the only reason I can think of, the one that wouldn't be my business, doesn't seem to come into it. So why else would he do it? You tell a good story, and I get the little catches in your throat as you tell it, but I'm damned sure that wasn't enough. He was taking serious risks, wasn't he?'

'Maybe he just wasn't the little gobshite you are, Sergeant.'

She said it with a smile, but there were no tearful catches now.

'I believe what you've told me, but that's not all of it.'

She looked at him hard now, her eyes narrowing, trying to get behind what that word 'trust' from John Cavendish had really meant when it came to this man she didn't know. Then she realised he had stopped searching.

'There's nothing here, is there?' she said.

'Not in the way of transatlantic tickets, no.'

'Or in the way of what you're looking for,' she replied.

It was his turn to look at her harder now. She had more to say; there was more she knew too. Whatever he was walking into, somewhere, somehow, at the moment she knew a lot more than he did. She might not know the same things, but she was unquestionably ahead of him. And somewhere, somehow, there had been something important in this for John Cavendish, in her, in this bizarre plan to get the crazy sister out of America.

'So what am I looking for, Miss O'Donnell?'

She smiled at him more confidently now; he already knew she knew.

'I was always good at charades. Is the answer IRA ciphers?'

Stefan Gillespie and Kate O'Donnell walked down the stoop to the sidewalk. Whether it was a good idea or a bad idea they were going to go to John Cavendish's office at the World's Fair together. He wasn't going to leave her to search it on her own. He had some sort of explanation for what she was doing, but it didn't really tell him why the G2 man had been helping her to do it, or how she knew what he was looking for. Did that mean she was someone the captain trusted or someone he had to watch? She was going to go anyway; Stefan couldn't stop her. And she had a key to the Irish Pavilion.

'We'll walk up and get a cab,' said Stefan briskly, but as they turned away from the house the door of a black Pontiac Eight, parked almost directly in front of them opened. A young man in a grey overcoat and a light brown hat stood in front of them, fresh-faced and smiling. He raised his hat.

'Mr Zwillman would like a word with you.'

Stefan and Kate simply looked; the words meant nothing. The man moved to the Pontiac's rear door and opened it.

'He'd very much appreciate it.'

Sitting in the back of the Pontiac was a man neither of them knew. He was older than Stefan, but not much. He had sharp, dark features, and small, enquiring eyes. There was a kind of smile, a half smile. He didn't look very appreciative; he looked like he expected people to do what they were told.

'I think you must have mistaken us for someone,' said Stefan.

It wasn't very good; he could see Kate didn't think so either.

'Get in the fucking car,' said the man in the back.

The young man in the overcoat was still holding the door open, and still smiling, but his other hand was in his coat pocket. Stefan knew it was holding a gun.

The Pontiac pulled away towards Vanderbilt Avenue. In the front the man with the gun lit two cigarettes. He passed one to the driver. No one spoke. In the back Stefan sat beside the sharp-featured man; Kate sat on the other side.

244

'I know who she is,' said the man. 'Who are you?'

'This is a mistake,' replied Stefan. It still wasn't very good.

'Let's hope it's not yours. My name's Zwillman, Longie Zwillman. That's the introductions. You tell me who you are and what the fuck you're doing. We'll take it from there.' He snapped at the driver. 'Keep driving.'

Stefan glanced round at Kate. She shook her head. She had no idea what was going on either, but she did have some idea who Zwillman was.

'Mr Cavendish and me had some business together. It was unfinished business. I liked him too. I'm disturbed by what happened to him, naturally. I'd like to know why it happened. So when people start breaking into his apartment and going through his private affairs, I don't think that's right.'

Stefan had no idea who Zwillman was, but he didn't need to know to work out that the truth, or some version of it, was going to be a better bet than any kind of evasion, or that smart answers needed to stay in his head.

'I knew John Cavendish too. I'm an Irish policeman. I'm liaising with the NYPD, in the investigation into how he died. I'm here because the Irish consul general asked me to look through his things, for anything personal, anything that ought to go back to Mrs Cavendish in Ireland – when I leave.'

'What do you call yourself?'

'Stefan Gillespie.'

'Lieutenant, Captain?'

'Sergeant.'

'OK. He didn't give me a name. He said there was an Irish cop.'

Zwillman took a leather cigarette case out. He offered one to Stefan, ignoring Kate. Stefan shook his head. The American pulled out a cigarette.

'So, with all this liaising, where are the Headquarters detectives? I mean what are they saying? They been looking at this a couple of days.'

'He was drunk. He got up on to an empty floor. He was drunk. There was a terrace without any railing. He was drunk. It was dark. He was drunk.'

Finally Zwillman's smile looked like a smile.

'New York's finest haven't impressed?'

'I'm not saying it's not true. But he didn't look pissed to me.'

'And they're not looking too hard, is that right? I hear that.'

'What's to look for?' said Stefan. 'They've made up their minds.'

'So did you get anything personal then, Mr Gillespie?'

Stefan Gillespie frowned, not understanding for a moment.

'Captain Cavendish's belongings.'

'There were some letters from his wife, some photos of his children.'

'OK.'

There was silence.

In the middle of all this, there really was a dead man.

'You were in there a long time. I'm told you were moving furniture. The captain must have kept his personal items in some fucking odd places.'

Stefan didn't offer an explanation.

'And what were you looking for, Miss O'Donnell?'

Longie Zwillman leant round to look at Kate.

'Boat tickets, boat tickets to Ireland. I've told him already.'
She looked at Stefan. 'Do you need to know why? What
does it matter to you?'

'It's all right, Miss O'Donnell, boat tickets is fine. I know
about boat tickets. They make a lot more sense than moving
the wardrobe to find Mr Cavendish's photographs of his
kids. Or is that just me, Mr Gillespie?'

'If I asked you what this is about, Mr Zwillman, I don't
suppose you'd tell me, would you? Maybe I should know
who you are. I've got no idea.'

Longie Zwillman offered no explanation.

'So where are you two going now?'

Stefan looked across at Kate; she understood no more
than he did, but she felt the danger even more acutely. She
didn't wait for Stefan to answer.

'The tickets weren't in the apartment. I'm going to the
World's Fair, to look in his office. They must be there. I
have to find them, Mr Zwillman.'

'And you're helping her?' Zwillman looked at Stefan.

'Yes.' There didn't seem much else to say.

'You know your NYPD friends are looking for her, and
her sister?'

'Yes.'

'Well, you're a helpful sort of guy for a cop, I'll say that
for you.'

Stefan said nothing. He still didn't know what any of
this meant.

'I'm a helpful sort of guy too. What if I come with you?'

Kate and Stefan exchanged glances; there was nothing
they could do.

Longie Zwillman leant forward towards the driver.

'Get us to the Fair. You need to find the Irish Pavilion.'

247

He stubbed out his cigarette in the ashtray and sat back in the seat.

'It'll be closed I guess, Miss O'Donnell?'

'It will be now.'

'That's OK then. You haven't been to the Fair, Mr Gillespie?'

'No,' replied Stefan.

'It's something else, I tell you, some-fucking-thing else!'

As the Pontiac drove through Queens towards Flushing Meadows on the Grand Central Parkway the nightly firework display that closed each World's Fair day began. The night ahead of them was exploding with light and sound. The sky was full of bursting stars of every colour, appearing and disappearing only to be replaced by more. For a moment, just a moment, Stefan saw only what was in front of him. Kate, tense and uncertain next to him didn't have even those seconds to spare; she had seen enough of the fireworks to be unsurprised. But the two men in the front seat were laughing, enjoying the show, talking about when they were going to bring their children out to see the Fair.

The car turned off the Parkway.

'We'll take the Corona Gate,' announced the driver. 'I guess the broad'll know where we're going once we're in the place. OK, boss?'

'All right, Miss O'Donnell?' asked Zwillman.

'They won't let us just drive in,' said Kate. 'I have got a pass –'

Nobody seemed interested.

The Pontiac approached the main gate along the highway that skirted the Fountain Lake, looking across to the lights of the rides and roller-coasters and theatres and restaurants of the Amusement Zone. Cars were heading in the opposite direction, away from the Fair, leaving the parking lots on the outskirts of the grounds. Fireworks were still shooting up and filling the night; red, white, green, yellow, blue; light and smoke, fountains of fire, star clusters. At the gate a World's Fair policeman flagged them down with lazy irritation. The driver wound down the window, smiling.

'We're closing. If you want the Amusement Zone, you turn round, go back down the Parkway and you put your car in the Boulevard Field or the 69th Road parking, like everyone else. You don't just drive in the place.'

'Mr Zwillman is here on business.'

The driver was still smiling. The policeman's irritation had gone. He looked past the driver to the back of the car where Longie Zwillman sat. Zwillman nodded a greeting. There was no expression on his face except the same expression Stefan had seen. He expected people to do what they were told.

'I guess that's OK. You know where you're going?'

'Yeah, we know where we're going.'

The car drove on through the gates. Quite suddenly there was silence. The night sky was black and the lights of the World's Fair around them brought everything back to earth. Crowds were walking towards the gates. To the left, in front of them, Stefan registered the narrow, tapering spire of the Trylon and the great ball of the Perisphere beside it, startlingly white against the night sky, the Trylon rising up, taller than anything else at the Fair, like a white needle. Further on he could see something else that was floodlight-white, a head, the top of the sixty-foot-high statue of George Washington, and beyond it the lights of the tree-lined avenue that was the centre of the Fair. It was something else he had read in the paper. He tried to remember; the Lagoon of Nations and the Court of Peace. John Cavendish had said something about the Four Freedoms, somewhere on that mall. He had wanted to show Stefan some of this. He was seeing it now, at gunpoint.

Kate directed the driver right, on to the Avenue of Pioneers, past the General Cigar Company and American Tobacco and the Triangle Restaurant. The streets and avenues were almost empty away from Constitution Mall now. Stefan registered some things. The clean, square lines of buildings; the white stone of statues and sculptures; as they drove through the Court of States a great circle of flags he thought must be countries he didn't know, then realised were the American States.

They turned into an avenue dominated by the gigantic figure of a man on top of a towering plinth. The sculpture was as high as the Trylon. The man was the colour of bronze; he wore a worker's overalls over bulging muscles; his right hand reached to the sky, holding a star. It was the pavilion of the Soviet Union. They passed a low building of glass and concrete panels. There was nothing very distinctive about it, except for its bright and simple modernity.

'That's something you won't see anywhere else,' said Zwillman.

Stefan looked round.

'The flag, the little red, white and blue one there.'

He looked back towards the low building as they passed.

'The Czechoslovak Pavilion. They got no country to go with it now.'

Just beyond the Soviet Pavilion the Pontiac stopped.

The driver got out and opened the door for Longie Zwillman.

The young gunman got out and opened the other door.

The Irish Pavilion was a high, curved wall of glass, brightly lit inside. Three tricolours fluttered in front of it. At one end there was a wall of stone and a sculpture of a naked woman rising out of the sea. The building was in the shape of a shamrock, though no one would ever see it was, except by flying over it. Stefan Gillespie, Kate O'Donnell and Longie Zwillman walked to the doors. They were locked. Kate took a key ring from her bag and opened one of them. She seemed very calm, but Stefan had felt the tension in her body, sitting next to her in the car. As they walked into the pavilion a woman was walking through the entrance, pushing a cleaning trolley. She was black, in her fifties. She seemed unsurprised to see them.

'They've all gone, Miss.'

'Yes, I know,' said Kate, trying to smile her most normal smile.

'You see the main lights go off? I ain't meant to leave them on.'

'I will. Thank you.'

The woman carried on, pushing the trolley of buckets and mops.

Kate walked through a door into a short corridor. She passed several more doors then stopped at the last one. She tried the handle. It was locked.

'Obviously I don't have a key to –'

Longie Zwillman moved her aside. He put his shoulder to the door, pulled it back a little, and then smashed against the wood above the lock.

They walked into the office. Kate turned on the light.

As the two men looked round she sat on the desk.

'So, I guess you two are the expert searchers, one way or another.'

Stefan attempted a reassuring smile; she was on her way back.

Zwillman was walking round the room. John Cavendish had been a man of orderly habits. It wouldn't be a difficult room to search. He stopped, looking down at a small safe that was built into the wall behind the desk.

'You start with the desk, Mr Gillespie. I need to get Sam in.'

He walked out.

'Who the hell is he?' demanded Stefan. 'You seem to know him.'

'He's a criminal, a gangster. I don't know him. I've heard the name.'

'I suppose I'd worked out he wasn't John's bank manager.'

'Why ask me then? You know as much as I do. If you think I've got the faintest idea why he was waiting for us outside John's flat –'

'Why, is one question. How, is another. But that's easily answered though. The caretaker you got so much sympathy from as a bereaved sister!'

Kate felt that one hit; but she was still on her way back.

'I don't think he's here because of my bloody boat tickets, he's –'

She stopped as Zwillman came back in with the driver.

'Drawers,' he snapped. 'Get it done. We haven't got all night.'

Stefan turned to the desk. He started to look through the paperwork. Kate was still perching on the edge. She opened her handbag and took out her cigarettes. Whatever was happening she felt safer. Stefan did too. Whether explanations were likely to come or not, it felt less dangerous now.

Longie Zwillman was in front of the safe with Sam.

'It's no big deal,' said the driver. 'It's a piece of crap.'

He knelt down beside the safe, pushing his ear up against it. He took the dial between his fingers and began to turn it, slowly, evenly, caressingly.

'So, how are you going to get to Albany now, Miss O'Donnell?'

'Are you just trying to show me how much you know about me, Mr Zwillman,' replied Kate, 'or do you have a special interest in my welfare?'

'Let's say I have an interest in your sister's welfare.'

'And why would that be?'

'The same reason Mr Cavendish did. I know what the deal was. Like I told you, John and me had some business together. The deal was he helped you get your sister out of New York, out of the country, and on a boat to Ireland. You were going to hide up at his apartment, after you got her out of the psych ward, and then he was going to drive you to Albany. You were going to pick up the New York train to Montreal in the middle of the night, when everyone on it was asleep. He got you the fake passports you needed, and the boat tickets in the fake names to go with them. And you had something to deliver in return. Or your sister had. Death notwithstanding.'

The depth of the detail surprised Kate, even after everything that had happened. She said nothing for a moment. It made no sense to her; it was evident Zwillman wasn't about to provide any. Stefan, still looking through the desk drawers as he took this in, understood more than he had done. He had some part of what had been missing from the story Kate had told him.

'OK, boss.' The driver stood up. The safe door was open.
'Let's see,' said Zwillman.

As he crouched down by the safe, Sam walked out with
an air of professional detachment. Longie pulled several
files and papers out of the safe. He put them on the desk.
Stefan stopped what he was doing. Kate got off the desk and
turned to face it. The gangster leafed through several documents quickly. He pushed them across to Stefan.

'They don't seem to mean much. Take a look though.'

As Stefan scanned the pages he could see only figures
and accounts.

Zwillman opened a small envelope. He smiled.

'The *Empress of Canada*. There you are, Miss O'Donnell.'

He continued to smile as he put the tickets in his inside
pocket.

'What are you going to do with those?'

'I hope I'll be able to give them to you later.'

He turned back to the papers on the desk. He opened a
sealed manila envelope. Inside were the torn pages from
a notebook, stapled together. He looked through the pages
and then he handed them across the desk to Stefan.

'From your IRA pals. This is what the ciphers look like.'

Stefan peered down at the pages. Rows of capital letters,
in Cavendish's tiny, meticulous hand; groups of five letters
in columns. Some took up only a few lines of a page; others
carried on over several pages.

'So, that's what you're after, right, Mr Gillespie?'

There was no point saying it wasn't. Whatever the
reasons, Longie Zwillman had been trusted by John
Cavendish, enough to know all this.

'That's what he wanted to get back to Ireland. But I want
to know what's in them too. I'll take a copy of them.'

He held his hand out. Stefan gave him the pages. If Cavendish had trusted him, he had to do the same. And it wasn't as if he had any choice.

'All we need now, is the key, right?'

Zwillman wasn't looking at Stefan now; he was looking at Kate.

'Like I say, the deal still stands, Miss O'Donnell.'

'The deal was with John Cavendish. It's got nothing to do with you.'

'You'll have to take my word that it has.'

'We've found a way to get out of New York. We don't need help.'

'That'll be Jimmy Palmer's friends, the band that's playing a dance in Buffalo. You go in the truck with the musicians. They drop you at Albany?'

She stared at him, no longer surprised, but still disbelieving.

'I got that from a couple of detectives in Harlem, and they got it from somebody at Headquarters Detective Division. I don't think they know where you're holed up yet, but they know you're in Harlem. You're not going to get out of New York, sweetheart. I doubt you'll get out of Harlem.'

She sank down on to the edge of the desk again. The bit of fire she had started to find again had just had a bucket of water thrown over it.

'So maybe you need some help after all.'

She didn't answer; it was answer enough.

'I can get you out. I can maybe get you into Canada. But forget about trains from Albany. If they know you're going in a truck with a bunch of Harlem jazzers, they'll know where those boys were going to kick you off.'

'Jesus Christ,' said Kate, reaching for another cigarette.

'So the deal's still there. You get the key to these fucking codes out of your sister, for Mr Gillespie and me, and I get you to the boat. I don't know how long you think you've got, but if your sister isn't out of Harlem pretty damn quick, she'll be back in the psych ward, and your friend Mr Carroll will be making sure it's one with bigger doors and bigger bars, and I don't think you'll be doing any visiting there. That's if she makes it back to the psych ward in the first place. Headquarters Detective Division isn't looking for you because it's their call. They're in Dominic Carroll's pocket, and let me assure you, Miss O'Donnell, I know whereof I speak, when it comes to having cops in your pocket. I have to pay. Mr Carroll just has to be Irish.'

Kate O'Donnell looked at Longie Zwillman and simply nodded.

'You go and get her now, and you bring her where I tell you.'

She nodded again.

'You better go with her, Gillespie,' said the American.

Stefan caught Kate's eyes as she looked at him. She had no words now; she was out of her depth and she knew it. But she wanted him with her. And he nodded too.

He wasn't exactly sure when he had moved from trying to find the envelope John Cavendish had asked him to take back to Military Intelligence in Dublin to helping a gangster smuggle a wanted woman out of the United States, but he was struggling to find the point at which he'd had any choice in the matter. Cavendish's death hadn't given him any choice. Kate O'Donnell didn't really offer him much choice either now. As for Longie Zwillman, he didn't look like a man who ever gave anybody any choice, at least not the kind of choice that would leave you with any choice.

As they walked out of the pavilion Stefan spoke quietly to Zwillman.

'There's a German intelligence man here, pretends he's a tourism –'

'Katzmann,' replied the gangster. 'I know.'

'He knows something about this.'

'Not as much as me, so don't shvitz, my friend!'

'So nisht kefelecht?'

Longie Zwillman roared with laughter.

'Nisht kefelecht!' he said, slapping Stefan on the back.

He was still laughing as he got into the car.

'Keep it clean, boys, we've got an Irish cop who speaks Yiddish.'

'Not much, that was about it.'

Sam looked round, amused.

'He's all right then, boss?'

'So far,' said Zwillman quietly. He looked at Stefan. 'You in this?'

'It looks like it.'

'Then I guess you'll do then, Sergeant.'

As the car pulled away from the Irish Pavilion, Stefan Gillespie looked out at the three Irish tricolours, drooping now after the breeze had dropped. The Soviet Pavilion towered above, massive and triumphant. Germany wasn't represented at the Fair, but it would have produced something strangely similar. There was a lot that towered above Ireland of course, all around, in all sorts of ways, everywhere. He looked out as the Pontiac passed the Czechoslovak flag; all that was left of a small, broken country. It was likely there would be a lot more broken countries, and the broken bodies to go with them. Whatever this was about it met all that, somewhere, out in the darkness.

Stefan didn't want any of it, but then nobody did. He had to trust what John Cavendish had left him with that night at the Hotel Pennsylvania: this mattered to his small country. He could still walk away from Kate O'Donnell even though he didn't want to. He could probably walk away from Longie Zwillman too; there was nothing he knew that the Jewish gangster didn't know already, and know more about. It was still the dead soldier who ultimately left him with no choice. Maybe the Abwehr man had been right after all. With no intention of doing so, Garda Sergeant Stefan Gillespie had taken over from Captain John Cavendish.

The Pontiac exited the deserted avenues of the World's Fair on to the Grand Central Parkway; the signs proclaimed its message everywhere: The World of Tomorrow. Kate put her arm through Stefan's. She leant closer to him. She had needed him there; now it felt as if she wanted him there too.

16. A Hundred and Twenty-Fifth Street

Negro Harlem started at 125th Street. If New York was the biggest Jewish city on earth and the third largest Irish city, Harlem was the world's greatest black city, in fact its only great black city. And like any other great city it teemed with the rich and not-so-rich and the poor, the idle and the ambitious, the builders and the breakers. Like any other city, it had its high-maintenance boulevards and its back-street tenements, and it threw them together, dancing cheek to cheek, like everywhere else in Manhattan. Nothing distinguished Harlem from any other low-rise part of New York in the appearance of its houses, apartment blocks, shops, theatres, churches, libraries, schools, gas stations, restaurants, diners. The dance halls and clubs weren't any different to look at; there were just more of them, though pouring out of them, apparently with about as much ease as it took to smoke a cigarette or drink a beer, was some of the most vital, new, original music the world had ever heard. It was only really the colour of people's faces that changed.

Riding uptown on 7th Avenue, for twenty-five solid blocks north of 125th, almost everybody on the streets was black. There was nowhere else like it; it had a faster heartbeat than anywhere else in the world's fastest city. Harlem wasn't a creation of concrete and steel; it was re-made every day by the people who walked its streets. It had none of the skyscrapers of lower and midtown Manhattan, but it also defined what New York City truly was.

At fourteen storeys the highest building in Harlem was the Hotel Theresa, on the corner of 125th and 7th. People called it the Black Waldorf-Astoria. There wasn't too much Waldorf-Astoria about the unimposing white building with too many small windows; the gables and columns that sat on top, that the architect might have called Renaissance if he'd been pushed, were facades that looked like they'd been lifted up from another building, maybe a rail terminus, that should have been twelve storeys lower. The Theresa was more big hotel than grand hotel, but it did something no other big hotel south of 125th Street did, all the way through Manhattan down to Battery Park; it was a big hotel a black man could walk into and get a room to sleep in. When you hit the Hotel Theresa, you were in Harlem.

Longie Zwillman's driver pulled left off 7th Avenue into 124th Street and stopped the car just past a row of garbage bins and some high wooden gates. Stefan and Kate sat in the back. She knew where they were, at the back of the Hotel Theresa; he had no idea. Sam had said little and explained nothing. He was doing what his boss had told him; his passengers would do the same. Zwillman and the gunman they now knew as Rick had been dropped off over the Brooklyn Bridge before the Pontiac headed north to Harlem. Longie's last remark had been curt; it had been an instruction, not a suggestion. Stefan could feel Kate's anger, though Zwillman spoke to him.

'Dump the Negro. He's a fucking neon sign. Tell him to

get out of the city for a bit. He's not important, but the cops won't give him an easy time.'

Stefan and Kate got out of the car and followed Sam back on to 7th Avenue, into the lobby of the Theresa. It was busy and noisy. People spilled out of the bar into the foyer; most of them were black. Sam walked to the reception desk. A young black man recognised Kate and smiled. As he eyed Sam he looked more serious and more wary. He had no idea who the man in the overcoat and the homburg was, but he knew what he was without a word being spoken. Sam spoke quietly and quickly; this was his boss's business.

'You had any cops sniffing round in here tonight?'

'No, sir, I haven't seen any.'

'You will. They'll be looking for Miss –' He glanced round at Kate, then back at the receptionist. 'Her and the woman with her, whatever they're calling themselves. The cops'll have another name. They'll be after the horn player too, Jimmy Palmer, whatever he's calling himself. Are they upstairs?'

'I don't think they've been out of the room. I can ring –'

'We're going up anyway. They need to get out. You've got gates on 124th Street. How do we get out that way? I don't want to go through here.'

'If you find the service stairs, at the end of the hall, here –'

The receptionist produced a plan of the upper floors of the hotel. He spoke as if he was telling them how to get to the nearest subway station. Stefan and Kate simply looked on; whatever was happening was outside their control; they were in a world of rules everyone but them understood.

'The room's here. All the floors are the same. You go right, right again. There's a door at the end of the hallway. You go all the way down and it'll bring you to the kitchens. You go straight in. I'll tell them you're coming, and someone'll show you the way. You come out into the yard –'

'I've got you.'

Sam took a roll of dollar bills from his pocket and peeled several off.

'OK. That checks them out,' he said, 'and there's a bit left over for you on top. I don't know how long before the cops get here, but you tell them the dames left a couple of hours ago. They won't believe you, but you might as well waste some of their time. They've got plenty of it, all right?'

'You need to get dressed and out of here. If the cops don't know you're here there's going to be somebody who's going to tell them. They know plenty already. I don't know if we've got minutes or hours, so let's say minutes.'

Niamh Carroll and Jimmy Palmer stood by the bed they had just climbed out of, a few hastily grabbed clothes draped round them, surprised and disoriented; only a moment before they had been asleep. Jimmy was suspicious, puzzled; like the Theresa receptionist he only had to look at the man in the homburg to know what he was. The other man hadn't spoken; he didn't go with the gangster though. Niamh was holding Jimmy's hand. She looked afraid. There were two men she didn't know; one giving them orders.

'I don't understand, Kate, who are –'

'This is Stefan,' said her sister. 'He's a friend of John Cavendish –'

'And I'm Sam,' said Zwillman's lieutenant, 'and I'm here to get you out before the paddy wagon arrives. So now we all know each other, and we all know what's happening, just get your fucking clothes on, sweetheart.'

'Don't talk to the lady like that,' growled the trumpeter.

Sam shook his head wearily, and turned to Kate.

'You tell these people why they got to fucking shift, in three words.'

'The police know we're in Harlem. They know about the band getting us out. They know where we're going, Niamh. They know Jimmy's with us. We've got to find another way. Stefan and someone else Captain Cavendish knew, Mr Zwillman – I've got the boat tickets, if we can get to Montreal. I can't explain now, Niamh. But we have to leave. We don't have a choice.'

Now Niamh looked cornered and frightened. She looked at Jimmy.

'Longie Zwillman?' asked the trumpeter in disbelief, staring at Sam.

'Mr Zwillman is making alternative arrangements,' nodded the driver.

'For fuck's sake! What is this?'

'Minutes, I said. You're not playing a solo now, brother.'

'Don't call me brother, Jewboy.'

'We're all brothers under the skin, Jimmy,' grinned the gangster.

Palmer wanted to lay one on him; instead he reached for his clothes.

'Niamh, please, you have to trust me,' said Kate.

'Your sister's right, Mrs Carroll,' Stefan spoke quietly. 'We're here to help you get back to Ireland. The plans have changed. They have to. There really isn't any time.'

His voice surprised Niamh, because it was an Irish voice when she didn't expect one. And it was an Irish voice talking about going home. She felt calmer.

Stefan looked at Jimmy. 'If the police come –'

The trumpeter nodded. It wasn't an easy nod, but reality was a wall in front of him now. Talking wouldn't take him over it. He smiled at Niamh.

'Harlem's a crazy place, I told you. We do what the man says.'

That smile hadn't been an easy smile either.

Kate bent down to pick her sister's clothes off the floor.

'You go in the bathroom.' She pushed the clothes into Niamh's hands. 'I'll put a few things in a bag, as much as I can. Just be quick, sis, please.'

She took Niamh's arm and pushed her into the bathroom, then she picked up a leather bag and started to take clothes from a suitcase and stuffed them into it. Palmer was almost dressed now, buttoning his shirt.

'Mr Zwillman recommends you take a trip out of town, Jimmy.'

Again the horn player produced a nod he didn't want to give.

'I guess I can work it out. Even one nigger's a nigger too many.'

Sam shrugged; that was about it.

The telephone by the bed rang. Sam walked across and picked it up.

'OK. Keep them talking and then send them to another floor.'

He put the phone down and grinned at Stefan. He liked his job.

'They're here now. So what do you think of New York, Sergeant?'

For a moment Niamh Carroll and Jimmy Palmer stood at the open door of the hotel room. There was no time to speak. Maybe that was best. She stepped forward and held him for another precious second. There was no time for tears either. They could wait. 'We'll find each other. I'll write when I'm in Ireland.' He nodded.

He knew she believed they'd find each other. He would have liked to believe it too. He knew that wasn't the way the world worked. He smiled to tell her it was true. And then she was gone. They were all gone. He shut the door. He walked to the bed and pulled on his jacket. He looked at the bed. He reached out his hand and touched the sheet where she had lain. The telephone rang again. He picked it up. It was the receptionist.

'Yeah, I know, I guess it wasn't going to take the assholes long.'

He put the phone down. He took a cigarette from the packet by the bed and lit it. He took in a long draw of smoke then walked to the door. He looked back into the room once more, and smiled. He turned out the light.

*

Longie Zwillman's driver led them through the Hotel Theresa's kitchens. Amidst all the noise and smoke and steam, the shouting and cursing and laughing, the crash of pans and crockery, no one took any notice at all of four people who very obviously had no place there, but each time they came to a door, or a turn, or a passageway, someone would look up from chopping vegetables or grilling steaks or washing dishes or wheeling a trolley, to point the way and send them on in the right direction. It wasn't long before they were walking past the garbage bins at the back of the hotel, out on to 124th Street. And

265

minutes later the Pontiac was heading south down 7th Avenue.

*

As Jimmy Palmer sauntered towards the elevators, he was in a good mood. He wasn't looking forward to what was going to happen downtown, but he'd been beaten up by detectives before. Years ago in the Prohibition days, when a speakeasy was raided, the cops always let the white customers leave and then beat up the black barmen and busboys and musicians, so that nobody could say they weren't doing their jobs properly. And every punch that was going to be thrown at him now was going to be more time they weren't out there looking for Niamh. There wasn't a bigger thing he'd done in his life than this.

For a long time he'd thought he'd never see her again. He'd found out where she was; he'd found out they had her locked away, because of the heroin or because she was crazy, but he knew that wasn't it. Yet there was nothing he could do, except remember, and hope that she remembered.

Then he'd met her sister; she'd been looking for him. She'd known who he was and she'd known what he was to Niamh. And somehow the plan they'd talked about one long night in Small's Paradise hadn't seemed so wild, even when the sun came up. Kate had found someone who could help too; a man who could get passports, real ones. He didn't understand what was going on between the Irishman and Kate; he didn't know what the Irishman really wanted. But he knew what Niamh had been doing when they met on the boats, when he was playing in a band back and forth across the Atlantic, and she was singing. They'd both

266

brought some drugs across now and again; everybody did. But she'd been doing something else.

She was carrying messages for the IRA. It didn't mean a lot to him. Nobody was going to lock you up for it as far as he could tell; definitely not in New York. What he knew about the IRA he'd read in the papers. It was a big thing where the Irish lived in New York, but what it was about, and what kind of army they had, he never really got a handle on. He'd played a few Irish dances and he knew they sang a lot of songs about it when they were pissed; that was about as far as his interest extended.

There were plenty of people in Harlem, if you wanted to listen, who hadn't got much time for the British. They'd stolen most of Africa after all, and black people weren't going to take that forever, any more than they were going to take white shit in America forever. Ireland was another place the British had stolen and if the Irish wanted to kick their arses out, there was nothing wrong with that. The same thing was going to happen in Africa; it was already starting to happen. It was how Niamh had met Dominic Carroll though, all that IRA stuff. He was a big man. He did what big men do. He took what he wanted and pissed on everyone else. There was nothing surprising about that. That was how it was everywhere; it didn't matter whether you were black or white, except that if you were black there were more people out there to piss on you.

Sometimes Niamh could seem hard, but she never was, not inside; he knew that. And when Dominic Carroll found out she wasn't what he wanted after all, he broke her, in every way a man could break a woman. But Jimmy had found her again. He'd found her and now he'd brought her away from it. She would find a way to put the pieces together.

That night in the Hotel Theresa, holding her again, he knew there was something that hadn't been broken. There was what she felt for him. He knew there would be a place, one day, where she could put the pieces together. Even if he never saw her again, he'd made that happen.

He was smiling as the elevator doors opened. A white policeman came out. He was wearing an overcoat over his uniform. The white shirt told Jimmy the man was a senior officer. It was Captain Aaron Phelan. On another day it might have occurred to him that he was more senior than anybody might expect on a job like this. But all that surprised him was that it was quicker than he'd thought. Not many minutes earlier there would have been nothing to smile about. A black, uniformed officer and a white plain-clothes man stood beside the captain. It was the black officer who spoke.

'Jimmy Palmer, right?'

'You looking for Jimmy Palmer?'

The game was on.

'Where are they?' asked Aaron Phelan quietly.

'Where's who, Captain?'

They looked round as two more officers appeared, coming up the stairs next to the elevator; another black officer and another detective.

Phelan looked at Palmer for a moment. The expression on the trumpeter's face told him that the room would be empty. He walked back along the corridor. The detectives followed him with one of the black officers; the other black officer stayed with Jimmy. When they reached the room Phelan nodded. One of the detectives kicked open the door. They all went in; and seconds later they all came out, heading back to the elevator.

'Check the rest of this floor. Get downstairs and check the service stairs and the service elevator. Get some men in the kitchens. Get outside back and front. We don't know whether they're still here or they've already gone. And when you've got a spare minute take the fucking receptionist out back and lose him some teeth. Somebody made a call, is that right Jimmy?'

As the captain turned back to Jimmy Palmer the two black officers were running down the stairs; one of the detectives was walking back down the corridor, heading for the service elevator. There was a door behind the trumpeter; a brass panel said 'Housekeeper'. The captain walked forward, opened the door, switched on the light and waited. The detective took Palmer's arm and pushed him through it. Inside the room there were shelves filled with perfectly folded and ironed bedlinen, from floor to ceiling; towers of white towels were piled on a table and on the floor. Aaron Phelan followed Jimmy and the detective into the small, windowless room. As the door swung shut the detective stepped back and the captain stepped forward.

'How long since they left?'

'Who left, Captain?'

'Shall we make it short, Jimmy? Niamh Carroll, Kate O'Donnell. You drove the cab that took them from the Bayville Convalescent Home. You brought them here. You've been staying here with them. That's about it.'

'You're right, they've gone. It was a couple of hours ago, I'd say.'

'It's not hours,' said Phelan. 'Where are they going?'

'I don't know, I just drove the cab. They didn't tell me.'

'You know how I got here?'

'A squad car?'

'I see,' smiled the captain. 'I got here because one of your friends, one of your trusted brothers, who was going to help you get the women out of New York, and upstate to catch a train to Canada, wasn't much of a brother.'

Jimmy Palmer took the blow. It wasn't the biggest surprise in the world. It's how things were; there was always somebody to piss on you.

'Is it worth what's coming, Jimmy?'

The horn player said nothing. He didn't need a diagram.

'You think that white whore gives a fuck about you?'

It wasn't the right thing to say, because as it happened, Jimmy Palmer knew that that white whore did give a fuck about him. He knew she loved him. Maybe because of that there was really no right thing for Aaron Phelan to say. The trumpeter was never going to tell him anything. Well, he was going to tell him quite a lot; it's just that none of it would be true. He had already got a series of stories in his head. Some of them would even be convincing; some of them he would keep till they were beaten out of him.

'All I need to know is where they are, and where they're going?'

'I drove the cab. I got paid for it. I brought them here to hole up. I don't know where they're going now. There was a train in it somewhere. I don't know about Albany. Maybe the Chieftain, maybe it was Chicago.'

'That's crap, isn't it Jimmy?' Phelan shook his head.

'They wanted my help, Captain. They didn't trust me though.'

'That's funny, because I don't trust you either.'

The trumpeter shrugged. He wasn't smiling, but there was a smile in there. And Aaron Phelan could see it. He wasn't such a bad judge of men.

'You're not going to tell me anything, are you? It won't matter what happens downtown. It won't matter how much shite we kick out of you.'

Jimmy said nothing. He wouldn't be able to waste as much police time as he'd hoped. But at least when the beating came it would be shorter.

'There's not a lot of point in this,' said Phelan. 'You know what they do with a nigger who fucks a white woman in the South, don't you Jimmy?'

'I don't spend a lot of time in the South, Captain.'

'Don't worry, you're in New York. We'll leave you your balls.'

Aaron Phelan turned abruptly and walked out. The door swung shut again. It was Jimmy and the detective now. The captain obviously didn't do his own beating. But if it was here, if they weren't taking him downtown, it wouldn't last that long, thought the horn player. It didn't. The hand the detective drew from his coat was holding a gun. He fired three times. Jimmy Palmer collapsed on to the towels neatly piled beside the shelves, scattering them across the floor. Red blood spread out across the white.

*

They were back under the Brooklyn Bridge now, driving beside the East River. Longie Zwillman's driver pulled into Fulton Street and wove his way through the fish trucks and forklifts, blasting his horn and responding enthusiastically to the curses that blasted back in return. Sam stopped the Pontiac in Front Street, behind the market. He pushed in through the open doors with Stefan, Kate and Niamh. The cold ice-and-blood air hit them along with the roar that was the noise of the market.

It was dark now and the market was gearing up for the night. Sam turned up a stone staircase just inside the doors. They walked up two flights of stairs and into a dimly lit office. The windows had been whitewashed over in places; cracks in the glass were papered over. There was a desk full of skewered bills and invoices; a table with unwashed coffee mugs and overfull ashtrays. One side of the room was piled with wooden fish crates. The smell was the smell of the market below, along with half a century of cigarette and cigar smoke and sweat, and it was as cold as it was downstairs.

A telephone started ringing. Longie Zwillman, walking up and down and rubbing his hands, ignored it.

'Mrs Carroll,' he stepped forward and stretched out his hand.

Niamh shook it, cautiously, nervously. She had no idea who he was, but fear had given way to a kind of bland, unquestioning acceptance now.

'Longie Zwillman. Call me Longie.'

'This is all very confusing, Mr Zwillman.'

'Let's hope we can make it less so.'

He smiled, and it seemed to be a smile that genuinely recognised Niamh Carroll's fragility. She was less nervous. She still didn't know who he was; she didn't know what he wanted; she didn't know whether he was going to help her or what he was going to do. But her life had been in other people's hands for a long time now; she was used to doing nothing herself.

The gangster looked hard at Stefan.

'You wouldn't want to have been any later out of there, Sergeant.'

'You've heard something already?'

'I got some of it back, yeah.'

He said no more, but Stefan realised there was more to say. He turned back to Niamh, still standing there as an onlooker to what was all about her.

'We have some business to conclude, Mrs Carroll.'

Niamh looked at him blankly.

'We need the deal, that's how business is done.'

She still didn't understand.

'Things are different, you know that of course.' The half smile was still the half smile no one could ever quite read, but the voice was kind. 'It's not in Captain Cavendish's hands any more, I'm sorry to say. It's in mine and Mr Gillespie's. But it's your part of the deal first. You know what your sister discussed with the captain. And you know what he wanted from you.'

Niamh was no longer puzzled. She remembered; she wasn't easy.

'Is there a problem with that, Mrs Carroll?'

Zwillman's expression didn't change; the voice was harder though.

'I don't know. I'm not sure what's right –'

'Niamh, we have talked about this,' said Kate softly.

The look of deep confusion was back on her sister's face.

'Look, Mrs Carroll, let's say in the absence of the captain, Sergeant Gillespie is representing the Irish government, and I'm the shipping agent. I can get you out of New York and I can get you into Canada. No borders involved. But you deliver first. People are taking considerable risks for you.'

'I know,' Niamh answered. 'I'm just not sure – it was a long – it was three years ago, more. Things change. Everything I knew then could be –'

273

'Buyer beware, no such thing as a sure bet. I've got you.'

Kate knew that if the deal had ever been an option it wasn't now.

'Niamh, it's what we all agreed.'

Niamh nodded, but she was still struggling with something.

'If it was just about Dominic, it wouldn't matter –'

Stefan knew what was happening; the idea of betrayal went deep in Ireland, very deep. It was that idea that Niamh Carroll was confronting. Longie Zwillman had some sense of it too, but he didn't have any time for it.

'Do me a favour, Mrs Carroll, one day, when the world seems bright and gay, maybe we'll get together and you can sing me "When Irish Eyes Are Smiling" and I'll sing you "My Yiddishe Momme". In the meantime you want to make sure a room in the psych ward's all your husband and his friends have got in mind. John Cavendish never struck me as the sort of man who'd take a walk off a thirty-storey building. So we'll cut the crap.'

Kate reached out and took her sister's hand.

Niamh looked at her for a moment. As she turned back to Longie Zwillman and Stefan she spoke more clearly, as if her mind was stronger.

'Can you let me see one of the ciphers?'

Stefan took an envelope from his pocket. He handed her a piece of paper. A short message; a date; two lines of capital letters grouped in fives.

Niamh gazed at it for some seconds, seeing another time.

'It looks the same. That doesn't guarantee –'

She stopped. When she spoke again her voice was clearer. These were facts. She had pushed away the emotions they carried with them. There was something in the back of her mind that was engaging. They were only facts.

'There's a date on each message,' she said slowly, but as she spoke her words became more confident. 'It won't have anything to do with the real date or even the real year. That's partly to confuse, but it's also because the date tells you how to use the key. You take the date. Then it's the month. You multiply the month by ten and add the date.' She looked back at one of the ciphers Cavendish had copied. 'This one is the 14th of August. The number you get is 94. The keys are in the Everyman edition of *The Scarlet Letter*. So you go to page 94.'

She stopped for a few seconds, running it all through her head. It was there.

'You add the last two numbers of the year. This is 1935, so that's 8. The first twelve letters of the eighth line, that's the key. You write out the message, with no gaps between the words, a letter at a time, under those twelve letters. You start a new line with every thirteenth letter. The message ends up as long columns of letters under the key. You switch the columns round by putting the key into alphabetical order, then you type out the letters in the columns. They're always in groups of five but that doesn't mean anything. If you're deciphering, once you've got the key you work backwards and you end up with the message. It can take a while.'

'Really? You're kidding me, Mrs Carroll,' laughed Zwillman.

Niamh smiled. It was easier than she had thought. And it was done.

'Sam, go and get a couple of copies of the book,' said Longie.

'What book?'

'Nathaniel Hawthorne, *The Scarlet Letter*. It's the Everyman edition. It's got to be that edition or it won't work. Is that how it is, Mrs Carroll?'

She nodded.

Sam frowned.

'Where am I going to find a bookstore open at this time of night?'

'Wake someone up, use your head, I don't know!'

'I'd have to go back to Jersey for anyone paying protection, boss.'

'You think we shake down bookshops now? You need to talk to your rabbi a bit more. What are we, Italians? You just buy the fucking things!'

Sam, looking a little put out, shrugged his shoulders and left.

'So, did you get all that cipher baloney, Sergeant?'

Stefan Gillespie laughed.

'I think you need to explain it again, with pictures, Mrs Carroll.'

'It's not so hard, Mr Gillespie. It's just tedious. I'll write it down.'

Niamh sat at the desk and took some paper and a pencil. She wanted to do it now. Perhaps she just wanted something to do. She needed to stop thinking about what was happening. She needed to stop her mind racing. She needed to stop thinking about Jimmy, finding him and losing him. She looked up at Kate for a moment. Kate gave her a reassuring smile. It didn't reassure her, but it did matter. They were together; that mattered more. Niamh turned back to the desk and started to write down the instructions for using the cipher key.

Kate looked at Stefan and then turned to Zwillman. 'The

deal's done. So where do we go from here, Mr Zwillman?'

'Well, the horn player didn't have such a bad idea. I mean a truck going somewhere. There's thousands driving in and out of New York, day and night. That's why I got you here. There's fish deliveries leaving Fulton Market all the time. You won't smell too sweet at the end of it, but a bar of soap should sort that out. Forget the train. And forget the border crossing.'

'That gets us out of New York,' replied Kate, 'not into Canada.'

'Ten years ago I was bringing a lot of liquor in from Canada, by boat, across Lake Ontario. It was Prohibition. I made a few trips over myself, it's no big deal. I still have some Canadian business associates who owe me a favour. It'll take a day or so to sort out maybe. I mean there's nothing organised now. No one's set up to do it. But I can find someone to bring a boat across the lake at night. The only question is where. You need to get some place you're holed up, out of sight, somewhere a boat can get to, so maybe some kind of jetty, right? That's harder but we'll get there.' He looked at Stefan. 'What do you think? They disappear. No one knows how.'

Stefan saw that Zwillman's insistence on asking him annoyed Kate.

'I guess it's up to Kate and Niamh.'

'I'm not offering options here. You're the one going with them.'

'Yes, I suppose I am.'

It didn't entirely come as a surprise to Stefan that he was going to take Kate and her sister across the border, but he hadn't quite got it into his head that he had replaced John Cavendish so completely.

277

'As you're not offering options, Mr Zwillman,' said Kate, 'a fish truck sounds just perfect. I wouldn't want to put Sergeant Gillespie out though.'

Longie Zwillman grinned.

'I'm already put out,' smiled Stefan, 'unless you want rid of me?'

'It's entirely up to you, Sergeant.'

She didn't smile, but he still knew she was glad he was going.

'Dominic has a house on Lake Ontario.'

It was Niamh who spoke. She had stopped writing now and had been listening to them. Her mind really was calmer now; she was thinking hard.

'We used to go there when we were first married. It's not far from Syracuse. It's a place called Mexico Bay, an old wooden house, right on its own. There's a boathouse on the lake. I couldn't tell you exactly where it is, but I could find the house if we got close to it. I don't know if anyone even goes up there any more, but it was always shut up till the spring anyway.'

'That sounds like something, Mrs Carroll,' nodded Zwillman. 'If you get across that end of the lake, you're close to Kingston. I know people in Kingston. You take a train to Montreal from there and the boat's waiting. Or we can just get a car to take you. You got almost three days till the boat sails. I don't think that should be a problem though. Maybe the tighter the better.'

As if he had only now remembered that he had them in his pocket, the gangster took out the envelope containing the boat tickets. He handed them to Kate O'Donnell. The deal had been done; it would be honoured. He turned to a bookshelf that was lined with telephone directories and box files. He ran his fingers along the shelf and pulled out several battered and stained road maps. He looked through them, then opened one up and spread it out.

'Can you show me where this place is, Mrs Carroll? Or near it?'

Niamh got up from the desk and joined him.

'It's not big, Mr Zwillman. I don't know about a boat finding it –'

'Don't worry, they'll be guys who know the lake backwards.'

As Longie Zwillman and Niamh Carroll pored over the map, Stefan moved closer to Kate. Nobody was speaking. The noise of the fish market below filtered up through the floor. Stefan watched Kate for a moment. She was watching her sister. It was a strange place to be, in strange company, but there was more animation in Niamh's face than she had seen in a very long time. She turned, aware of Stefan looking at her. She looked up at him.

'I'm glad you'll be with us.'

'I'm glad I'll be with you too.'

In what was not said in the moment that followed those words was something that neither of them had expected, but both of them understood.

Two hours later Stefan, Kate and Niamh were in the back of a fish truck, heading out of Manhattan to New Jersey. The ice that had been packed round the boxes of fish still made the truck bitterly cold. They huddled together against the wall between them and the cab, where they could feel a little heat from the engine through the panelling. The two sisters wore men's coats and boots, hats and gloves, collected up from porters at the market. It would be a long journey, six or seven hours, to Upstate New York.

Sam was in the cab driving, after returning to Fulton Market with two very expensive copies of *The Scarlet Letter*; he had Rick, the gunman, to keep him company; the truck, like the clothing, was borrowed.

For the time being no one spoke in the back of the fish truck. Too much had happened; there had been too much talking. All three of them needed the silence of the journey, for a time at least. Stefan's thoughts, as the truck pulled away from Fulton Market, were ones he didn't want to share, not yet anyway. He had been right that Longie Zwillman had more to say about the Hotel Theresa.

Zwillman had walked down to the Fulton Market coffee stall with him and had told him then. Jimmy Palmer was dead. It seemed a bad idea to let Kate know right now, let alone Niamh; he left it to Stefan to decide when was a good time and what story to tell. When Stefan asked Longie Zwillman why he was doing all this, Zwillman shrugged, as if he wasn't really doing anything at all, then he said it was because John Cavendish had given his word. Someone had to honour that.

'So I'm honouring it, Sergeant. Aren't you doing the same?'

'Why do you care about IRA ciphers? That's what you wanted too –'

'We all pick up shit on our shoes. It's spread pretty even these days. The captain and me just found out what was on our shoes was the same shit.'

*

280

The Harlem police weren't pleased that detectives from downtown had shot a Negro on their patch. Not that anyone was very bothered about a dead black man. It had no significance; but if there was a Negro to be shot above 125th Street the Harlem cops preferred it if a black officer did the shooting; it didn't cause so much resentment that way. Longie Zwillman had got it straight from a detective in the 26th Precinct; Jimmy Palmer was shot while resisting arrest, though everyone knew he'd been shot for fucking Dominic Carroll's wife. He had been shot by a Headquarters detective of course, but everyone knew that the man who gave the order was Captain Aaron Phelan.

17. The Waldorf-Astoria

Micheál Mac Liammóir took a long time getting himself ready that morning. He lay in the bath for almost an hour. He shaved meticulously and precisely. He oiled his hair with Murray's Pomade and dabbed himself with the bergamot-scented cologne that should have soothed his temper but only gave it a sharper, citrus edge. He paused only once in the five minutes he spent staring into the mirror, brushing his teeth; it was to stretch out his foot to crush a cockroach that had been unwise enough to scuttle out from under the bath. He laid out a pale blue soft-collared shirt and a crimson tie, the pair of lemon silk socks Hilton Edwards, his partner and co-producer, had bought him at Bergdorf Goodman for luck (unsuccessfully as it turned out); also the pale grey suit that he liked because it was slightly too big and made him look thinner than he really was. He dressed with the intensity he gave to the delivery of words on stage; he retied the tie three times. Then he picked up the black Malacca cane that offered both elegance and assistance with his sciatica, and went out. He was furious. Hilton Edwards, ever patient, but aware that today patience would not be rewarded, had already gone, leaving his lover in the bath, deciding that a morning at the Museum of Modern Art would be good for his soul. The other actors had gone too, because someone would have to take the blame, and their director wouldn't care who it was.

Emerging from the Markwell on to 49th Street Mac Liammóir didn't walk west, to the diner that had become the company's green room. He might be hung for a ham here, but not for being cheap. He turned towards 8th Avenue, then walked the bottom end of Central Park to the Waldorf-Astoria. He ordered eggs Benedict and a bottle of champagne. When the waiter offered him a copy of *The New York Times* he shook his head curtly. Yesterday had been the first night of *John Bull's Other Island*. He had sat with the cast in Sardi's till midnight, waiting for the first editions to arrive. He would not be reading that mealy-mouthed bollocks of a review again.

Mac Liammóir had often felt that disaster was preferable to faint praise; anything was. He abhorred the whimper of ordinariness and that was what lurked between the bland platitudes of the gobshite from *The New York Times*. He should have seen it coming. A man who wore a cravat in Manhattan could hardly be trusted. Probably *John Bull's Other Island* had been a mistake. Shaw thought his plays were about ideas, but they were about words; words that needed to be juggled like knives in some kind of frenetic circus act. And if the knives weren't as sharp as hell, then it didn't work. The *Times* review stuck in his craw; he couldn't get the damned thing out of his head. 'Although the Dublin Gate Theatre company is amiable, it is not brilliant enough to make so much talk continuously incandescent.'

He looked round at the wealthy breakfasters. What could you say about a city whose claim to fame was its height?

It swam in a sea of dollar bills, proclaiming its endless vulgarity as the future of the world. At least Ireland wasn't vulgar; nobody had the money for it. He drained the glass of champagne then laughed, because he loved this city and everything it was. When petulance and spite were about to consume him it was his ability to laugh at himself that brought him to earth. It was then that he thought of Owen Harris in a police cell at the end of Manhattan. He needed something to do. He called the waiter and held up the two-thirds-full bottle of Moët.

'Could you put this in a bag?'

'A bag, sir?' The waiter looked at him, puzzled.

'You do that very well,' said Mac Liammóir. 'Do you act?' The waiter looked more puzzled.

'I want to take it with me. Isn't a brown bag the usual thing?'

'I don't think we have brown bags, sir.'

'You surprise me. I'm sure the Markwell has brown bags.'

He smiled. The waiter smiled too, and went to find a brown bag.

Clutching the champagne in the brown paper bag, Micheál Mac Liammóir strolled through the morning crowds on 7th Avenue to the Hotel Pennsylvania. Stefan Gillespie wasn't there. Mac Liammóir thought nothing of this, but having set his mind on doing something he carried on down to Centre Street and Police Headquarters. It was a long walk, but he was enjoying it. He had a new sense of the size and shape of the city. He liked the way it dwarfed him and absorbed him at the same time. Its scale shouldn't have been human and yet it was, entirely and utterly human. When he arrived at Police Headquarters he was surprised to find himself in a foyer that was a smaller version of the Waldorf-Astoria. Whatever lay behind the dark front desk, the NYPD at least possessed a halfway decent chandelier.

Mac Liammóir had been important for as long as he could remember. Even as a child, before anybody else realised he was important, he had commanded his family's attention effortlessly, with the same authority that he commanded a stage. His explanation of who he was didn't amount to much, but he mentioned the Irish consul general and Sergeant Gillespie. It was enough to establish that he had some official role. His own expectation that he would see Owen Harris was enough to convince Inspector Twomey; in fact the inspector didn't even pause to be convinced. Wasn't it enough that your man was Irish, and so self-evidently a man of some importance?

It was the same bare room that Stefan Gillespie had sat in with Owen Harris. Now Micheál Mac Liammóir sat across the table from the fresh-faced matricide. They drank from white cups, stained brown with coffee. Harris had not asked why the director of the Gate had arrived with champagne. He smiled vacantly. Mac Liammóir couldn't remember why he'd come. It had been a moment of responsibility perhaps; the man did work for him. Or maybe it was just curiosity. Charlie Mawson did keep talking about it. That was the problem. And Mawson really didn't believe Owen Harris had killed his mother. As Mawson was one of the better actors he had in New York, the Gate director had found himself listening to the conversation more than he wanted; it had lodged in his brain. Mawson was a fool when it came to pretty boys, and Harris was pretty, but he was no bad judge of character.

'You're all right then, Harris?'

'The bed's rather uncomfortable. That is getting on my nerves.'

'Well, it won't be for long. Do you know when you're going back?'

'I'm not quite sure. Sergeant Gillespie –'

'I gather you're flying?'

Mac Liammóir felt the inanity of the question. Harris ignored it.

'How did the first night go, sir?'

'Oh, well, it went.'

The Gate director's lips were tight; the conclusion was obvious. It hadn't gone as well as it should have done. But Owen Harris was not someone who could read what other people were thinking, however obvious.

'How was the grasshopper?'

Mac Liammóir didn't know what he meant.

'I was the grasshopper understudy. I did think Helen did it rather too quietly. It's got to have some feeling. Not just a noise. I felt you could have got rather more out of it, if you don't mind me saying, Mr Mac Liammóir.'

Harris put down his champagne and coughed, clearing his throat.

He made a shrill clucking, sucking sound with his lips.

'Then he says, "Ah, it's no use, me poor little friend. If you could jump as far as a kangaroo you couldn't jump away from your own heart an' its punishment. You can only look at Heaven from here: you can't reach it!"'

He made the noise again, louder this time, his face red with effort.

'Do you see?'

Micheál Mac Liammóir nodded, now wishing he hadn't

come. He shifted in his chair and grimaced, as a pain suddenly shot through his leg.

'Are you all right, sir?'

'A bit of sciatica. It comes and goes, like an old friend.'

'You must see my father then. He's quite the expert on the sciatica front. I can take you to Pembroke Road myself. He'd be delighted. Moloch's not keen on the theatre, but anybody who's somebody is always welcome!'

Harris chuckled, as if sharing a joke.

Mac Liammóir picked up the bottle of champagne and poured the last dregs into the cups. He had always found that anything that smacked of taking responsibility for anything, let alone anybody, was usually a mistake.

'Sciatica is an indefinite term applied to conditions associated with pain in the region of the sciatic nerve. The public think that sciatica is a disease of itself, of course, and if you tell a patient you wish to examine his pelvis, hip joint, or his bowel, he will invariably inform you that he cannot understand the importance of being examined for other more serious diseases, of which his trouble and pain is, in reality, only a symptom.'

Owen Harris's words came in a voice quite different from the one Micheál Mac Liammóir had been listening to; it was deeper, more resonant, richer. Harris was not a good actor, by any standards, but the Gate director had no doubt that this was the voice of Doctor Cecil Harris, his father, and probably a very good imitation. When Harris stopped it was with a slightly sheepish grin, like a child waiting to be congratulated for a party trick.

'I can do the whole lecture, you know!'

Mac Liammóir quickly asked Harris if there was anything he needed. He wasn't sure how long Doctor Harris's lecture on sciatica lasted, but from the pride he could hear in the son's voice he suspected it might be a considerable time. But the question got no answer. As Harris drained the last, flat champagne from the porcelain cup, he wasn't even listening.

'It's the fuss Moloch won't be able to abide. Name in the papers and all that. I think they'll be respectful though, given who he is. "First Moloch, horrid King besmear'd with blood!"' He laughed. 'I'm sure you know all that. "Of human sacrifice, and parent's tears." Medea and I used to shout it at the moon, dancing in the garden, whenever there'd been another great, fat, screaming, Moloch row! A kind of "Hubble, bubble", and we were the two witches, sending him into the fires of hell! I always had too many parts to play though. "Death take you all, you and your father!" That was me too!'

Again a shared joke, almost a shared past, as if Mac Liammóir was on the inside of it all. The actor was distinctly uncomfortable now: 'besmear'd with blood', 'human sacrifice', 'death take you all'. Harris spoke as if he was remembering a fond and funny family picnic. And it was barely a week ago that his mother had been hacked to death, in almost everyone's view by him. The smile stayed on his lips briefly, then he looked at Mac Liammóir.

'I didn't do it. I hope you know that, Mr Mac Liammóir.'

'I know that Charlie Mawson is very sure –'

'It is a mess though, isn't it? A really frightful mess.'

Harris spoke over Mac Liammóir; he didn't want a conversation.

'And of course I do keep wondering about the Lost Boys.'

The Gate director said nothing. He didn't know why the man was talking about *Peter Pan*. By now he knew who

Medea and Moloch were, and he had some sense of the world Owen Harris inhabited, somewhere in the hatred and mutual dependency his parents fed off. He had been the glue that held them together; the stick they never stopped beating each other with. He still looked like a boy, but not a boy who had never grown up, thought Mac Liammóir; a boy who had grown up a very, very long time ago and had spent his childhood pretending that he hadn't. He was still pretending now.

'I'm sure they'll be all right. Spring's here,' continued Harris, as if Mac Liammóir knew what he was talking about. 'I always left out anything we had – wood, a bit of turf. They're sharp you know, especially Slightly. When I think of some of the idiots who surrounded me at Shrewsbury! Well, that was a mistake from the start. Medea always thought so. I'm sure Moloch did eventually, though he could hardly say so. An English public school was the worst of all worlds. The only thing it taught me was that I didn't belong in England and I was just English enough not to fit in Ireland. Money well spent! Slightly is the bright one. Tootles is very Tootles. I've always felt he'll miss out on anything that comes his way. Not that anything's likely to come his way, or Slightly's. But if you're warm, at least if you're warm –'

Micheál Mac Liammóir took a cab back uptown, but as he passed the Hotel Pennsylvania he got out. He left a ticket for the play at reception for Stefan Gillespie, not because he wanted him to see it, but because he wanted to see the Garda sergeant. With the exception of Charlie Mawson there was nobody who knew about the murder of Leticia Harris who didn't believe her son had killed her. The consul general had said as much. It was probably true. The boy was clearly disturbed, and that disturbance had its roots in his relationship with his mother and father; it took only minutes of listening to him to see that. But it troubled the actor that no one seemed to have any doubts. He sensed that nobody in Ireland was asking any questions.

It wasn't that he knew what questions needed to be asked; he had no idea. But he was a man who was often full of doubts; easy certainties troubled him. He felt that Owen Harris believed in his own innocence if nobody else did. He could put it no more strongly. Maybe it was because the poor boy was mad enough not to know what he had done. Maybe it was true; he hadn't killed her. If it was true it troubled Mac Liammóir how easy it would be to ignore that, because of who he was, because of what he was. When he stood in an Irish court no one would like what he was; it already made him guilty of something. More than anything it troubled Micheál Mac Liammóir what a small step it might be from that unspoken guilt to a noose.

18. Route Eleven

Through most of the previous night the fish truck from Fulton Market had carried Stefan Gillespie, Kate O'Donnell and Niamh Carroll into Upstate New York. It took the Holland Tunnel out of New York City, under the Hudson River, into Jersey City and Newark. It drove west along state roads to the Delaware River and into Pennsylvania where it picked up Interstate 11 at Scranton and finally turned north towards Lake Ontario. South of Binghamton it crossed the line back into New York State, and rattled on through Cortland to Syracuse. East, in the darkness, were the Appalachians and New England; west, the Great Lakes and the Plains and all of America.

In the back of the truck Stefan, Kate and Niamh had little idea where they were going. They tried to sleep and sometimes they managed, for minutes rather than hours. The cold and the rattle and sway of the truck would always wake them, even on the Interstate.

It was completely black; there was nowhere for any light to come in. Only the flame from a lighter or a match and then the dim glow of cigarettes occasionally lit the boxes that were piled up all round them. The fish that had been emptied out had been fresh enough. The smell of the sea it left behind wasn't so unpleasant, but there was a deeper, rancid stench behind it that every so often filled the air and sent a wave of nausea through them. That was when they all, as one, reached for another cigarette. They would be long hours travelling north.

Three times Longie Zwillman's men, Sam and Rick, stopped at a gas station and brought them hot coffee, always driving on and turning off the road to find a dirt track and some trees before they opened up the back and let them out. For ten minutes they could walk a little bit of warmth back into their legs. No gas station pump man or passing driver could remotely know who they were, but it was better that no one saw them. They were a strange cargo for a truck still dripping out melting ice and rank with the smell of fish. It was only after they turned off the Interstate beyond Syracuse, heading for Oswego County, that Niamh went up front to direct Sam to the Lake Ontario shore, through fields and woods and the sleeping towns of Mexico and Texas. Stefan and Kate stayed where they were in back.

Niamh said very little that night. She was absorbed in her own thoughts and it was best to leave her there. Stefan and Kate wanted to know where they were, how far there was to go; she seemed to want to know nothing. It was enough that it was happening and somehow simply letting it happen was the easiest way to deal with it. Talking about the journey across the lake and getting to the boat in Montreal made her anxious. She didn't want to think ahead, even a few hours ahead; the fear of being snatched back into empty captivity was never far away. Being with Jimmy Palmer had pushed it from her mind, but it was all around her again now, and much closer without him. She did what she could to shut it out, and whatever she was thinking about, it kept her calm at least. She had spent eighteen months in a room on her own, barely speaking to anybody except the nurses and cleaners who came in and out to do their work. She was used to silence.

Some of the time Stefan Gillespie and Kate O'Donnell talked, but they avoided what was about to happen; they both knew Niamh wasn't sleeping. They asked each other questions, aware that it was something to do to pass the time, but aware too that they were interested in the answers in a way that was about more than passing time.

In the throwaway shorthand Stefan was good at, Kate found out about the farm at Kilranelagh, and Tom, and David and Helena, and Maeve's death, so long ago now that there was nothing really to say about it except that it explained some things and not others. She felt that the reasons he had stopped working in Dublin as a detective four years earlier were brushed away too quickly; they were about more than a decision to be with his son. She sensed too, with surprising ease, the restlessness that lay behind his jokes about a country policeman's life.

When the conversation stopped and they tried to sleep, before it started again because they couldn't sleep, she thought he was comfortable with the way he talked about himself, and she liked that. But she wondered if the words didn't come too easily, because he wasn't really talking about himself; he was talking about his son, or his parents, or where he lived, or telling a funny story about missing cattle or raiding dance halls that was almost too well rehearsed. Maybe he was trying to keep her spirits up, but he talked more than he needed to for the kind of man she felt he was, as if he was offering her a surface there wasn't as much behind as he might have liked. But he did keep her spirits up. And she liked his voice. Several times, as she dozed off for a moment, she woke abruptly to find her head on his shoulder. The first few times she moved away, shuffling sideways along the back wall of the truck, but after a while she only lifted her head. She felt better for being beside him, better for feeling him there.

If there were things Kate O'Donnell didn't talk about, they seemed obvious enough to Stefan for the most part. She didn't talk about her sister because her sister was there. She talked a bit about growing up in Dún Laoghaire, with a mother and father who had both been teachers and with brothers and a sister who were all a lot older. If there was more to say about that and about how she felt when, quite suddenly, they had all left home, it wasn't said. Her words didn't disguise the fact that it had been sudden and that she remembered that still. It had mattered when she found herself the only child in a house that was unnaturally empty. He was an only child; it wasn't something he could ever feel in the same way.

She told him she had left school and had gone to the National College of Art; she had worked as a designer and artist for a time with an advertising agency; for a time at the Gaiety Theatre; for a time dressing windows at Clery's in O'Connell Street. When the opportunity to work at the Irish Pavilion at the World's Fair had come she had fought hard to get it, harder than she had ever fought for anything.

As Stefan tried to understand her, in the gaps in their talking, he knew she had been driven by more than her career. It was the woman who sat on the other side of her, staring into the darkness.

For both Stefan and Kate the intermittent conversation was something to do, but the time each of them spent piecing together what the other said wasn't idle. There was a kind of intimacy in the darkness; they felt closer to each other than anything they talked about warranted. And there were things both of them waited for and didn't hear. If there was a woman in Stefan Gillespie's life, Kate O'Donnell had no sense of it; if there was a man in Ireland, waiting for her, he had no sense of that either. The unspoken, unanswered questions seemed foolish enough. And as the long time-out-of-time journey came to an end they each pushed them away.

It had already started to get light as the fish truck turned off Interstate 11. The land was flat; a thin mist hung in the air. It was very quiet; for a time even the birds had not yet started to sing. There were empty, straight dirt roads and small fields backed by clumps of woodland, barely in leaf, fragile and ghostly in the mist. There were clapboard houses strung out along the highways where no one was awake. The only eyes that watched the fish truck belonged to Holstein cows. The town of Mexico was empty too as they drove through it. Three miles on they turned off the road that ran from Mexico to the lake, just before the boatyards and the jetties along the Little Salmon River at Texas.

Niamh Carroll knew the roads well enough to find the way but something about being there had increased her anxiety. She was in the cab with Sam and Rick, and even they felt it. It wasn't a happy place for her; she was only remembering how unhappy it was now that she saw it.

The house was at the end of a wedge of flat, wooded land between the Little Salmon River and the small, brown stream that was called Sage Creek. The dirt track ran in a perfectly straight line through the trees, which were thick here, until it reached the lake. Then Ontario stretched out across the horizon like a sea. The track turned right along the shore. There was a small painted sign that read 'Loch Eske'; it was the name of the tiny lake in Donegal where Dominic Carroll had fished with his grandfather as a child.

The truck stopped outside the house. Rick opened the back up; Stefan and Kate climbed down, blinking in the morning light. Niamh was on the wooden veranda, kneeling down. She pulled up a loose plank and reached down to produce a key. She made no move to go in. She stood with the key until Kate took it from her and opened the front door; she didn't go inside until her sister grabbed her hand and pulled her into the house. Longie Zwillman's men said their good-byes, tired themselves now, and the truck turned in front of the house to make the long journey back to New York.

'One in the morning at the jetty, with a light,' shouted Sam. 'You got it?'

'They are going to be there?'

It was said with a smile, but Stefan still wanted the reassurance of the answer. This was a long way from anywhere. There was no phone and there was no way out. They were completely reliant on people they didn't know.

'If Mr Zwillman says they'll be there, they'll be there!'

Then the truck was gone. It disappeared almost as soon as it pulled into the trees, and by the time Stefan reached the door the noise had gone too. He looked around. The only sound now was the sound of birds. As long as the boat came it was a good place to wait. No one would see them here.

The house smelt damp and musty; no one had been here for a long time. It was a small, two-storey clapboard house that had stood beside the lake for maybe a hundred and fifty years. Farmers and fishermen had lived there, but now it was the vacation home of a man who almost never used it. There were two rooms downstairs and three bedrooms upstairs. A single-storey extension had been added to one side. There was no electricity, and in the years when Dominic Carroll had brought his first wife and his young sons there, he had made a point of keeping everything as simple as possible; it reminded him of where he came from.

The years when his sons had cared about the simple life hadn't been very many; and after his wife's death he hadn't cared much about it either. He had visited the house by the lake as a shrine, not a home. When he finally remarried and brought Niamh there, it was where he discovered that he had made a mistake. It was where Niamh discovered that she had married a man who wanted her for two things; to ornament his life in New York when required and to provide the sex he despised himself for wanting with any woman other than his dead wife. Some of those thoughts were in Niamh Carroll's mind as she stood in the living room.

Kate clattered back down the stairs just as Stefan came in. 'There's a stove in the kitchen and there's a fire in here. Niamh says there's wood in a shed behind the house. Please God, let's have some heat!'

'I'll get some in,' said Stefan. He walked across to the fireplace and picked up a wicker basket. He turned to Niamh. 'What about oil lamps? We'll need to show lights tonight. How far is this jetty from the house?'

'It's just through the trees. There's a boathouse there.' Niamh answered quite brightly suddenly, pulling herself from the past into the present. Getting away was all that mattered.

She moved across to the stairs. There was a small door underneath them. 'There's a cellar. There should be lamps down there and some drums of kerosene.' She unbolted the door and pushed it open, then walked to the sofa in front of the fireplace and sat down. She laid her head back and closed her eyes; she would try to sleep.

'You can get out to the back from here,' said Kate.

She walked through a door into the kitchen; Stefan followed.

'Is Niamh all right?'

'She doesn't like being here. I don't know why, just unhappy memories. It's Jimmy too, leaving him behind. She felt safe with him. I know she thinks there's some way they can be together, somewhere. She was talking about London. I know he played there. It's not that easy, is it?'

She shrugged, shaking her head. He didn't reply.

He walked to the door and went outside. It wasn't that easy, a black man and a white woman. It was a lot harder when the black man was dead.

There was soon a fire in the big grate in the living room and there was the smell of ham and eggs frying on the stove in the kitchen, and the aroma of coffee driving out the mustiness of the house and the stink of fish that was in their nostrils. Rick had picked up some food at a gas station near Syracuse, and they sat round the living room fire eating the ham and eggs and drinking the coffee, as much to get rid of the cold that was still in their bones as because they were hungry.

They all felt more alive, even Niamh. Warmth made the house more comfortable, but it was full of things she didn't want to think about again. Kate could feel some of it, but she had no idea how deep it went for her sister. This was Dominic's place; even the musty smell reminded Niamh of him. Upstairs the master bedroom was still as it had been when his wife Maureen was alive. When he had brought Niamh here she had been allowed to sleep in it; when he wanted sex he took her to another room.

'There are some bedclothes in a cupboard upstairs,' said Kate. 'I can air them and make up the beds. We should try and get a bit of sleep. I don't know how long we'll be on the lake tonight. We all need to get some rest.'

'I'll stay down here.' Niamh curled up on the sofa again.

'I'll look at the jetty.' Stefan got up.

Behind the house the grass sloped gently down to a line of trees along Lake Ontario. As Stefan Gillespie walked towards the lake shore the sky was clear above him. There had been cloud earlier, but now most of it had gone. The spring sun was warm on his face for a moment. The birdsong was loud and full of life. Among the trees the grass petered out into mud-grey, pebbly sand, and the sand disappeared into the lapping water of the lake. To the right, along the shore, there was another building, a wooden boathouse, almost at the water's edge; there was a rickety jetty reaching out a dozen yards into the lake.

He stepped on to the boards of the jetty and went to the end. The tree-lined shores of Mexico Bay stretched out on either side, but across the water he thought he could see something dark on the horizon; it was land, and it had to be Canadian land. He could have no idea how long it would take but it didn't seem so far. Everything depended on Longie Zwillman and Longie's contacts in Canada. They would be, presumably, in the same line of work as Zwillman himself, what the gangster referred to as 'business'. But their business wasn't Stefan's business, not here anyway, and whatever it was that motivated Longie Zwillman and had drawn him and John Cavendish into an unlikely alliance, he seemed nothing if not reliable.

He turned back to the boathouse, set just back from the jetty. Inside it was dark. There were three boats; two rowing boats and a small dinghy. There was a workbench at the back of the boathouse; oars hung from the wall behind it; there was a heavy, padlocked sail chest. None of it looked like it had been used in a very long time. Underneath the workbench, rusty and dust-and-dirt-covered from years of neglect, were two children's scooters, a toy wheelbarrow, a tricycle with one wheel, a bundle of small fishing rods tied together. He turned round and walked out to the light.

In the cellar beneath the house Stefan was filling lamps with kerosene. When he had returned, with another basket of wood, Niamh was asleep on the sofa. Kate was in the kitchen washing the dishes they had used. He heard her footsteps above him now, walking towards the fire, throwing on more wood.

'Sorry, I didn't mean to wake you.'

It was Kate's voice. Underneath the rugs the floor was bare boards on joists. He could have been in the room.

'I wasn't really asleep, just dozing,' said Niamh.

'I've made up some beds. Try and get some proper rest.'

'No, it's bad enough being down here.'

'What do you mean?'

'It doesn't matter, Kate. It's not somewhere I want to be. The first time I came I thought it was beautiful. Within a day I hated it. That's when I found out I could never be anything to Dominic because I wasn't her – Maureen. He'd always been kind. That stopped. Here. The first time we –'

'Come on, sis.' He heard Kate walk over to the sofa.

'You don't have to think about it any more. In two days we'll be on a boat, heading home.'

'I don't want to go upstairs. I used to think she was still up there! I thought she'd be mounted on the wall above the bed, like one of his fish.'

'Niamh, that's terrible!' laughed Kate.

Her sister laughed too; Stefan could hear she had to work at it.

More wood was thrown on the fire.

'Pity to waste those clean sheets though,' said Niamh, giggling now.

'What?'

'So where is he, Kate?'

'Niamh, don't be so stupid!'

'Well, you seem to like him. I do know when you like someone.'

'He's down in the cellar.' Kate lowered her voice, but he could still hear her perfectly. He smiled. 'So shut up! He'll be back up any minute.'

'Well, he's nice enough.'

'I don't believe you sometimes. He's nice enough! Is that all it takes?'

'What do you want it to take?'

He had finished what he was doing. The lamps were filled. But he stood still where he was. It was hard not to want to hear the answer to that.

'Anyway, of course I like him. He didn't have to do this.'

'That's not why you like him. You know that perfectly well.'

'Whether I like him or not, whatever the reasons,' snapped

Kate, 'I've got more important things to think about now.'

'Are there more important things to think about, little sis?' Niamh's laughter was more natural now. She was enjoying teasing her sister. It was a moment of something between them that hadn't happened in many years.

'At least you sound like Niamh again.' Kate's voice was happier. He knew she was smiling. 'Let's say I'd rather get to know Mr Gillespie first, not jump into bed and then find out if he's worth knowing afterwards. Shh!'

Stefan had moved, just a fraction, but Kate had heard something.

'What?'

'What's he doing down there? Do you think he can hear?'

He moved quickly and quietly to the stairs and clumped noisily up.

He pushed open the door from the cellar.

'I've got three lamps. I need to get the wicks trimmed right and make sure they're working for tonight.'

As he carried the lamps through to the kitchen Kate eyed him suspiciously, not at all sure he hadn't heard something. He looked slightly awkward, but he kept walking. The lamps clattered on to the kitchen table.

'Don't you think you ought to help him trim his wicks?'

'Niamh!' Kate hissed at her sister.

She just giggled, then lay back on the sofa and closed her eyes.

Kate was standing at the back of the house, looking out towards the lake. It was late afternoon. West along the lake the sun was low in the sky. Stefan was loading logs into the basket again. He looked up from the barn door, watching her.

Niamh had been talking about Jimmy Palmer again. The idea that there was some way she could be with him was still pushing its way through all the confusion in her head. She kept coming back to London. London was a place where people didn't care what you did. There were parts of London where you could live how you wanted to live, just like there were parts of New York. Jimmy had played in London before, when he was working on the boats. He'd played in Soho; he knew people there.

Kate didn't think this was any time to argue with her sister. Anything that kept her positive, anything that kept fear away, anything that made her strong, anything that gave her purpose, was something she would listen to.

Stefan understood that, but he knew he had to tell Kate what had happened to the trumpeter. Maybe as soon as they got across the lake, when they were in Canada; maybe that was when Niamh had to know. Or maybe he should say it now, so at least Kate understood. He couldn't go on nodding every time Niamh mentioned Jimmy Palmer. Kate would have to make the decision about telling her; it couldn't be his. There wouldn't be a right time, but she would know what was the best time. He walked over the grass towards her.

'I wish we could get on with it,' she said.

'I guess it has to be night time.'

'I know.'

'How's Niamh?'

'She's OK. Up and down. I don't know really, I mean inside.'

He nodded. Whatever was inside her, it was a mess.

'I think it'll take her a long time. The truth is, I only know a little bit of it. What he did to her. I don't know why he married her at all. I know she wanted security more than anything, a place to be safe. She thought he would give her that. It probably wasn't very clever, a man twice her age. But she thought he'd look after her, and she could give him, I don't know, companionship, affection. It wasn't enough, for either of them. He was, he was just – it was as if he felt nothing but contempt for her. She did try –'

Kate was crying, quietly. Her sister's pain had become very close.

'She's still such a long way away.'

'It'll be over soon,' said Stefan; he knew it wasn't much to say. He knew it wasn't the truth either. One journey would be over, but only one.

'I don't know. I look at her and I don't know when it'll ever –'

He knew it wasn't the time to tell her about Jimmy Palmer now.

She looked up at him.

He stepped closer and put his arms round her.

She pressed her body against his. She needed him to hold her.

It was a long kiss that neither of them wanted to end.

She broke away and laughed awkwardly.

They looked at each other uncertainly, unsure.

'So what now?' he said quietly, looking into her eyes.

'I don't know, Stefan.'

'Well, since you went to the trouble of airing all those sheets –'

'You bastard, you did hear!'

'Well, maybe a bit,' he smiled.

She nodded, and for another moment they looked at each other.

'All right, so what now?' she said.

'You did say we should try and get some proper rest.'

She took his hand and they walked back to the house.

*

It was almost midnight. Niamh Carroll stood on the veranda of Loch Eske, looking into the darkness. Clouds had rolled in off the lake; the sliver of a crescent moon that appeared occasionally between them gave almost no light. There was an owl in the trees nearby, waiting for something too; there was the shriek of a vixen further away along the shore; there was the rhythmic lapping of Lake Ontario, almost too quiet to hear.

Niamh was smoking a cigarette; she felt easier now. Soon the boat would come. And across the lake the journey home would begin. Earlier that day the idea of crossing that water in the darkness had been another fear to add to all the fears she carried with her, not just the simple fear of being taken back to a room with bars, but the fears she had no names for that had broken her hope and her spirit down the years. Those were the fears that had driven her into Dominic Carroll's arms in the first place. The life that had drifted away from her because she had always thought there must be more; loves she had snatched at too hungrily, too many times, that had lifted her up and then crushed her; the empty places where she had left her family and her childhood; the alcohol and the drugs that had made being awake like sleeping, and yet never let you sleep.

When all she had wanted was a safe place to be, and someone strong to put a wall around her, Dominic Carroll seemed to have that strength. She only met him because she had carried messages for the IRA, for no great reason except that another man she thought she loved asked her to and because, for a time, she thought it was something that mattered when nothing mattered. She had met Dominic on the boats she worked on, as he travelled back and forward to Europe. He had been kind; he had been funny. He had trusted her; he had made her feel what she was doing for the IRA did matter after all, that there was something bigger than her own obsessions and fears.

In New York he had taken her to the theatre, to restaurants like the Rainbow Room. He was always a gentleman when every man she met expected to sleep with her for the price of a drink. He was a decent man; a man who revered his dead wife. She liked him for that and she had had no intention of replacing the first Mrs Carroll. He would give her the safety and strength she needed; she would try to take away the loneliness in his heart. And when he asked her to marry him, it seemed a way out of the darkness that was always threatening to swallow her. It was only when they were alone together for the first time that she saw what she had never seen, that marriage was simply his way of paying her. There would be no friendship, no companionship; what mattered was how she looked on his arm and satisfied him in a dark bedroom, in a furtive, loveless act of sex.

She stubbed out the cigarette and immediately lit another one. She wasn't afraid of crossing the lake now. It felt right that it was taking her away, not just from her imprisonment, but away from this place, the place she first understood the man she had married. It would be a journey that would begin in the dark, but there would be light at the end of it. She didn't know what would happen. She didn't know what it would mean to see her mother and father again. But Kate had found her; she had found Kate. It was a beginning. And all these new things, all these new questions, were about decisions and choices. They were things to be afraid of, but they were real; they carried hope in a way nothing had for a long time. She heard her sister laughing in the house, calling to Stefan; ordinary things, ordinary laughter. She smiled and took a deep breath.

Then she frowned.

In the darkness along the bay, right at the end of Lakeview Road, where it turned into the County Road, there were lights, flickering through the trees. It was still too far for the sound to carry, but she knew it was a car.

And there was only one place to drive along that road.

19. Mexico Bay

Niamh burst into the house. Kate was packing the few clothes they had into a bag. Stefan was walking lazily in from the kitchen with a cup of coffee.

'There's a car coming. Someone knows we're here!'

Kate and Stefan stared at her. It had been so quiet all day. They had seen nothing, heard nothing. They had all felt it was over; even Niamh had started to feel she was safe. Helplessness and terror were in her eyes again.

'There's nowhere else to go,' she said. 'They're coming here!'

'How long before the boat comes?' Kate pushed aside the shock.

'Get your coats on,' said Stefan quietly, nodding. It wasn't over, whatever the car meant. 'Go out the back door and get down to the jetty.'

Kate closed the bag. She picked up Niamh's coat from the sofa. She had to help her on with it. Niamh was frozen. Stefan went to the oil lamp on the table and turned it off; he hurried back into the kitchen and put the lamp out in there too. He came back in, carrying it. Now they were standing in the darkness. He put the lamp down and walked to the window. He could see the headlights in the trees clearly, still some way off along the road.

Kate walked to the front door, pulling on her own jacket, and turned the key in the lock. She turned back to pick up the bag and take Niamh's hand, pulling her through into the kitchen. Stefan left the window and followed her. They could hear the sound of the car now. As they moved through into the kitchen the headlights swept across the living room windows and lit up the room behind them. None of them spoke now. The kitchen door was open. Kate and Niamh were already outside, heading to the lake. Stefan came out afterwards. As he caught up with them he suddenly stopped, cursing under his breath. He had forgotten the lamp they needed; it was still inside.

'Behind the boathouse, in the trees. I left the lamp. We have to –'

Kate nodded and ran on with Niamh.

He turned back inside.

He walked quickly, quietly through the kitchen to the living room again. The lights of the car were still on, pointing towards the house, shadow-lighting the room. He reached the table where he had left the lamp they had to signal the boat with. As he picked it up there were voices. Two men were on the veranda, at the door. There was more light on the veranda. One of the men was shining a torch. A key was being pushed into the lock.

'I can't turn it. There's something already in –'

'I've got a back door key, I'll go round there,' said the second man.

Stefan froze. He knew the last voice well enough; he thought he knew the other one too. Footsteps were already moving off the veranda. He might make it out of the back door before the second man got there, but he would be moving across the grass when he came round the side of the house. He wouldn't make it to the trees without being seen. He had no time left to weigh the risk. It was too late; he couldn't get out. He walked to the stairs and opened the door down to the cellar. He stepped in and pulled it shut behind him. As he reached the bottom of the cellar steps footsteps sounded above him, through the kitchen to the living room. The key was turned in the front door and the first man's footsteps creaked across the floor above him.

'The back door was open,' said the man who had let him in. 'There's a fucking fire in the grate! Some bastard's living in the place! Jesus Christ!'

Stefan knew who he was listening to. He had recognised the voice immediately. It was Dominic Carroll. But Carroll seemed surprised to find someone had been in the house. There was no sign he knew who that was. There was no sense that the two men were looking for anybody, expecting anybody to be there. It made no sense but what they'd found was a surprise.

'Fucking hobos! Let's get some lamps on. You take a look round.'

'I'll start upstairs, Mr Carroll. I'll do the house first.'

Now Stefan knew the second man; the voice was Aaron Phelan's.

He heard footsteps climbing the stairs. Meanwhile Carroll's footsteps moved across the floor above him. He was at the table, lighting the lamp. The cellar was solid black. There was nothing to see. Then, looking up to the bottom of the door to the living room now, there was a thin line of light from the lamp. Stefan knew there was a way out of the cellar. A pair of trap doors opened up at the back of the house, outside. He could find his way to it and get it open. He would need to climb up on something, but it wouldn't be difficult. It might make some noise though. He couldn't do it now, but he had to do it soon. Now they were looking through the house. They were bound to come down to the cellar.

He tried to remember what was there. It was big, running almost the length of the kitchen and living room. It was piled high with packing cases, old furniture, empty oil drums, fishing tackle; there was a line of free-standing shelves at one side, full of tools and timber off-cuts and rows of canned food that must have been there for years. He felt his way slowly to the shelves and moved along till he got to the end. He squeezed in behind them and crouched down. As he did so the door from the living room above opened.

There were feet on the narrow stairs; lamplight lit the cellar; then someone moving across the room; the sound of metal and glass. He assumed it was Dominic Carroll. He had come down for more oil lamps; now he was filling a can with kerosene from one of the drums. There were more feet on the steps. Aaron Phelan was coming down too. Stefan reached into his coat pocket. Whatever happened he wouldn't be another Jimmy Palmer. The gun he had been given at Police Headquarters was there.

'There's a bed made upstairs, Mr Carroll. They can't have gone long.'

'Some fucking time to play Goldilocks in my house!'

'What about in here?'

'They must have been down for the lamps. I guess they've run now.'

'I'll look outside,' said the NYPD man. 'If they're still around —'

'Assholes!' muttered Carroll.

'Has this ever happened before?'

'Once Aaron, years ago. I think it was fishermen or a couple of hobos like I said. I remember they made a bigger mess than this lot. Look, just make sure the grounds are clear. If you see anyone, fire in the air, that should see the back of them. But I'd say they'll be on their way now.'

Dominic Carroll handed a lamp to Phelan and the two men walked back up the stairs. The light went with them and as the door to the living room closed the bolt outside slid across. Stefan was undiscovered, but there was still only one way to get out.

As he moved from behind the shelves he heard a car horn sounding outside. There was another vehicle arriving; more people. But whoever they were more people would mean more movement and more noise, and that meant more distraction. It would be cover. He had to use that to get the trap door open. He felt his way along the cellar in the darkness, very slowly, feeling with hands and feet for anything he might knock over, anything that might make any sound. He heard more voices.

'You know Eric Bauer, Mr Carroll.' Aaron Phelan was speaking.

'Good to see you again,' said Carroll. 'We met at the bookshop.'

'It was easier to get to than this!' The voice that answered was a New York voice. 'You said it was the middle of fucking nowhere, Dominic! It is!'

There was polite laughter. These weren't old friends.

'You haven't met Paul Eisterholz though,' continued the captain. 'He's the Bund leader in Brooklyn and Queens. He knows what Eric's men are doing at the World's Fair. Well, the thing's pretty much done, isn't it?'

'It's a real pleasure, Mr Carroll.' The voice was another New York voice, but Stefan came from a German family; he didn't need the name to hear the bit of Germany that was still there, somewhere behind Brooklyn.

'We're not here to talk about any of that, Mr Eisterholz,' said Carroll. 'It's going ahead and it's going to mean big things. It's going to change everything, for all of us, Ireland as well as Germany. But it's out of our hands. Barely anyone on our side even has a whisper of it. That includes people who will be here tonight. So it won't be mentioned. That's how you want it, right?'

'On that matter business is closed, Mr Carroll. Here or anywhere else.' Whatever they were talking about, Eisterholz was more clipped. He didn't seem to like the fact that this unknown issue had been raised at all.

'It's Dominic, please. We're all friends,' replied Carroll.

'You were in Berlin?' continued Eisterholz.

'Yes, I'm not long back.'

'I hope it was successful.'

'I think it was,' replied the Clan na Gael president. 'Very successful.'

There was silence for a moment. Stefan Gillespie could almost feel Carroll and Eisterholz looking at each other. If there were things Eisterholz didn't intend to talk about, he could tell that the details of Dominic Carroll's recent visit to Berlin weren't about to come pouring out now either.

'You'll understand that I was speaking to people at a very senior level of course, Paul. A lot of it concerns our activities in Britain and Ireland.'

In the silence that followed two men had established their importance.

'I'll go and check outside, Mr Carroll,' said Aaron Phelan quietly. 'Before the others get here, OK? Just to make sure everything's in order –'

Stefan heard the policeman's footsteps move to the front door. He had reached the trap door himself. He could feel he was underneath it. But he couldn't open it with the NYPD man outside. He stood in the darkness. He was next to a wooden barrel. His hands moved over it, tracing out its shape. It would do the job. If he stood on the barrel he would be able to reach very easily. When there was more noise he would slide it under the trap door.

'Let's open some whiskey, gentlemen,' said Dominic Carroll.

The three men moved into the kitchen; the voices were still clear.

'You read about Seán Russell's arrest, in Detroit?' Carroll continued.

'I certainly did,' said Bauer. 'That's quite a stir you've made.'

'I was at the station with him when he was arrested. Windsor was the latest stop on the English king's tour of Canada. We only had to say Seán was going there, set up a few secret meetings that weren't very secret, and say we were heading across the Ambassador Bridge. If looks could kill he might have been dangerous, but the British didn't like him being there –'

'It seems to have come off well,' laughed Eisterholz.

Stefan was almost underneath them now. The trap door opened up just behind the kitchen. He could even hear the whiskey pouring into the glasses.

'It was enough. The FBI leaped on him and hauled him in. They've been questioning him about a plot to blow up Georgie that never even existed, which means they've all done their job and everybody's happy. And we're happy too. Because as for the rest of it, Seán's become a hero overnight, for doing nothing! We're up to seventy-two furious Members of Congress now, demanding an explanation and an apology from Roosevelt for trampling on Seán Russell's rights and Irish sensibilities. If they don't get it they won't be at the Congressional reception for the king when he gets to Washington. Not that there'll be much of a reception to turn up for!'

The last words were met with silence again.

'The end of the conversation,' said Eisterholz.

Stefan could feel irritation being held back by the Bund man.

'We don't need to say it a third time, Dominic. We will be in the company of friends tonight but friends can only be trusted so far. Your friends in the IRA, even mine from the Abwehr.'

'Don't sweat, boys. Here's to the future! Sláinte!'

The chink of glasses. The German American returned the toast.

'Sláinte!'

'And I can hear our other guests!' said Dominic Carroll.

Stefan could hear too. There was a third car arriving, and another close behind. The three men left the kitchen. They walked through the living room and went outside. He heard car doors slamming and the sound of new voices. He strained to push the barrel across the cellar floor. It scraped across the cellar floor, but there was no one above to hear it. He climbed on top of it. Reaching up in the darkness, he could feel the two trap doors. His fingers found the bolt that held them shut. He pulled hard. For a moment it wouldn't move. He pushed this time, using both hands. It shot back as the sound of footsteps on the floor above him filled the cellar again.

The floor was shaking slightly. He wasn't sure how many people were in the room now, eight, nine, ten. The buzz of conversation was loud. He was sure it ought to be enough to cover any sound he made opening the flaps and climbing out. But there was a voice he needed to hear first; Captain Aaron Phelan's. The policeman had been outside, looking for signs of intruders. If he was still there now Stefan might be opening the doors in front of him.

'Gentlemen, before we begin!' Dominic Carroll's voice was loud. He was calling the gathering to some sort of order, and the conversation dropped. 'I'd like to introduce Bob Monteith to you. Some of you may not know who he is. If you're Irish you damn well should do!'

There was some laughter.

'Bob lives in Detroit now, but in 1916 he was commanding the Irish Brigade that Irish patriots formed to fight against British imperialism, and to stand alongside Germany in that battle. He was the man Roger Casement chose to land with him from the submarine that brought him from Germany to Banna Strand, to join the Easter Rising. When Roger Casement was betrayed, Bob Monteith escaped. He lives in Detroit now, where he's still fighting for Ireland and still fighting British imperialism. He's one of Father Coughlin's leaders in the Union for Social Justice, and he's a man who knows well what a true friend Ireland has in Germany and its Fuehrer!'

There was a murmur of approval; and scattered applause.

'We're here because we all know war is coming to Europe,

because we know that for the freedom of Ireland, the true freedom of America too, Germany must win and Britain must lose. We're here to do what we have to, to make that happen. But before we chew the fat, Bob has a message from the Shrine of the Little Flower. He brings us all Father Coughlin's blessing.'

There was silence in the room. Stefan knew who Robert Monteith was. He had some idea now of what this meeting really was. Clan na Gael and the IRA, the German American Bund, maybe German Intelligence, maybe the Abwehr man he had met in Central Park. For a moment he thought he heard some words in German.

This was all part of what John Cavendish knew, but only a part of it. Stefan had heard some of it. He didn't know what was happening in this meeting, but he knew what everybody knew. The King of England was on a tour of Canada; after Canada George VI was coming to America, days from now. And somehow there was something about that that wasn't to be talked about here, in front of people joined by nothing except their hatred of Britain. Somewhere in there was what John Cavendish had been scraping away at. Somewhere in there was what he was looking for in IRA ciphers. Somewhere there perhaps was the reason he was dead.

Dominic Carroll had joked about a bomb plot that didn't exist. It wasn't much of a stretch for Stefan to imagine one that did.

The voice that spoke next was an Irish voice. It wasn't an old man's voice, but the fragility of age was in it. There was an American twang too, but Stefan could hear the accent of his own county over it. Monteith was a Wicklow man. He spoke quietly, but there was a sense of excitement and intensity behind it. Stefan heard how much this moment mattered to him.

'Father Coughlin asked me to say these words: My prayers and my blessings are always for peace, but if peace cannot come except by the destruction of everything we hold holy, then we have to stand against the warmongers, against Britain with its capital and its empire, against Jewish gold, against the Red Terror. We have to join together, America and Germany, Germany and Ireland, and all the people of the world who see the evil that eats away at our true democracy, the democracy of faith. Britain cannot be allowed to push America into war, and no true American will stand by and watch as politicians bay for blood. To fight the warmongers is not only our work, it is God's work, and may his light shine upon you all.'

A few murmured amens filtered down into the cellar; feet shuffled, and then the buzz of conversation picked up again in the room over Stefan's head; the floorboards creaked. He had to get out to find Kate and Niamh.

'Find a seat!' Dominic Carroll called out. 'There are more chairs round the house. Aaron, there's a cupboard full of glasses in the kitchen and half a dozen bottles of Bushmills on the table. See to the drinks, will you?'

'OK, Mr Carroll. They're on their way.'

So Phelan was inside; Stefan knew that now. He couldn't wait any longer. He pushed up one of the flaps of the trap door, holding it so that it didn't drop. He pushed the second one open and lowered it as quietly to the ground. He was standing on the barrel now. He pushed the lamp up on to the ground and then levered himself through the opening.

He was outside, at the back of the house, just to one side of the kitchen window. He knelt down and closed the trap

318

doors. He could see Aaron Phelan through the window, taking glasses from the cupboard. He crept forward, out of the pale light thrown out by the lamp in the kitchen, and he walked away, into the trees.

When he reached the boathouse Stefan stopped, looking out at the lake. He could see nothing; he could hear nothing. There was a slight shimmer on the water, but it was just a great stretch of greyness spreading out to meet the greyness of the sky. There was no horizon to see. There was certainly no boat to see. He moved on into the trees beyond the jetty and the boat house. There was a kind of path but after a few yards it stopped. The trees hadn't seemed so thick in daylight. But they were dense now. He had to risk his voice. He was a long way from the house now. He threaded his way into the wood. He called out in a low whisper. It still sounded louder than he wanted it to sound; but it had to be loud enough for Kate and Niamh to hear him.

'Kate!' he hissed. 'Kate! Niamh!'

He waited.

There was only the lapping of the water.

'Where are you? It's time! Come on!'

He heard a noise behind him. He looked round to see Kate. She was holding a heavy iron bar. Niamh stood behind her, dazed and silent still.

'Where the hell have you been?' demanded Kate.

'I couldn't get out. I had to go through the cellar.'

'Is it the police?'

'No.'

'Are they looking for us?'

'No.'

319

'Then who –'

'It doesn't matter. They don't know we're here. I'll tell you later.'

Kate looked at him a moment. She wanted a better explanation than that, but he had to have a reason for not giving it. She knew that. She knew too how hard it was to keep Niamh calm. But she had to know something.

'So what do we do?'

'We can't stay here. If someone came down – we need to get out on to the lake. We can't let the boat come in to the jetty. Once we're away from the shore we can light the lamp. They'll see us. There's a boat we can use –'

He walked away, heading to the lake and the boathouse.

'Come on.'

Kate took Niamh's hand and followed.

'But who was in the car? I'm sure I heard another one too.'

'We haven't got time. It's a kind of party. But it's not our kind.'

The look Stefan shot Kate seemed to tell her, finally, that any more would not help at all, not now; in particular it would not help her sister.

Niamh sat on the edge of the jetty, staring out at the lake that was still her only hope. Kate carried a second oar from the boathouse. Stefan was inside, clearing a path for one of the rowing boats. As Kate put the second oar down beside the first it slipped from her hands and clattered loudly on the boards.

'Shit,' she exclaimed.

Niamh grinned. 'You never were very good with boats.'

'Thanks Niamh, you can do the rowing then!'

It was the first time Niamh had smiled since they had run from the house to the lake shore. Kate bent down and kissed her forehead. As she looked up she found herself looking straight at Aaron Phelan. For a moment she was surprised more than she was shocked or frightened. Stefan had said there were no police. But she knew Captain Phelan. She had met him at the Hampshire House. And as Niamh turned round, she knew him too; he wasn't any policeman, he was her husband's policeman. And he was holding a gun.

'You're a noisy bitch, Miss O'Donnell.'

Kate stood very still. Niamh got up and stood beside her.

'I didn't put two and two together,' said Phelan. 'I was just uneasy. Still checking to make sure there wasn't some drunken hobo round the place. But there was something nagging at me. Sheets! Where the fuck would you find a man who'd break into a house and kip there, and go through the presses looking for sheets to put on the beds? Now it makes sense.' He shook his head, laughing. 'So what you going to do, girls, row to Canada?'

'Does it really matter to you?' said Kate quietly.

'It matters to Mr Carroll, that's the thing. I don't know what he'll want to do. I know what I'd do and there's plenty of water out there to do it in. But Mr Carroll's a lot nicer than me. I'm sure he'll be happy to put you on a boat back to the Emerald Isle and your sister back where she can be looked after. But for the moment, he won't want to be troubled. Since you like it here, you can wait till he's finished his business. I'm sure we'll be able to find something to tie you up with so. But it could be a long night.'

It was only now that Aaron Phelan sensed there was someone behind him, but he didn't have time to find out

321

who it was. The barrel of a Colt Police Positive hit the back of his head and he collapsed.

Stefan Gillespie had crept out from the back of the boat-house, into the trees, and had got behind Phelan. The gaze of fear the NYPD detective had seen on the face of the two women really was about fear, but it was the fear that he would turn round as Stefan inched his way towards him. It was a good job he didn't. Stefan still remembered Jimmy Palmer; he knew Phelan would have fired.

Stefan bent and picked up Phelan's gun. He threw it into the lake.

'Let's get the boat.' His voice was quiet, but urgent now.

He went back into the boathouse. Kate and Niamh followed quickly.

'Niamh, you push it out with me. Kate, see what you can find to smash the bottom of the dinghy and the other boat. There's maybe a hammer on the workbench. Make sure they're holed, that's all. I don't know how long we're going to be sitting out there, but we don't want anybody coming after us.'

Kate hurried over to the bench to get on with the job.

Stefan and Niamh pushed the small rowing boat. It wasn't heavy. The shock of what had just happened, the idea that her husband was there, at the house, hadn't yet found its way into Niamh Carroll's head. The action in front of her was all she could see; what she had to do to get away was all she had room to think about.

The sound of breaking timber echoed through the boat-house as Kate took a hammer and chisel to the other two boats.

The rowing boat was moving now, grating over pebbles and cracked concrete, out towards the water lapping round the lakeside entrance to the boathouse. There was thick mud there and suddenly the keel wouldn't shift. Stefan and Niamh pushed hard, their feet sinking into the mud.

Kate came out to join them. Still the boat wouldn't move. Then abruptly it shot forward, sending the three of them sprawling into the water, laughing. They got up and shoved the boat again and it was floating. Stefan pulled the oars down from the jetty. He held the dinghy as Kate and her sister clambered in, wet and muddy but somehow excited, then he got in himself. He took the oars and pulled away, past the jetty now, out into the lake.

Kate looked back. Niamh looked determinedly at the dark water ahead. She took a deep breath; she felt free.

'We'll keep going until we can't see the shore, then we'll light the lamp.' He looked at his watch. 'Fifteen minutes. Just pray they're coming.'

Kate did pray. Niamh didn't. She knew they were coming.

By the time Captain Aaron Phelan came to the boat had already gone. He couldn't see anything out on the lake. He thought there was a light, but it was a long way out now. There was some mist coming in and the cloud had thickened. What little light there had been had gone. It wasn't going to be easy to explain it to Dominic Carroll. He'd had them there; he'd had a gun on them. And he'd been suckered. He'd been lazy. When he heard the noise of the oar, the last thing he expected to find was the two women he'd been scouring New York for. But when he did he hadn't followed it through. He thought he was only dealing with Kate and Niamh. It wasn't just lazy, it was sloppy. There had to be a man there. Why the hell hadn't he realised that?

As he turned away from Lake Ontario he swept his torch

across the path. He saw something glinting. He bent down. It was a Colt .38 Police Positive Special, short-barrelled. He assumed it had fallen from his hand when he had been hit from behind, but as he picked it up he knew it wasn't his. It was exactly the same, but it wasn't his. He shone the torch on to the barrel. There was a dark mark, and several hairs stuck to it. The gun might not be his, but the blood and the hair were. Whoever had come up behind him had dropped it, or it had fallen from a pocket.

It wasn't an unusual gun of course, at least not if you were a policeman. But it was new, almost brand new. There was no reason why a gun like thousands of police guns should feel so familiar, yet somehow it did. It wasn't an accident it was here. He already knew that it came from Police Headquarters in Centre Street.

20. The Empire State

The small boat bobbed gently about on the lake. Every few minutes Stefan Gillespie pulled on the oars two or three times to keep it where it was. The Canadian boat would be looking for the jetty at Loch Eske; they had to stay as close to it as possible. The mist was heavier now, and in the white silence that surrounded them they would lose any sense of where they were if they drifted out further into Lake Ontario. Kate was in the bow, gazing out at nothing, holding the lamp in front of her. Niamh seemed to be looking out too, but as so often she had retreated inside herself. They said nothing; their voices would carry back to the shore across the water. The minutes passed slowly, until almost half an hour had gone; it seemed much longer.

Then there was a sound.

At first Stefan and Kate could barely distinguish it from the sounds inside their heads; it was so quiet they seemed to hear the beating of their hearts. But the noise was real and it was growing louder. There was light moving through the mist. Kate stood up and held the lantern. They were all shouting, Niamh as well. And then the light was coming towards them, cutting through the haze. They could see a white hull and the shape of a wooden wheelhouse. The engine cut quite suddenly and the boat swung round in front of them. A searchlight beam picked them out, momentarily blinding them. And a man shouted: 'Bonsoir, mes amis, ça va?'

The Elco Cruisette was somebody's pride and joy; inside it was all polished mahogany and brass. If the *Temeraire* had ever carried liquor across the lake during Prohibition, it lived a quieter life now. The two crewmen said little, and when they did say anything there was no reference to what was happening; they might have all been on a tourists' midnight cruise. The men's accents mixed Canada and France; when they spoke to each other they spoke in French. They took Stefan, Kate and Niamh down to the saloon and left them there with a bottle of rum. But the closed-in cabin wasn't where any of them wanted to be and most of the time they sat on deck with the open night around them.

It was another long journey. It took almost five hours, north across the lake past the small islands that marked the end of America, over the invisible border, skirting round Wolfe Island, into an empty corner of the harbour at Kingston.

It had been light for a while, but they saw nothing of the city. A black Hudson waited for them at the dockside and they were soon on the road that followed the St Lawrence River, and the American border, through Ontario and Quebec, to Montreal.

By midday Stefan, Kate and Niamh were in a room in the Ford Hotel on Dorchester Boulevard. It was where the Hudson had brought them. They were asked no questions and they were not asked to register. Whoever Longie Zwillman's friends were, everything had been paid for and there would be no record of their stay at the Ford. They would not be there long anyway. Kate and Niamh went out to buy the suitcases and clothes they needed for the trip home; not only because they needed something to wear but to make sure they looked like the ordinary passengers they were meant to be.

By the time the ravages of the last few days had been brushed off, at least off the surface, there was only an hour to go until the cab came to take the two women to the boat. There would be no dockside goodbyes though. Kate and Niamh felt safe, finally, but it was important that when they got to the boat the faster they moved up the gangway, unnoticed and anonymous in the crowd, the better. So Stefan would not go to see them off. And when he took Kate for a drink in the bar, and left Niamh to finish packing, it wasn't about farewells either; it was to tell her that Jimmy Palmer was dead and to leave her with the task of telling her sister.

Kate understood why he had said nothing before, but she was very quiet. She knew what it would mean to Niamh. The news seemed to cut away anything that Stefan and Kate might have had to say to one another too, and in the end they said very little. What had happened between them at Lough Eske had taken them by surprise; neither of them knew whether it was anything or nothing. It was jammed about with other things, bigger things. It had been a moment of need. Did it have to be more?

Stefan had no explanation to give Kate about Dominic Carroll's presence at the lake. It was better that she and Niamh knew nothing about what was going on. He said it was all to do with Clan na Gael; she didn't want to know more. She had no interest in anything Dominic Carroll did now. He was something to be thrown away, as quickly as possible.

And then Kate O'Donnell and Niamh Carroll were gone; several hours before Stefan Gillespie went to the Gare Windsor for the overnight train to New York they were moving down the St Lawrence towards Quebec and the sea on the *Empress of Canada*, bound for Belfast.

For Stefan, there was no space to wonder about Kate. And for the time being he didn't much want to. He didn't know what it had meant to him; or perhaps he didn't want to think about it because he didn't know what it had meant to her. If there was going to be a time to ask, it would come later.

Now the words he had heard in the cellar at Loch Eske were in his head; he felt the ghost of John Cavendish was still at his shoulder. He phoned the number in New York that Longie Zwillman had given him to use in an emergency. Ten minutes later Zwillman phoned back. What Stefan said was oblique, but the urgency of it was clear.

'When you get back to New York,' said Longie, 'the first thing you need is some fish.'

In the sleeper on the Montreal Limited, Stefan knew he wouldn't get much sleep. He was tired enough, but Dominic Carroll's words had stuck, and the words of Paul Eisterholz, the German-American Bund leader, and the unspoken words that weren't even for an assortment of pro-German and anti-British zealots at the lakeside meeting.

He had had no great interest in George VI's tour of Canada and America, but it was news that had been in the air for weeks, even in Ireland. Now the American newspapers he had bought at Windsor Station were full of it. King George and Queen Elizabeth had crossed the border at Niagara Falls; he was the first reigning British monarch ever to visit America. He had been met by President Roosevelt and he would be moving on to Washington soon, but he would be stopping off in New York first to visit the World's Fair.

The king's itinerary was in *The New York Times*, minute by minute. That was how these things worked. The minutes for the motorcade, the minutes for photographs, the minutes for inspecting the troops, the minutes for admiring the exhibits in the British Pavilion, the minutes for a speech and some more anodyne pleasantries, the minutes for shaking some hands and smiling at children. These things had to run like clockwork.

As he sat in the diner Stefan reflected on the big reception in Washington that would take place several days later; the reception there wouldn't be much point anybody turning up for. If Dominic Carroll's throwaway words meant what they could mean, there might be clockwork, real clockwork, somewhere in the king's New York itinerary.

The Delaware and Hudson train had left Montreal at half past ten; an hour later it crossed the border into New York State at Rouses Point. Stefan would see almost nothing except the night for much of the journey as the train moved south, following the Adirondack Mountains and the Hudson River to New York.

In the sleeper he took out John Cavendish's notebook pages and the copy of *The Scarlet Letter*. He looked at the last entry, the most recent of the IRA dispatches. He followed Niamh Carroll's instructions and got a page number and line from the date at the top of the message. It was page 239; the seventh line. It read: 'There is good to be done! Exchange this false life.' He wrote the first twelve letters at the top of a sheet of paper, then started to write the apparently arbitrary letters of one of the last ciphers Cavendish had obtained in columns underneath them. After an hour of writing and rewriting and transposing he began to see the first few words emerging. It was a short enough message, but it was three o'clock in the morning by the time he had enough of it on paper to make any sense of it.

AGREED. NO MORE DISPATCHES RI IN US. ARMY COUNCIL PLANS ABANDONED. CEARNOGA HAVE IT. ENSURE EVERYTHING DONE TO GET MR HART WATCHED AND ARRESTED TO PROVIDE SIDESHOW. HAPPY HUNTING TO OUR FRIENDS. SO BLACKBIRD RI ABU. JESUS.

Together with the conversation at Carroll's lakeside house that wasn't even for the most approving IRA and pro-German ears, the message had to confirm what Stefan was beginning to believe. There was no indication of when the message had been sent, but from its place in Cavendish's notes it was recent. It was a message from Ireland; it was a reply to instructions from America, maybe from Seán Russell or Dominic Carroll.

He stared out at the darkness and listened to the rattle of the train. This was John Cavendish's 'something big'; the assassination of the King of England in New York. That was what it was. It was hard to think of anything bigger. He took a clean sheet of paper and put it in front of him. He looked at the night again, conscious he was only seeing himself reflected back from the glass. He began to copy out the letters of the next cipher.

When he looked out again two more hours had passed. It was morning and the train was running along the west bank of the Hudson River. On the opposite shore a long, low line of hills followed the river, falling steeply to the water's edge.

It was a wall of trees, deciduous and pine; not all in leaf, but the hardwoods were starting to colour with coming spring. Stefan sat back from the table and looked out. They were not far from New York now but the trees of the Hudson Valley stretched on endlessly it seemed. He knew the oaks and beeches well enough, and the birches and ashes, the red maples too; there were others he couldn't quite name; sugar maples and hickories and wild fruits, and all sorts of pines that didn't grow at home. But it was what it all made in the morning light that held him; little colour yet, but still a tapestry of soft, intense light, mile after mile after mile.

It was enough to push what he had been doing to the back of his head for a time at least. It was enough, however different it was, to take him home to mornings at Kilranelagh and the scruffy ashes and hazels in the valley below the farm. Enough to make him wish he was there with Tom, with his mother feeding the hens, his father bringing in the cattle from the fields and the air still cold enough to mist their breath.

It surprised him how close the Hudson Valley forests took him to Manhattan, but then, very suddenly, there were buildings and factories. The trees were gone; the river was gone. And the train plunged underground into the darkness, to tunnel its way beneath New York's streets.

*

In the office above the Fulton Street Market Stefan Gillespie sat at the table with Longie Zwillman and a small, fat, balding man who wore a pin-striped suit that was too tight for him. He had taken a cab straight to the fish market from Grand Central Station. Zwillman was waiting for him. The gangster introduced the other man, unexpectedly, as a Federal Special Agent. He gave him no name and offered no explanation. The FBI man blinked at Stefan through milk-bottle-thick glasses and offered a handshake limper than the dead fish being loaded in the market hall below. Now he was gazing at the two deciphered IRA dispatches. He had been looking for several minutes.

'You understand "ri", Mr Gillespie? And "ceorn—", what's that?'

'I think so,' replied Stefan. 'The word "rí" is the Irish word for king. So there was an IRA plan that had something to do with a king, and it's all off. No more dispatches about it. Nothing more said about it. Whether that's an instruction from here to Ireland or from Ireland to here, I don't know, but it's "abandoned", that's for sure. As for who the king is, it says the king in the United States. There's only one king who's going to interest the IRA very much, the English king, who's just crossed the border from Canada.'

'So we take king literally?' asked the FBI man.

'He's here, isn't he?' shrugged Stefan.

'Right here, in New York, tomorrow,' replied the Special Agent.

'But the plan is only abandoned as far as the IRA is concerned. Somebody else has it. "Cearnoga" is Irish again. It just means squares. But maybe the word you'd be looking for here would be more like squareheads.'

'Germans,' smiled Longie Zwillman.

'And you think the plan is a bomb, Mr Gillespie?'

'I can't say that. It would have to be my guess. One way or another it seems to involve George VI not being around. Not being around for a reception in Washington anyway. That's what Carroll was joking about.'

'You would think so.' The man in the glasses still didn't raise his eyes. 'So what is the blackbird rí? Does that tell us anything else? Presumably words aren't wasted given the amount of time it takes to encode these messages.' He pushed the message back across the table to Stefan.

'I won't sing for you, but it goes like this: "In England my blackbird and I were together, Where he was still noble and generous of heart. Oh, woe to the time that first we went thither – Alas, he was forced soon from thence to depart." Is that enough?' said Stefan with a grin.

The expressions on the faces of Longie Zwillman and the FBI agent told him it wasn't.

'It's an old Jacobite song. The blackbird was the King over the Water, the king who would return when whoever was on the throne of England was defeated, mostly some Hanoverian with the name George as often as not. I'm not suggesting anyone's interested in that now, but I guess the English do have a King over the Water again, in the shape of the abdicated Edward. And from what I've read in the papers, he's very pally with Adolf Hitler.'

The Special Agent nodded; there was very nearly a smile.

'Yes, I think I've got hold of that. And "abu", Irish again?'

'Forever. The Blackbird Rí Forever! Followed understandably enough by "Jesus", which would probably be short for something like, "Jesus Christ what the fuck are we doing blowing up one English king on behalf of another one!" It might take a bit of explaining in the IRA and Clan na Gael.'

'You're a useful man to have around, Sergeant Gillespie. Deciphering these things only seems to be half the battle, unless you've got some Irish.'

The Special Agent looked at the second cipher Stefan had decoded.

'There are two people who feature in these messages. Mr Brown and Mr Hart. From what we know about who's calling the shots I'd guess Mr Brown is Dominic Carroll and Mr Hart is Russell. Do you agree?'

He pushed the paper with Stefan's workings on it across the table.

```
MR BROWN MR HART AUTHORISED NEGOTIATE
WITH BUND FRIENDS. NO ONE ELSE. NOT
ALL MR BROWNS GERMAN PALS ON BOARD.
NEW CONCERNS ABOUT COURIER INTEGRITY.
IF INFORMATION LEAKS DISPOSE OF ALL
LOOSE ENDS.
```

'Seán Russell's the one you arrested in Detroit. That's what the message says was meant to happen. That's why he went there with Carroll. To get arrested.'

'On the basis that if we thought anybody was going to try anything it would be him. And if we've dealt with him there's no more to worry about?'

'A sideshow's what they wanted. I don't know about Bund friends versus German pals.' Stefan looked from the FBI man to Zwillman. 'Some people can be trusted and some people can't. All that's more your area.'

Longie Zwillman shrugged. 'Don't ask me.'

'I don't know what German Intelligence would make of this,' said the Special Agent. 'It doesn't smell like anything

334

official. I mean if you wanted to start a war tomorrow morning, and maybe undo all the work you've put in persuading most Americans to stay out of it – this would be no bad way to go about it. I should think the German government's as likely to be in on this one as the Irish government, which is not to say it wouldn't suit them of course.'

'And the loose ends?' continued the Special Agent.

'John Cavendish would be one,' said Longie Zwillman quietly.

The FBI man stood up.

'Thank you, gentlemen. I don't know what we'll get from the rest of these ciphers, but your people are probably looking for different things, Mr Gillespie. We're not in a hurry, except for the matter of a bomb, of course. There are a number of possibilities but the most public one is the World's Fair. As for the rest of it, just now we're more interested in watching what the IRA and the Nazis are up to in America than catching them. Safe home.'

He took his briefcase, put on a hat that was too big for him, and left.

Longie Zwillman stood up, thoughtfully; he took out a cigar and lit it.

'You keep unexpected company, Mr Zwillman,' said Stefan.

'Given my line of work?'

'I wouldn't think you often sit down with the FBI.'

'The wolves are coming out of the forest, Stefan. It's a good time for friends and neighbours to leave off strangling each other. We can go back to that when they've gone. In the meantime there's things people like me can do that fine upstanding people can't. I didn't think I'd be in the

335

business of saving an English king's life though. You neither, I reckon?'

'It wouldn't have been high on my list of things to do in New York.'

'A Jew and an Irishman! The Empire's fallen on hard times.'

'It looks like it,' smiled Stefan.

'Not too hard for now, I hope. They're all bastards as far as I'm concerned. I might have men in the docks now, finding out what the IRA and the German-American Bund are planning to do to sabotage arms shipments to Britain, but when I'm not doing that I'm smuggling guns out for Jews to use against the British in Palestine. It pisses me we've got the same enemies, you know that? I think it pissed John Cavendish too. He didn't have much doubt what was coming though. And it is coming. We're going to be a big neutral and you're going to be a small one, but sometime we'll all have to decide what side we're neutral on.' He smiled and sucked in cigar smoke. 'If you're Jewish it's not a hard decision.'

The two men said nothing for a moment.

'You know how I met John?' continued Zwillman. 'It was a meeting above a German bookshop on 3rd Avenue, the usual crew, America First, the German-American Bund, Silver Shirts, Coughlin's Christian Front. There's always some IRA men too, to add a bit of anti-British to the anti-Jewish, anti-Negro, anti-Communist, anti-Democracy, anti-fucking-anything-you-can-think-of stuff they like. That's what he was interested in, what the IRA was up to in all that. But what does he do? He takes fucking notes! So they think he's a reporter. And what they do with reporters is send them away with enough cracked ribs to make sure they don't come back. He was lucky. I had some boys come over from New Jersey to break up the meeting. The Bund had to leave him out the back. They hadn't really got started on him.'

Stefan began to gather up Cavendish's notes and the ciphers.

'But somebody got started on him eventually,' he said. 'They got finished too. I doubt I'll ever know any more than that, not now. It's about the beginning and the end of what I'll be taking back to the Garda Commissioner. He was a loose end somebody needed to dispose of. Someone'll have to think of something else to tell his wife and his kids.'

*

'I can't say New York was everything I expected,' said Owen Harris, 'but I haven't been able to get out as much as I'd hoped. I'm not complaining. I've met some fascinating people. Frightening, but with their own New World charm. I do admit that I'm rather glad to be going home though, Sergeant.'

Stefan Gillespie sat across the bare table in the bare room at Police Headquarters as he had the day Harris had been arrested in the bar on 52nd Street. He knew what to expect from him, and he wasn't in the mood for it.

'I'll pick you up in the morning, Mr Harris.'

'I suppose I'd better pack. I didn't bring a lot with me.'

'I have your things. They've been sent over from the hotel.'

'The dear Thesps! How are they? Mr Mac Liammóir was kind enough to come to see me, for what it was worth. He didn't have very much to say.'

'The plane takes just over –'

'You know Yeats rejected it?'

'We'll be at Foynes –'

'The play, *John Bull's Other Island*,' continued Harris, 'it was commissioned for the Abbey originally. Too controversial, too long, he said. Now it's not controversial at all, but it's still too long. I always think Shaw had a problem with his comedies. The trouble is they're not remotely funny.'

'Tomorrow then,' said Stefan.

'I've found myself relating to Synge in here. I should have said that to Micheál. I'd never thought much of him before, Synge I mean.' He sat back, frowning and giggling at the same time. 'All that English that's meant to sound like Irish and doesn't sound like anything on earth. But I've become quite a celebrity in here, just like in *The Playboy of the Western World*, a kind of Christy Mahon of Broadway. "Is it killed your mother?" "With the help of God I did surely?" It should go down even better in Ireland!'

Owen Harris looked up smugly, as if he was waiting for applause.

Stefan stood up.

'You don't think it will then, Sergeant?'

'No, Mr Harris, I don't think joking about your mother's death will endear you to anybody. You'll help yourself more by shutting your mouth.'

'My God, you're right, the story of my life, Medea versus Moloch. Only two parents to choose from and I couldn't even murder the right one!'

Stefan turned and walked out, leaving Owen Harris chuckling.

338

When he came into the Headquarters Detective Division room it was almost empty. Two detectives hurried out as he walked in. Michael Phelan was at his desk, strapping on his shoulder holster, with the boyish look of gung-ho enthusiasm that had accompanied him into the 52nd Street club with Stefan.

'Can't stop, Stefan, we're heading for the World's Fair.'

'I heard something,' said Stefan.

'Something's a bomb, that's the word, at the British Pavilion.'

'They've found it?'

'I'm not sure.' He grinned. 'The thing is, what's going to happen when we do? Are we going to get rid of it or set the thing off? It's asking a lot of an Irish cop not to see a bit of England blown up. Maybe those lions!'

'Come on Mikey!' Aaron Phelan appeared in the doorway in uniform. 'If you want a lift over to Flushing Meadows, I'm going now!'

'Keep your hair on, Captain!' Michael Phelan turned back to Stefan. 'I say that because he's lost a chunk. Right about there.' He pointed to the back of his own head, more or less where Stefan Gillespie's revolver had hit his brother. 'And he's got a bump the size of a duck egg. If I didn't know better I'd say he'd been out on the piss. That's usually my job in the family.'

'I said move!' Phelan laughed. 'You want to come, Stefan?'

'No, I need to get everything sorted out before I go.'

'We'll be glad to get your prisoner out of our cells,' said Captain Phelan cheerfully. 'He's taken to singing in the middle of the night. Much more and you'd be taking him home in a box. And it'd be a cop who strangled him! We've got to go. There'll be a car to get you to La Guardia tomorrow. Can you do it, Mikey?'

'Fine with me,' said Michael. 'I'll see you then, Stefan.'

The two brothers were gone. The room was empty. Stefan smiled a quiet smile which was all relief. He had had no choice but to go into Police Headquarters; that's where Owen Harris was. But bumping into Aaron Phelan was something else. It was something he had hoped wouldn't happen. There was no reason why the NYPD captain should connect him with Kate and Niamh. He had thought it through a dozen times. Nothing had happened to let him make that connection.

The captain couldn't have seen him, even in that last moment by the jetty as Stefan had smashed the gun barrel down the back of his head. But the revolver was nagging at him. Somewhere he'd lost it. It could have been by the boathouse at Mexico Bay; it could have been in the rowing boat, or on the *Temeraire*; it could have been in the big Hudson, or in the Montreal hotel.

So far no one had asked for it back at Centre Street. He didn't want to say he'd lost it; the thing had been given to him so casually he was simply hoping the question wouldn't arise. But there was nothing odd about Captain Phelan's behaviour, and by tomorrow Stefan would be gone.

*

Richard Langham, who was responsible for such things, hadn't thought it mattered much when the big bald-headed black cleaner they called Cab (he didn't know his surname, but it was written down somewhere) hadn't turned up for work at the British Pavilion at the World's Fair one night in early February. A small white-haired Negro who said he was Cab's cousin turned up instead (Mr Langham didn't remember his name at all, but it must have been written down somewhere).

The Fair would be opening in a matter of weeks and the cleaners needed to be in place; one black cleaner was the same as another black cleaner. They weren't a part of the Fair anyway; they were an invisible army that would only appear when the Fair closed. Buses brought them from Harlem every evening and took them back in the early hours of the morning, about the same time the garbage trucks left. Who they were didn't matter. And as it happened someone whose job it was to notice such things mentioned that the new cleaner was a damned sight better than the old one, whatever his name had been, whatever the name of the new man was.

The cleaner's name was actually Louis Marshall. Two men from the German-American Bund had taught him how to put the bomb together and how to set it. The meetings his Ethiopian Pacific Movement had had with the pro-Hitler groups had been few and far between, but he had tried to establish contact, because he knew they had things in common under the skin; and something remarkable had come of those efforts. They wanted to work with him; they wanted him to work with them.

He had brought the bomb parts into the British Pavilion one at a time, in pieces small enough to fit under the sandwiches in his lunch box; he had hidden them in sealed packets in the toilet cisterns and in empty tins of polish in the cupboard where he kept his trolley, mops, brushes, buckets. The false bottom in the cleaning trolley was more difficult than the bomb. That had to be good; so good it was solid. It had to stand up to the search that would happen before the English king got to the World's Fair. Marshall had had to carry the metal plate in and out of the Fair three days running before the Bund men got it to fit right.

He was to assemble the parts of the bomb two nights before George VI's visit; they told him the time to set it; the tiny clock, almost silent, could run for forty-eight hours. The Bund men were as biggity and astorperious as every other white-ass Louis Marshall had met; he certainly wasn't dumb to the fact that they despised him all the time they were patting him on the back. But they were no better than rednecks anyway; whatever they called themselves they weren't real Germans; real Hitler Germans didn't come from Queens and New Jersey. But they were paying him well, and what he was doing was bigger than them. It was as big as Louis Marshall's dreams.

It was the British Empire that had stolen Africa from Aunt Hagar's children, and once the British were out of Africa it would be a home for every black man on earth. He didn't know much about the English and their kings. He knew about the man who'd stopped being king because they wouldn't let him marry some American woman, though he had no idea why anybody gave a damn. But when the king they had now was dead, the old one would come back. And this one didn't even want Africa. He was a friend of Adolf Hitler's; he was Hitler's man all the way. And when he'd kicked out all the Jews who controlled the British Empire, it would be the way Hitler said it would be. The whites would have their place. The brothers-in-black would have theirs, and it would be Africa, without a white ass on the continent, from Cairo to Cape Town. The way God intended it.

342

So when Louis Marshall aired out back to Harlem after setting the bomb, he knew that what he had done was as righteous as rage itself. He had stood on a box at the corner of 125th Street and Lenox Avenue for four years. He had borne witness to the days of wrath that would change the world, and now he was a part of it, now he was driving it.

The world Hitler wanted was the world he had seen too, when every dusty-butt, jar-head nigger in Harlem couldn't see further than jooking and jelly and juice. Oh, Little Sister, Babylon would fall, because she made all nations drink of the wine of the wrath of her fornication! Everybody said big things were coming; the great battles and the great storms would sweep Babylon away.

When the Bund men came to pay him that night Louis had got in some bottles of Budweiser. He didn't drink a lot, but he wouldn't see them again, and whatever he thought about the Germans they were the only people he could celebrate with. He knew he couldn't tell anyone else, not yet; one day, one day his brothers would know what he had done. But as it happened there was little likelihood of him telling anyone, either now or at any point in the future. While one of the German Americans held him down, the other one stuck him in the chest with a knife, and then cut his throat.

He wasn't the only one the bomb killed.

The next day, when the FBI and the NYPD poured into the British Pavilion at the World's Fair, it took a while to find the bomb, but it was discovered eventually, in the almost invisible trolley of the completely invisible black cleaner.

Two detectives from the NYPD's Bomb Squad took it to a stretch of waste ground at the back of the Fair to defuse it. When it went off it killed them instantly. The two men had worked together at Police Headquarters on Centre Street for a long time. When they were drunk in McSorley's they had a party piece; they sang 'When Irish Eyes Are Smiling'. Joe Lynch would sing in English; Freddy Socha was the only NYPD officer who knew it in Polish.

When the bomb exploded most Fair visitors assumed some of the evening fireworks had gone off by mistake.

*

In the Statler Bar at the Hotel Pennsylvania Stefan Gillespie sat in a booth with Micheál Mac Liammóir and another actor, Charlie Mawson.

Mawson was tall, with a thin, angular face and dark hair. He smoked continually and had very little to say except that if Owen Harris had killed his mother he would have known. They had shared a cabin together on the boat from Cobh to New York; he would have known. The fact that he didn't even know that his ex-lover's mother was missing at all until they arrived in New York and that there was no question that Harris had, at the very least, dragged his dead mother's body out to her car, driven it through Dublin to the sea, and there disposed of it, didn't seem to alter Mawson's certainty about his innocence.

He said several times that Owen Harris was a 'troubled young man but not that troubled, never that troubled'. He said he had asked him directly, at the Markwell, what had happened. Harris's answer had been that he didn't know, but that his mother had been threatening suicide again. Mrs Harris apparently went through phases of threatening suicide and she had even told Mawson himself,

344

several times, that she intended to kill herself, because her son hated her and her husband despised her.

Charlie Mawson also said that although he had felt some sympathy for the lonely, self-pitying figure of Mrs Harris when he had first met her, he had come to the conclusion, very quickly in fact, that she was cruel, manipulative, vindictive and incapable of telling the truth about anything, particularly about her son and her estranged husband.

Then he stopped saying the same thing over and over again, and gave a dry smile; he knew what Stefan Gillespie was thinking anyway.

'I'm not helping, am I, Sergeant?'

'I appreciate your concern for your friend –'

'But I've got bugger all to say.'

'I'm not in a position to take statements, Mr Mawson.'

'Naturally I'd speak for him in court.'

Stefan nodded. Mawson's declaration that his friend had not only lied to him all the way across the Atlantic, but had spent most of his time drinking and playing pranks on the other actors, while showing no sign at all of grief or remorse about the mother he had thrown off a cliff, even if he hadn't stabbed her to death, was definitely unhelpful to anyone except the prosecutor. His description of Leticia Harris as manipulative, spiteful and violent sounded more like a list of motives for her son to kill her than an explanation of dry he didn't. The only mitigating factor in there perhaps, somewhere, was that mother and son were probably as mad as each other.

'I wrote this down after I, saw him at Centre Street.'

It was Mac Liammóir who spoke now.

'It's the same mix of confused and sometimes unfeeling remarks, the same leaps back to his childhood, or to things he seems to consider complete strangers ought to know, that the actors who sat with him at the Markwell have talked to me about, but it's what he said. I don't know whether there's anything in there that means anything at all, but somewhere in that conversation I felt that when he said he didn't kill his mother, he meant it. I've thought about it a great deal since. I keep telling myself that probably the boy is mad enough to mean he didn't do it and mad enough to have done it all at once. But I wanted to say –'

He laughed.

'The truth is I don't know what I wanted to say, except that someone should listen to him. Either there is some truth in there, or he really is as mad as a hatter, and if he's that, then it needs to be said too. People won't like him, Mr Gillespie. Jurors won't like him. I don't like him myself.'

Micheál Mac Liammóir shrugged.

'He could hang himself, just because of the man he is. He has no sense of how people respond to him. I'd like to think that you won't let him do that. That if there are questions to be asked, they will at least be asked.'

He glanced at Charlie Mawson. They both stood up.

'You won't make it to the play, Mr Gillespie?'

'I go back tomorrow.'

'Ah, you read the reviews!'

'I haven't seen anything about it.'

'You're too polite for a policeman. I've always thought that.'

'Not great?'

'It was the wrong play. That was the problem.'

Stefan nodded, as if he agreed.

'And a reviewer who arrived in a cravat.'

346

Stefan looked puzzled.

'It's a questionable choice at the best of times, Sergeant, but in Manhattan it shows all the imagination you might find inside a gnat's arse!'

The three men shook hands. They were standing in front of one of the mirrored pillars in the lobby of the Hotel Pennsylvania. There were a lot of people, but for a moment Stefan Gillespie's eye was caught by a brown suit in the mirror. As the director and the actor walked away he turned. The suit had gone, but he was sure he had recognised it, along with the man in it. It was Katzmann, the German intelligence officer he last saw in Central Park.

In the Statler Bar Stefan had almost forgotten about what had been happening around him. He was almost back on the Yankee Clipper. It was what waited for him at home that was at the front of his mind; the man he was taking back to Dublin to hand over to Superintendent Gregory. But maybe it hadn't been Katzmann at all.

It was a suit and a man who was slightly too big for it. He couldn't see him anyway, and he had something to do that pushed even Owen Harris away. He had the top of the Empire State Building to go to. He had promised Tom he would do it. He wanted to himself. He wanted to look out at New York at night. He wanted to clear his mind of everything that had happened and to let the city give him something he could share with his son. And something that would also be his own.

He walked out on to 7th Avenue and stepped to the kerb to hail a cab. It was all busy, noisy, bright; he wanted that too. He smiled as the cab pulled up, remembering the moment with Kate O'Donnell outside the Hampshire House, when he couldn't get her a cab, before the Hampshire

House became a very different memory. It was only a couple of blocks to 5th Avenue, but it would be his last New York taxi. He would walk back. As it pulled away he was thinking about Kate. It wasn't everything he wanted to clear his head of when he stood at the top of the Empire State.

He was unaware of the dark saloon that inched out behind him, following the cab into 34th Street. But it hadn't gone entirely unnoticed.

Rudolf Katzmann stood just down from the Hotel Pennsylvania, in the brown suit Stefan Gillespie had recognised, lighting a cigarette. He had watched Stefan come out. He had watched him get into the yellow cab. He had watched the dark car pull out behind. Now he walked quickly back into the lobby of the Pennsylvania. He went to the Bell Captain's desk. He put a dollar bill down and picked up the telephone.

21. A Hundred and Sixteenth Street

Last night in New York. The picture on the front is right
where I am, nearly at the top of the Empire State
Building. You told me I had to come up here, so up here
is where I am. Looking out at the city at night is like
nothing else on earth. You have to see it for yourself. One
day you will. I know you will. I'll post this tomorrow.
Then we can both wait for it to arrive. Love to everyone
at home, love to you Tom.

He felt those last words very deeply tonight. They weren't
words he was used to writing as simply and as straight-
forwardly as that, but he needed to say them. He wanted
to be home again. There was nothing he wanted to see
now, surrounded by so much he had wanted to see. There
were things he wanted to remember, and things he wanted
to forget. As the elevator carried him down to the street he
wondered about Kate O'Donnell again. He wondered what
she would want to remember. He hoped he was on that
list.

He came out on to 5th Avenue and walked towards the
kerb, simply looking up and down before turning to walk
back to the hotel. There was a car straight in front of him.

Standing by it was Captain Aaron Phelan, no longer in uniform, watching him. He smiled as if he had been waiting. Stefan knew that he had been. Phelan dropped a cigarette on to the sidewalk.

'I thought you might want a lift, Stefan?'

He stepped forward and pulled open the back door of the saloon. There was nothing threatening about it, but it was still threatening; it was the rear door, not the front. Stefan's surprise had already given way to something else. Phelan couldn't have guessed he would be here. And why would he want to anyway? He hadn't bumped into him by chance because he happened to be standing by a car outside the Empire State Building, smoking a cigarette. Stefan Gillespie knew he had been followed. Aaron Phelan's behaviour at Police Headquarters had been an act. However unlikely the connections to Kate and Niamh were, he had made them now.

'I'd like to walk. It's my last night in New York, Captain.'

Immediately he was aware that there were two men on either side of him. One took his arm, pulling him into the car after him; the second grabbed his other arm and pushed. It was done so quickly that before he could even start to resist he was on the back seat of the dark saloon.

The second man was already in behind him; he was wedged between the two of them. The first man had a gun in his hand now. The barrel was pressed hard against Stefan Gillespie's temple. The second man grabbed his hands and pulled them up. He snapped a pair of handcuffs over his wrists. Aaron Phelan was in the driver's seat. He started the engine. No one said a word.

The car pulled into the 5th Avenue evening traffic. It drove two blocks south and into East 32nd Street, then north on

350

to Madison Avenue. No one spoke. There was nothing to say. There was only the radio, and as the car headed uptown the man on Stefan's left leant back beside him, whistling tunelessly through his teeth with the Andrews Sisters. 'Zing boom tararrel, ring out a song of good cheer. Now's the time to roll the barrel, for the gang's all here.'

He knew he was just north of Central Park now, somewhere off Lexington Avenue, towards the East River, but that was about it. The car had pulled up in an alleyway behind a row of flat-fronted tenements and shops. There had been no point struggling as he was bundled down steps into a dark corridor and then a dimly lit cellar room.

He was sitting on a chair, surrounded by string-bound piles of newspapers and boxes of what looked like books. The two men who had pushed him into the car sat across the cellar at a table. The one who had grabbed him from behind was rolling a cigarette; the other was half-reading a newspaper. Captain Phelan had left as he had been deposited in the chair, still handcuffed. Above he could hear voices. A man was talking. There was applause, cheering; a lot of people. There was a kind of echo. Above it had to be a big room; some kind of meeting was in progress.

It was the cellar of a bookshop. A lot of the books were in German; a few of the newspapers too. Stefan took in some of the titles as he looked round. They didn't mean much, but they gave him a sense of where he was, and who the people sitting opposite him were. They certainly weren't Irish.

To his left piles of the *National American*, with a headline, 'Sterilization for All Refugees Entering America'; to his right the *Christian Mobilizer*, 'Will Your Sons Die for England's

Empire?'; at his feet the *American Vindicator*, 'Guard Your Womenfolk from the Pollution of Jews, Blacks, Browns and Bolsheviks'.

It came as no surprise when the two men started to speak quietly to each other in German. Stefan assumed it must be because they didn't want him to know what they were saying; from their accents it was clear they were Americans. It wasn't their first language. They had no reason to know that he spoke German, but their desire to keep the conversation from him was something, a straw. After all, no one minded what dead men heard. Besides, he could see that they were uncomfortable.

'Come on, what the fuck is this?' said the man smoking the roll-up.

'Someone Phelan wants to teach a lesson to,' answered the other one.

'He's Irish, isn't he?'

'That's what Phelan said.'

'So what's it got to do with us?'

'He said he needed a favour.'

'Hasn't he got enough cops and Micks to do him that sort of favour?'

'The guy trod on his toes – he wants to give him a lesson.'

The man with the roll-up shook his head.

'I would have thought we'd be better keeping out of each other's way at the moment. If this is some IRA thing then it's nothing to do with the Bund – if it's some Irish shit who's pissed him, what the fuck do we care?'

'It's no big deal.'

The man with the roll-up still didn't like it.

'You should have told him to fuck off. We've got enough shit to clean up without working for the Micks. You're not telling me they haven't got something to do with this fuck up in the first place. He shouldn't be here.'

'He said he needed to ask this guy some questions.'

'He doesn't give us orders.' The man smoking the roll-up shook his head as he spoke. The conversation wasn't making him any happier. He took out another paper and some tobacco. He was tense and uneasy. 'He was thick with Paul before, but now Paul's not – after what happened to Paul –'

For a moment neither of them spoke. The other man was tapping his fingers uneasily now too, no longer looking at the newspaper. As the man rolling the cigarette put it in his mouth and lit it, he wouldn't let it go.

'We don't have to take Phelan's orders. It's over, isn't it? It's over and Paul's paid the fucking price for going behind the Abwehr's back. It doesn't look so clever now any of it. And isn't this guy some kind of cop?'

'An Irish cop.'

'There's enough fucking Irishmen in New York to do him over then.'

The conversation stopped. In the quiet Stefan could hear the voice of the man addressing a meeting above more clearly. He was shouting now.

'America will not fight a war in Europe, and it's our job to see she doesn't. America will remain neutral, even though the King of England is parading through our streets. He won't be parading anywhere when Hitler's tanks are in London! But things are going to change here too. There's a revolution coming! And it's going to start in the streets. We'll clean up this goddamn democracy! This is New York not Jew York! We won't let this city be run by a stinkweed like Guardia or leave our country in the hands of a Jew-bum like Roosevelt. Don't put your trust in Democracy. Will America continue on the Low Road of Democracy, on to slavery and national suicide, or will we regain the High Road of true freedom? Will Democracy drag us back into the Dark Ages, or will Nazism lead us to the New Dawn? The same question lies before every man in every country in the world today. Is America on the road to the true Republic? Is Ireland on the road to the true Republic? Is any country on that road? Yes, one country is. Germany! Germany is already there. We want it too! Freedom! And if we have the courage, we will take it! Freedom!'

Applause had grown as the speech reached its crescendo, and it ended with roaring and shouting from the audience above Stefan Gillespie's head. The floor shook as hundreds of feet stamped out the rhythm of the word that the audience kept repeating. 'Freedom! Freedom! Freedom!' And then suddenly it stopped. The shouting was replaced by the murmur of excited conversation, and several hundred feet shuffled in one direction, out of the hall above. It was silent.

The two men at the table seemed to take no notice of what was going on above them. Then a phone rang. They looked up. The man who wasn't smoking got up and walked to a shelf. He picked up the phone.

'Yeah, he went out. He'll be back though.' The man glanced round at Stefan. When he spoke again he spoke in German. 'We picked up the guy outside the Empire State. Phelan said he needed the shit kicking out of him.'

The door opened and Aaron Phelan entered. The Bund man put down the phone. It wasn't hurried or awkward, but the way he looked at the NYPD man was somehow different now. He walked back to the table and sat down.

'Not giving you any trouble?' said Aaron Phelan cheerfully.

'He hasn't said a word.'

Phelan took a step forward and stared at Stefan, half smiling. The NYPD captain took a .38 Colt Police Positive from his pocket and held it up.

'Thanks for letting us have it back.' He rubbed the side of his head.

He walked up and down slowly. He seemed unaware of the two men at the table. They watched like an audience not sure they're at the right play.

'I knew it was the gun we'd given you, so I knew you were the one with them, with Mrs Carroll and her sister, I couldn't work it out. Why would you be helping them? How did you even know them? But you'd met the sister. I saw you with her on Patrick's Day. It didn't make sense, but there was something. Had to be. It nagged me all the way to New York.'

He looked at the gun again then put it back in his pocket.

'I helped them, that's all,' said Stefan. There was no point denying that. 'It was the sister who pulled me in, Kate. I guess it was pretty stupid.'

'She's a looker. You're right about that,' smiled the policeman.

'She got me hooked,' shrugged Stefan. 'It got out of hand.'

'Thinking with your cock, that's an Irishman for you.'

Phelan looked round at the German Americans and laughed. They smiled uneasily. Stefan could see they had no idea what the captain was talking about. He turned his eyes back to Aaron Phelan. He didn't know where this was going but he knew what the policeman was capable of. He knew Jimmy Palmer had died after a conversation with him, maybe a conversation like this. But surely the NYPD man only knew about Niamh and Kate. He couldn't know what Stefan had heard in the cellar under Dominic Carroll's house at Mexico Bay. He couldn't know Niamh had provided the key to John Cavendish's IRA dispatches. He couldn't make that leap. Surely all he wanted to know was where Niamh Carroll was.

'So where are they, Sergeant Gillespie?'

Stefan felt a sense of relief; the truth made for easy answers.

'On their way home to Ireland.'

'How?'

'A boat, what do you think? Why can't you leave it at that?'

'And the sister sorted that out?'

'That's it. She just needed help getting out of New York. There was a plan. I don't know what went wrong. She came to me with a sob story –'

There was no need for him to say he knew who Jimmy Palmer was. His part came with the journey to Mexico Bay. It was no more than that.

'How did you get up to the lake? There was no car?'

'We paid a couple of guys with a fish truck. From Fulton Market.'

It was an unlikely reply, but it sounded unlikely enough to be true. If Aaron Phelan wanted to take that any further Stefan wished him the best of luck in a market run by Longie Zwillman's associates. Stefan was starting to breathe more easily. It was all about Niamh. Phelan knew nothing about the rest of it. He could know nothing about how Stefan had really got involved.

'Is it such a bad thing? Whatever's wrong with Mrs

356

Carroll, her sister wanted her home. I shouldn't have got involved, but maybe it's for the best.'

The shrug that accompanied the words wasn't reciprocated.

'The sister couldn't have got her out without you.'

'I should have walked away. But does Mr Carroll really want his wife locked up for the rest of her life? So she disappears? So he's shot of her.'

'I think that's Mr Carroll's business, not some culchie gobshite's. But how did you manage it so? You didn't row the fucking boat across Ontario.'

'Kate had plenty of money to pay her way,' said Stefan. 'I told you, I helped them get out of the city. She'd arranged for a boat to come over and pick us up. She phoned the guy before we set off. She'd been working it out for a long time, ever since she got to New York. I left them in Montreal. She said that was the end of it as far as I was concerned. The bitch dumped me.'

Stefan tried a man-of-the-world smile; it wasn't reciprocated either.

'What about the Free State soldier, John Cavendish?'

This was the conversation Stefan Gillespie didn't want. He didn't know whether the NYPD man had just been waiting to ask that question because he knew more all the time, or whether he was only fishing.

'What's he got to do with it?'

'You knew him.'

'I can hardly say I knew him. I met him at Mr Carroll's party, on Patrick's Day. We didn't have very long to get acquainted, as you know.'

'You didn't know him better than that?'

'No, but I know a lot more about him now. I've been

sitting at Centre Street with your brother reading the reports on the investigation into his death, as requested by the consul general. Yes, I should've stuck to that.'

'I think Kate O'Donnell was pretty friendly with Captain Cavendish,' said Phelan slowly. 'They were working together, over at the World's Fair.'

'I wasn't very interested in who else she was friendly with, Captain,' said Stefan. 'I was interested in how friendly I could get her to be with me.'

'You think that was all he did, Sergeant – Mr Cavendish?'

'All he did what?'

'Someone told me he was in Military Intelligence at one time.'

'I wouldn't know.'

'A Free State soldier and a Free State detective would have a lot in common, the way things are in Ireland now, with de Valera cracking down on the real Republicans. If he was G2, maybe you're in Special Branch.'

'You know who I am. You know why I came to New York.'

'You tell a good tale, Sergeant,' replied Phelan. 'And it seems to hang together. I know you're not Special Branch. I know you really are a sergeant in Baltinglass. Mr Carroll wanted you checked out. But you still worry me. The IRA never really got anything on Cavendish, but there were things going on, there was information going out some-where, and he was in it somewhere. Maybe it's just a coincidence, but that's the impression I've got. Now, out of nowhere, there are things that have gone wrong, very wrong.'

'So a woman gets out of a nut house and goes home to her family?'

'That's not what I'm talking about.'

'Then you've lost me, Captain.'

Aaron Phelan looked at Stefan Gillespie for a long moment.

'Mr Carroll is still pretty pissed about his wife.'

'You've told me.'

'That would be enough,' continued the NYPD man. 'It would be enough to teach someone a very serious lesson. Mr Carroll doesn't get involved in that sort of thing. I deal with all that for him. I make my own decisions. He doesn't like to know. Why should he? I could almost have decided to let it go, even though I'm pretty pissed too. You made me look like a real jerk, because he had to know some of it. He had to know she'd left the country. I don't like being humiliated like that, Sergeant. But when I put being pissed together with, well, other things nagging me –'

He took the gun out of his pocket again.

Stefan tensed himself; he could do nothing. And it was unexpected. Whatever his fears outside the Empire State Building, he had felt them ease away as Aaron Phelan's words had focused so much on Niamh Carroll. That was all the NYPD man really knew. What he hadn't understood was what he had done to Aaron Phelan in the only eyes that mattered to him, Dominic Carroll's.

The two German Americans stood up. They didn't like this at all now.

'Look, Mr Phelan, a bit of roughing up –'

'Don't worry, boys. I told you, we're doing Mr Carroll a favour.'

'All you said –'

'All you need to do is clear up the mess!' snapped Phelan.

Suddenly the door opened. Aaron Phelan spun round,

surprised and irritated. But he knew the man who walked in. And so did Stefan Gillespie. It was the Abwehr man he had met in Central Park, Rudolf Katzmann. It was the man he thought he had glimpsed in a mirror at the Pennsylvania only two hours earlier, watching him. Now he knew he had been right.

'It's Captain Phelan, isn't it? We have met before.'

'I work for Mr Carroll.'

'Of course,' smiled the intelligence officer. 'What is this?'

'There's a problem to attend to here, Mr Katzmann, that's all. It's not your problem though. If you've got some interest in it, then get on to Paul Eisterholz. I spoke to him about it on the phone yesterday and he cleared it. You know these things need doing sometimes. It's not German business.'

'I see,' said Katzmann softly. 'He's an informer?'

'It's close enough.'

'An IRA informer?'

'It's between me and Paul, Herr Katzmann. These are Paul's men.'

Phelan was impatient now; he jerked his head at the two Bund men.

'Paul is no longer here,' said Rudolf Katzmann. 'He has no men.'

'I spoke to him yesterday.' The captain looked at the two German Americans. 'Tell this guy to fuck off. You don't take orders from him.'

'They do now,' smiled the Abwehr man. 'There has been, well, let's say a change of management. Paul has disappeared. Unfortunately no one knows where he is, but he was dabbling in things that were really beyond his competence. Sometimes there is a price to pay for that. I don't know enough about the IRA to know whether that's true of you and Mr Carroll, but I'm sure you know what I'm talking about. So, I really think you need to tell me why you've brought Mr Gillespie here, and what you intend to do with him.'

'You know who he is?'

'As a matter of fact I do.'

'Well, he's fucked off Mr Carroll, and maybe more –'

'So you're going to shoot him.'

'I think you want to go a bit higher up before you start throwing your weight about. You need to talk to Mr Carroll and Seán Russell. You might want to remember that Mr Carroll was in Berlin two weeks ago. If you don't want to watch, go outside. I can get rid of the body without anybody's help.'

Aaron Phelan turned to Stefan, holding out the gun.

'He's a loose end. You'll have to trust me, Mr Katzmann.'

'All right, Captain,' shrugged Katzmann. 'It's your decision –'

Stefan flung himself off the chair at Phelan. His hands were still cuffed. But it was all he could do. As he moved he heard the explosion that filled the room. His head hit Aaron Phelan. For a moment he didn't know that it had actually hit Aaron Phelan's dead body. The NYPD man was a bloodied sack of potatoes. Stefan was on the ground next to him. He felt nothing. Surely Phelan couldn't have missed him at that range? He was staring into the policeman's open eyes. But they were the eyes of a dead man. There was blood trickling from his mouth. He started to get up. Katzmann was standing over the body with a gun, looking down.

'Unfortunately, you are the loose end, Captain Phelan. I wouldn't necessarily feel obliged to act on that, but you don't seem to know when to leave well enough alone.' His eyes moved to Stefan as he put the gun back into his pocket. 'Is that an Irish trait, Sergeant Gillespie? I rather think so.'

Stefan said nothing. The Abwehr man turned to the two American Bund men. He spoke to them in German, sharply. They stood to attention.

'Get rid of the body. The river will do. The IRA need know nothing. But I don't think he has to disappear as completely as Paul Eisterholz. I know the Irish like a good funeral. I wouldn't want to deprive him of that.'

Without a word the two men walked across to Captain Aaron Phelan's body. One of them reached into his pocket; he handed Katzmann a small key. Katzmann stepped over the dead man and undid Stefan's handcuffs.

'You'll probably want to get back to your hotel and pack, Sergeant.'

Stefan sat beside Katzmann as the German's crossed into 7th Avenue from the park. He glanced left at the tower of the Hampshire House along 59th Street.

'It seems you took over from John Cavendish after all, Mr Gillespie.'

'I don't think I did, Herr Katzmann. It was about a woman who didn't get on with her husband, and another woman I liked. That's it. I don't know what else Captain Phelan had in his head. All I know is I couldn't get it out.'

'We should probably leave it at that then, Sergeant. You won't know anything about a bomb that was planted at the World's Fair today, in the British Pavilion. In anticipation of King George's imminent visit it seems.'

'I heard about it when I was at Police Headquarters earlier today. And I heard they'd found it, on the radio. Two cops were killed, isn't that right?'

'No one knows who did it, of course,' said the Abwehr man.

'I guess between the FBI and the NYPD they'll find out.'

'I very much doubt it.'

'You very much doubt it or you hope they won't?'

'It was certainly nothing to do with the Abwehr. My superiors would not be altogether enthusiastic about replacing the present English king with a man who is quite as captivated by our Fuehrer as the Duke of Windsor. There will be a war, as any fool knows. When it comes we fully intend to defeat Britain, and we will, as any fool knows too, even American fools, with the exception of the biggest fool of all, President Roosevelt. But defeating Britain and turning it into a Hitler-worshipping satellite of our Thousand Year Reich are two very different things. One day Germany may have to get rid of Hitler and the Nazis, and we may want the world to resume something more like normal service. When that day comes it will be useful if the rest of the world still exists. Not that any of those thoughts are mine. I am as loyal to the Fuehrer as any German alive.'

'I hope more Germans are as loyal as you, Herr Katzmann.'

The Abwehr man laughed; he drove on for a moment saying nothing.

'I don't know whether Captain Cavendish knew about the bomb,' continued Katzmann, 'but he did know something was going to happen. And he knew it involved, well, shall we call them rogue elements. I don't know whether rogue elements applies to the IRA, who seem to be under the impression that a king calling himself Edward VIII would hardly be on the throne five minutes before handing the island of Ireland over to them in its entirety. However, it certainly applies to anyone who thought killing the English king was in Germany's interests. One way or another Captain Cavendish had decided I was probably worth talking to. Whatever he knew about bombs, he didn't believe the Abwehr would have countenanced it.'

'He was going to tell you something?' said Stefan.

'Tell me what? What you know nothing about, Sergeant?'

'Something like that, Herr Katzmann.'

'He spoke to me that night at the Hampshire House, St Patrick's Day. I had suggested we talk before, but he had been, well, standoffish, let's say. In our line of work you can be sure anyone in the same line who suggests a conversation is looking for more than he intends to give. As of course I was. He asked me to meet him that evening, on one of the empty floors. Naturally it wouldn't have been good for either of us to be seen talking to each other.'

Stefan realised what the German was telling him. It wasn't about a bomb or an IRA and American Bund assassination, it was about Cavendish.

'You were there.' It was all he said.

'Yes.'

'You know who killed him?'

'I walked up the stairs. I was a little late. When I got there I could hear voices, angry voices, and sounds I recognised. I didn't go much further, but I saw enough. It was a fight, well, not a fight. It was dark, but I could see John Cavendish was being held and he was being hit. There were four or five men, from the team that had been playing some game. The hurlers, isn't that the word? I'd seen them at the party, drunk from the start.'

'And you walked away?'

'Any public contact of that sort would have embarrassed us both.'

'Maybe John would have preferred being embarrassed to being dead.'

'My job doesn't offer much in the Good Samaritan line. Obviously I had no idea at all how it would end. If I had I would have found a way to mention it to somebody. There were enough policemen there. I'm sorry, that's all I can say. In our profession it doesn't do to get into awkward situations. How he got into a scrap with a bunch of drunken ball players –'

'They followed him up there,' said Stefan simply.

'Do you know something about it?'

'I know something. I can't make any sense of it though. It seems –'

He shook his head. He remembered the party. He remembered the anger in the face of the hurler who had spoken to John Cavendish. He remembered the look on the captain's face too. He had felt the darkness, even though he had no idea what it was about. And he still had no idea, though he now knew it had cost the G2 man his life.

He didn't believe Rudolf Katzmann was the only person who knew something though. Someone in the NYPD did. He didn't know how high it went; he didn't know how many detectives knew. But the runaround he had been given was all about covering up what happened. There was no unpicking that now, at least not in New York. Katzmann would not be walking into Centre Street to make a statement. But it wasn't over; he owed John Cavendish more than that. He was taking what he knew back to Ireland. The people who killed the intelligence officer didn't have a police force to cover up for them there.

In the Statler Bar at the Pennsylvania Stefan Gillespie bought a bottle of whiskey. He took it up to his room. He put it down on the desk and walked into the bathroom to get a glass. He found himself shaking. He went to the sink and stared into the mirror. Suddenly he threw up. The telephone was ringing. He splashed his face with water and went back to the bedroom.

'This is Roland Geoghegan, from the consulate.'

'And how's it going, Roland?' he said, coughing.

'The consul general wants to speak to you.'

'I'm grand too, Roland.'

'Mr McCauley would like to speak to you now. If you could –'

'Are you sure?' interrupted Stefan.

'What do you mean, am I sure?' said the third secretary shortly.

'On the Owen Harris front I'm hoping to get him on a plane tomorrow without him getting killed in an NYPD cell or giving an interview on what's funny about killing your mammy. As for the rest, tell Mr McCauley he'll need to decide how much he wants to know, on a variety of subjects relating to dead intelligence officers, Clan na Gael presidents, bombs in World's Fair pavilions, the IRA and German Intelligence, and what the NYPD never got round to telling anybody about the Cork hurling team. He won't want to know everything. He might not want to know anything. But without your diplomatic training, Roland, I'm too fucked to guess what bits to leave out.'

'Just get a cab to the consulate, Sergeant!'

'Tell him to come here,' said Stefan.

'What?'

'You heard me, you gobshite. I'm not going anywhere.'

'Have you been drinking, Gillespie?'

'No, Geoghegan, but by the time he gets here I'll be well on!'

He slammed the phone down and picked up the bottle of Jameson.

22. Saint Patrick's Cathedral

When Stefan Gillespie left his room at the Hotel Pennsylvania he left the NYPD cap that Michael Phelan had given him on St Patrick's Day in the wardrobe. He knew that Tom would love to have it. It would be the source not only of excitement and pride but of endless games of cops and robbers. Played in that cap, with toy guns and pretend deaths, those games would never sit very easily with him, however far away from New York the fields and woods of Kilranelagh were. Too much real blood came with it now.

*

In St Patrick's Cathedral Mass was in progress. The pews in front of the altar were full of New Yorkers, among them the dark uniforms of far more of New York's finest than anyone would expect to see except on Ash Wednesday. The thick overcoats the detectives seemed to wear whatever the weather were there too. And as the Mass proceeded many more officers came and went at the back. They knelt briefly to say a prayer in the pews near the great doors; they walked to the shrines that lined the walls and lit candles.

Three policemen had died the previous day. Joe Lynch

and Freddy Socha were blown to pieces in Flushing Meadows; Aaron Phelan's body had been seen floating in the Hudson River just after dawn, by a passenger on the Hoboken Ferry, as it came into the Christopher Street Pier. He had died from a single bullet. There was nothing to say where he had been shot, let alone who had shot him. The manhunt that was already cranking up would be no more successful in finding out how he died than the investigation into the World's Fair bomb would be.

But even all that was on hold for reasons that didn't sit easily with many of New York's police officers. No one would investigate any death, however deeply it cut, until the English king had paid his scheduled visit to the World's Fair and was on his way to Washington.

Stefan Gillespie stood in the entrance to the cathedral, listening to the Latin words he knew so well, though they had never been his words. The stone pillars and arches and the vaulted ceiling high above were familiar enough as well. There was the smell of incense as well as the smell of cold stone, but it could have as easily been the Anglican St Patrick's of his Dublin childhood as New York's Catholic cathedral. 'Adiutorium nostrum in nomine Domini.' Our help is in the name of the Lord.

Michael Phelan, standing next to him, spoke the response. 'Qui fecit caelum et terram.' Who made heaven and earth. Then he turned away and walked across the narthex to the flickering candles of the shrine of Saint Anthony. As he did several officers stopped him and shook his hand. He seemed not really to notice.

Stefan watched him bow his head and cross himself. He watched him use a taper to light a candle. He watched him pray. He bowed his own head and let words he still held close trickle through his mind. He didn't want to be here. He was not a man who prayed. But this was a place that demanded something of him. It even demanded that those words were not only for him, and for those he loved, but that somewhere they were for the man who had tried to kill him as well. 'Lighten our darkness, we beseech thee, O Lord; and by thy great mercy defend us from all perils and dangers of this night.'

It was daylight outside and the noise of the New York traffic drifted in through the cathedral's heavy doors, but for Stefan Gillespie the previous night still felt close.

It hadn't been easy to walk into Police Headquarters in Centre Street that morning. The mood was as grim as anyone could expect it to be with three police officers dead. The Headquarters Detective Division knew the two Bomb Squad men well. And they had lost one of their own. The son of Inspector Ernie Phelan and the brother of Sergeant Michael Phelan had been shot down and his body had been tossed into the river. Aaron Phelan had been an administrator, not a detective; no one even knew what questions to ask yet.

The only person in Police Headquarters that morning who did know said nothing. He had no choice but to say nothing. All he wanted to do was get his prisoner out of the cells and leave the city of towers and lights behind. Its wonders had become a cellar room on 116th Street and a dead body in the Hudson that ought to have been his own.

Stefan had hoped that the last thing Michael Phelan would want to do that day was to drive him to the Marine Terminal at La Guardia, but drive him he did, intermittently raging, silent, bewildered, tearful, but in his grief feeling a sense of connection with Stefan's Irishness that Stefan himself found hard to bear.

370

Owen Harris followed behind them in a squad car, but there was to be a diversion that Stefan had not expected. The two cars headed north from Centre Street to St Patrick's Cathedral. With all that connectedness Sergeant Michael Phelan expected that Sergeant Stefan Gillespie would want to say a prayer for his brother, as probably every other police officer in New York would do that day.

Stefan understood; he understood how much it mattered that other people felt something too. And all he could offer was silence.

As he waited for Michael Phelan to finish his prayer, he was aware of someone standing at his shoulder. He turned to find Dominic Carroll there. It was clear from the cold expression on Carroll's face that the usual pleasantries weren't to be pursued. The question was what the Clan na Gael president knew about the previous night. Aaron Phelan had made it clear enough that what he was doing was his own decision. It was no more likely that he would have involved the man he solved problems for in Stefan's death than in Jimmy Palmer's. And Phelan had tried to dispose of him without any of the usual Irish connections. There was no police involvement, no Clan na Gael involvement, no Irish involvement at all. Killing an Irish policeman was not something anyone would like. But Dominic Carroll would surely know about Niamh; he would know about Kate; he would know Stefan had helped the women get across the border to Canada.

'You're here with Mikey.'

'I am,' Stefan nodded.

'Aaron told me. He knew you were there.'

'This wouldn't be the place to talk about it, Mr Carroll.'

'I don't intend to talk about it, Sergeant Gillespie.'

'She'll be with her family. Does how that happened matter so much?'

'And that's the whore of a sister's story, is it?'

Stefan could see Michael Phelan walking towards them.

'I'm sure you'll think what you think, Mr Carroll. But it's over.'

'No, it's not over. Remember that. When you see my wife, tell her.'

*

'The honeymoon suite, Sergeant Gillespie, I'm touched.'

At the rear of the Yankee Clipper's passenger deck there was a separate, self-contained cabin. Now it provided a place for Stefan Gillespie to keep Owen Harris out of sight of the rest of the flying boat's passengers. The plane was an hour out of New York, over the Eastern Seaboard and the New England coast. Harris was drinking a glass of champagne. Stefan had only coffee; he would not be drinking during the journey home. But he saw no reason not to let Owen Harris have something. It might be the last drink he had for a very long time; it was very possible that it might be the last drink he had before he was offered a glass of beer the night before an appointment with the English hangman. And maybe it would keep him quiet. Stefan was in no mood to listen to his endless meanderings about murder, mothers and Owen Harris.

The steward entered the suite at the back of the flying boat with a nervous knock. Apart from the fact that Stefan Gillespie was an Irish policeman, returning to Ireland with a prisoner, the crew weren't meant to know who Owen Harris was, but naturally enough they knew everything.

The steward carried a bottle of champagne. Stefan shrugged and nodded. He poured another glass. Harris looked up, smiling broadly; then he sang.

"'As he walks along St Stephen's Green
With an independent air he
Can hear the boys declare he
Must surely be a fairy – "
Do you know that one?'

'I'm afraid I don't, sir,' replied the steward with grit-like politeness.

'I'm sure you'd pick it up in no time.'

The steward walked out.

'She has to be, Sergeant, wouldn't you say?'

Stefan had already had enough.

'I'll give you two choices, Mr Harris. You can shut up and spend the next twenty hours in here, free to move around, free to go to bed when you want, free to eat when you want, free to have a drink, or you can carry on with the bollocks and I can cuff you to the seat, and I'll just spend the rest of the journey sitting out there in the main cabin. It's entirely up to you.'

Owen Harris scowled petulantly. He looked out of the window.

'All right, but it's going to be extremely boring either way.'

Stefan picked up a copy of *The Irish Times*.

Owen Harris sipped his drink, gazing at the Atlantic. He picked up a map of the flying boat's journey. He idly traced his finger along the route.

'When do we get to this Botwood place?'

'It'll be the early hours of the morning.'

'Do we get out?'

'No.'

'It says here we can.'

'You don't leave this cabin.'

Harris groaned. He put his head back, looking at the ceiling.

'Newfoundland is a rather wonderful name. "O my America, my Newfoundland, My kingdom safest when with one man manned." But Botwood leaves a lot to be desired, as names go, don't you think?'

Stefan turned a page of the newspaper and continued reading.

The authorities in Washington have announced that Seán Russell, the IRA leader, has been released from detention, following his arrest at Detroit at the time of the Royal visit to Windsor. He is officially at liberty on five thousand dollars bail, guaranteed by Mr Dominic Carroll of New York. Mr Russell was recently seen at a Clan na Gael meeting in New York, where he called on Americans of Irish birth to lend their moral and financial support to the 'organised will-o'-the-wisp' bombings of English cities. Russell said that all the bombings had been arranged so as to avoid loss of life but, he added, 'if any of our men are executed we cannot give assurances that we will exercise the same care'. At the meeting Mr Russell predicted that the English would be so terrified in the next few months that the government would grant all IRA demands and leave Northern Ireland.

Owen Harris still stared up at the ceiling, mouthing words to himself, slowly, rhythmically, quietly, and snorting

374

as if what he was saying was extraordinarily funny and he was forcing himself to hold back his laughter. 'Botwood, Spotwood, Blotwood, Rotwood, Clotwood, Begotwood, Snotwood, Dotwood, Shotwood, Whatwood, Notwood, Totwood, Sotwood.' After several minutes he stopped. And as Stefan looked round he was asleep.

When the flying boat landed at Botwood in Newfoundland, most of the passengers disembarked. Stefan Gillespie stayed in the suite with his prisoner. Owen Harris had said little after the first hour of the flight. He had slept until dinner and had eaten in sullen silence. When the beds were made up he climbed into one of them and pulled the curtains shut. Stefan still sat in his seat, sometimes trying to read, sometimes trying to bring some clarity to what he would have to tell Military Intelligence in Dublin; he still had John Cavendish's work to finish. It had almost cost him his life. He wasn't pleased when Harris opened the curtains and got out of bed. The fact that he felt he had to stay awake didn't mean he wanted company, let alone Harris's company. But when the almost-actor asked if he could have a brandy, Stefan called the steward.

Owen Harris sipped the drink and looked out at the lights and the fishing boats in the harbour at Botwood. Then he started to speak, very quietly, in a voice so unlike the shrill, mocking tone Stefan had always heard before, that he hardly recognised it as belonging to the same man.

'My mother had been in hospital since Christmas, after a nervous breakdown. She quite often had a nervous breakdown at Christmas, usually around the time my father was sitting down to Christmas dinner with his mistress. I came home two weeks after my father decided they could let her out of the convalescent home. I'd been sharing a flat with Charlie Mawson, from the Gate. That didn't work out. Just because you enjoy being in bed with a man doesn't mean you can bear sitting across a table eating toast with him every morning, listening to him tell you what a grand feller he is. Of course, Medea didn't want me back. She told me to go and live with my father. Well, the only thing worse than living with Medea is living with Moloch. The thing was I needed money, desperately. I'd been waiting for an opportunity to really start acting, and the Gate tour was my chance. I had to have the money for the passage though. I really did think Medea would cough up. Yet she wouldn't give it to me. She told me she didn't want me in the house, but she wouldn't give me the money to go. That's Medea, of course. She's never got any dosh, because Moloch doesn't give her enough. Well, he gives her a damned sight more than he gives me, and she has ways. She has her little tricks for getting her pointy fingers on some cash when she needs it.'

He turned to Stefan and shook his head.

'You don't need all that. You only need to know what happened.'

Stefan said nothing. He had been told that questioning Owen Harris wasn't his business. But it wasn't his business to stop him talking. The first time a suspect told a policeman his story mattered a lot. Whether every word was true or every word was a lie, or whatever mix of the two it presented, it was as much a key to a crime as any piece of forensic evidence. He didn't know Harris, but he had seen enough to realise that if the man wanted to speak, he had to be allowed to speak. He had heard the different voices Harris put between himself and the world; this sounded like the man himself. For all Stefan knew it might be the only time that voice would be heard.

'We'd been rowing, which was the usual state of affairs. A lot of crockery had been thrown, along with a lot of smelling salts sniffed and threats of suicide from Medea. She was always under pressure, you see. Pressure from me, pressure from Moloch, pressure from her nerves, pressure from the Hospitals' Sweepstake about the money she collected for them. Well, enough said about that. She was more than a little naughty on that front. But it was the same old failed life and failed marriage and a son who was the biggest failure of all. It was all hopeless and she wished she was dead, and bla, bla, bla. I went out to get drunk, as any sane man would. It was all quiet when I came back. I thought I'd better say sorry, and try to wheedle the money out of her by crying. Sometimes it works. I found her on the bed. She must have cut her throat. It wasn't easy to tell. It was such a mess, blood everywhere. You wouldn't think there could be so much. God, the smell!'

He got up and started to pace slowly up and down the cabin.

'I did think about the police. I thought about a lot of things. It was disconcerting. She'd been threatening to kill herself since I was eight or nine. The last thing I imagined was that she'd do anything about it. I realised I had to do the decent thing by the old stick. Medea was rather religious in her own way. She wouldn't have wanted anyone to know she'd killed herself. Most of all she wouldn't have wanted Moloch to know. It would have meant he'd won. She said it's what he'd been trying to do since he left her, get her to kill herself, so he could marry his nurse. I had to find a way to get rid of her. That's when it came to me, the sea! A Viking burial! If I could clean the place up and get her into the Irish Sea with the Austin. The body would drift off and if the car was found it would be clean as a whistle. No one would know. She would be a mysterious disappearance. Let Moloch put that in his pipe and smoke it!'

He stopped and looked round at Stefan triumphantly.

'Of course cleaning up all that blood wasn't easy. Everywhere! I rolled Medea up in a carpet and got her out to the garage and into the car. I drove her out to Corbawn Lane. But there was some idiot parked there, right at the end. And they'd put up some barrier too, God knows what for, so I couldn't drive all the way. But there was the garden at the house. I could get to the sea there. But the damned car got stuck in the hedge. The only thing was to carry her down and drop her in. But do you know what? The parked car was still there, at the bottom of the lane. I'd have been spotted, even in the dark. I crept along the cliff, to see what the hell was going on. They were copulating of course. I mean, honestly! They were over an hour! I sat in the back with Medea. I put my arm round her and talked to her. It was odd being where we lived when I was a boy, before Moloch and Medea went their separate ways. I don't think I ever really talked to her after that, or my father. They had each other to destroy, you see. Life was the great battle, the eternal battle. Moloch versus Medea!'

He suddenly sat down again, laughing. Stefan could hear the note of shrillness in his voice again; the real Owen Harris was beginning to fade.

'Anyway, the copulators eventually finished copulating and drove away. I carried her to the edge of the cliff. I climbed a little way down, and dropped her into the water. The tide was quite high. And that was it. Except that I still couldn't budge the fucking Austin. I got a lift to Ballsbridge from a very helpful chap and his wife. But the mess there, the –'

He stopped as suddenly as he had started.

There was a knock on the door. The steward looked in. 'We'll be taking off again in five minutes.'

As he closed the door Owen Harris looked round at Stefan.

'Haven't you got any questions?'

'No,' said Stefan simply.

He had a lot of questions, but his orders were that he didn't ask them.

'Is that a technique of detection you developed yourself, Sergeant,' grinned Harris, 'not asking any questions, I mean? It's certainly original.'

'The questions will have to wait for Superintendent Gregory.'

'Is he any fun?'

'I doubt you'll find him a great deal of fun, no.'

'It's all going to be very tedious, isn't it?'

Stefan said nothing; this was the Owen Harris he didn't want to hear.

'Do you think I should call character witnesses?'

'What?'

'At the trial. People do, don't they? You wheel out some influential friends to say what a fine fellow you are and you couldn't possibly have committed unspeakable crimes. You'd be quite surprised how many chaps I've encountered, in pursuit of fun as it were, who are rather influential, so many in fact that I could imagine them performing as a

kind of chorus for me.' He frowned a moment then gave
a childish grin. 'I'll draw up a list –
James Gordon Deale, so fond of rugger,
Loves to scrum down hugger-mugger,
Hairy cheeks, skin like a slug, a
Nicer chap you couldn't bugger.
Now sixty, Doctor Larry Brady,
Likes to dress up as a lady,
Rotten sex, but still, he paid me
Not to snitch to old Ma Brady.
In Dáil debates A.P.'s not seen,
But in the Gents' on Stephen's Green –'

The great propellers of the Yankee Clipper turned and
clattered several times; then the engines roared. It was enough
to stop Owen Harris in mid flow. Minutes later the flying
boat was racing into the darkness, away from the lights of
Botwood, cutting elegantly through the waters of the Bay of
Exploits.

It lifted into the air quite suddenly, the motors straining
and whining, caught in that goose-like moment between
clumsy take off and soaring flight. And then the wings were
lifted up, effortlessly, by the power of solid air beneath them.
And there was only the night outside, and the high horizons
of distance, and the low hum of the now calm engines.

In the dim light, Stefan picked up his note pad and
started to write down what Owen Harris had said. Whether
Superintendent Gregory wanted him to do it or not, that
was his job. And Stefan had other things to think about.
He needed to see his son again. And he wanted to see the
woman who must be asleep on a boat now, somewhere on
the ocean below him.

Owen Harris was silent, staring at nothing. He would

not speak again until the plane started to descend to the Shannon Estuary and Foynes, hours away on the other side of dawn. He made no sound and no movement, yet Stefan knew that he was crying; but crying for who or for what he could have no idea.

PART THREE
Upstroke

Last night an Irish Times reporter spent two hours in O'Connell Street and other main thoroughfares in the city. He sat in restaurants, rode on tramcars, mixed with the people in the bus queues, and listened; but the one subject about which people were not talking was the war that had started that day. The weather was the favourite topic of conversation. Everyone agreed the like of it had never been seen. Lightning and loud peals of thunder had preceded torrential downpours; roadways were torn up and there was much flooding. In Dublin it was amid thunder and lightning that 40,000 people saw the Kilkenny hurling team beat the best team Cork could field, by one point, at Croke Park, in a match continually interrupted by the weather. Thousands were driven from the uncovered stands, drenched to the skin. Throughout the city, anybody who had been caught out-of-doors had a real experience to tell. Dear Dublin! London, Paris, Berlin and Warsaw are living in fear and terrible dread, but Dublin remains just the same inconsequent, 'aisy-going' Dublin. The Irish Times

23. Dún Laoghaire

Home was not as easy as Stefan Gillespie wanted it to be. The journey to New York had ended in darkness and in things he either didn't want to speak about or couldn't speak about. The excitement everyone expected him to show about the city could not be as natural and effusive as it should have been, and despite his best attempts, for the first few days anyway, he felt like he was avoiding the subject that should have been all there was to talk about. His mother and father couldn't understand his distance, especially when conversation about something, really anything, that was new and bright and full of great things was what the farmhouse kitchen needed, because if Stefan was making a poor job of wanting to talk about New York, Tom Gillespie was making an equally poor job of wanting to listen. Tom knew now that his friends Jane and Alexander were leaving Ireland, along with their mother, and that the path through the woods between Kilranelagh and Whitehall Grove wouldn't be trodden that summer. It hit him as hard as his grandmother knew it would, and postcards of the Empire State Building wouldn't soften the blow. He pretended it mattered less than it did, though the long faces and the unnerving silence from all three children told its own story. Both Stefan and Tom were unusually quiet; unusually they couldn't share what they were quiet about with each other.

Stefan had been working hard since his return. Anything that needed doing that he would normally do at the Garda station in Baltinglass had been left for his return, and a bit besides. And now that he was back Superintendent Riordan, still irritated by his sergeant's absence in the first place, wanted it all done immediately. Lambing was coming to an end at the farm but there were still long nights to spend in the fields with his father that meant little sleep. And after two meetings with Ned Broy, and with the Garda Commissioner and Commandant Gearóid de Paor of Military Intelligence, he had been instructed to conduct an investigation into Captain John Cavendish's death in conjunction with G2, in the light of information he had brought back from New York.

It was a delicate inquiry; there were no witnesses; only the uncorroborated statement of a man who appeared to be a German intelligence officer and certainly wouldn't appear in Dublin to repeat what he saw. Left to himself the Garda Commissioner would have put the whole thing on the long finger for long enough to let it drop off and be forgotten. If nothing could be proved, opening up the sore had little to recommend it. That wasn't how Gearóid de Paor saw it. John Cavendish had been his friend. Even if it led to nothing he wanted to know what happened.

Now Sergeant Gillespie was in Dublin again. Superintendent Terry Gregory wanted to talk to him about his conversation with Owen Harris on the Yankee Clipper. He had been told before that no one wanted a report from him, and that he was a courier not a detective, but he had put one in anyway. Terry Gregory could do what he wanted with it. Nothing changed Stefan's opinion that the first story a suspect told mattered, and there should be a record of it at least. Nothing changed Superintendent Gregory's opinion that the sergeant from Baltinglass was an interfering pain in the arse either.

'Do you believe this?' asked Terry Gregory.

He was turning the pages of the report Sergeant Gillespie had sent him. It consisted of not much more than an account of the conversations he had had with Owen Harris at NYPD Police Headquarters and on the flying boat; attached to it was Micheál Mac Liammóir's scribbled note of the conversation he had had at Centre Street which was even more wall-to-wall nonsense. The superintendent skimmed the pages with a half smile and raised eyebrows that he kept raised throughout. It was less the content that he found funny than the idea there was anything in the way of serious information to be extracted from this bollocks. It puzzled him that Stefan had even bothered to write it all down, let alone type it up and send it to him.

'When I say, do you believe this, I suppose what I mean is, are you telling me I should take all this bollocks, extract the words "I didn't do it", and put it up as some kind of proof of innocence? I can just about see your friend Mr Mac Liammóir being mad enough to see the sense in that, but even four years down among the sheep shaggers can't have addled your brain that much, Sergeant. Or maybe you're just doing it to take the piss?'

They sat in a room off Lower Castle Yard at the back of Dublin Castle, where a collection of garages and tightly hemmed-in buildings made up the headquarters of the

Garda Síochana's Metropolitan Division. It also provided the cramped rooms of a Detective Branch that was more or less indistinguishable from the Special Branch that dealt with threats to the security of the Irish state. They were the same cramped rooms that the Dublin Metropolitan Police's Detective Branch had used, when it too had been virtually indistinguishable from a Special Branch that dealt with threats to the security of the British state. The ceilings were black with more than a century of tobacco smoke; Terry Gregory was adding to it as usual.

'Do you need to know if I believe it?'

'I'm interested.'

'You'll have a better idea what's true, sir. And maybe what looks like nonsense might relate to something. If you haven't got it, you can't make any judgement. Even if you're just trying to get into his head –'

'I've spent long enough talking to the man to know that's the last place I'd want to be. But with friends like you and Mac Liammóir, I don't know if Harris needs anybody to prosecute him. You two could do a grand job by yourselves. You've a man accused of killing his mammy, singing songs, cracking jokes, telling us she was robbing the Hospitals' Sweepstake, and when he's not parading the fact that he's a fairy, he's explaining that the old lady stabbed herself to death a dozen times and he dumped her in the sea to save her any embarrassment about it. How does that sound as a defence?'

'It does have its weaknesses, sir.'

'Then there's Mr Charles Mawson of the Gate Theatre Company, who is of the firm opinion that Mr Harris couldn't have killed his mother because he didn't say a word about it during the six days they shared a cabin across the

Atlantic. Mr Mawson does tell us, according to his boss Mr Mac Liammóir, that he's prepared to come forward as a character witness. Maybe you can imagine a line of questioning when Mr Mawson assures the court that his friend Owen Harris couldn't possibly have murdered his dear oul sainted mother, who he'd never said a bad word against. "You know Mr Harris well?" "I should do. Haven't I been up his arse enough times?"'

'I just put down what Harris said. I don't know if what's there proves he did it or not. But some of the time he was talking about what happened. I thought there might be something he wouldn't say again –'

'Well, he's said it again all right. Again and again. Word for word. That's what's odd about it. It really is word for word. Did he memorise it?'

'I think that's the kind of mind he's got. It's a performance.'

Stefan Gillespie watched Terry Gregory for a moment. The half smile had long gone; the eyebrows had not been raised in some time. He hadn't just been called in because he'd irritated the Special Branch man. However clear it all seemed, Gregory didn't know what to make of Owen Harris. While pretending Stefan's opinion didn't matter, he was asking for it now.

'You don't believe the suicide stuff? He found her dead –'

'I don't know, sir. Nobody would believe it. But it's as if he does.'

'Maybe that's just good acting.'

'I don't know if there's anything Harris is good at, but the one thing Micheál Mac Liammóir said he can't do is act. I did feel that he believed it.'

'Which means he's mad.'

'Or telling the truth.'

'Suicide with a wood axe?' Superintendent Gregory shook his head.

'He never mentions the axe.'

'No. He says a razor. Not that there was a razor.'

'So why didn't he take the axe and dump that in the sea as well?'

'He'd hardly have been thinking very clearly –'

'He was thinking clearly enough to try and clean the blood off. He didn't do that, but I heard he managed to get rid of any fingerprints on it. Why bother? Why not dump it with the body? But he didn't. He got his mother into the back of the car, then all he could think of doing with the axe he'd killed her with was to stick it under a pile of turf. If there was a cat in hell's chance of anyone believing the suicide story, the axe is solid evidence that contradicts it.'

'There's one thing worse than no analysis, Sergeant, and that's too much. If he'd been behaving rationally he wouldn't have killed her at all.'

'All he wanted was money, and she had a box in her wardrobe with hundreds of pounds in it. That has to be where he got his fare for the boat from Cobh. But he only took what he needed. If he killed her for the money why not take it all? It didn't matter then. He knew where it came from. He knew it was money she'd stolen from the Hospitals' Sweepstake –'

'There's no evidence about where that money came from.'

'And there won't be, will there?'

'It's not an issue in this crime, Sergeant.'

There was silence for a moment. It was a silence that told Stefan Gillespie he had crossed a line the superintendent didn't want crossed. Terry Gregory closed the file on his desk and stood up. He walked to the window and looked out. He turned back to Stefan.

'So is that it, Sergeant?'

'What do you mean?'

'You've got some doubts about the story a madman's telling us, because there are bits that don't make sense.'

'When he was talking to me on the plane, it was the nearest I got to hearing a voice that wasn't, well, someone else's. It seemed worth saying.'

'I thought there might be more, Sergeant.'

The half smile was back on the superintendent's face, but Stefan could see that somewhere, behind that, there was a slight sense of disappointment.

'I need to put together a case out of what's in front of me. If I find any evidence that makes sense of the shite you've given me, I'm always happy to change my mind. And on the subject of shite, why were you in New York so long? Why have you been talking to Commandant de Paor?'

It was an abrupt change of tack, spoken as if it followed on from the question of the guilt or innocence of Owen Harris, but Stefan felt that this was probably the real reason he was at Dublin Castle, the real reason Terry Gregory had been talking to him as if his opinion mattered.

'Ned Broy didn't seem to think it was worth telling me why my prisoner had to sit in an NYPD cell for another week, after he'd spent a fucking fortune to get you to New York and back on the flying boat. Why?'

'He must have told you about the death of Captain Cavendish?'

'Wasn't that an accident?'

'It had to be investigated.'

'I heard he'd been celebrating Paddy's day too enthusiastically.'

'The consul general wanted someone to liaise with the NYPD.'

'Do you know, I've never liaised. I'm not sure I can even spell it.'

'I happened to be there, sir,' said Stefan.

'So was it an accident?'

'I'm not sure.'

'I heard the Detective Division in New York was sure.'

'There were still some details –'

'Is that why you're going down to Cork with the head of G2?'

'I'm doing what the Commissioner's asked me to do, Superintendent.'

'So fuck off, Mr Gregory, is that it?'

'You'd better ask the Commissioner.'

'And he'll tell me to fuck off?'

'That'll be up to him, sir.'

Superintendent Gregory laughed.

'You won't make yourself very popular in Cork.'

Stefan said nothing. He didn't think any more replies were needed.

'Cavendish was a G2 man, wasn't he?'

'He was working at the World's Fair.'

'There you go again with the bollocks, Sergeant.'

'I'm sorry, sir.'

'You know the IRA chief of staff was in New York?'

'I read something about that, yes.'

'I thought you met him at a Clan na Gael party on St Patrick's Day.'

'I forgot. We didn't have much of a conversation.'

Superintendent Gregory took the last cigarette from his packet of Woodbine and lit it. He asked no more questions, but he looked at Stefan Gillespie for a long moment without speaking, the half smile on his face.

As he left Superintendent Gregory's office a man was waiting in the corridor. He was probably sixty, tall and heavy-set, with a dark beard, neatly trimmed. His hair was dark as well, a little too dark to be quite its own colour. He wore a black jacket and pin-striped trousers, and an already old-fashioned wing collar. He carried a hat and a pair of gloves in one hand. He looked overdressed for the Castle Yard, or maybe he just looked overdressed. He eyed Stefan curiously, as if he knew him, and as Stefan walked towards him he stepped forward and held out his hand, smiling.

'I gather you are Sergeant Gillespie.'

'That's right.'

'You brought my son back from New York.'

'Doctor Harris.'

'I was concerned about him there of course. I know he had friends, but not really reliable people. He was very vulnerable in a city like that.'

Stefan realised Doctor Harris was still shaking his hand.

'You brought him home safely. And for that I thank you.'

And finally the doctor let go of his hand.

Stefan was at a loss for a reply. The usual kind of thing, 'Well, he's safe home!' or 'He's in safe hands now!' didn't apply, however safe those hands might be. He said nothing, but simply returned the doctor's smile.

'We're rather going round in circles at the moment. Owen

will keep decorating the basic facts with all sorts of gibberish. I want him to keep to the facts as far as possible. He's trying the superintendent's patience –' He stopped abruptly. 'I'm sorry, Sergeant. You'll understand how difficult this is. Obviously you were very good to him. He speaks very highly of you. But a lot of the time he doesn't seem to understand how serious the situation is.'

'I think he does when he chooses to, Doctor Harris.'

The smile that was still on the doctor's face faded. What was left was somehow a more honest expression. He nodded. He understood his son.

'You seem to know rather more about my son than most people here.'

'I doubt that.'

'I'm afraid I don't, Sergeant. Do you get any sense of how it's going?'

'I don't know. I'm not working on the case.'

'You can't say, of course you can't. The superintendent is very good. I think he's being as helpful as he can. He wants to find the truth, whatever that is. I have only one concern. I can't undo what has been done. I'm not interested in truth. I'm not interested in justice. I don't really know what that is in a case like this. I simply want to save my son's life, and everything I know about him suggests that the less he says, the more likely he is to live.'

He looked at Stefan, questioningly, as if he wanted his opinion now. At that moment the door from Terry Gregory's office opened and the superintendent looked out. He was expecting Owen Harris's father.

'You're here, Doctor. Come in, will you?'

Cecil Harris reached out his hand and shook Stefan's again.

'Will you be giving evidence?'

'I'm not sure. I may have to –'

The superintendent had walked back into his office.

'Good,' said the doctor. 'Owen will like that. I think you'll do well.'

He walked away, into the superintendent's office, smiling again. The door closed. As Stefan Gillespie walked out into Castle Yard, up towards Dame Street, he couldn't help feeling he had just been interviewed for a part.

He met Dessie MacMahon in Neary's in Chatham Street. It was well off the beat of Special Branch and the Castle detectives. Dessie was still at the Castle, still attached to the case, still working for Superintendent Gregory.

'The super's been asking a lot of questions about you.'

'I know. He told me.'

'He had you followed when you went to G2.'

'It doesn't surprise me. I'll take it as a compliment.'

'I don't think it's got anything to do with Harris. He wanted to know what you were up to in New York. That G2 man who died there –'

'Well, I don't think he'll follow me down to Baltinglass.'

'What did you make of the old man, the doctor?'

'Doctor Harris?'

'I saw he was in.' Dessie took out his packet of Sweet Afton.

'He's set on keeping his son's neck out of a noose. That's about it. There's not much else he can do, as a father, whatever sort of son he's got.'

'Do you remember the two lads we saw, in Herbert Lane?' said Dessie. 'When I took you there, before you went to see Terry Gregory?'

For a moment Stefan couldn't remember.

'Collecting sticks for the fire.'

'I remember.'

'I was talking to them the next day. They were in a tenement in Dominick Street. There was a route they did every couple of days, to get firewood. They always went along the back of Herbert Place. They knew your man Harris, Owen I mean. He always put something out for them.'

'The Lost Boys,' said Stefan, smiling.

'You know who they are?'

'Slightly and Tootles. Harris mentioned them, to Mr Mac Liammóir.'

'Well if they weren't lost then, they are now.'

'I'm not with you.'

'They've left Dominick Street, nine of them. The whole family's emigrated. A week ago now. No one in the tenement's exactly sure where they went. It begins with A though, America or Australia. They came up on the Sweepstake. One minute I was talking to them, the next they were gone. The only thing is, when I asked around a bit more, they never did win anything on the Sweepstake. But the oul feller did come into a good bit of money.'

'What made you want to find all that out?'

'They were in Herbert Lane that afternoon, when Mrs Harris disappeared. Five o'clock, maybe a bit later. They saw a car pulling out at the bottom of the lane. They knew it. It was the old man's. Doctor Harris's. Now I do know Terry Gregory's spoken to the doctor. He's got the details of where the doctor was that day. But Herbert Place isn't on the list.'

'Has the superintendent spoken to them?'

'I suppose he would have got round to it eventually.'

'So how sure were they?'

'I went back to Dominick Street with them. The little one gave me this, from his collection. There wasn't much he didn't know about cars.'

Detective Sergeant MacMahon took out his wallet. He opened it and put a Gallaghers' cigarette card down on the table. It was a drawing of a big, square saloon, light green and dark green, a Sunbeam Dawn.

'Doctor Harris's was blue. Unfortunately he doesn't have it any more. He sold it to a dealer three days after his wife disappeared. The dealer took it to England.'

'What does Superintendent Gregory think about all that?'

'Well, he did think about it.'

'And?'

'And you brought Owen Harris back, so he stopped thinking about it.'

Dessie MacMahon stood in one of the two rooms at the back of the tenement in Dominick Street where the Lost Boys had lived. It was empty. It was like thousands of other rooms across the centre of Dublin that filled the rotting hulks of houses in the carefully choreographed streets that had been the homes of the wealthy and the well-heeled, and not much more than a hundred years earlier. They had been graceful, elegant avenues that ought to have been one of the city's greatest treasures; an entire Georgian city of a size and scale and beauty unlike anywhere else. Instead they were its dark and constant shame.

This room was like all the others, except that now it didn't have eight, nine, ten people living in it. The plaster had fallen from the walls. The stuccoed ceiling had long since crumbled to reveal the bare lathes looking through to the floor above. The panelling had gone from the walls for firewood. The broken window panes, patched with torn paper, sat in rotting frames. When you breathed you breathed in the damp, clammy, mould-stale air. Dessie knew the smell of the place well enough; the smell of smoking fires from blocked chimneys; tobacco and something like boiling cabbage; refuse from the yard below, and somewhere, always, urine and puke. There were the same noises he knew too. A crying baby, a man and a woman arguing loudly, violently, a drunken voice singing, a woman shouting for her children, and laughter; there was always that too.

There might have been a few pieces of furniture here a week ago, but whatever had been left behind had already been burned or sold by the other nine families who packed the other rooms of the house. Dessie gazed down at the yard below, where three raggedy children were chasing each other through the rubbish and rubble. He turned as footsteps echoed across the bare, stained, creaking wooden floor. Stefan Gillespie had walked up from the floor below.

'You're right. Best bet is America. No one knows where they are.'

'You think they would with a guard asking the questions?'

'So that's it?'

Dessie nodded.

'Maybe they'll hear from them when they get there?'

'I lived in a room like this till I was twelve,' said Dessie. 'My father died in it. He was thirty-seven. The day they took his body away was the first time I ever had a bed. No one paid my mother to get us out, but when she found a way, no one heard from us again. They're gone. That's how it is.' He walked out.

As he did so it was as if a shutter had come down.

When Stefan went back into town he crossed Grafton Street and walked through to Hodges Figgis in Dawson Street. He was looking for a book. He wanted it to be special, but not so special as to be embarrassing. He wanted something with pictures, or drawings, but he didn't want it to be ordinary; he wanted something that Kate O'Donnell would be surprised by.

He looked for a long time along the shelves in the bookshop, and when he found it he liked the fact that it wasn't a new book at all, but a battered book of poems, illustrated by an artist whose work he recognised without needing to see the name. There was a book of Hans Andersen's Fairy Tales at home that his mother had bought for Tom two Christmases ago, with similar pictures; though the rich, intricate, swirling figures in Harry Clarke's drawings had slightly alarmed him. Stefan smiled as he flicked through the pages. The style was the same, but the female figures in this book would have alarmed his mother this time; he didn't think they would alarm Kate. She would know Harry Clarke; she would know his illustrations as well as his stained glass windows. The poems were by Algernon Charles Swinburne. Nobody read Swinburne any more, but somehow he felt that made the book less ordinary too.

It cost a lot more than he had intended to spend. The assistant in Hodges Figgis eyed him awkwardly as he paid, then put the book in a heavy paper bag, folding the top securely twice. He started to tie string round it.

'There's no need to tie —'

'It's all right, sir.' The assistant kept tying. 'It's not a book that should have been on the open shelves so. It must have been put there by mistake.'

Stefan looked puzzled; the man was whispering.

'The illustrations,' mouthed the assistant without any sound at all.

Kate O'Donnell had been back in Ireland for almost a week, since the *Empress of Canada* had docked at Belfast. She and her sister were staying with their parents in Dún Laoghaire. Kate was trying to find a job and somewhere to live with Niamh. The kindness of their parents would be something that neither of them would be able to take for very long. They wanted to help, but they also wanted to know nothing about anything, and from the moment the two women arrived at the high flat-fronted terrace in Monkstown Road, Mr and Mrs O'Donnell were in constant fear that their kindness would involve them facing things they expected Niamh and Kate to leave at the door. For Kate and her sister, who didn't want to talk anyway, except to each other, it was still a cloying, claustrophobic, nervy atmosphere, where any ill-timed word seemed to reduce everyone in the house to silence.

The first thing Kate had done was to send a postcard to Stefan Gillespie in Baltinglass. She wanted to see him as soon as possible anyway, but she needed to see him too. He was the only person who knew everything, and that meant he was someone she could say anything to. She told him to call as soon as he could. And she knew he would come soon. But by the time Stefan got off the tram in Dún Laoghaire something had changed. No one had considered it his business what Military Intelligence intended to do with the information Niamh Carroll had given him. That was over. G2 had the IRA key and it would open up all the ciphers

John Cavendish had collected. But they had all – Stefan, Kate, Niamh – been naïve to think that would be the end of the matter.

Commandant de Paor had arrived at the house in Monkstown Road two days after Kate and Niamh came home. Niamh spent eight hours the next day in the G2 offices at Portobello Barracks being questioned. De Paor wanted anything else she had; names, places, courier routes. It had been three years since she had had any contact with Clan na Gael or the IRA; the key to the cipher was all she had to give. The questioning wasn't harsh, but it was more than enough to break the fragile confidence Niamh Carroll was struggling to find. The news of Jimmy Palmer's death had already made her withdrawn and tearful. It had already made her want to run again. The feeling that she couldn't shake off what she had already run from, that there was just another set of people to watch her and follow her plunged her back into a black, unmoving depression that not only filled Kate with anger, it would make staying at her parents' home even more impossible than before.

So when Stefan Gillespie stood on the doorstep at 18 Monkstown Road the reception he received was very different from the one he was expecting. It was Kate's mother who answered the door. When he gave his name she looked at him slightly oddly. He thought she must have heard it and couldn't quite place him. So it was only for a joke that he said, 'Just tell her it's Sergeant Gillespie.' The joke didn't go down well. Mrs O'Donnell stared at him for a moment, almost with a look of fear, and turned back into the house, shouting Kate's name at the top of her voice, and leaving him on the doorstep.

A moment later Kate appeared; she wasn't smiling; she didn't ask him to come in. She walked out on to the path and pulled the front door to behind her. Stefan was smiling, clutching his parcel from Hodges Figgis.

'It's good to see you.'

She didn't reply.

'I got you something, I thought –'

Something was wrong. He didn't know what to say.

'Why couldn't you leave her alone?'

'What?'

'Have you got more questions? What's it going to be today?'

'I don't know what you're talking about, you said I should –'

'I went to the barracks. Eight hours we were there. It was like she'd been arrested. I don't know whether they were soldiers or policemen. They kept asking questions she couldn't answer. They kept mentioning you. "Mr Gillespie told us . . . Sergeant Gillespie said . . . In the sergeant's report . . ." Aren't they satisfied yet? Have they sent you back for more, is that it?'

'Kate, I've come to see you.'

'No flowers then? Really, Sergeant!'

He was glad he had abandoned the idea of flowers.

'I had no idea, Kate. I didn't know –'

Her face was flushed with anger; but he could see tears too.

'Leave us alone. If you need some more thanks – thanks! Fuck off!'

She strode back into the house. The door slammed shut.

He stood for a moment, holding his hat and his parcel. He stepped off the path and put the Hodges Figgis bag down on the sill of the bay window. She could do what she liked with it. He put on his hat. And he walked away.

24. Béarra

When the two cars drove into the farmyard at Pallas Strand, Colm McCarthy was watching. He had been driving the cattle out to the Long Field, the closest field to the sea, the one that almost met the beach. Walking back he had heard the sound of the engines over the quiet pulse of the breakers and the lazy calling of the gulls. They were expected.

Dinnie Purcell had cycled from Horan's at the crossroads to say they had left the Garda Barracks in Castleberehaven just after ten o'clock.

The Garda sergeant and the army commandant had been in County Cork for three days now; in the city, in Cobh, in Macroom, in Drimoleague, in Kealkill. They had spoken to almost all the hurlers who had travelled to New York. Some knew nothing, and those who did said nothing at first; several remarked that although they knew nothing the man who had died had had it coming. There were no witnesses however to challenge the empty statements of ignorance and righteous indifference, real and unreal.

It was what Stefan Gillespie had expected; it was what the Garda Commissioner had told Commandant Gearóid de Paor to expect. But de Paor had his duty to do, to his friend John Cavendish and his fellow officer, Captain

Cavendish. And in Cobh one of the young hurlers finally found the death harder to ignore than he wanted it to be. He told Stefan and the G2 commandant that four of them had followed Cavendish up to the empty thirty-second floor of the Hampshire House from Dominic Carroll's apartment, where Colm McCarthy had confronted the man who had murdered his father seventeen years before. There had been hard words and a short, ugly argument, and then a fight. But it hadn't been much of a fight; they had held John Cavendish down and they had beaten him.

If he hadn't denied it all, maybe it wouldn't have happened; if he hadn't told Colm McCarthy that he had nothing to do with the death of his father all those years ago, nothing to do with the body half-buried on Pallas Strand, maybe they wouldn't have hurt him so much. It was the lying that turned Colm McCarthy's anger into fury. So, yes, they had given the captain a beating like hell; nothing like the hell the man deserved. But they'd stopped; they'd stopped and they'd walked away from it.

No one wanted it to go any further. Even McCarthy had had enough by then. And they had left him there alive. They went downstairs again and left the party. They had nothing to do with John Cavendish's death. The first any of them knew was when they were briefly questioned on the way to the boat next day.

After that it was easier for Stefan Gillespie and Gearóid de Paor to get the others to talk, but what they said was the same, exactly the same. They left him alive.

Commandant de Paor had always known that the last place they would come to would be the farm on Pallas Strand, right at the end of Cork on the Béarra Peninsula. It was where it had all begun, during the Civil War, and where the truth about how it had ended lay now. On the last night, in the hotel at Castleberehaven, the G2 commander had shown Stefan three hand-written pages from a note-book. They were the records John Cavendish had kept as a young Free State intelligence officer in 1922. It began with the afternoon that Luke McCarthy, a farmer of Pallas Strand, Cappanell, a well-known IRA man, had been taken to the police barracks in Castleberehaven for questioning about a bomb attack the previous day, in nearby Kenmare.

The two cars stopped in front of the farm. In the first car were a detective from Castleberehaven and two uniformed Gardaí. The detective was armed and in the back of the Austin there was a rifle. They weren't expecting trouble, but they were uneasy. This investigation wasn't something anyone in Cork wanted. The McCarthys were an old and respected Republican family; it was no secret that they still had close ties to the IRA. No one needed the past stirred up, whether it was by the young McCarthy or these outsiders, the Garda sergeant and the army commandant. The dead were dead, and the decent thing was to leave them dead. Some things needed to be buried with them. But the local men had no say in this. They preferred it to be left that way as well. The two men from Dublin would ask the questions.

Stefan recognised the young man who was standing in the farmyard watching them with defiance and undisguised contempt. It was the hurler who had launched into that strange, drunken conversation with John Cavendish on St Patrick's Day in New York. He looked sober enough now. And now Sergeant Gillespie knew what that conversation had been about; he knew what its consequences had been. He walked forward and spoke briskly. He was fully aware that their arrival was no surprise to anyone here.

'I'm Sergeant Gillespie. You may know why we're here.'

Colm McCarthy said nothing. He wasn't afraid of these people.

'We met in New York, on St Patrick's Day, when you were talking to Captain Cavendish,' continued Stefan. 'I don't know if you remember me.'

The young hurler was surprised. It wasn't something Stefan had said to anyone else in the team, and no one had recognised him so far. But he wanted McCarthy to know he had been there. It would unsettle him. And it would cut through all the pretence and evasion that had had to be cleared out of the way with the others. It wasn't about what had happened across an ocean, out of sight. Stefan was there. And even if McCarthy didn't remember much of that night very clearly, he was unsettled. The Garda sergeant's words took him back. The questions that he expected to be at a distance were very close.

There were two more people in the farmyard now. Maura McCarthy, Colm's mother and an older man Stefan Gillespie knew; the man who had broken up the argument in Carroll's apartment and had pulled the hurler away from the drunken confrontation. He was also the man who had looked so hard at the army officer, the man he was sure John Cavendish had recognised. Aidan McCarthy was Colm's uncle; he had married Maura McCarthy two years after her husband's body was found on Pallas Strand.

'Since you'll know every move we've made through County Cork, we can dispense with the formalities.' De Paor spoke now, stepping in front of Stefan. He wanted to

407

get on with this. 'Sergeant Gillespie is investigating the death of Captain John Cavendish. I am Commandant de Paor. I was the captain's commanding officer. You'll know the questions, so there's no need to waste the sergeant's time on shite. We'll want your front room, so.'

De Paor stepped past the woman and the older man by the door, ignoring them as he walked into their house. Officially he was there to observe, but though he had never given Stefan an order, it was done his way.

'We'll start with you, Mr McCarthy,' said Stefan to Colm.

The hurler shrugged. Despite the disturbing presence of the policeman who had stood beside the Free State soldier at the Hampshire House, the defiance was still there as he passed his mother and his uncle. His mother smiled in reassurance. Stefan followed him inside. Maura and Aidan McCarthy stayed outside. Neither of them spoke. There were two cars, and there were men in uniforms watching them. There were guns, even if they couldn't see them. For a moment it was seventeen years ago. Mrs McCarthy was standing with her dead husband and the man who was his brother, and the small boy who was now a man. Aidan McCarthy was back there too. Bile rose in his throat. It was not a place either of them was happy to be.

Stefan Gillespie sat in the small, cramped sitting room of the farmhouse. Like the one at Kilranelagh it wasn't used every day, but this one felt like it wasn't used at all. There were the usual family photographs, but over the fireplace and on the mantelpiece they were bigger, much bigger; and they were all of the same man, not much older than Stefan. He didn't need telling it was Luke McCarthy, Colm's father. The room was a shrine.

Colm McCarthy had decided to tell the truth. Silence

408

had been the original plan, but other people in the team had spoken now. It didn't matter anyway. He would say what had happened and he would say what he felt. He hadn't killed John Cavendish, but he wasn't troubled by his death. This was the man who had shot his father in the head, seventeen years ago, because he wouldn't give away his IRA comrades. This was the man who had ordered his Free State soldiers to drag Luke McCarthy's body to Pallas Strand and bury it there in the sand, to show the people of Béarra the price of being an IRA man; to show what might be in store for those who sheltered the rebels and lied for them and hid their guns.

He had known John Cavendish's name since the day he ran down to the beach and saw his father's body, and the black holes where his eyes had been. He remembered it all. Would anyone deny a son the right to beat the hell out his father's killer? If that's what they were there for, he had no problem telling these Free State gobshites what he had done. And he would have done more; maybe he should have done more. If his friends hadn't dragged him away, maybe he would have killed John Cavendish. And if he had done he'd have told them to their faces. As it was he was happy to tell them he hoped the man was rotting in hell. However his father's killer died in New York that night, it was a better death than he had given Luke McCarthy, his father.

It wasn't much more than Stefan Gillespie and Gearóid de Paor had anticipated. What the hurler had to say added no new information. It was the story they already knew. It was consistent in a way that Stefan recognised as being unpractised, unrehearsed. He stopped the questioning abruptly; they had heard it already. If there was more to say, McCarthy was hiding it well. And if Stefan had unsettled him by his presence at the Hampshire House that night, it had achieved nothing.

Gearóid de Paor had sat in the armchair across the room from the hurler, simply watching him. He had said nothing.

Now the older man, Aidan McCarthy, sat in the room, looking far less easy and far less defiant than his nephew. He glanced at the photograph of his dead brother, forever thirty-five, on the chimney breast. It was the deep past that was closer to him today than anything that happened in New York.

'When the lads came back down to the party, they told you what had happened to Captain Cavendish,' asked Stefan. 'Wouldn't that be right?'

It was a question, but he wasn't asking Aidan McCarthy to deny it.

'And you told them to clear off out of it, back to the hotel?'

'Yes.'

'And then what?'

Aidan McCarthy frowned, as if he genuinely couldn't remember.

'What did you do? Did you go and see if the captain was all right?'

'No.'

'You didn't think that might have been a good idea?'

'They'd given him a beating, that's all. I believed what they told me. And I still believe it. They gave him a going over, that's all there was to it.'

'You were meant to be keeping an eye on these lads. Am I right? That's why the Cork Board sent you, to help the bainisteoir and keep them out of trouble. Did you think it was all right for them to wander round New York, pissed as fucking hell, beating up anybody they took a dislike to?'

'As far as I knew he wasn't badly hurt. And he wasn't just anybody, was he? You've heard enough to know who he was, and what he did here, to Colm's father, to my brother. We don't apologise for remembering. I don't know how he ended up dead, but I know they didn't do it. That's the truth.'

Gearóid de Paor got up slowly. He had been sitting in an armchair, watching Aidan McCarthy as he had watched his nephew, lighting a series of cigarettes that he hardly smoked and stubbing them out in an ashtray as the ash dropped off. He walked across the room and looked out of the window.

'I know better than that, Mr McCarthy, and so do you.'

'I don't. The man was good enough when they left him. How many times do I have to say it? I'm sure there was blood and I'm sure he was hurt, but he wasn't dead. I just sent them to the hotel and then I went back too.'

'I'm not talking about that night,' said de Paor, turning round, 'though I'm sure you know more about that too. I'm talking about something else.'

'I'm not with you, Mr de Paor.'

'You know very well John Cavendish didn't kill your brother.'

Stefan knew it would come at some point; he had seen the notebook.

Aidan McCarthy stared. Then his face was red with anger.

'What? What the fuck are you talking about?'

'You heard me.'

'Everybody in Béarra knows it!' shouted McCarthy.

'I wouldn't say everybody. There'd be some old IRA men

who know better. Wouldn't you be one of them, Aidan? Weren't you there for it all?'

McCarthy frowned in a kind of disbelief, but he wasn't shouting now.

De Paor sat on the arm of the sofa and lit another cigarette.

'But that's history. Know your history, that's what we're always told. Know your history and never forget it. Well, I know more of yours than you seem to remember yourself. Now answer the sergeant's fucking questions!'

Aidan McCarthy's head dropped down. There was a long silence.

'What happened in New York, Mr McCarthy?' said Stefan quietly.

'I didn't go up there. I didn't want to see him. I just told –'

Stefan waited.

'I don't know how he died and that's the truth of it. I wanted to get out of the place. He said there wouldn't be any trouble. He said he'd sort –'

'I see. You told someone what had happened. Who was that?'

'It was a policeman, a New York cop. Mr Carroll introduced me to him at the Polo Ground, before one of the matches. He was a friend of Mr Carroll's and he was a Clan na Gael man. We had a drink with him in McSorley's one night. He said if there was a scrape or a mess, the lads –'

'What was the man's name?' asked Stefan; but he knew already.

'He was a captain, Aaron, I think it was, Captain –'
'Phelan.'
'Captain Phelan, that's him.'

'And you told him the story?'

'I told him about the fight –'

'No, I mean the whole story. You told him why they'd followed him up there at all, what it was he'd done. You'd have wanted him to know that.'

Aidan McCarthy didn't reply.

'You didn't tell him?'

'I told him something. I needed to explain –'

'What did you think when you heard Mr Cavendish had fallen thirty-two floors off the Hampshire House? Some way to tidy up a mess! But there was more than one mess being tidied up for you. It must have been a relief?'

'I promise you I didn't know.'

'No, I don't think you did. But you'd have wondered.'

McCarthy shook his head.

'All right, now get out,' said Stefan sharply.

Commandant de Paor looked round, surprised.

McCarthy stood up. He looked at them. It was a strange look, as if he was asking for their help in some way. He didn't want to be in the room and yet something stopped him leaving. He didn't want what was outside either.

'I said get out.'

McCarthy went. He was more afraid than when he had walked in.

'Explain,' said de Paor.

'You know who Aaron Phelan was,' answered Stefan. 'The NYPD captain I've told you about. Clan na Gael, IRA, and the man who cleaned up after Dominic Carroll, and not only where politics was concerned either. You might remember he was the man who was going to shoot me, before Mr Katzmann decided to do some cleaning up of his own. So I'd believe Aidan McCarthy. I'd say he really did think Aaron

413

Phelan would smooth things over with John Cavendish and make sure there wasn't a fuss. I don't suppose it entered his head the man would walk up there and throw him off the terrace. But that's what I'd say he did. I don't know why. Maybe it was an opportunity he couldn't resist. Maybe somebody in the IRA had suspicions about John. Phelan was part of a plan they couldn't take chances with. Or maybe he just bought Aidan McCarthy's story, the way everybody in Béarra bought it for seventeen years. Maybe he thought it was a fitting end to St Patrick's Day. He'd have been drunk enough. I don't know who knew what in the NYPD. I'd guess they just thought they were covering up for the hurlers.'

'So now we know,' said de Paor.

Stefan nodded; for what it was worth, they knew.

'It doesn't make me feel any better, Sergeant.'

'Did you think it would?'

The G2 commandant smiled, shaking his head.

'I'm sorry, sir. There's no crime here. There's nowhere to go with it.'

Gearóid de Paor looked up at the photograph of Luke McCarthy.

'There's still the truth.'

He got up, stubbed his cigarette into an ashtray, and walked out.

In the farm kitchen Maura McCarthy was putting peeled potatoes into a pan on the range, with a kind of intensity that she rarely wasted on potatoes. Colm McCarthy was at the window, just looking out at the guards in the yard, drumming his fingers on the sill. He turned round as de Paor entered.

'Are you going to fuck off now?'

'Yes, Mr McCarthy, we are going to fuck off. Where's your uncle?'

'He went for a walk.'

'Maybe down to the beach,' said the commandant, coldly.

'You've had your say.' Maura McCarthy stepped from the stove. 'Leave us alone. If you stay in Béarra any longer you might need a gun to protect you.'

'I'll leave you this, Mrs McCarthy,' replied the G2 officer, 'not that I think you need it. I'm sure you know. I'm sure you've always known.'

He took a paper from his pocket; a carbon copy of a typed page.

'A report from a Lieutenant Cavendish, two days after he arrested your first husband and brought him to Castleberehaven for questioning. A guard had been killed at Kenmare. You've maybe forgotten about that bit.'

'For fuck's sake!' exclaimed Colm. 'What's this now?'

'That's right, Mrs McCarthy. Know your history. I said the same thing to your second husband, just now. Well, that's your history, there.'

He looked round at Colm McCarthy. 'This is what happened to your father. He was questioned at Castleberehaven, where he said nothing at all, not a single word, as you might expect. He was a brave man, though that's only John Cavendish's opinion. He was released around midnight. He was picked up outside the town by the IRA brigadier, Sullivan. Then he was court-martialled as an informer and shot, all in the space of fifteen minutes.'

'You ignorant, fucking gobshite!'

Colm moved forward. Stefan stepped in front of him.

De Paor wasn't looking at the son; he was looking at the mother now.

'Lieutenant Cavendish doesn't record the evidence presented against Luke McCarthy. He didn't know of course. It couldn't have been much though, in fifteen minutes. Anyway, some bright spark thought, why waste a body when it could be turned into another Free State atrocity? And why not? There were some real Free State atrocities to go with the IRA atrocities after all. We've nothing to be so proud about. We were all at it then. So they buried your husband on the beach, and the word went round that it was all the work of Johnny Cavendish and the boys in Castleberehaven Barracks.'

The commandant threw the piece of paper on to the kitchen table.

'I'll leave you to tell your son why that isn't true, Mrs McCarthy.'

The only sound in the kitchen was the ticking of the clock.

Commandant de Paor turned to the door. Stefan opened it.

In the doorway the army officer stopped and looked back.

'I forgot to say why Lieutenant Cavendish was so well informed about what happened at an IRA court martial. The real informer was there for Luke McCarthy's execution. That would be his brother, Aidan McCarthy.'

De Paor walked out; the truth hadn't made him feel any better either.

There were no words for a very long moment. It was only as the sound of the cars was fading into the distance that Maura McCarthy spoke.

'A man can only give what he has. Sometimes it's not enough. It doesn't change who we are.' They were the only words she would ever say.

She walked out of the kitchen, taking off her apron, and went upstairs. The bedroom door shut. When she came back down it would be as if nothing had changed. The only thing she had to throw in the face of it all was her silence. She had made a similar decision seventeen years earlier. And she still had her hate. Her son would still have his too; she had given it to him after all. But for the rest of his life he would not know what to do with it.

*

It was late when Gearóid de Paor dropped Stefan Gillespie in the farmyard at Kilranelagh. They had driven straight from the Béarra Peninsula, barely stopping, saying little. De Paor had children, and a lot of the time he was thinking about them. Just as Stefan was thinking about his son. They both wanted to be home; they both wanted to hold their children. But as the car pulled up at the farm and Stefan nodded goodbye, he was surprised to see so many lamps on in the house and Valerie Lessingham's car parked there. It was late enough that something had to be wrong.

He hurried into the kitchen.

'It's the children,' said Valerie as soon as he walked in.

'Tom's gone,' continued his mother.

They were dressed in coats and carrying torches.

'They're looking at Whitehall Grove. We'll start here,' said David.

'What are you talking about?'

'Jane and Alexander have just gone. I thought they must have come over here, but when Helena went up to wake Tom, she found he'd gone too.'

'Will you stop saying "gone"! Gone where?'

David Gillespie was a lot less anxious than Helena or Valerie.

'Well, I think Tom went out the window over the pigsty roof.'

Valerie Lessingham thrust a piece of paper into Stefan's hand. He recognised her daughter Jane's very best handwriting.

We don't want to go to England. We want to stay here. This is our home. Tom doesn't want us to go. So we are going to do something about it. We will stay away until you stop it! Love Jane, Alex, Tom.

'Jesus,' said Stefan. 'I didn't know it had got this bad.'

He caught the look from his mother; she had tried to tell him.

'It's just a prank. They won't be far,' replied David.

'It's not a prank for Tom,' said Stefan's mother quietly.

'I know what you're saying, Ma, but let's not make too much –'

'Come up here,' she snapped. 'Would you too, Mrs Lessingham?'

Helena turned on her heel and went to the stairs. As she walked up to the bedrooms Valerie looked taken aback. Even if there had been a certain coolness between the two women, Helena had never given her orders before. Stefan looked at her and shrugged. They both followed his mother upstairs.

A lamp was on in Tom's room. The window he had climbed out of was still open. Helena was leaning over the small drawer in the table by the bed. Stefan and Valerie stood behind her, impatient to get outside to find the children, but feeling slightly foolish and awkward and unaccountably adolescent. Helena Gillespie took a piece of folded paper from the drawer.

'I'm sure no one else has seen this except me.'

She opened it up and handed it to her son. There was a picture of a hill, with trees and flowers; on the hill five stick-like figures – a man, a woman, three children. The children brandished a sword, a bow and arrow and a fishing pole. On either side of the hill was a house, one very big, the other small. Next to the small one were two more figures, a man and a woman, Helena and David. It was a picture of Tom Gillespie's world; the motte, the woods between Kilranelagh and Whitehall Grove, the houses where he and his friends lived. Some of it was what he was about to lose. Underneath were the words: To Mrs Lessingham Happy Mothering Sunday.

Stefan looked at the picture and his son's almost joined-up writing.

After a moment he gave it to Valerie.

'Mothering Sunday was two weeks ago, of course,' said Helena. 'The fact that he wouldn't even give it to you, couldn't, it makes it even more –'

She was crying. Stefan put his arm round her.

Valerie was still looking at the drawing.

'I hope he'll let me keep it now.'

She looked hard at Helena.

'He means a lot to me. I'm sure you know that.'

'That doesn't make it easier for him, does it, Mrs Lessingham?'

There was silence for a moment.

David Gillespie called from downstairs.

'Are we looking for them or not?'

Stefan gave both women a reassuring smile.

'Pa's right. They won't be very far.'

Valerie smiled too. She knew it. But she felt more than she showed.

'It's finding them. In the middle of the bloody night, where on –'

Stefan was looking at Tom's bedside table; he walked forward and picked up the copy of *Tom Sawyer* he and Tom had read together twice now.

'I think if we held a funeral for them tomorrow, we might find the three of them looking down from the gallery. What do you think, Valerie?'

Helena looked at him in shocked incomprehension.

'Jesus, Stefan, what sort of a thing is that to say!'

But Valerie Lessingham laughed. They wouldn't be far.

They found them quite easily, on the far side of the motte, where there was a small clump of trees above the stream that separated Kilranelagh land from Whitehall Grove. By then Tom, Alex and Jane were not that sorry to be found as it happened. It had started to rain; the blanket that had formed their tent was sodden, and so were they. The fire they had tried to light had refused to be lit and the matches they had brought with them were as wet as they were themselves. The food they had taken from the kitchen at Whitehall Grove had fallen into the stream when Tom tripped over and grazed his shin. They were cold, wet, hungry, and they all felt that after two hours, two hours that seemed like the whole of the night, the point had been made. They knew it would change nothing of course, but it had been one last adventure, and as they sat round the open range at Kilranelagh and ate bacon and eggs and drank hot, sweet tea, they felt it had been worth it.

Stefan watched his son, happy and warm and laughing; it wasn't the night that would stay in his heart for a long time though, it was the drawing and everything that went with it. He didn't often waste time wishing that things were different but it was there tonight. His father filled his glass with beer and walked across to fill Valerie Lessingham's, as she made a point of helping Helena wash up.

She stood close to Stefan's mother for a moment and spoke very quietly.

'Do you think it will help if we write to him when – if we all write?'

Helena Gillespie nodded.

'I'm sure it would.'

It wasn't quite a smile, but it was as close to one as Valerie would get.

A mattress and blankets had been dragged into Tom's room and that night Jane and Alex slept there instead of going home. Having announced that they had no intention of sleeping and were going to stay up all night, it was little more than twenty minutes after they went upstairs that the three children were fast asleep. Helena and David had gone to bed shortly afterwards.

Stefan sat in the kitchen with Valerie. He poured her another glass of beer. For a moment they sat looking at the fire in the open door of the range. There was nothing much to say. The sense of an end was there between them. Not the end to what they had been to each other sometimes. That had already gone, and more easily than the friendship that remained.

'I shall take one great failure to England with me, Stefan.'

'And what's that?'

'I never got your mother to call me anything but Mrs Lessingham.'

He laughed. 'That's how she sees things.'

'We've never talked to each other, but I like her.'

'She'd be more likely to call you Valerie if she didn't like you.'

She looked at him sceptically.

'It's how she is,' he said.

She sipped the glass of beer, still looking at the fire.

'We're starting to pack up. I suppose that's why this happened.'

'When do you go?'

'The week after next. Maybe sometime Tom could come and stay?' she said.

'We'll see.'

'You don't sound very sure. Is it a bad idea?'

'I don't know how things are going to be. I don't know how easy –'

'No. I keep forgetting why we're going. I'm like everybody else. I don't really believe there's going to be a war. I suppose, if I'm honest, I imagine a long holiday in Sussex and we all come back here for Christmas.'

'Maybe if enough of us imagine something like that –'

She looked round at him.

'You've always seemed to be expecting a war. You never say very much about it, but you never say it might not happen. Even Simon doesn't really think it's going to happen half the time and he's going to be fighting in it.' She laughed. 'I wonder if those German connections of yours aren't a little bit suspicious. Not that there's very much to spy on in Baltinglass –'

He smiled, but he did feel those German connections.

'I'm German enough to know Germany. I'm German enough to have cousins in the Nazi Party who don't write to us any more. I'm German enough to know my mother has a reason for not listening to German radio any more and won't talk about Germany. And I'm German enough not to be able to pretend that when Hitler says one thing he means something else. So it's hard to agree with the people who are kidding themselves.' He poured more beer. 'But apart from all that, well, I'm hardly German at all, surely?'

'Thanks. And so much for Christmas at Whitehall Grove!'

'Christmas in Sussex shouldn't be so bad. Isn't it home?'

'I'm not sure it is,' she said quietly.

He looked at her. He could see tears welling in her eyes.

'It's not just Jane and Alex. I'm probably not doing a good job of enthusing them about going to England. I keep saying it's going home. But it's not their home. This is. And I suppose – I've never thought about it – I'd never realised. You know I spend all my time complaining about Whitehall Grove – it's falling round our ears – and the farm's a disaster – and we're all going to hell in a handcart while Simon swans around the Empire and leaves us all to rot here – well, you've been on the receiving end of enough of it.'

'That doesn't sound like you at all.'

She smiled, but the smile was only on her lips.

'The truth is – it's my home too. I don't want to go. It's nothing to do with the war. It's nothing to do with Simon. I don't mean that the way it sounds. I want us to be a family again. I want the children to know their father, for all of us. I wish it was here. I wish it was all the other way round.'

'Whatever happens, it won't go on forever.'

'Is that the best you can do, Stefan?' Now she laughed. It wasn't very good, even for a platitude.

'You'll have the children.'

She nodded; that was better; that was true.

For a moment they both looked at the fire.

It was still the children that held them together.

'Can I sound like your mother, Stefan?'

'How the hell do I answer that?'

'I've never been very good at making wishes for other people. I wish you – I wish you and Tom – I suppose what I mean is I hope anything that happened between you and me – didn't get in the way of anything else –'

He sat back and shook his head.

'Unfortunately there was nothing to get in the way of.'

Then he laughed. It was a throwaway from the list of throwaways he had in stock for the occasions when people said such things. Valerie never had in the past; he liked her because she didn't push those lazy ideas at him. It didn't much matter that she had now. But he was conscious of the trip he had taken to Dún Laoghaire the week before. There had been a few days, just a few days out of years, when he had thought differently. It hadn't lasted very long. And even that tiny, fragile hope, maybe only barely there, had been broken, not by anything in him, not by anything in Kate O'Donnell, but by other people's battles, other people's memories, other people's rattle bags of righteous-ness and revenge, other people's wars. The past didn't only come up at you out of the ground in Ireland; it walked around the streets, following you, and if you turned round to complain it spat in your face.

Stefan stepped out into the farmyard with Valerie. She kissed him on the cheek and got into her car. As she drove away he watched the headlights move down the road towards Woodfield and Whitehall Grove. Then they were gone.

The yard was dark. There was no moon. He heard a high-pitched shriek suddenly break the stillness. It lasted only a few desperate, agonised seconds, but it was enough to fill the night. A fox and a rabbit; the rabbit would be dead. He turned back into the house. He poured himself a last glass of beer. He thought about the three children sleeping upstairs and smiled. He thought about the mother his son had never known and wished, helplessly, pointlessly, as he never allowed himself to do, that something would change.

25. The Four Courts

The rhythm of the summer brought the ordinary business of life back to the farm at Kilranelagh. Valerie Lessingham had left Whitehall Grove, and with her Jane and Alexander. Every few weeks a letter or a card would arrive for Tom from Steyning, in Sussex where they were now living. But the Norman motte on the edge of the wooded valley between Kilranelagh and Whitehall was still whatever kind of castle, or ship, or camp it needed to be for Tom and Harry Lawlor, and other children soon assumed at least some of the roles Jane and Alexander had played, though Huckleberry Finn was never enjoyed as much or as enthusiastically as it had been when Valerie Lessingham had joined in as Aunt Polly, Judge Thatcher, Jim, and, in her finest performance, Huck's drunken Pap.

Baltinglass was busy with what mattered, as new lambs and new calves fattened on new grass, as hay was made and crops were harvested. There were days in the Garda barracks when almost no one was there. There were guards who had gone home to Kerry and Tipperary and Galway to help with the hay making, and local guards like Stefan Gillespie who were doing the same on their family farms outside the town; and there were the rest of the guards who came to look at the hay-making and the harvesting anyway, and watch their dogs chasing the rabbits that fled the fields in their hundreds as the crops were cut.

There was war and the rumour of war in the background, of course, but it was a long way away, in small countries or places nobody knew very much about. Slovakia and Hungary; a piece of Lithuania called Memel Hitler had annexed, apparently by registered letter; Italy and Albania; Japan and Mongolia.

There was good news too. The war that mattered most in Ireland, the Spanish war, had finally ended. And as the summer faded prayers were said from the pulpits for the fascist government of Generalisimo Francisco Franco. The peace pact between Adolf Hitler in Germany and Josef Stalin in the Soviet Union sounded slightly strange in the light of this. It was the communists who had murdered priests in Spain; it was to protect Christianity from communism that German and Italian planes had bombed Spanish cities. But surely peace was better than war, and if there were parts of Poland that had once belonged to Germany, or that Germany needed, were a few green fields on the other side of Europe worth anyone fighting and dying for?

There was a sense through the course of that summer that it was all too far from Ireland to matter and that as so many times before, when they'd all stopped shouting in London and Paris and Berlin and Warsaw, nothing at all would happen.

Stefan Gillespie remained one of those who was a lot less sure about that. He read the newspapers more than he had before; he listened to the radio news quite late into the night sometimes, from London as well as Dublin, and sometimes from Berlin as well. He wanted no more to do with it all than most of his neighbours; but he was already a part of it. It had touched him twice now, in Danzig and Dublin four years ago, and now in New York. He said little, but when he listened to Adolf Hitler on German radio he didn't hear what the Reichkanzler said, but what he meant.

*

It was at the very end of August that Stefan was called to Dublin to give evidence at the trial of Owen Desmond Laserian Harris, for the murder of his mother, Leticia Grace Harris. He put his account of his conversation with the defendant on the Yankee Clipper into evidence and as he had not been involved in the investigation questions were few. But he would have to stay in Dublin for almost a week in case anything else arose, and in case he had to be recalled to answer more questions from the jury once it had retired.

By the time he took the witness stand he had already sat through the evidence of the State Pathologist and several senior detectives, including Superintendent Gregory. The State Pathologist's evidence revolved around what conclusions could be drawn from the amount of blood found in Mrs Harris's bedroom and in her car, and whether strands of cut hair were the result of an undiscovered razor blade or the axe found in the garage. There was a lot of information about tides from the Dublin Harbour Master, which attempted to explain why Leticia Harris's body had never been found. Information about when and where Owen Harris had been seen on the night of his mother's death was less than conclusive, though the maid, who had been away at the time, gave evidence about furious arguments between

428

mother and son in the preceding days, on the subject, endlessly familiar in the home, of money. The only definite sighting came from the motorist and his wife who had given Harris a lift from Shankill to Ballsbridge that night.

The prosecution asked Sergeant Gillespie no questions. Owen Harris's barrister, Lawson Fitzgerald, looked at him lazily, as if not entirely sure whether what he was about to do was worth the effort, and decided it was.

'Would you say Mr Harris's demeanour, when you arrested him in New York, was consistent with a man who had recently killed his mother?'

Stefan saw the scene in the Dizzy Club on 52nd Street. It was clear that Owen Harris saw it too; he snorted as he restrained his laughter. Smirks, snorts and yawns of boredom had been a part of his court performance since the start of the trial. They alternated with long periods during which he gazed up at the ceiling and seemed completely unaware of what was going on, and times when he drew sketches of witnesses and jurors on pieces of scrap paper.

The jury-alienating snort was enough to make Harris's barrister wish he had left the question alone, but he had to pull something back now.

'What did you think, Sergeant?'

'I was there to bring him back to Ireland, that's all. I didn't think about it. I'm sorry, I don't know whether Mr Harris killed his mother, and I don't know how people who have killed their mothers are meant to behave.'

'Well, shall I simplify it? Do you know what grief is?'

'Yes,' replied Stefan quietly. 'I know what grief is.'

'Well, was Mr Harris's attitude when you met him, his demeanour, even remotely within the range of what could be described as "grieving"?'

'No, not really.'

'How would you characterise it?'

'I'm not sure.'

'Well, eccentric?'

'Yes, by most standards.'

'Your standards will do perfectly well, Sergeant.'

'Then by my standards eccentric would be the word.'

'As if he didn't really comprehend what had happened?'

Martin Maguire, SC, stood up to interrupt.

'My Lord, Mr Fitzgerald keeps asking every policeman who takes the stand what he thought about the defendant's behaviour, clearly with a view to raising questions about his sanity. But I do wish he'd tell us what he's trying to prove. Will he be asking the jury to believe Mr Harris *did* kill his mother because he's insane, or *didn't* kill his mother because he's insane?'

Mr Justice Henry Hanna, KC, smiled.

'He might be happy to make do with either, Mr Maguire. But I think we all have the point, Mr Fitzgerald. And I feel sure there is more to come.'

There was more to come, and as Stefan had to spend the rest of the week in Dublin he passed some of that time in court.

No one believed the explanation Harris had given about finding his mother dead; the fact that he had taken her body to Corbawn Lane to throw it into the sea made the idea of suicide, and a son desperate to protect his mother's reputation, unlikely by any normal standards. In the end the defence wasn't about whether Mrs Harris had killed herself, whether her son had taken an axe to her, or even whether someone else had come into the house and bludgeoned her to death before he found her. It was the weakness

430

of the defendant's mind that the focus of the defence.

The decision had been made that Owen Harris would not testify; it was as his father had hoped and as Superintendent Gregory had anticipated. His arch gestures, his snorts of laughter, his groans of weariness, were enough to unsettle the jury without letting him speak.

Stefan knew perfectly well why the defendant couldn't be allowed to take the stand. Nothing would stand in the way of a performance, and his words were as likely to hang him as demonstrate his insanity.

It was all very cursory. The turmoil of family life that had existed between the supposed axe-murderer and the parents he called Moloch and Medea was touched on, but Stefan knew its disturbing depths were not being trawled. The issue of Mrs Harris's breakdowns and her real threats of suicide were only skirted round. People who might have given evidence about her son's behaviour in the months leading up to the murder would never be called; not only was the prospect of opening up the disturbing world of Owen Harris's sexual life disconcerting for others, his barrister had concluded it was enough to hang him in the minds of any jury of decent men. Mrs Harris's theft from the Irish Hospitals' Sweepstake was still never mentioned. The possibility that Doctor Cecil Harris's car had been in the lane at the back of his wife's house on the day she died had vanished along with the Lost Boys.

Various psychiatrists and alienists described the consequences of Harris's unhappy life in the vaguest way possible, and half-recognised the self-obsession of his ever-quarrelling mother and father. Cecil Harris accepted some small responsibility for that, and pleaded with the court to show compassion; he seemed to have abandoned any idea his son might be innocent. The only time Stefan

Gillespie saw Owen Harris pay attention to anything during the trial was when his father testified. It was the only time he had seen him cry. The tears were silent.

When the verdict came it surprised no one. The hangman really had seemed less and less likely as the week had passed. Owen Harris was found guilty, but insane. And he would be detained at the Central Mental Hospital in Dundrum, indefinitely.

Stefan Gillespie left the courtroom and walked down the steps to the cells, to collect the coat and hat he had left in the Garda meal room earlier. In the corridor Superintendent Gregory and a crowd of noisy detectives and Gardaí were heading towards him, in celebratory mood. Terry Gregory saw him and walked forward, slapping him cheerfully on the back. It had been a big case, and a big trial; it had been handled in the way everyone wanted it handled.

'Are you coming for a drink, Stefan?'

'No thanks, sir.'

'I don't think anyone wanted him strung up in the end,' said Gregory.

'I'm sure he'll be pleased to hear it,' smiled Stefan.

'Go on, have a fucking drink. I'm paying.'

The detectives around him laughed, moving on past them.

'It's almost enough to tempt me, sir. But I've got something to do.'

'You can't always be sure, Sergeant. That's not our job.'

He was surprised Gregory knew or cared what he was thinking. But he did. And for some odd reason he wanted to explain himself to Stefan.

'Do you think if I'd wanted him to hang I couldn't have got it?'

There was a smile on the superintendent's face, but Stefan saw something he hadn't expected to see behind it; the weight of responsibility.

'I'd have done things differently if I'd been Owen Harris though. I'd have killed them both, and done it fucking years ago! I'll be seeing you so.'

Terry Gregory moved off to join the other detectives.

Stefan walked past several cell doors. One was open. As he looked inside he saw Owen Harris in there, quite alone, quite calm, smoking a cigarette. He looked up and saw Stefan. He smiled and raised his hand. Just across the corridor two warders from Mountjoy Prison and a uniformed guard were also smoking. Stefan nodded at Harris, who beckoned him in.

'Can I talk to him?' Stefan called, looking at the guard.

The guard shrugged and went back to his conversation.

'I thought you were very good, Mr Gillespie,' said the prisoner.

'Well, it's over anyway,' said Stefan simply.

'There were some very shoddy performances, I thought. At least you had the part prepared. And, what was it you said? "I don't know how people who have killed their mothers are meant to behave." Not bad! My father was very wooden, workmanlike but wooden, but then that's Moloch, of course. My mother would have given a very different account of herself. Oh, by the way, I've decided I did kill her now. It seems easier that way, and really I've got to have some sort of career. I don't hold out much hope for the acting. I think I have too much presence. Micheál Mac Liammóir told me as much once. It was either that I had too much presence or he wished the fuck I'd get out of his presence.' He roared with laughter. 'So, I might as well be

433

what I'm told I am. I think it should give me some status in Bedlam as well. And of course, it means the final victory over Moloch. I believe Medea would almost approve. No longer the idiot son of a famous doctor! Now he's the unremarkable father of the notorious, mad matricide! It has a Greek quality.'

The cigarette had gone out. Harris let it drop to the floor.

'I've spent the week trying to decide whether I believe what you told me on the plane,' said Stefan after a moment. 'I thought I did believe it in the end, despite everything, but now you're telling me you really killed her.'

'I'm not telling you I did. That's not the point at all.'

'So she did kill herself?'

'Of course she didn't!'

Stefan frowned. Harris looked at him with some irritation.

'It was the old man, wasn't it? Moloch! Knocked her out, then cut her throat. That was my guess, anyway. He'd had enough. She was getting nuttier by the day. And if all that stuff about stealing the money had come out, well, she'd have ended up in prison. That wasn't on. I didn't see it, of course, but I'm damned sure he did it. You couldn't really blame him. Something had to give, didn't it? I always thought she'd kill him though.'

'So that's the new version. Your father did it.'

'It's not a version. That's what happened.'

Stefan recalled the Lost Boys, Slightly and Tootles, and the Sunbeam Dawn. There could be an answer to the badly hidden axe; Owen Harris hadn't hidden it.

'This time you mean it?'

'Of course I mean it. Why wouldn't I? I've just told you.'

'So you did it for him? You're going into Dundrum –'

'I'd have done the same for her,' replied Harris, quieter. 'Truly.'

Stefan didn't reply; the words sounded utterly, pathetically real.

'I really couldn't have seen him hanged.'

Owen Harris looked intensely serious, but then he smiled broadly.

'I take the Master's words very seriously, Mr Gillespie, as any child should. I'm sure you know what I mean. As he said, "To lose one parent may be regarded as a misfortune, but to lose both looks like carelessness."'

*

As he walked along the Quays towards O'Connell Street and Clery's clock, Stefan Gillespie breathed in the evening air and listened to the laughter and noise of Dublin around him. It was a bright day still. The sun was shining, and what had happened that morning had already made him glad that Harris's trial had kept him in Dublin so long.

He had been coming out of the Four Courts when she had stopped him. She was standing in front of him, blocking his way.

'I was in the gallery just now. You didn't see me?'

'No,' he replied.

'I saw you were in the newspaper, when you were giving evidence. I only read it yesterday. I wondered if you'd still be here. I just came to see –'

Kate O'Donnell stopped speaking and laughed.

'Well, here I am,' said Stefan.

'Here you are.'

'So, here we are.'

'I should have sent the Harry Clarke book back.'

'I'm glad you didn't.'

'It's very beautiful. But my mother thinks you're a pornographer.'

'Does she mind?'

'We don't talk about such things. Look, I can't stop, Stefan.'

'I see,' he smiled. 'Is that it then?'

'Don't be silly. Can you meet me at Clery's later, under the clock?'

'What time?'

'I'm back dressing windows there. I'm finished at five.'

She leant forward and kissed his cheek; then she was gone.

They said little about New York and little about anything that went with it. There were things that needed saying as they sat in the upstairs room at Bewley's, at the table that looked out on to Grafton Street, but it wasn't much more than the simple business of geography.

Kate and Niamh had moved out of her parents' house in Dún Laoghaire, and since Kate had got the job at Clery's again the two of them had rented a house at Inchicore, a few streets away from the Phoenix Park. She didn't tell him that leaving Dún Laoghaire had been both rancorous and painful, except to say that when her mother started taking Niamh to Mass five days a week, she realised that being at home wasn't going to provide a solution to her sister's depression, even with the guaranteed personal intervention of St Anthony and St Thérèse of Lisieux. It was a joke, but he knew from the uneasy smile that accompanied it that it was something she would talk about another day.

In the end they spoke mostly about the things she only knew about him sketchily, that had nothing to do with those days and nights in New York; Tom and Kilranelagh and Baltinglass and the farm and what he cared about and what made him laugh. There would be a conversation to come when she found a way to say some of the same, ordinary things, about herself. But it wouldn't be now. He didn't need her to say more about Niamh to know that the way back wasn't proving easy for her sister; when she said Niamh was seeing a doctor, he didn't need to ask her what kind of doctor; he knew well enough.

Then it was over again, as abruptly almost as it had begun.

She had to get back to Niamh. She was running again, and she was late again. But when she kissed him goodbye outside Bewley's, she kissed him as he wanted her to kiss him. They didn't make arrangements to meet again, but he had her address and he had her telephone. It didn't seem to occur to her that anything else was happening other than that they were now going out together in some way they had both agreed to, in the easy ambiguity of that phrase.

He walked to Neary's to have a drink, to sit on his own and take in what had happened, and enjoy taking it in. As for what it meant, that would work itself out; for now he was happy enough to let it all take its due course.

He had been in Neary's for about half an hour, going over her words, and doing not much more, when something she had said as a joke struck him quite differently from the way it had when she said it. There had only been a few remarks about the problems Niamh was still trying to shake off. He heard one of them again now. 'I thought she'd at least left all that paranoia behind. She's been much happier since we got the house in Inchicore. She's been going shopping on her own. Now it's all gone haywire again. She won't go out unless I'm with her. Last week she suddenly started saying someone was watching the house!'

It had been another one of those half-joking asides that meant she needed to let him know something, and wanted to make it sound as if she was on top of it when she wasn't. He had thought no more of it, except to wonder what his reappearance would do in all this; would it help Niamh now or would it make things worse? But the words were in his head more disturbingly now, along with a conversation he had had with Dessie MacMahon when he had first got to Dublin for the trial.

Dessie had been stuck in Special Branch ever since being attached to the investigation into Mrs Harris's death in March. No one had ever told him he had been transferred, but Superintendent Gregory had said he would be there until the trial. He had been expecting to go back to Pearse Street since the beginning of August, but he was still at Dublin Castle, and Terry Gregory was treating him like any other Special Branch detective, even to the extent of putting him on surveillance operations on various IRA members and fellow travellers. Recently that had included watching someone Stefan Gillespie knew well enough.

Dominic Carroll was in Ireland, apparently on his way home after another visit to Berlin. He was there to see his sick father in Monaghan, but he had been trying hard to engineer a meeting with Éamon de Valera through Republican-leaning friends in Fianna Fáil. It had got him nowhere. The messages back from the Taoiseach's office had been polite enough, but they left no room for doubt.

What they told Carroll was clear: he was lucky he was allowed into the country at all; the only interest Dev had in him was when he was leaving. None of that mattered to Stefan; what mattered were the last words Dominic Carroll had said to him in New York.

Dessie MacMahon was still at Dublin Castle when Stefan rang, and it was half an hour later that he walked into Neary's.

Dominic Carroll was still in Dublin; he would be getting the plane from Foynes to New York in two days. There had been surveillance on him for most of the ten days he had been in the country, but Sergeant MacMahon wasn't impressed by what that amounted to. Carroll knew the men who were watching him, so much so that when Dessie had followed him from the Shelbourne Hotel to Mass at the Pro-Cathedral the American had stopped him, offered him a cigarette, and asked him if he was new.

It was common knowledge that there were Special Branch men who would take a back-hander from Carroll; Dessie already had a good idea who they were. But there was little doubt that if the Clan na Gael leader wanted to slip the leash he could do it easily. Everyone assumed he had had several meetings with the IRA Army Council in Dublin, and that he hadn't been troubled by anybody from the Special Branch about doing it.

It was almost dark when Stefan got off the tram in Inchicore. He had tried phoning the number Kate had given him, but there was no answer. She certainly didn't know Dominic Carroll was in Ireland, but she should do. And he needed to know whether Niamh Carroll's visions of people watching the house were paranoia or not.

439

He hammered on the door of the terraced house in Inchicore Square. No one came to answer. There were no lights on. There was no reason Kate and Niamh couldn't be out, but it didn't feel right. The impression he'd got was that Niamh didn't like going out; that most of the time they were at home, especially at night. He moved quickly round to the back of the row of terraces; then he scrambled over the wall into the yard. He walked to the back door and put his shoulder to it and pushed.

He saw Kate O'Donnell as soon as he entered the kitchen. She was tied tightly, hand and foot, and she had been gagged. Her face was bruised.

'They've taken her. They were here when I – I don't even know –'

He untied her hands and left her to do the rest.

'Where's the phone?'

'In the hall.'

Stefan called Dessie MacMahon at Dublin Castle for the second time.

'Can you get a car?'

'When?'

'Now.'

'I guess so.'

'Will anyone know?'

'Not if I don't ask. Where are you –'

'We're at four Inchicore Square North. And Dessie, bring a gun.'

26. Henrietta Street

It was almost midnight when Dominic Carroll was woken by the telephone in his room at the Shelbourne Hotel. He switched on the lamp and answered sleepily but within seconds he was fully awake, sitting on the side of the bed.

'Mr Carroll, there is a call for you.'

It was the Shelbourne operator. He wasn't expecting anyone to phone him here, not unless something had gone wrong. But what else could it be at this time of night? They knew where she was. Surely it wasn't hard to do.

Then another woman spoke. The voice was slightly muffled.

'Mr Carroll, this is the Taoiseach's office. I'm calling on behalf of Mr de Valera. He apologises for the lateness of the call, but he would very much appreciate it if you would meet him at Leinster House. He's waiting here.'

Carroll's heart was beating fast. This was what really mattered. This was what he had come for. It was what he thought had been thrown back in his face by the man he had once called a friend, a comrade and a leader.

'You mean now?'

'Yes, sir. We can send a car straight round to the Shelbourne. The Taoiseach is sure you understand that a meeting of this kind can't happen publicly at the moment, with the situation as it is in Ireland and in Europe. It wasn't possible for him to meet you any other way, but he doesn't want you to return to New York without at least making contact. He has to stress that this meeting is completely private, and no one else is to know about it.'

'I understand.' He breathed deeply. 'I'll be in the lobby, five minutes.'

'Thank you very much, Mr Carroll. The car will be waiting outside.'

He pulled on his clothes as quickly as he could. He was shaking with excitement; adrenalin was pumping round his body. Within minutes he was walking along the corridor to the lift. He had been wrong to believe that Éamon de Valera had shut himself off entirely from the past, and from the Republic that he had once been prepared to die for. The possibility of bringing the whole Republican movement back together, of repairing the rifts that everyone believed were irreparable, at a time when England had never been as vulnerable as it was, brought a flush of pleasure to his face. He had not wasted his time after all. The imminence of war had finally made Dev face facts. He would need the IRA; he would need Germany. And Dominic Carroll was the bridge. He felt, as he walked through the lobby, that this was the moment he had been waiting for, for many long years.

There was a black Humber Snipe outside the Shelbourne, the only car in sight. A big man got out from the driver's door and walked towards him.

'Mr Carroll?'

He nodded.

'I'm here to take you to Leinster House, sir.'

Dominic Carroll smiled and nodded again.

The man opened a rear door and he got into the car. Seconds later it was heading into Merrion Row; it was only a few hundred yards into Merrion Square and Leinster House, and the Taoiseach's office where Dev was waiting to talk to him. Last week he had been in Berlin, in Hermann Goering's office. That would be no bad place to start, telling Dev that; it would give him the proper sense of how much Carroll mattered. They had been friends once, good friends; maybe they could be friends again. But Dominic Carroll had only moments to start to rehearse what he would say before the car slowed and stopped. The driver shook his head and cursed.

'Jesus! Sorry, sir, you won't believe it, I think I've got a flat –'

The Clan na Gael president didn't have time to find this behaviour odd. It happened too fast. A man and a woman were standing under the archway of the Huguenot Cemetery, in an embrace. As the car pulled up they broke away from each other and walked quickly towards the car. Stefan Gillespie wrenched open the door of the car and got in beside Carroll; Kate O'Donnell pulled open the front passenger door and sat in. Stefan was already pointing a gun at the American when he slammed the door shut. The driver, Detective Sergeant Dessie MacMahon, pulled away at some speed.

Dominic Carroll stared at Stefan Gillespie in disbelief. For a moment it was less the shock of what was happening that hit him than the disappointment of what wasn't. He had believed every word of that phone call. There was no reason on earth why he shouldn't have done. He had tried to see Dev for over a week and he had been rebuffed. But the call had made complete sense, especially to a man who believed not only in his own importance but in the importance of his mission. And before he could take hold of what was going on now, of Stefan, Kate, the gun, he had to deal with the feeling in the pit of his stomach about what had been torn away from him. There was no meeting with Dev. It really had been a waste of time.

'I'm sorry, Mr de Valera still doesn't want to see you, Mr Carroll,' said Stefan. He held the gun with the barrel pointing up to Carroll's head.

The American was not a timid man. He didn't yet understand why Stefan was pointing a gun at him, but along with a deep sense of his own importance came a sense of his invulnerability. Crossing Dominic Carroll wasn't something anybody got away with, not in New York, not here.

'It was well done, Sergeant, but is there a point to this?'

'The point is Mrs Carroll. She was taken from her home.'

'I have no contact with Niamh. I have nothing to do with her, or with the sister.' The American spoke the last word with contempt. Kate looked ahead, tight-lipped; she had nothing to say, yet. 'And I'd have thought after all your shenanigans in New York you'd know that as well as anybody.'

'I don't, Mr Carroll, not at all. Didn't you tell me it wasn't over, that morning in St Patrick's? You're a man of your word. And I don't think anybody would take the Clan na Gael president's wife off for an IRA court martial without his say-so, in fact without his orders. That's what they told "the sister", a court martial. They told her she wouldn't see Niamh again.'

'I don't give orders here. If it's true, it's not my business.'

'Jesus, but you're a gobshite,' said Kate, lighting a cigarette.

'We'll see,' replied Stefan. 'One way or another you're going to have to start giving some orders to somebody – and I'd say pretty damn quick.'

The car drove south out of Dublin, through Donnybrook, Mount Merrion, Stilorgan, and Cabinteely, to Shankill. In Shankill village Dessie MacMahon took the long, straight road that led to the sea, Corbawn Lane. At the end he turned into the house on the right, Clifton, just before the beach, the house where Owen Harris had brought his mother's dead body. It was an empty place, that's all; that no one would think of, where no one would see or hear.

As the car stopped, Stefan took a pair of handcuffs from his pocket and snapped them on to Carroll's wrists. He was very aware that the last time this had been done the wrists were his and the gun was pointing at him. And a man had died. Dessie opened the boot of the Humber; he took out two Tilley lamps and a crow bar. He handed the lamps to Kate O'Donnell and walked to the back door. He pushed the crow bar in the door jamb and wrenched it open. He walked ahead along a black corridor. He took the first door he came to. It led into a kitchen. As Stefan prodded Dominic Carroll into the room, Kate was lighting the lamps. He pushed Carroll down into a chair.

The American was unimpressed by the show.

'So what now, Mr Gillespie? Are you going to shoot me?'

'No, I probably won't do that.'

'Perhaps your friend will.'

Dessie was sitting down, lighting up a Sweet Afton.

'I don't know that he will either. But we'd be happy to leave you in here with "the sister" and come back. She went

445

through quite a lot to get Niamh away from you. She's a serious woman when it comes to her family.'

'Is that it?' laughed Carroll. 'Is that all? You snatch me off the street and threaten me with a woman, over something I don't even know about?'

'You know well enough, Dominic.'

The words were the first Kate had spoken since Dublin. She looked across the room at him in the lamplight. The expression of amused contempt he threw in her direction wasn't quite as confident as he wanted it to be. He didn't really know Kate. He was sure about the two men. They might shoot him in a struggle, but they wouldn't do it in cold blood. They wouldn't do it if it achieved nothing. Saying nothing would be enough. He wasn't afraid.

'Well, I guess we sit here till you all get fed up with it.'

Kate walked forward to take the gun from Stefan. He hesitated as she put her hand on it, still holding on to it himself. He was trying to think how to push the threat hard enough to make Dominic Carroll talk. It wouldn't be easy. The Clan na Gael man wouldn't be softened up by a few punches. It would have to be more. But how far did he go? Kate smiled at him. He didn't know what she was going to do but he trusted her instincts; he let her take the revolver.

She walked slowly across the room to Dominic Carroll. When she reached the chair she lifted his cuffed hand and put the gun barrel against one palm. For the first time there was doubt, even fear in him. She didn't hesitate. There was no threat, no word. She fired straight through his hand. The gun deafened them, but Carroll's screams rose above the blast.

'Have you got anything to stop the bleeding?' she said. She turned round and handed the gun back to Stefan. 'If there are no bandages –'

'There should be some first aid stuff in the car boot,' said Dessie.

'I'll get it,' said Kate quietly, and walked out.

'Jesus Christ!' screamed Carroll. 'Jesus Christ! She's as mad as her sister! Look at what the bitch has done to me. The fucking whore! Christ!'

Dessie stubbed out his cigarette.

'I'll tell you where we are, Mr Carroll,' said Stefan. 'You'll remember the man I was bringing back from New York. The trial has just finished. You might have seen something about it in the papers? The man who killed his mother, or didn't kill his mother. Guilty but insane, that was the verdict.'

'What are you talking about? I'm bleeding here! Do something!'

'This is where he brought the body, Owen Harris,' continued Stefan, taking no notice. 'He dumped her into the sea, at the end of the garden. He chose a good place. Mrs Harris's body was never found. That's why we're here. In case we end up with a body. So, you give me a phone number and a message with all the right words in it, and we'll arrange for someone who's involved in your IRA kangaroo court to release Mrs Carroll. Then we'll release you too. If you can't do that we'll go out for a smoke and leave you with Miss O'Donnell. You've another hand, not to mention two feet, two kneecaps, a groin.'

Kate came back in.

She knelt down beside Dominic Carroll and started to clean the wound that was now bleeding profusely. He winced as she dabbed it with iodine and then started to wind a bandage round it. She was doing it in a way that almost seemed tender, but as she looked up at him he was in no doubt about the hatred he could read in her eyes. He believed she would kill him.

It wasn't long afterwards that Stefan stood in the AA box at the top of Corbawn Lane. He asked for the number Dominic Carroll had given him and read the message the American had written. It was an instruction to release the prisoner, Niamh Carroll, and to abandon the court martial. A man answered. Stefan read the message. It obviously contained words or phrases that verified its authenticity. He waited in silence for another five minutes; another man came to the phone. He asked for the message to be read again. He said nothing for almost a minute, then asked Stefan to identify himself.

'You don't need to know that. I'm sure if you do what you're told Mr Carroll will fill you in afterwards. If you don't, he won't be in a position to.'

'Are you Special Branch?' asked the man.

'After a fashion.'

'What the fuck's that supposed to mean?'

'It means Mr Carroll has made a mistake, and I'm just here to put that right. His wife didn't give information to anybody about the IRA. The only thing she did wrong was to sleep with a man who wasn't Dominic Carroll. If that's treachery, I don't think it's the sort that would normally involve an IRA court martial. If you're going on Dominic Carroll's word, you might want to ask him some more questions. Like why he had Mrs Carroll locked up in a psych ward for a year, and why she had to be smuggled out of America to stop him putting her back there for good. It's just a suggestion. Maybe it's one Seán Russell would want you to follow up. I mean you're soldiers of Ireland, aren't you? Unless you're in the business of helping men get rid of wives they don't want by blowing their brains out. She's a sick woman. She's under a psychiatrist. You've got her, fucking look at her!'

An hour later Stefan Gillespie sat with Dominic Carroll outside the entrance to the Convent of the Sisters of Mercy of St Vincent de Paul. Dessie was in the driver's seat. Stefan still had the gun in his pocket. The handcuffs had been taken off the Clan na Gael man and he clutched his bandaged, smashed hand.

The convent advertised itself as a free hostel for respectable women; it offered shelter when there was nowhere else to go. Kate O'Donnell was inside, waiting for Niamh. Stefan had already spoken to the Sister Superior. It was a place of safety; in Ireland no one would challenge that. There would be a bed for the night and there would be no questions. That was as far as anybody could go. The nun understood Stefan's shorthand enough to know that questions would give unwanted answers. She knew he was a policeman; she had a sense of who the people he talked about might be; it came with being Irish. It wasn't the first time the convent had been neutral territory.

Stefan was looking across Henrietta Street at the long dilapidated row of high Georgian houses. They were more tenements, just like the one the two boys he only knew as Slightly and Tootles had lived in. He thought of Owen Harris again and hoped that if nothing else, whatever money had taken the boys and their family away from Ireland, for whatever reason, had done something worth doing. Dominic Carroll was watching him, not understanding what was in his head, but knowing well enough what he was looking at.

'Dev's Ireland. You can get the smell of it, can't you, Sergeant?'

Stefan looked round.

'The same slums as England's Ireland,' continued Carroll.

'And you've the answer, Mr Carroll. A machine gun in every tenement.'

'England's still choking the life out of us. Everyone knows it.'

'I'd say we're big enough to choke ourselves,' said Stefan. 'We don't need England any more, except to blame.'

'That wouldn't be a very popular opinion.'

'Here or in New York?'

'Do you ever wonder if you belong, Stefan?'

'I belong enough to say what I think about my country.'

'Is that the same thing?'

Stefan looked hard at the American and shook his head, smiling.

'My son should be asleep now. My mother and father too. There's three mountains that look down on the house, Keadeen, Kilranelagh, Baltinglass Hill. If they're not our mountains, then they're nobody's.'

As he said the last words he looked back out of the car window.

Dominic Carroll didn't reply. For a moment in the darkness, just a moment, he felt more American than he was used to feeling when he was in Ireland.

Stefan looked at his watch; they would soon be there.

'If I were you I'd get to a hospital with that hand,' he said.

'She'll need to go a long way from Ireland before this is done, you know that?' replied Dominic Carroll. 'Do you think it really stops here?'

'I think your friends might have something to say about that. They might want to know a bit more about why you want your wife killed before they do this again. Whatever you've told them, she didn't know anything about bombs in New York. She hasn't betrayed anyone. If that's what you've told them it's not true and you know it.'

It was true of course, but he didn't believe the Clan na Gael man knew any of that, whatever story he'd made up to get someone else to exorcise the humiliation he had felt as a result of what his wife had done. This was personal revenge, nothing more than that.

'You know she hasn't been an IRA courier for years. You had her locked up for half that time. I know your comrades get excited about traitors. Just point the finger hard enough and almost anyone will do. There's a gun out before there's a question asked.' He was thinking about a night in Castleberehaven seventeen years ago. 'I know a little bit about that.'

It was the first time Dominic Carroll had really believed that Stefan Gillespie could be anything other than the man he met on the Yankee Clipper; a guard who went to New York to escort a prisoner and got caught up in an affair with his sister-in-law. A man who should have got a kicking, and one hell of a kicking, but a man Kate O'Donnell had used. Whatever was going on tonight, however it had turned around and put him where he was now, Carroll knew that Stefan had the authority here. With that knowledge came the belief that there had to be more; he had been tricked in some deeper way that had to do with more than getting Niamh out of America. He had taken the guard at his word about John Cavendish. But did he really not know the intelligence officer at all? Surely he must have done.

451

'And do you know a little bit about bombs in New York too, Sergeant?'

'Not very much. Let's say I knew a man who did –'

'Captain Cavendish.'

Stefan didn't need to say anything.

'You had me fooled. I really thought you were nobody.'

'That's because I am nobody.'

'It doesn't matter,' continued the American. 'Nobody can be a nobody in this war, Stefan. And nobody can stay neutral, whatever Dev thinks. People here need to know that. I've been in Berlin. I've seen what Germany is. Britain isn't going to stand in the way of Adolf Hitler. And as for bombs in New York, well, maybe I'm not so sorry the stuttering idiot's still in Buckingham Palace after all. I'd rather see England broken into a million pieces and wiped from the face of the earth than see it coming to terms with Hitler. No real Irishman would feel any different.'

Carroll was in his stride. This was his testament; this was what he believed.

'However you look at it England, Britain, the Empire, it's all finished. Germany is the future. You've seen New York. You know what it is. That's one part of the future. The other's Berlin. Put them together. Imagine if you put them together! And it's going to happen. And when it does we're going to make sure Ireland's at the heart of it too, on the right side, on the side of what's unstoppable. An earthquake won't go away because you don't like it, whether you're Éamon de Valera or some other nobody-to-be. The future has already been written.'

'I don't think New York and Berlin are going to fit together quite as neatly as you think, Mr Carroll. But I guess we'll all find out, won't we?'

Dominic Carroll's response was a shrug. It wasn't easy swallowing what had just happened, but he could see that he needed to. He had mended his fences with German Intelligence after the mess at the World's Fair. No one had told him that Aaron Phelan's life was part of the price of that mess; perhaps he chose not to think about it. In Berlin Hermann Goering had been polite and enthusiastic about the IRA's contribution to a war with Britain, but in the offices of the Abwehr it had been made clear that Carroll was there to take back a message: Seán Russell and the IRA were to do what they were told. Their day would come; but it would come when and where and how Germany decided.

The American didn't find it easy to admit his mistakes, but Stefan Gillespie had just turned his attempt to take revenge on the wife who had humiliated him into a mistake. Without the Garda sergeant no one in the IRA in Dublin would have cared what happened to Niamh Carroll; his word was enough to have her shot, and that should have been it. But Seán Russell would not like this; there was never any room for the personal where he was concerned. And it had been made clear in Berlin that some things had changed. However much Dominic Carroll meant in New York, the only leader the Abwehr was interested in now was Seán Russell.

A grey Austin pulled into Henrietta Street from Henrietta Place, past the black Humber. It turned round in front of the gates into the King's Inns. The driver got out and opened a rear door. Niamh Carroll stepped out, slightly shaky, clearly dazed and confused. She walked forward a few steps. The IRA man took her arm, holding her back. He was waiting. Inside the Humber, Stefan Gillespie leant across Dominic Carroll and opened the door.

'Do you know Longie Zwillman, Mr Carroll?'

'What?'

'You probably know who he is.'

The American frowned. He didn't know where this came from.

'I know who he is. So?'

'It's odd, I think it's odd, but he was a friend of John Cavendish's.'

'What the hell are you talking about?'

'He'd still like to know who murdered him.'

'Zwillman's a fucking gangster!' laughed Carroll.

'I did meet Mr Zwillman briefly. He asked me to tell him who killed John Cavendish, if ever I found out. As it happens I have found out now.'

'Really? And who was it?'

'Captain Aaron Phelan, NYPD.'

'Aaron Phelan's dead.'

'He was your man. You gave the order.'

'You're not as good as I thought,' smiled Carroll. 'That's shite.'

'Maybe it is. I'm not entirely sure. But I don't need to be sure. Longie Zwillman told me to stay in touch. You know New York a lot better than me, but I'd say if Mr Zwillman got it into his head that you were responsible for killing a friend of his, you'd need a lot more than Clan na Gael to stop him doing something about it. I'd say a better option would be to leave your wife alone, right alone, and forget about all this. Just go home, Mr Carroll.'

The Clan na Gael president frowned. None of that made sense. But the fact that it didn't make sense was disturbing rather than reassuring. Longie Zwillman's wasn't a name Stefan Gillespie could have plucked out of the air. It had to mean something. What Dominic Carroll did didn't bring him into contact with the Mob, but he knew there were people in the Mob who were no friends of Germany and no friends of the IRA because of that. He shook his head, smiling slightly, but the smile was by no means convincing.

'It's still shite.'

'Well, I'd take a long look before you step in it, a chomrádaí.'

Dominic Carroll got out of the car and walked towards the Austin.

The IRA man let go of Niamh Carroll.

She stood for a moment, not sure what to do; then she walked towards the convent. Between the two cars her path crossed that of the man she was married to. He looked at her with the disgust he had always felt for her. She didn't bother to look at him. She walked to the convent entrance. She stared for a moment, still disoriented, trying to find the bell. She found it and pulled it. The door opened immediately. A nun appeared. Then the door closed.

The Clan na Gael leader was now in the Austin. The headlights blazed and the car pulled out into Henrietta Street. It was gone.

Stefan Gillespie leaned across the back seat of the Humber and pulled the car door shut. Dessie started the engine and drove forward to turn the car round in front of the King's Inns gates.

'She's all right,' said Dessie MacMahon as they drove away.

'Who?'

'The one who shot your man in the hand. I like that in a woman.'

27. Reilig Chill Rannaireach

The night before Aidan McCarthy's execution, Thomas Pierrepoint, the English hangman, watched him through a secret window in the condemned cell at Winson Green Prison, Birmingham, in order to finalise his calculations. Although the Home Office provided a table that matched height and weight to the length of the noose required for an efficient hanging, the final judgement was the hangman's own; hanging was an intimate business and in the last seconds, when the hood was put over the head, there were only two people involved, the hangman and the to-be-hanged. Other judgements had, of course, already been made, and if there was another to come after the drop, well, that was in a different jurisdiction altogether.

As Pierrepoint watched him, McCarthy was kneeling at the side of the bed praying.

He prayed for the people he loved. For his wife and the man he had always looked on as his son. He prayed for the brother his silence had sentenced to death in another execution all those years ago on a stormy night outside Castleberehaven. He prayed for his country and the struggle for freedom that he was dying for. He thought of the places he loved. He remembered the sound of the sea; the breath of the cattle in the cold morning air; the rain on the Caha Mountains. He prayed for the places he loved too. He prayed for the man who had met a brutal death in a strange city because of the lies he had told, and because of the lies other people had made out of those lies, and because of what had been left inside a small boy's heart seventeen years earlier; but it would be an exaggeration to say that the life of a soldier of the Free State, even then, warranted very much praying.

He didn't pray for the five people who had died outside the jewellery shop in Coventry's Broadgate: a man of eighty-one, a man of fifty, a man of thirty-three, a woman of twenty-one, a boy of fifteen. He had heard their names many times in the course of the trial, but he didn't think of them now. He felt no remorse for what he had done. A war was being fought, and wars had victims; there had been enough Irish victims after all. How many of their names were on English lips?

He got up from his prayers and moved to the table where a plate of steak and roast potatoes and cabbage was waiting for him. There was a glass of Guinness. He had no particular love of stout; he was no great drinker; but he drank it out of politeness to the warder. And he was calm enough. What was happening now was what had to happen. He had known that from the moment he was arrested. And he had thought about it in the bare, damp room in Hammersmith, lying awake at night, listening to the rumble of the Underground. He would die for Ireland, and in doing that maybe someone else, someone younger, wouldn't have to die. In dying he would pay his debt too, and in paying it, finally, the past would be purged.

Aidan McCarthy had left Ireland for England the day

Stefan Gillespie and Gearóid de Paor returned to Dublin. He had not waited for goodbyes; he would not see the faces of the people he loved changed in the way they saw him forever. He had simply walked away with enough money to take the boat from Cobh to England.

In London he had gone to Hammersmith, for no special reason other than that there were Irish people there, but not too many. He called himself David Haigh. He had got a job on a building site and, after sleeping rough for two nights, a room in Cambridge Grove, overlooking the District Line; he worked hard and kept himself to himself.

The first night in Cambridge Grove he had walked down to the Thames; he had a drink at the Blue Anchor and drank it outside, looking at Hammersmith Bridge.

The IRA's attempt to blow it up was in Aidan McCarthy's mind that night. It wasn't difficult, over a period of months, for him to find his way to people who knew people in the IRA in London, and to make it clear that he was willing to work for the cause. He had soon sensed who he should talk to, and the habit of silence that characterised him recommended him. Since the bombing campaign had started in January the bombs had continued to go off, regularly and ineffectually; the IRA was now an illegal organisation in Ireland as well as Britain; more and more IRA men had been imprisoned. Volunteers were thin on the ground now, and because of that David Haigh was trusted sooner than he might have been. He moved very quickly from carrying messages across London to carrying explosives.

On 21 August he had taken a train to Coventry to visit James Richards, an IRA man lodging with an Irish family in Clara Street, to instruct him to prepare a bomb. The bomb would be collected by another IRA man and planted in the city. McCarthy had returned to Hammersmith the next day to supply explosives for three bombs destined for Scotland Yard, Westminster Abbey and the Bank of England. The bombers were caught before the bombs could be planted, but two days later, in Coventry, James Richards' bomb went off outside Astley's jewellery shop in Broadgate. Five passers-by died. The man who left the bomb was never identified, but James Richards was arrested immediately; Aidan McCarthy, as David Haigh, was already in custody in London. Now he was to hang.

A man can only give what he has, but as he faced death Aidan McCarthy found more than he knew he had. He had said little during the trial; he had answered questions where there was an answer he chose to give, but he said nothing that provided information, nothing that incriminated anyone. Only at the end did he say anything about himself.

'My lord, before you pass sentence of death on me, I wish to thank sincerely the gentlemen who have defended me. I wish to state that what I have done I have done for a just cause. As a soldier of the Irish Republican Army I am not afraid to die. God bless Ireland and God bless the men who have fought and died for her cause.'

He died under the name he had called himself in London, David Haigh. He made no attempt to communicate with his family in Béarra. There was no consolation to be offered to them and he didn't expect his death to give any; but he felt he had done his duty at the highest level, and in doing so he had tried to pay the debt he owed his brother; if there was forgiveness, please God, he had earned it. He died well for what he believed in; the five people in Coventry who had also died for what he believed didn't; but as tens of millions prepared to die all over the world, well and not so well, for what others believed, none of it mattered very much.

Many years later, Aidan McCarthy's body would be transferred from the grounds of Winson Green to Ireland for burial. His coffin would be draped in the Irish tricolour, just as Captain John Cavendish's had been, and just as, alongside the Stars and Stripes, Captain Aaron Phelan's had been.

Yet when Aidan McCarthy walked the cold stone corridor at Winson Green to meet Thomas Pierrepoint, his final thoughts were not as easy as he had hoped they might be. A priest walked beside him; his last confession was said; he had received his last Eucharist and he carried its promise of salvation. And he wanted to believe it, yet the words that came to him, not the priest's words but words suddenly there in his head, were not words of absolution. 'But whoso shall offend one of these little ones . . . it were better for him that a millstone were hung round his neck and he were drowned at the bottom of the sea.'

As the black hood went over his head, the sound he heard was a sound from that morning, seventeen years ago on Pallas Strand, somehow there with him now, at the end; it was the angry screaming of the gulls. And it wasn't the eyeless face of his brother that he saw, buried in sand almost to the shoulders; it was the face of the small boy staring at it.

*

Garda Sergeant Stefan Gillespie was eating breakfast in the otherwise empty dining room of Annie O'Neill's Private Hotel in Westland Row, on the morning of 3 September. It was late, already after eleven o'clock, but the events of the previous night meant that he had slept in; not that he had slept very much in the end. Kate and Niamh would have left the convent now; Kate was going to take her sister to an old friend's in Kildare, somewhere she could stay for a while and do nothing and say nothing to anybody. Dominic Carroll would be on his way to Foynes to take the flying boat to New York, with whatever messages he had brought back from Berlin. As Stefan ate there was music on the radio, not loud enough to listen to but too loud to ignore; he found himself humming John Ryan's polka.

Suddenly Annie appeared, bustling and businesslike in a way that was quite unlike her; with her was Superintendent Gregory. As senior officers didn't stay at Annie's, she was always dismissive of them; she had known them before they were jumped up and full of shite and she usually knew things about them they weren't comfortable with. Terry Gregory was unusually polite as he sat down; there were things she knew about him in his younger days. He made a laboured joke about the grand old times and said he'd love a cup of tea; sure, didn't he know no one made tea like Annie after all? It was true enough, although it wasn't exactly the way he remembered it. As he would shortly recall, Annie made some of the worst tea in Dublin.

'She gives me the shivers,' he said, taking out a cigarette. 'She's got something on all of us, even Ned Broy. I wish I had her in Special Branch.'

He lit the cigarette and glanced down at the newspaper on the table.

'Will it be war today, then?'

'I can't see why not.'

'You wouldn't think so walking through Dublin, Sergeant.'

461

'Well, they keep telling us it won't be our war,' shrugged Stefan.

He kept eating, not really noticing what he was eating now, waiting for Gregory to tell him why he was there. He couldn't believe he knew anything about the previous night; he certainly wouldn't have got anything from Dessie MacMahon. But the Special Branch had informants in the IRA. It wasn't impossible he knew. However Stefan wasn't going to play the game. He had nothing to say to anybody about Niamh Carroll now. Whatever else happened, he wasn't going to hand her back to Special Branch for questioning in Dublin Castle. There was nothing more she could tell anyone anyway. She had more than earned the right to be left alone.

'I was talking to Ned Broy about you,' said Gregory cautiously.

'I see,' replied Stefan without looking up. He wasn't convinced the superintendent didn't know something, or that he wasn't being questioned.

The next words, however, were no species of question.

'You start in Special Branch next week. You'll be working for me.'

When the surprise had subsided Stefan shook his head.

'I'm happy enough where I am, sir.'

'I'm not here to ask you how happy you are, Gillespie.'

'The reason I'm in Baltinglass –'

'I'm not interested in your family problems either,' snapped the superintendent. 'Some of it's going to be our war too. It's not a request.'

'I have responsibilities –'

'You'll have to sort that out yourself. The Commissioner tells me I need you. And he's probably right. I've got a couple of German speakers, and if I was going on holiday

462

with them they'd be great boys for ordering beer and sausage. I need someone who can not only tell me the difference between the Abwehr and the Sicherheitsdienst des Reichführers-SS, but can actually say it.'

Stefan noted that Terry Gregory had no trouble saying it.

'Besides, you've got a nose for it, Sergeant, maybe it's all those relations in Germany you don't see any more.'

Stefan was well aware that the superintendent was letting him know, as he had before once, exactly how much he knew about him.

'And people like you, Sergeant, you know that, people who don't like me very much at all. I think you'll be very useful.'

'What does that mean, sir?' asked Stefan.

'You know a lot,' Gregory continued, 'about all sorts of things. From German spies in Ireland to what Captain Cavendish had on the IRA in New York. So the first thing you're going to do is fill in some gaps in my education. We're all going to be working with Military Intelligence now, like we're old pals. I don't need to tell you I've got too many ex-IRA men to make it easy for G2 to trust us, and G2's got too many anti-Treaty soldiers with long memories. But it seems you feature very low on the list of policemen Commandant de Paor doesn't trust, unlike most of Special Branch. That's how the Commissioner put it. I'd put it like this. You tell me everything. You're working for me. And don't you ever fucking forget it.'

He smiled, but there was nothing idle about those last words. He looked at his watch. He got up and walked to the radio. He turned the dial. There were whines and crackles as 'The Boys of Bluehill' turned into distorted, isolated words in Irish, German, French. Then there was an English voice. It was Neville Chamberlain's, the British Prime Minister.

'. . . unless we heard from them by eleven o'clock that they were prepared at once to withdraw their troops from Poland, a state of war would exist between us. I have to tell you that no such undertaking has been received and that consequently this country is at war with Germany . . .'

Gregory retuned the dial to Radio Éireann; the sound of applause.

'From the horse's mouth. Right so, Dublin Castle, Monday week.'

On the radio the band was playing 'The Maid behind the Bar'.

The superintendent headed for the door.

'And by the way, you're an inspector now. About fecking time.'

Stefan sat back in his chair.

'I'll want my own sergeant, sir.'

Terry Gregory turned round.

'Not one of my two-faced lying hacks you mean?'

Detective Inspector Gillespie smiled; it was exactly what he meant.

'Well, that fat eejit Dessie MacMahon's no use to me.'

*

When Stefan Gillespie arrived home from Dublin, the news of war was already there, and he left his own news until later. He needed to tell his mother and father before he talked to Tom. For a time it was going to be like it had been once before. He would have to live in Dublin and come home when he could on weekends and days off. It

464

would have to work, however little anyone liked it; the farm was still the right place for Tom. Stefan still wanted it to be a home for both of them, even if he could not be there all the time.

His move to Special Branch wouldn't be something his father liked either. Years ago David Gillespie had worked in Dublin Castle too, as an inspector in the Dublin Metropolitan Police. He had left because staying would have meant deciding who to inform on. Either he would have had to inform on men he knew were secretly working for the IRA, to British Intelligence in the Castle, or he would have been expected to hand the names of British Intelligence and Special Branch officers to the IRA. As he saw it he had to choose between joining one side and maybe getting shot by the other, or pretending he could really stay out of it and possibly get shot by both sides. He had never believed that spying on your neighbours had anything to do with being a policeman and however Stefan might rationalise what he would be doing, to himself, he would be spying on his countrymen.

The dark corridors of Dublin Castle had left a mark on David Gillespie that had never quite washed off. He wouldn't approve of what his son was about to do.

When he came into the kitchen Stefan could see that his mother had already been crying. And he knew why. She had a family in Germany still, however little contact there was now. They felt closer, inevitably, at this moment. He had felt it himself, walking past St Patrick's Cathedral on his way to Kingsbridge, remembering when he had been chosen to sing a verse of 'Silent Night' in German one Christmas Eve, while he had been in the choir there as a boy, because of his good German and his family ties. He had cousins he hadn't seen since his teens who would soon be fighting. And he knew other people who would soon be fighting too. There would be tens of thousands of Irishmen ready to fight for Britain, not because they were British but because they were Irish; he knew men in Baltinglass who would be going, quietly, slipping away, barely telling their friends. Everyone knew it but no one said it.

There was already a lot going on in the farmhouse under Kilranelagh, most of it unspoken yet too. Tom felt the uncertain mood. His first concerns were for his friends in England and for Valerie Lessingham.

'Will people be bombed in Sussex, Daddy?'

'I'm sure they won't. They're in the country, aren't they?'

But people would be bombed; the adults knew it would be about that.

'Harry Lawlor's dad said the Germans are bound to win.'

'I don't know, Tom. I don't suppose it'll be that easy –'

Tom looked round uncertainly, almost guiltily at his grandmother.

'I'm sorry, Oma, I'm not sure I want the Germans to win.'

'Oh Tom, that's not how it is.' She walked over and put her arm round him. 'I don't want anybody to win. I don't want a war at all. Nobody does.'

'Doesn't Hitler?' asked Tom.

'We don't, Tom, remember that.' Helena was fighting back tears.

'But aren't we German as well, a bit I mean?'

'Let's make do with being Irish, Tom. God knows that's hard enough.'

It was David who spoke, smiling as he did. And they all

tried to smile, as if a few easy words put an end to the real questions hanging over them. But then Tom suddenly left the conversation, and all the awkwardness and concern in his grandparents' and his father's minds. He sat down at the table, absorbed in the comic his father had bought him at Kingsbridge Station earlier, *The Magnet*.

'How do you say this, Daddy?'

Stefan looked over Tom's shoulder. 'Mapledurham.'

His son read on and for a few seconds Stefan followed the words below the picture of a fat schoolboy falling into a river. 'Nobody was in a hurry. Past Reading, and getting on towards Mapledurham, the surroundings were beautiful, especially on a gorgeous August day. The Famous Five of Greyfriars found life worth living. "What about a walk?" asked Bunter. They looked in astonishment. Not once since that holiday on the Thames had started had Billy Bunter wanted a walk!'

As he turned away Tom started to chuckle, and by the time Stefan and his father went out to bring in the cows for evening milking, he was laughing aloud.

When the cows had been milked that evening Stefan Gillespie walked up to Kilranelagh Cemetery and Maeve's grave. It wasn't somewhere he went so often now. Needs changed and there was no sense that she was there in the almost physical sense that she had been in the first years after her death. He didn't go to talk to her in the way he did then, and as Tom still did, but when something important happened he went up on to the hillside of tussocky grass and tumbled stones that was the graveyard. At times, as you walked along the slopes of Kilranelagh, it was hard to know where the cemetery ended and the broken walls of ancient fields began; it was the same scruffy, wind-blown space. The graveyard had no neatness or order about it, and Stefan still liked that, as Maeve had once liked it too; it tried to make no sense of death. He put some late roses from his mother's garden on the flat grave stone that simply bore his dead wife's name, and he thought for a moment, not of her, but of how Tom would cope with him not being there.

As he turned to walk home he noticed a smudge of white and brown at the side of the grave. He knew what it was immediately, in all the undergrowth around him. It was a lily, the rotting trumpet of a single, large arum lily. It had been placed on the grave several weeks earlier, since he had last been there, as a single arum lily had been placed every year at some point and left to rot there. The time of year changed. It could be March, June, September; once it had been Christmas; but it always happened.

At first he had assumed it was a neighbour, or a friend. People didn't forget here, and that mattered. But as the years had gone on the regular arrival of the lily had begun to trouble him. He had asked eventually whether a neighbour or a friend left a lily there each year; or a relative who came by only occasionally. But no one knew anything. He wasn't really sure why it had started to trouble him. It was an act of remembrance; that was all. But he felt there was a determination in the anonymity of that act, and a strange claim to intimacy that he knew nothing about; not only to an intimacy with Maeve, but somehow with him too.

It was as if there was someone else who shared his grief, who stood outside and yet was there, once a year, every year. He picked up the slimy remains of the trumpet as he walked off. He didn't know why but he didn't like it being there. He felt as if in that empty place, that had for so long been entirely his and Maeve's and Tom's, he was being watched in some way. He dropped the thing suddenly and laughed at himself. Clearly going to work in the Special Branch was having its effect.

As Stefan walked back into the farmyard there was a car he didn't know. It was a black Ford Prefect. Helena rushed out of the kitchen as he stood looking at it, with his father ambling behind and a wry smile on his face.

'For goodness sake, why didn't you say something?'

He had no idea what she was talking about.

'We've nothing in! I was there in an apron and slippers!'

'It's true,' grinned David, 'apron and slippers!'

'Who is she?' demanded Helena.

'Who's who?'

'Maybe there are lots of them, Helena, we should give him a clue –'

'David!'

'She's called Kate,' explained his father.

'Oh,' said Stefan, pleasantly surprised.

'Why didn't you tell us?' continued his mother.

'I suppose I didn't really know there was anything to tell.'

'Then you don't know much! God save us!'

Helena turned and stalked back into the house.

'I don't know what she'll think of us!'

As the kitchen door slammed David Gillespie shrugged.

'Tom's taken her to see some lambs. He doesn't seem flustered at all.'

*

When he reached the Moatamoy field he couldn't see Kate or Tom. He stood looking down at the stolid, barely moving ewes and the furiously energetic lambs chasing round them. He looked across towards the wooded mound that was the Norman motte on the far side of the field. He looked up, beyond it, to the pyramid point of Baltinglass Hill in the distance. Then he heard Tom's laughter.

He clambered over the fence and walked down the slope of the field towards the motte. He saw Kate and Tom emerging from a dip where the field stopped and the land plunged down into the steep, scrubby valley below the mound. They were deep in conversation and they didn't notice him until he had almost reached them. Kate smiled broadly then.

'I was just learning about Huckleberry Finn's drunken Pap.'

'Any resemblance is purely coincidental.'

'That's some good news then, Stefan.'

'Kate came to see you, Daddy. She knows all about Tom Sawyer.'

'I certainly do now,' she grinned.

They felt the rain that had suddenly started.

'I think we'd better get back,' said Stefan.

'Oma's making something special for tea!' enthused Tom.

'I didn't want anyone to go to any –'

'That's not how it works,' Stefan replied. 'Surely you know that?'

They walked towards the gate, ewes and lambs parting ahead of them as Tom led the way, sweeping the stick he was holding in front of him, talking to himself, engaged in a game that Stefan and Kate could have no idea whether they were a part of or not. The rain was falling more heavily.

'I think I was a bit of a shock to your mother,' said Kate.

'Worse than that, I'm afraid. A relief!'

She laughed. He found himself watching her doing it.

There was a roll of thunder; the rain poured down now.

'Isn't this a lovely day to be caught in the –'

'No it isn't! Run!' he shouted.

'I don't mind at all!'

She stood in the rain and let it wash down her face.

He snatched her hand and started to pull her across the field.

'We'll be soaked!'

'I'm already soaked!' she shouted.

As they reached Tom, who had abandoned his game and was now running too, Stefan grabbed him with his other hand. The three of them ran on through the sheeting rain together, drenched to the skin, running and laughing, and getting wetter and wetter. The rain stopped as suddenly as it had started, but they kept on running, and laughing, all the way back to the farm.

28. Royal Oak

Detroit, November 1939

It was the First Sunday in Advent and the winter's first snow was falling lightly on north Detroit and Lake Saint Clair. In Royal Oak the tower that marked the Shrine of the Little Flower didn't so much look up to the grey heavens as it broke out of the surrounding suburban streets like a fist; ancient limestone that was as raw as new concrete. Despite its height it was squat; despite its sacred heart it was belligerent; it spoke a faith that was solid, impenetrable, immovable. It was a testament to certainty, not to the quiet hope of a night in Bethlehem. On the other side of the Atlantic another cross, broken and crooked, could have replaced the square-cut, crucified Christ facing out from the tower and it would not have looked out of place; the superhuman muscles of Soviet Labour would have sat comfortably there too.

Seán Russell didn't much like the place. He bowed his head as Father Charles Coughlin raised the host before the packed church and throughout the Mass he felt the electricity of the faith that was all around him, but unlike most of the Radio Priest's congregation, including Dominic Carroll who

472

sat beside him, he listened with irritation rather than enthusiasm to the homily.

It wasn't that he disagreed with the venom Father Coughlin brought to bear on the evils of British imperialism; the thieves of Africa, the thieves of India, the warmongers and the wasters of the earth. It wasn't that he objected to the priest's half-hearted criticism of Adolf Hitler; the blame for war lay heaviest where it always had, on English greed, English capitalism, English deceit. It wasn't that he couldn't join wholeheartedly in the Radio Priest's prayer that above all else America was not dragged into Britain's war. But if democracy was a sham he had no great conviction that fascism, or anything else that was on offer, wasn't a sham as well. He had no time for politics and he despised politicians, even the Republican politicians of his own movement. They were the ones, after all, whose arguments and petty squabbles had broken the IRA into fragments and factions and left it weak and ineffective in the face of the Irish Free State's half-arsed democracy.

He was a soldier. His only purpose was to remove the stench of England from the island of Ireland; not only from the occupied six counties of Ulster but from every corner of the still-infested Free State that Éamon de Valera now wanted to call a republic. When Ireland was free, how the people of Ireland chose to govern themselves was their business. The IRA was there to give them the right to choose, no more than that. Priests had a lot in common with soldiers, true soldiers; to serve your country and to serve God required the same kind of self-sacrifice, the same kind of purity of intention. It wasn't a priest's job to spout politics and Seán Russell didn't much like the air of self-importance that came off America's most famous priest.

However, Father Charles Coughlin was important, not only because of his love of Ireland and his hatred of England, but because he, more than almost anyone else, really did speak for the tens of millions of Americans who demanded neutrality. And as everyone knew, without America Britain's war was lost before it started. So at the end of the Mass, when Robert Monteith introduced him to Father Coughlin at the doors of the Shrine of the Little Flower, the IRA chief of staff shook the priest's hand with all the appropriate reverence and respect.

Seán Russell had been staying with Monteith in Royal Oak for a week. It was time to move. He was on the run now. His visa had expired and if he was picked up he risked extradition, to Ireland or even to Britain.

However the reality was that the FBI wasn't looking for him very hard, and in the cities that gave him the sea of Irish America to swim in, Detroit, Chicago, Philadelphia, New York, Boston, there would be no police forces scouring the streets for him. If his presence was an embarrassment to the government in Washington, arresting him would be a bigger one still. Irish-American politicians wouldn't let him be extradited to England to face trial over the bombing campaign, nor would they have him sent back to Ireland where he would be locked up for the duration of the war Ireland had no part in, as an enemy of the state, without even a trial. On the other hand the British wouldn't stomach him leaving the country to go wherever he wanted, only to end up in Berlin, where the alliance between the IRA and Germany was now his sure and certain hope for the achievement of Irish freedom.

But Germany was where he fully intended to go.

As Robert Monteith watched the IRA leader drive away

474

from the Shrine of the Little Flower in Dominic Carroll's car he crossed himself; he prayed that what he and Roger Casement had failed to do twenty-three years ago, Seán Russell would do now. Irish America would hide the man easily enough, but it was the Abwehr that would spirit him out of the United States. It was German Intelligence that would get him to Berlin. And when England was breaking, as even the American papers said it must, under Germany's irresistible machinery of war, a U-boat would take the IRA chief of staff to Ireland, as one had once taken Robert Monteith and Roger Casement to Banna Strand. He would reunite the IRA's warring factions and make the Republican movement the soul of Ireland again; he would hold out the hand of old friendship and old comradeship to Éamon de Valera. And they would win.

The same thoughts were in Seán Russell's head as Dominic Carroll drove towards Detroit. The words of the First Sunday in Advent's Preface to the Holy Trinity were there too; it was a kind of omen. 'Dominus dabit benignitatem.' The Lord will grant us his blessing to make our land yield its harvest. The snow was heavier; it was settling on the windscreen. He was a lot less sure than Robert Monteith about how Éamon de Valera would react to his outstretched hand when the Abwehr eventually got him to Ireland. But if Dev's neutrality ended up doing England's work instead of Ireland's, it was clear enough what would have to be done. If the Long Feller really had turned himself into Michael Collins over the years, then there would be an IRA bullet for Dev, just as there had been one for the Big Feller before him. And Seán Russell knew he would have no hesitation in pulling the trigger himself.

THE END

War and the Rumour of War

Neutral Tones: Ireland and America in 1939

As war between Britain and Germany looked more and more inevitable in 1939, a lot of people thought it could still be avoided. Even the British government, despite the warmongering imperialism that apparently lay behind all its tedious democratic whingeing, reckoned that throwing Czechoslovakia under the German bus might do the trick. A lot of small countries in Europe didn't much like that, but they consoled themselves with the fact that, well, they weren't Czechoslovakia, and what was happening there, as the British Prime Minister Neville Chamberlain so reasonably put it, was a quarrel 'in a far-away country between people of whom we know nothing'. Only a few out-of-power British politicians and the irritatingly Polish Poles, with most of their country to lose, still seemed concerned about Hitler's plans to expand his bus routes. Everyone else said the threat of war had gone. Everyone said it, and there may have been some who believed it.

On either side of the Atlantic two predominantly English-speaking countries, still with the closest familial ties to Britain, were busy announcing their intention to stand aside from any forthcoming conflict, as neutrals.

In Ireland where the Second World War, once it started, would be referred to euphemistically as the Emergency, neutrality would always be a strange beast, best summed up not by anything Irish politicians had to say about it, but by what actually happened. Small things tell the bigger story. Once the war was underway any German aircrew landing in the Republic of Ireland were interned for the duration of the war; British and Allied aircrew were given a cup of tea and put on a bus for Belfast. The transatlantic flying boat service that had started up in June 1939 didn't really stop, as popular history has it, in September; the Clippers flew from Foynes throughout the war, out of range of German fighters, carrying British and American diplomats, politicians, industrialists and military officials, who were all about the business of planning war, even while America was supposedly neutral. The flights were an open secret. But tickets weren't available for any Germans who might have wanted to make the trip.

The rhetoric was very different of course. Éamon de Valera had a lot to say about how meticulously neutral Irish neutrality would be, and he kept on saying it as the war continued. From time to time Winston Churchill had a lot to say on the subject too, about Irish betrayal and all that frolicking with fascists in Dublin, though he usually said it after lunch and his daily bottle or so of champagne. Talk of occupying Ireland to gain control of 'essential' Atlantic ports was also thrown around a bit, though it was President Roosevelt who would eventually get most exercised about Ireland's refusal to join the Allies once America was in the war, and would seriously suggest invasion. Churchill had to calm him down and tell him it was grand to shout about invading the bloody-minded Irish, but no one intended to do it, not even after a few drinks too many. The truth was, at least in the early stages of the war, that Irish neutrality suited Britain in many ways. The idea that, say, after Dunkirk, regiments of British troops and at minimum a squadron or two of fighters could have been spared, not only to protect Ireland from German invasion but simultaneously to fight a rejuvenated IRA, rescued from disarray and unpopularity by a new English incursion, was something most of the British military establishment saw starkly and realistically as unhelpful, to put it at its politest. They were right too. There was a day in the Battle of Britain when air cover that might have been needed for Ireland would have given sure victory to the Luftwaffe.

The hope of the IRA and Republicans generally that a swift German victory in the upcoming war would bring about a free and united Ireland was shared by a relatively small part of the Irish population. Tens of thousands of Irishmen would volunteer for the British forces; IRA membership barely increased. German hopes that Ireland could become a serious threat to Britain, either as a base for sabotage or as a platform for invasion, were ill-informed and ill-founded. For de Valera though, neutrality was really the only option he had, and naturally enough plenty of *realpolitik* came into that. It looked very unlikely in 1939 that Britain and France could beat Germany. Much of the world saw Hitler's victory as inevitable. Ireland itself was in a fragile situation economically and it simply had no resources to draw on to fight any kind of war, with anybody. But if Ireland would never join a war against Britain, as some in German Intelligence believed it might, it could not, in the light of its recent history, fight beside its neighbour either, let alone invite British troops back into Ireland.

Supporting Britain was probably never in de Valera's head; it would certainly have divided the country and given new strength to his Republican opponents; it could have meant a serious renewal of civil war. Yet de Valera's sympathies, scrupulously kept in a box as they were, were by no means as neutral as he made them appear. Whatever his bitterness towards Britain he knew well enough that what there was of democracy in the tired decline of British imperialism, was still all that was available of democracy to fight against totalitarianism. And although de Valera isn't noted for his democratic instincts, a belief in the freedom of small nations was something that mattered to him a lot. That had been forged not only out of the struggle for Irish freedom but out of his years working in the League of Nations.

Real freedom, in a world where small, independent states would not be under the thumb of great powers, was not something de Valera could seriously imagine being realised by Adolf Hitler's march through Europe. He didn't talk a lot about democracy but it is probably no coincidence that he was an Irishman born in America. Irish neutrality was far more one-sided than it suited either Éamon de Valera or Winston Churchill to admit. The fact that Winnie and Dev hated the sight of one another usefully helped disguise that.

In America in 1939, where neutrality was being much debated, the atmosphere was very different. While de Valera had most of Ireland behind him in his vision of a neutral stance in the event of war, Franklin Roosevelt was fighting to take sides openly, even if the official American position was loudly proclaimed neutrality. President Roosevelt saw the coming conflict very clearly as a struggle between democracy and totalitarianism, and he had no doubt which side America should be on. How far ahead he saw in terms of

America's involvement in a war itself is arguable, but he fully intended to do everything he could to arm and aid Britain and France and their allies. If America wasn't fighting, it would nevertheless be the arsenal of democracy.

A lot of Americans didn't agree. Most simply didn't want to get dragged into another European war. Some genuinely supported Germany and the other fascist states, in the belief that 'democracy wasn't working' and that the coming war was about defending civilisation from socialism and communism. There were powerful pro-German advocates on the right, and there was also a strong and influential Irish-American lobby too, that saw the prospect of war not in terms of America itself, but in the same way the IRA saw it, as an opportunity to finally kick the English out of Ireland. In early 1939 opposition to Roosevelt's pro-Allied policies was in the ascendant; his plans to arm Britain in particular had been scuppered in Congress, though those decisions would eventually be reversed. For a lot of Americans it wasn't only Czechoslovakia, which many had not even heard of, that was a far-away country 'of which we know nothing'; it was the whole of Europe. It didn't only suit the isolationists to keep it that way. It also suited the pro-Germans and the pro-fascists, the anti-Semites and the anti-socialists and anti-communists, and even those like many Irish Americans who were none of those things, but who saw an opportunity for Britain to get its comeuppance at last in a way surely no country on earth so richly deserved.

History and Mystery: Real and Imaginary Friends

Raymond Chandler said that one of the characteristics of crime fiction, for want of a better name, is the unnatural squeezing up of timeframes. The same thing applies to history when it is dragged, willingly or otherwise, into that world. This book, like *The City of Shadows*, contains, alongside fairly straightforward fiction, real events and real people, as well as characters and events that skim history a little more loosely. I hope that from time to time there is some truth to be found in what may often be inaccurate, but as it is not unknown for untruth to insert itself into what passes for meticulously accurate history, I can only say that I make no claims at all in the truth area.

The book opens with a myth. The story of a man buried alive on an Irish beach during the War of Independence first appears in *Tales of the RIC*, essentially a work of populist pro-British propaganda designed to expose the brutality of Irish Nationalists. It never happened; the death of a magistrate called Alan Lendrum lay behind the story, though there was never a beach. The myth survived the years to be included even in historical accounts of the War of Independence and the Civil War. Whatever brutality it reflects here is the lazy, sometimes unthinking brutality of any war, especially those wars in which there is righteousness to hand.

The Coventry bombing that connects to the way this story is told did happen, though no one called Aidan McCarthy was involved. The real nature of the bombing remains unclear to this day. It does not reflect Seán Russell and the IRA's determination to avoid civilian casualties, and it feels as if it emerged out of a dangerous mix of desperation and incompetence as the Sabotage Campaign in Britain fell apart. Two IRA volunteers were tried by jury and hanged for their involvement in the bombing in 1939. The executions were protested widely in Britain and naturally enough in Ireland. It is no defence of the capital punishment generally accepted at the time to say that the Irish government's protest has to be taken in the context of its own executions of several IRA prisoners during the Second World War, also using the English hangman.

In terms of squeezing up history a number of real events in America have been brought together to make the story of *The City of Strangers*. The flying boat service from England to New York via Foynes didn't start operating commercially till June 1939, but trial flights had been running for some time before that. The World's Fair opened at Flushing Meadows several weeks later than is suggested here. Seán Russell, the IRA chief of staff, was in America from the early summer of 1939 and was arrested in Detroit on suspicion of planning some kind of attack or disruption during George VI's visit to America, which took place at the beginning of June. The king did go to the World's Fair in New York. There was a strong suspicion that his visit to the USA was secretly about cementing an alliance that might eventually drag America into war; it was absolutely true.

In 1940 a bomb exploded at the British Pavilion at the World's Fair; two NYPD police bomb squad officers were killed. It was clear even in a surprisingly lacklustre NYPD investigation that the suspects were likely to be pro-German or pro-IRA, or both; no one was ever arrested. The various pro-German, pro-fascist American organisations mentioned in the story are for the most part real, as are the links between them and some Irish-American groupings. There was an organisation called the Ethiopian Pacific Movement that believed that Hitler and Japan had an interest in promoting black freedom and turning Africa into a kind of black-apartheid paradise. Father Charles Coughlin, the Radio Priest, was for a time the most powerful voice of isolationist neutrality in America but, as his notorious miti-gation of the events of Kristallnacht had demonstrated, his stance was often more pro-German than it was anti-war. Robert Monteith, the almost forgotten survivor of Roger Casement's U-boat landing in Kerry in 1916, did work for Father Coughlin.

Longie Zwillman was a Jewish-American gangster oper-ating out of New Jersey who played an active part in the uglier side of anti-fascist protest in both New York and Jersey City; street fighting was promoted on both sides. Such activities were the unlikely prelude to the equally unlikely but well-documented liaison between the FBI and the Mob, in all its various forms, during World War II.

When Seán Russell was arrested in Detroit, as a potential threat to George VI, then across the river in Windsor, Ontario, he was with the Clan na Gael leader Joseph McGarrity. It was McGarrity who put together the IRA Sabotage Plan in Britain with Russell, and McGarrity whose visits to Berlin laid the foundation of IRA links with German Intelligence when war came. The character of Dominic Carroll draws significantly on McGarrity, but as I have no reason to think McGarrity's personal relationships were as bitterly played out as are my character's, it seemed unreasonable to use his name. The IRA's ciphers did use lines from a cheap edition of Hawthorne's *The Scarlet Letter* as a basis for a transposition code, certainly into the late 1920s; messages using this code were not decrypted until a few years ago.

Conspiracies involving the Duke of Windsor, the abdi-cated Edward VIII, are ten a penny. This one suggests no involvement by him of course. The duke's longstanding admiration for Hitler was well known, as was his predilection for keeping company with people plotting against Britain and his brother, even if he didn't plot himself. There were those on the fringes of Irish Republicanism, especially in America, who thought quite irrationally that the ex-king's pro-Nazism somehow translated into sympathy for Irish Republican aims. Errol Flynn was one of them, though he may have been mixing the duke up with King Richard returning from the crusades and himself with Robin Hood. What I remember is a conversation with someone who was at the time the queen's press secretary. He said that while Queen Elizabeth would 'carry her silence on it to the grave', what she could never forgive the Duke of Windsor for had nothing to do with the abdication; it was his willingness, declared repeatedly to a ragbag of Britain's enemies before and during the war, to replace her father 'in the interests of peace'.

Owen Harris is a fictional version of Edward Ball, tried and convicted of the murder of his mother, Lavinia Ball, in 1936; he was found guilty but insane. The circumstances were very much as the story describes, down to the details, including the undiscovered body dumped into the sea. Ball, like Harris, was an occasional employee of the Gate Theatre, and the argument that may have provoked the attack on his mother was about her refusal to fund his boat ticket for a Gate tour, though it was to Egypt not America. The first Gate tour to the US didn't happen until 1948. Ball was eventually set free but among campaigners for his release many believed him innocent. I don't know what Micheál Mac Liammóir made of Edward Ball, but he was probably very glad that, unlike Owen Harris, Ball never did make it on tour.

Acknowledgements

As before, the number and variety of books, etc. that contributed something to this story is greater than I can remember; this time even pieces of jazz. There is one particular book, however, that has contributed uniquely both to the atmosphere and the substance of the story. *Decoding the IRA*, by Thomas G. Mahon and James Gillogly, deciphers and contextualises a collection of IRA messages, many of them between Ireland and America, which have not been read since they were sent in the 1920s. The book is a masterful work of decryption that could almost certainly not have been achieved without the imaginative use of modern computers, but it is its vivid re-creation of time and place through these cryptic communications, and its window into the IRA, that is unlike anything else. Only the message I have quoted at the beginning of the book is real, but in the casual content of that message, 'annihilation of all spies', it sets the tone of *The City of Strangers*. Another remarkable book of immersion is John Roy Carlson's *Under Cover*, an investigative journalist's contemporary journey through the pro-German and pro-fascist underground of America in the late 1930s. A book to read simply because it is a remarkable piece of writing is Richard Cobb's *A*

Classical Education; it is the story of the friendship between the English historian Cobb and Edward Ball, the character Owen Harris is based on. It is the content of this book that enabled me to write Harris as I have, though there is far more strangeness to find in Cobb's writing. The poem declaimed by Owen Harris in the Dizzy Club is Louis MacNeice's 'Bagpipe Music'. As ever, the archive of *The Irish Times* provided starting points throughout that only the atmosphere of its inky pages can give; *The New York Times* delivered the underwhelming review of *John Bull's Other Island* that so infuriates Micheál Mac Liammóir. The story Tom Gillespie reads in *The Magnet* is one of the last Greyfriars' tales Frank Richards published before the outbreak of war. Full of the usual absurdities and Bunterisms as it is, it also captures, in a boat full of schoolboy friends floating lazily up the River Thames in the bright summer of 1939, something of England that, for better or worse, was about to disappear forever. But it is, as always, the deep countryside of West Wicklow around Baltinglass that remains, wherever Stefan Gillespie may happen to find himself, somehow at the heart of it all.